THE WOMAN
DETECTIVE

Also By James K. Rone

SHERRY RUSSELL THRILLERS

No Nice Girls: A Sixties Noir Thriller

Klavern

NONFICTION

The Thyroid Paradox
How to Get the Best Care for Hypothyroidism

What About My Weight?
An Endocrinologist's Unorthodox, Irreverent, Politically Incorrect, Practical
Guide to Losing Weight and Combating Obesity

THE WOMAN DETECTIVE

Also By James K. Rone

SHERRY RUSSELL THRILLERS

No Nice Girls: A Sixties Noir Thriller

Klavern

NONFICTION

The Thyroid Paradox
How to Get the Best Care for Hypothyroidism

What About My Weight?
An Endocrinologist's Unorthodox, Irreverent, Politically Incorrect, Practical
Guide to Losing Weight and Combating Obesity

THE WOMAN DETECTIVE
A Sherry Russell Thriller

JAMES K. RONE

Arno Press, College Grove, TN 37046

Copyright © 2017 James K. Rone

All rights reserved. Published 2017

ISBN: 0-692-92745-X
ISBN-13: 978-0-692-92745-8

For Susan, Baxter, Aubrey, and Emma.

As we look at America, we see cities enveloped in smoke and flame. We hear sirens in the night. We see Americans dying on distant battlefields abroad. We see Americans hating one another, fighting each other, killing each other at home…Did American boys die in Normandy and Korea and Valley Forge for this?
—Richard Nixon

A woman must have money and a room of her own…
—Virginia Woolf, *A Room of One's Own*

The dignity of movement of an iceberg is due to only one-eighth of it being above water.
—Ernest Hemingway, *Death in the Afternoon*

As we look at America, we see cities enveloped in smoke and flame. We hear sirens in the night. We see Americans dying on distant battlefields abroad. We see Americans hating one another, fighting each other, killing each other at home…Did American boys die in Normandy and Korea and Valley Forge for this?
—Richard Nixon

A woman must have money and a room of her own…
—Virginia Woolf, *A Room of One's Own*

The dignity of movement of an iceberg is due to only one-eighth of it being above water.
—Ernest Hemingway, *Death in the Afternoon*

CHAPTER 1

ELECTION DAY.

I voted for Hubert Humphrey—"Humpty Dumpty" to my mother, whose father had considered FDR's election to be the beginning of the apocalypse. I'd have sooner vomited than vote for Richard Nixon—"Tricky Dick"—or, God forbid, George Wallace's traveling political circus. I'd have rapturously voted for Bobby Kennedy, who would've stopped the war. Truth be told, I'd have married Bobby Kennedy, given half a chance, though Ethel might've put up a squawk.

Except, Bobby Kennedy was dead.

Shot to death.

Out in California.

A tense election-night vigil followed, ending with Nixon carrying not one major city, but nevertheless capturing the White House with the lowest percent of the popular vote since Woodrow Wilson. In the wake of it all, the press said, of the three once-upon-a-time Democratic hopefuls—Kennedy, Humphrey, and Gene McCarthy—it was said of them, respectively:

One dead.

One lost.

One missing.

What a year. My own father, forcrissake, teargased in Chicago, and two months, nearly to the day, prior to RFK being

3

cut down by that assassin's bullet in Los Angeles, at the Ambassador Hotel, the same fate befell Martin Luther King, in Memphis, at the Lorraine. And while I mourned both, personally as well as for what their deaths might bode for us all, it was King's killing that hit closest to home for me, and for reasons beyond simple in-state geography.

It so happened that I had in a minor way helped to quash a King assassination plot by the Klan down in Mississippi last year. I felt pretty good about that, damn proud, in fact: *I am woman, hear me roar*, and all that rot… (*I know, I know*… That song wasn't out yet, but it's apropos—so, you'll just have to, as the hippies say, go with the flow). Anyway, James Earl Ray having laid waste to all my efforts, and half-plunging the whole country into a race war to boot—130 rioting cities—well, that all felt to me pretty much like a kick in my own stomach.

I LEFT THE POLLING PLACE rather numbly and jammed on some Foster Grants and drove to a noon meeting I had with a potential new client, a stockbroker named E. Hillard Harris. He worked at J. C. Bradford, and called me on Monday on the business line I'd installed in my new home office, complete with an Ansafone system. He wouldn't tell me what he wanted with a private detective.

That wasn't unusual.

What was unusual was him wanting to know the color of my hair.

"Blonde," I replied, with an arch of tweezed brow, elaborating no further. Must have been enough, because he asked if we could meet for lunch, on Tuesday, at the Nashville City Club. I told him I looked forward to it.

Shrugging, I maneuvered downtown in traffic. I still thought the hair issue strange, but there could be a reasonable explanation. He needed me to pose, for instance, as someone known to be blonde, in a negotiation, or something, and not knowing my powers of disguise, he'd worry about hair color. In any case, I wasn't in the habit of refusing gainful employment without a better reason than E. Hillard Harris had given so far. I was especially keen on his potential value as a referral source for other clients, assuming I impressed him, given his connections with the likes of J. C. Bradford, the only Nashville firm with a seat on the New York Stock Exchange.

As for the Nashville City Club, it had formally been housed in the Maxwell House Hotel—of good-to-the-last-drop coffee fame—but it burned to the ground in 1961. The reopened club sat atop the gleaming new aluminum-and-glass Third National Bank Building, on the same site, Fourth Avenue and Church. *Nashville* magazine proclaimed it the most beautifully built thing to hit Music City since Miss Universe, rising "high above Nashville's soot-covered plain."

I parked and entered carrying my purse at my side through a lobby of waterfalls and pools, escalators up to the "modern" banking room, with tellers and loan officers sharing a single open space. Men in the elevator, as I squeezed on, examined me carefully. I wore a purple cowl-neck dress, and a pink, purple, and green pillbox hat, tasseled on top. On the top floor, the twentieth, threading through tinkling ice, clinks of flatware on good china, the hostess delivered me to E. Hillard Harris's table. He wore a blue suit, was in his late forties, of average build. He rose, pushing his chair out, wiping his mouth. "I'm Sherry Russell," I said, cross-table handshaking, registering a funny way he gave me the eye, saying nothing, then deflecting his look.

Smoothing my skirt, I let the hostess seat me, and ordered iced tea when she asked. I then watched the stockbroker watch her go sinuously away, showing considerably more interest than he seemed to have for me. Not that I thought I was all that great to look at, but I knew men who didn't mind the view too much. "Thank you for coming," he said, at long last, rubbing the back of his neck. He took out a Viceroy. Lit it with a Zippo. He made me no offer of one, seeming to be making up his mind about something. *Little ol' me?* People who needed private detectives commonly had things they were nervous about. Patience is a virtue, therefore, in these meetings. It was a window-seat overlooking the famous rooftop NOEL HOTEL sign. Diagonally across was Harris's firm, and on the remaining corner stood the L&C Tower, Nashville's first skyscraper, and tallest. I recalled a conference room over there on the fourteenth floor, I believe it was, three years ago, where I'd signed onto my first big case as a PI. I drank some water. Looked at Harris up from under my eyelashes. Vanderbilt ring. Clean-shaved, dark-haired, neat, not unlike Clark Kent in an actuarial sort of way. He had a small straight mouth, silver-blue eyes, small and close, behind round horn-rims. There was some distinguished gray at the temples. "Well," I said, breaking the silence, which wasn't getting either of us anywhere, "I should look at the menu. Was I late?"

My host was halfway through a hearts-of-lettuce salad. A tall Negro waiter with gunmetal hair brought my tea, and I was ready, trading him the menu: "I'd like the French Toasted Ham and—"

"Sorry, Eugene," Harris interrupted, "but the lady can't stay."

I screwed my hazel eyes to the sticking place.

"Bring me, a double Seagram's, rocks."

"Right away, sir."

"Won't work out, I'm afraid," he flickered, slicing back into his salad.

"I don't…"

"Please, stay, have your tea, if you like."

"I don't need tea," I said. "I'm here about a job."

He glanced up, questioningly. Knife and fork poised, lettuce crunching.

He swallowed.

"As I said—"

"It won't work. I heard that."

I drank some tea to wet my throat. Snagged up my black gloves. Exhaling, I pulled them through my fist, then slapped them back down, jutting my pert chin:

"You knew I was a woman, Mr. Harris."

"Oh, it's not that."

He kind of shrugged with an eating utensil.

"Told you, in fact, I was looking for a woman."

"You told me, in fact, you were looking for a blonde."

"More platinum. Or…a brunette."

My mascaraed eyes narrowed.

"I have a stellar collection of wigs. What, sir, is this about?"

He stopped eating, picking up coffee, studying me over its brim.

"Really? Must we go into this?"

I tightened the corners of my mouth, and snatched my pocketbook, clawing out my pack of Kents. I ripped a match from the NASHVILLE CITY CLUB book, from an ashtray of cut-glass crystal, struck it, and fired up. I whipped out the match, darted it viciously, then twisted in my chair. Hazel-eyeing Harris, I crossed my thighs with a lot of fabric swishing, and tugged the hem of my skirt, and blew smoke out one side of my pink-lipsticked mouth.

I said:

"Yes. We must."

My elbow was on the table, wrist cocked, cigarette poised between curled fingers.

Then, smiling lightly, I fingered an earring.

"Least tell me what kind of problem you have."

"My wife wants a divorce." He splayed fingers.

I gave a nod.

"I cheated on her."

"Ahh," I said. "We're getting somewhere." I tapped my cigarette ash, glided the ashtray nearer me. "I'm an expert on divorce. Divorce is my specialty, if I have a specialty." I shrugged with the cigarette. "Like most solo detective operations, I have to be a jack of all trades. Or, Jill, in my case." I flickered eyes, a twinkle of mischief. "Want me to see what I can get on her, to help you in court? I can do that."

He seemed bored.

Leaned over to stub out his cigarette.

Then sighed.

"I know she has a lover."

"That's a start."

"I know perfectly well who he is. He's…let's say…an associate."

"At Bradford?"

A nod.

"You need…? *Proof*, then?"

"I don't *want* a divorce. If I got a divorce my girlfriend would want to marry me. And that, if I may say Miss Russell, would ruin a very pleasant arrangement." He was getting animated, comfortable. My feminine magic, what made me a great detective. I was a listener, unthreatening, men liking to talk about themselves, assert their masculinity, even things best kept under wraps, and they all felt the need of a soft shoulder. "Besides," he added, sweeping an open palm, "my wife only wants a divorce so she can marry…"

He drained his black coffee.

Tinked the cup in its saucer.

"Your associate," I said, smiling out one side of my mouth. Too much *Peyton Place*, methinks.

I flicked my cigarette.

Eugene, who wore a red jacket, brought Harris's double whiskey, dark amber, alive with ice, and replaced his salad with a plate of grilled calf's liver with bacon, okra and tomatoes, and fried corn. My stomach growled, even after seeing the liver, worse yet, Harris sawing into it. Smelled better than it looked. Typically I could eat the tires off a Jeep but I had never espoused liver. My mother was big on liver and onions when I was growing up. A girl needed her iron. I could espouse one of those whiskeys of Harris's. Didn't seem, however, I was getting my ordering privileges back. Harris bent closer, once Eugene sauntered out of earshot, picking up the threads of his infidelity entanglements:

"But if he cheats on her…"

"If the associate cheats on your wife…"

"Yes. And she finds out… She's insanely jealous…"

I swallowed tea.

"Hard to imagine."

"She'll dump him. And I'm back in like Flynn."

I scowled confusedly, leaning on both elbows.

"So…you called, wanting me to prove *he's cheating on her?*"

"He's not."

"I'm lost." Sighing, pulling at my forehead.

"Really, Miss Russell, must we keep on? I really must have my lunch and return to the office." He swallowed some whiskey, slurping it softly from the ice. I reminded him he'd called me. "Your name and number"—an edge of disapproval grating here—"were in the Yellow Pages."

"Under DETECTIVE!" I said. "Why call, if not to prove your…associate…is cheating on your wife? Think you could get me to manufacture evidence, something like that? Well, you couldn't. I wouldn't."

"Never suggest anything of the kind. But…"

"But?"

"If he really *were* cheating…"

"You said he wasn't."

"That could change."

And with that he began to move serpentinely, dancing a creepy little bebop, seated all the while, adding:

"Given sufficient inducement."

"*Inducement?*"

My head jerked.

Slowly I straightened, getting the picture, slow on the uptake as I was, stiffening as I did. I drew in some smoke, then smashed out my cigarette. "I see." My voice crackled, eyes roamed wild over the silent piano, empty dance floor, off into the vivid blue through the picture windows along the opposite wall. When they stared back at Harris, like the cutting of a scythe, they were damp and hot. "Inducement," I said, tight voiced, "I was to provide."

I took to my feet not knowing I was doing it.

"I'm sorry," Harris pled.

Hand against his necktie.

"You were in the Yellow Pages."

"Not under CONCUBINES!" Surrounding tables' heads twisted. The stockbroker squirmed, face red and shiny. I hooked my pocketbook in the crook of an elbow, gathering up my gloves. "Right after all, Mr. Harris. Won't work out. I don't play seductress. If were I to, not for penny-ante damn stakes like these. I am a licensed private detective, licensed by the district attorney's office." I was whispering through my teeth. "Not some Lower Broad slut ho. Thank you, sir, for wasting my time."

I stormed for the exit. Heels stabbing through gold-and-burgundy Persian carpet. Then I spun back. On impulse. Returned, same path, same brusque pace. Planting the fist holding my gloves and handbag, back on my left hip, glowering down, my chest pumping in and out, couple of hard breaths. Speaking of, *I am woman, hear me roar.* Out the picture window, the lazy curl of the Cumberland, the Shelby Avenue Bridge, the old Nashville Bridge Company's sheds on the east bank. Harris, chewing liver, leaned back, placed his knife and fork carefully together on his plate, and put his hands on the table, either side of the plate. He waited.

"Just curious," I said, coldly now, but calmly, "what made you decide so easily it wouldn't work? I suppose I should consider that a complement."

He swallowed, wiping around his mouth.

Spread the napkin back upon his lap.

Sighed.

"Truthfully…"

There was the lilt of a question there. "Yes."

"Hoped you were one of those bra-burning kooks. Like Atlantic City."

I gave a slow nod.

Protest march. The Boardwalk.

Sign proclaiming:

WELCOME TO THE MISS AMERICA CATTLE AUCTION.

Another:

Picture of a kneeling nude woman with her body marked off as cuts of beef. "It'd be a mistake, sir," I said, "to assume feminism and free love to be parts of the same cause."

"I wouldn't know."

"Sorry to disappoint."

He looked at me squarely.

Brows gathering.

"Not at all"—he shrugged—"it's to your credit, as you say. You're a young lady, it would appear, with class. I have a daughter—

"Well," he went on, distractedly, "never mind that—"

He ate some fried corn.

"Sorry we couldn't do business," I said.

As feminists went, I was less Gloria Steinem, more Marlo Thomas, with a skosh of Mamie Van Doren/Jayne Mansfield swirled in, spicing things up, which probably would get me banished from the clubhouse. Feminism, though, was more than skin deep. I asked: "The hair thing for real?"

"Yes and no."

Again he circled his lips with the embroidered napkin.

"Your friend really wouldn't have gone for"—I swiped, coquettishly, my bangs—"*mousy* blonde?"

"Look, Miss Russell, I am sorry. But—"

He lifted the steel-blue eyes, like twisting drill bits when they were really looking at you, into you, which his were.

"Yes," I said.

He interlaced his fingers. "At risk of aggravating my already severe foot-in-mouth affliction, I must say, I figured if I mentioned hair color on the phone, and you didn't bristle too much, I might not be barking up the wrong tree. If you see my point."

I rolled eyes.

Then settled them, sighing.

Slightly nodding.

"I guess so."

I was turning to go again, more elegantly this time. "Hey," he called me back. Had out his black wallet, snapping out a crisp ten. Extended it. "Assume this will pay for your confidentiality—and, wasted time?"

My smile was faint. "I could use the money, Mr. Harris. But don't worry. I'd be mortified to tell this story."

"Feel better if you took it."

The faint smile became acidic. "Sure you would."

"Wait."

Quaking voice.

We locked eyes.

His glistening, all of a sudden. "What is it?" I said.

Moving closer, knitting brows.

"There may be…after all…something you can do for me."

"For you?"

"Legitimately. As a detective."

I waited, shifted weight to one hip, and rubbed up and down the flesh at the back of one arm. "Why is it," I said, twisting my mouth, "Rick Nelson singing 'Poor Little Fool' pops into my head?"

"Please. Sit down."

He shoved his plate aside, ground his palms together.

"It's my daughter."

I sat, arranging myself, pocketbook held two-handed on my lap.

I listened.

CHAPTER 2

S HE WAS TWENTY-TWO, STILL living at home, cum laude
art-history graduate, Vanderbilt. I told Harris he must be
very proud. He said he was. Then he said she didn't go out
on dates with men. I nodded.

Adding quietly:

"Most fathers, of daughters, would be ecstatic."

"Perhaps," he said, slightly breathless. He started to smoke a
cigarette. "She has a friend, a female friend. University classmate.
Nice girl, good family. They go out, together, couple nights every
week. I've followed them, twice. At my wife's urging."

I nodded.

They thought the girls, he added, might be meeting boys their
families wouldn't approve of.

"Were they?"

He told me he didn't know...

Maybe...

Both times he followed, they went straight to some dive.

His phrasing, not mine.

The dive was the CC Club.

Dickerson Pike, past the Starlite. I knew the place. Snapped
open my bag, took out my Kents, and lit one. I ran the tip of my
tongue along the edges of my front teeth, thinking what to tell
him. A year back the pious branch manager of a local bank
proclaiming to have been founded by two godly men, hired me

12

to investigate suspicions about an natty young male teller, who'd worked there a year, and by all accounts, was a stellar employee. For a week, I tailed him, from when he left work, until he seemed in for the night. He didn't always sleep at his apartment. I documented two separate addresses, besides his own, where he slept over. Both were residences occupied by bachelors living alone. I followed the teller twice to the CC Club. Both times he sat at one corner of the bar, drinking wine, talking to and laughing with a man, a beat-generation-type, who wore turtleneck sweaters, and a goatee.

Most other couples, drinking and dancing, as I scanned the club—though not all—were heterosexual. In fact, while I sat there, nursing a Scotch on the rocks, I got propositioned, twice, by men. When I typed my report, submitted it to the bank manager, it confirmed his suspicions.

The teller, in spite of being a stellar employee, was fired.

He was also blacklisted from every bank in Nashville.

"Did you go inside?" I asked E. Hillard Harris.

"The CC Club? No. Afraid she'd spot me. That's what I want you to do."

I nodded, closed my eyes, exhaled.

Eaten up with guilt all over again about the bank teller.

Like a scab torn off.

I looked Harris in the eye.

"CC's is a straight club," I told him, "but at one end of the bar, they let gay people sit and drink."

"I...don't understand."

"I think you do. It's what you suspect, but can't admit to yourself."

"I don't like your tone."

"Hire me, you're *going* to get my tone. Part of the service, no extra charge. And, perhaps your wife does believe they're going off on some illicit rendezvous with men, *as if that would be better?*" I shrugged, drew on my cigarette. He snicked a dark ash from his. "I don't know your wife," I went on, "but I know you a little, and I'm not sure what I think of you, but I don't think you're naïve."

"Miss Russell—"

"I'm not going to take your money, or this job, because I

know what I'm going to find. Ninety-nine-point-nine-percent sure, anyway."

"Saying my daughter's queer?"

My head gave a jerk.

I didn't like, on some gut level, the sound of that, so when I glanced back it was with a frown. "I'm…saying…I believe she is going to that club, to enjoy a snippet of time, relatively undisturbed, in a social setting, with someone, a person, she cares about, enjoys being with, just as you would with your wife—or your paramour—just as I once did, with my husband."

"It's against nature."

I shrugged. "Perhaps. I don't know."

"It's illegal."

"If that's your approach," I said, "call a cop, not me."

"Not going to call a cop, on my own daughter."

"Delighted to hear that."

"The friend, perhaps."

He motioned Eugene, rattling ice, for another drink.

"Even if your daughter didn't disown you, sir, you wouldn't be able to keep it just about the friend."

"Suppose that's true."

He nodded, sighing.

Then looking up again: "She *could* get in trouble."

"Sure she realizes that, but it probably doesn't change her feelings."

"Top of everything," Harris ranted, at a whisper, "it's blasphemy."

"I know." I looked at my cigarette, studied the corkscrewy smoke off the tip. Clicked the polished nails of my thumb and middle finger.

"Homosexuality is a sin, Miss Russell, roundly condemned in Scripture."

"I know."

"I'm a deacon in my church. You *know* that?"

"No." I was looking at him again. "How could I?" And as if to offer proof of his deaconship—not that there was any trouble believing it, hard as it was to swing a dead cat in Nashville, without smacking *some* church muckety-muck—he produced a small black leather-bound Bible from inside his suit.

"How could she do this…?"

Fanning well-worn membranous pages.

"To me," he went on, "to her mother?"

I blew smoke through pursed lips.

"I don't know your daughter, Mr. Harris, but I seriously doubt she, with malice aforethought, set out to do *anything*—to you, or her mother."

"Here it is," he announced:

And began to read from his little Bible, as Eugene replaced his old glass with a fresh one, heavy-bottomed, brimming with whiskey. "The unrighteous shall not inherit the kingdom of God…neither fornicators, nor idolaters, nor adulterers'"—my mouth gaped at that—"'nor effeminate, nor abusers of themselves with mankind'—et cetera, et cetera—'shall inherit the kingdom of God.'"

"You *seriously* quoted *that* to me?"

"There's more: Romans 1:26. 'For this cause—'"

"You are a hypocrite, sir."

His gaze lifted.

"*Excuse me*, young lady."

"That first verse: you conveniently ignore *adultery* on the list, even before *homosexuality*? Yet, you freely admit, both you *and* your wife are adulterers."

"Totally different."

I laughed bitterly.

Tapped my cigarette.

"*How?*" I said.

"You can't see that," he said, swigging from his new drink, "we have nothing to talk about."

I shook my head rapidly, incredulously. "Okay, sir, I get this is a difficult subject, and I'm no expert. But before I was a detective I was a registered nurse, so I know little bit about this from the medical side. The American Psychiatric Association considers homosexuality a sexual deviation, a type of…of sociopathic personality disturbance. Now, I don't know if I agree with that or not, but if it might be a medical diagnosis, doesn't it deserve the same compassion as any other—like, say, what if your daughter had *diabetes*?"

"Be serious."

"I am. Said I'm no expert. But your daughter deserves compassion, I know that, not condemnation. Not a Bible banged in her face, no offense. Unless it is your goal, to chase her away."

He swallowed.

Sighed from his nostrils.

"It isn't."

"Good."

I drank some of what remained of my tea, put down the glass. "Now, if I did what you asked, followed her into that bar, confronted her, or gave you ammunition to confront her"—I shrugged elaborately—"she'd be mortified. My advice, for what it's worth, and it's free, is this: if you can't find a way to deal with her, regarding this, her friend, compassionately, then don't deal with it at all. Let her live her life. If you can, though, be compassionate, avoid treating her like something *perverse*, or needing to be *fixed*, talk to her, ask her feelings, invite her friend over. Get to know them. As people."

"This is going to tear my family apart."

I blinked, and puffed from my cigarette, breathed out the smoke. "Considering, Mr. Harris, why you called me up in the first place, asked me here: I say, *how dare you*, lay that blame on your daughter."

He leaned back.

I snubbed out the cigarette. Slid out my chair, and stood to leave. "Maybe it's just my Pollyannaish streak," I said, stretching on gloves, "but figuring out how to deal with this issue—*issue*, not *crisis*—in a healthy way, is perhaps what ends up *saving* your marriage, your family."

"I…"

He sighed.

Shook his head, like he was trying to get a moth out of his ear.

"…don't know."

"Good luck." I opened my pocketbook, and thrust out one of my business cards.

"Call me if your wife does decide to divorce you."

He took it, thoughtfully, by a corner.

"I might be able to help."

CHAPTER 3

NOT HAVING GOTTEN MY BUSINESS lunch, nor even a buttered roll, I drove out along Church for two miles, tuning in the radio news, while threading through traffic. There was a lull in Vietnam, wake of the bombing halt, and there was more clucking about last month's Apollo 7 textbook space mission. First TV broadcast from an orbiting U.S. manned capsule. First U.S. spaceflight with a three-man crew. Unfortunately, both these feats the Russians had accomplished several times over.

Was an American moon landing viable in the coming months?
Could we beat the Russians to that?
Did anybody care?

Skirting the back of St. Thomas Hospital, where it still was then, and Mid-State Baptist, where ten years ago I was taking my nurse's training, I went to Rotier's on Elliston, and gorged down a cheeseburger and chocolate shake, belly up to the bar. Then, having the rest of the afternoon free, I decided to parlay that extra cheeseburger/milkshake poundage into some actual billable detective work, being that I was in the neighborhood. Next clinic on my list was on Hayes Street, down from St. Thomas, a drab suite on the third floor of the Altman building.

Dr. Ed Peebles—osteopath—weight control.

A fat doctor.

I apologized to the receptionist for coming with no

appointment, but said I was interested in losing weight.

I never asked for pills.

It was fine, she assured me, the doctor had an opening. They always did. The visit and medication would be $15, in advance, cash, no personal checks. I paid, gave my real name, a false local address, and said I was a secretary. The girl handed me a form with 195 questions on it, about my eyesight, hearing, nose and throat conditions, my liver and spleen, was I nervous?

Progressing to:

Did I feel alone?

Sad at parties?

Do I cry?

Do I wish I were dead?

Away from it all?

The girl took my completed questionnaire, asking was I allergic?

No.

What was my highest weight?

I answered honestly—138 pounds—I had put on weight when I was married, and lost some since separating from Fred. She weighed me with clothes and shoes on—133½ pounds—which I knew to be just about average for my age of twenty-eight, height of five-foot-six, according to the Society of Actuaries 1959 report. She took my blood pressure and pulse, and bust, waist, and hip measurements, recording twenty-seven inches for my usual twenty-five-inch waist, not seeming to notice me pooching my stomach out. She asked who referred me and I claimed to have heard about Dr. Peebles from a woman at a party whose name I'd, I was terribly sorry, forgotten. "Never heard that one before," she chortled, leading me into a small green antiseptic-smelling room where a white-clad technician had me kneel on a cushion beside a space-age-looking machine they called an *Achilleometer*. He tapped my Achilles tendon with a reflex hammer. The needle on the machine jumped into the middle range, which the girl told me meant I could take an average dose of their medicine.

"Of what medicine?"

I feigned surprise.

"All our medicine."

Last Friday, another fat doctor in Green Hills used an ankle-jerk machine on me they called a *photomotograph*. It had some extra knobs and dials, which, as a trained, licensed nurse, I can tell you were not real. Purportedly these devices were measuring how long it took my reflex to jerk then relax, a legitimate though not particularly reliable test of thyroid function. From there I waited in an exam room for Dr. Peebles, who came in after ten minutes with a box teeming over with pills, which had been prepared for me, without him ever having laid eyes upon me, nor spoken to me. "Congratulations, honey," he said, "on catching your weight problem early."

I batted my eyes.

"So, I have a weight problem, doctor?"

"Not a bad one. We caught it in time."

"What should someone my height and build weigh, doctor?"

I was beaming. Eager to learn from His Eminence.

"Wouldn't do you any good to tell you"—he fingered his eyeglasses more firmly up the bridge of his nose—"you people aren't going to get down to the weight you should anyhow, not and stay there."

You people?

I weighed 130 pounds naked that morning on my bathroom scale.

"My goal," he continued, "is to get you down to where you're more happy with yourself."

No one ever called me fat.

A bit hippy, perhaps.

Never fat.

A reliable size twelve.

Without an exam he gave me the box of pills, saying he would see me in a month and prescribe more. There were 252 pills, I later counted, to be consumed in thirty-days time. "What about diet?" I asked.

"We don't advise going on a diet," he said.

"Oh." I nodded.

Then, rattling the box, marveling:

"What *are* all these pills?"

"Oh, one is a kind of gland substance, there's an appetite depressant, a laxative—some people get constipated when they lose weight—vitamins and minerals that work with the pinks to reduce you, and something for your hips."

"My hips?" I swept my hands, looking, along the sides of my pelvis, down my thighs.

"My own preparation."

"Will there be side effects?"

"If you're not nervous," he said, "they won't make any difference. You might not sleep too well with the pink pills, but don't worry about it."

He opened the door for me. "Any other questions," he declared, "the receptionist can help you."

As I walked out there was another woman, an inch shorter than me, perhaps ten pounds heavier, paying $10 for her monthly checkup, and was led back. I drove home down Eighth Avenue with my crate of pills. I poured them onto a paper towel on my kitchen table in my small clean house, and broke open my 1968 PDR, setting about identifying this spectral array of pharmaceuticals, more out of interest, than investigative necessity. Chemists and pharmacists for the state would officially analyze and ID the pills. When done I shook that day's catch into its own baggie, twist-tied it, and labeled it with the date and Dr. Peebles' name. In the bigger bedroom I used for an office, I typed up and signed an affidavit detailing my visit to the doctor. I filed that with the others and dropped the baggie of pills into an old Jantzen shoe box with five other similar packages. My haul so far, from one visit each to six different fat doctors from one end of Tennessee to the other:

887 pills!

Average of 148 pills per doctor—some of whom, a state investigator told me, saw upwards of one hundred patients per day. The drugs included amphetamines, barbiturates, the sex hormone progesterone, diuretics, thyroid USP, and digitalis. The latter I knew very well to be deadly, if used carelessly, and had, in any case, no place in weight loss.

Oh, and Dr. Peebles' "own preparation…"

For my hips…

Prednisone.

A risky anti-inflammatory hormone.

I'd been hired by the State Department of Public Health to

spend a month going undercover visiting ten doctors across Tennessee who treated weight problems. This materialized after agents of the Bureau of Drug Abuse Control, with a deputy U.S. marshal, had raided a fat clinic in Atlanta, confiscating 2.5 million pills, mostly amphetamines, some barbiturates. And after the Tennessee State Medical Examiner reported he knew of ten, possibly as many as fourteen Tennessee women, ranging from 19 to 51 years of age, who had died—of potassium loss and cardiac toxicity—taking a "galaxy of drugs, in a rainbow of pills." This all on the heels of hearings in Washington, in January, of the Senate Antitrust Subcommittee, on the obesity business, shaping up to be a major scandal in American medicine.

I cut on Huntley-Brinkley, letting the TV warm up as I fixed a Scotch and water, and relished my first swallow of the day. I swirled tinkling ice cubes around cut-glass crystal, settling on my soft, deep sofa. By no means nonplussed about Dr. Peebles, and the rest. Hell, five years ago last Thursday, the most eminent doctor in Nashville—*still*, by the way, the most eminent doctor in Nashville—half tore my nurse's uniform off me in his plush office, making a most earnest attempt, to rape me.

He got a black eye for his trouble.

I came out of it with one shoe, my slip hanging out the front of my dress, and the start of a cascade of events, which got *me* blackballed out of nursing.

I sighed, slurping Dewar's, and got very drunk, staying up watching the election. By midnight NBC was reporting Humphrey 600,000 ahead. Yet it seemed Tricky Dick would win most of the remaining key states: California, Texas, New Jersey, Missouri. What Wallace was siphoning from Nixon in Dixie, depressingly, exactly offset what the racist ex-Alabama governor was bleeding from Humphrey in the blue-collar North. Nixon handily won Tennessee's electoral votes.

My own county, Metro-Davidson:

Went for Wallace!

I could scream.

I did scream.

By two A.M. it was looking frightfully good for Nixon. I dropped off to sleep, on my very own couch, in my very own bungalow, in my slip, under an Afghan, and awoke in time to hear all the networks conceding the election to Nixon. Not that I was any great LBJ fan. I just wasn't convinced the outgoing Democrat and incoming Republican weren't cut from the very same cloth. Did it really matter which party held the White House? Might they all be puppets on strings, serving the same masters.

My father would say I was crazy.

Wouldn't however be that long before I got a very bizarre hint I might just be right.

CHAPTER 4

Veteran's Day.

Ironically, though I didn't think of it at the time, no earthly reason to, it was one month to the day since Apollo 7 blasted off. Different from the Space Shuttle era, those days, NASA missions were a relatively big deal, worthy of much special coverage, Walter Cronkite demonstrating maneuvers with model spaceships, and so forth. And while more famous Apollo missions were in the offing, for the present Apollo 7 was a pretty big deal. America's first manned spaceflight in almost two years, since Gemini 12 launched on Veteran's Day, 1966. More significantly, it was the first U.S. space shot since the ghastly Apollo 1 incineration deaths, in a launch-pad fire, of three astronauts:

Grissom.

White.

Chaffee.

Anyway, on *that* Veteran's Day, 1968, I rode to Memphis in a Ford Galaxie with my father in spitting snow. "Glad you came, punkin," he said.

I smiled over, rubbing his arm. "Looked forward to it."

My father was fifty-five, short, plump, nearly bald, mostly Irish. He was also brilliant, a triple major in college in English, history, and economics, and a Vanderbilt Law graduate, who never practiced a day of law in his life. He was the Senior

Associate Editorial Page Editor of the *Nashville Tennessean.*

"Not every young lady," he mused, glimpsing between my pretty mug, his little Guinevere, and the interstate ahead, guiding the wheel one handed, "who'd spend the day with her ol' man, touring a rusting old airplane, listening to a passel of middle-aged—"

"Equally rusting…" I quipped, darting my head, flashing eyes.

"Let's say…*vintage*…war vets, swapping stories."

He was one of the few who knew and could tell my nose had once been broken.

By a man's fist.

"I can think," I sighed, "of worse ways to spend a day."

"Then we really must get you a more interesting life."

"Besides," I said, "I've buried my bridges with every other guy who's ever been important to me. Got to keep you schmoozed."

"You don't—"

"I'm kidding, daddy."

He wore red Ban-Lon, a brown fleece-lined nylon jacket, and a felt hat with a little red feather in the band. My getup was a copper-gold Shetland-wool sweater, twill pants, tall brown leather boots, and a pale-blue trench coat, with a belt and dark-blue stitching. "Hafta admit," my father said, several more miles down the road, "looking forward to seeing the old gal."

I asked, "The *Memphis Belle?*"

"Uh-huh."

I shook my head, snorting. "Didn't know better I'd think we were going to a riverfront whorehouse."

"*Sherry Lou.*"

"Kidding."

"Far as your mother's concerned," he said, "you aren't too old to wash your mouth out with soap."

"But you and I"—I smirked—"know better, don't we?"

He shrugged, forehead wrinkling, and after a pondering moment, I added…

"Mama sure wouldn't go on a trip like this."

I was gazing out, fingering my hair, the hilly strip beyond the Tennessee River, before the state dropped off to the Mississippi

Bottoms.

"Nooo," my father said. "Got that right."

I looked. "Evelyn either?"

"Don't see her in the car do you?"

"Too bad," I sighed, blinked. "Aren't marriages ever happy?"

He stared over twice.

"We're happy, punkin, just not welded at the hip."

"Okay."

"Happiness is a choice. Or…a…a warm puppy."

I shot him a weird look.

"*What?*"

He shrugged. "Couldn't come up with a Shakespearean retort, so I substituted Charles Schulz."

I laughed out loud.

Felt delightful, laughing, actually, being that my divorce from Fred Nates was just final, just last Friday. Ink barely dry. I, Sherry Russell, was officially a *divorcée*. We were quiet, passing Jackson, passing a sign saying MEMPHIS 78MI, when I remembered: "Oh, what'd Evelyn's brother want?"

Phone call my father took, just as we were leaving from his house in West Meade. "A favor."

"What else is new? Restaurant going under again?"

"Wants me to pull some strings, get his nephew in the reserves."

"Ahh…" I nodded significantly. "Can things get any more screwed up?"

"How so, punkin?"

"Men clamoring to get *into* the Army, to keep from fighting in a war. It's the Negro draftees who are going, and white kids not smart enough, or rich enough for college."

"Or a bribe, or a favor. I know."

"Going to do it?"

"Try." He shrugged, one shouldered. "Might, or might not be a slot available."

"Legal draft dodging," I groused.

MEMPHIS, TENNESSEE WAS PROUD BUT backward in 1968: big, rowdy, historically rich, gothic, weird, chockful of outlandish characters, one of whom I would soon meet. I wasn't a Beale

Street fan, but the music was said to be genius, a black/white melding, like the city itself. Only major American city named for an African capital, that of ancient Egypt, with the largest proportionate Negro population of any southern city.

Reeling, of course, from the King assassination, stained by that violent, convulsive bolt, as Dallas had been by JFK's killing. We were going to the National Guard Armory off Central by the fairgrounds, encountering protest marchers outside the security gate. Unwashed, unshaven, bell-bottomed, Afro'ed in some instances, leather-clad hippies, colored-glass love beads bedecking the men and the women, taunting, foolishly seemed to me, a phalanx of helmeted Memphis police, billy clubs drawn, eager for some head-knocking. The cops weathering epithets like "Pig," "Storm trooper," keeping the armory gates open for authorized visitors, like my father and me, the marchers hoisting signs:

MAKE LOVE, NOT WAR.

PEACE.

I was sympathetic.

To a point, but agreed with the billboards, saying:

BEAUTIFY AMERICA, GET A HAIRCUT.

"You know about that?" I asked, once we were through. Twisting back, I saw a Volkswagen Bus belonging to the hippies, psychedelically painted, a peace symbol in place of the VW logo on the nose. "No," my father replied, threading us toward the parking area. "Can't say I'm surprised." I looked at him grinning. "Go interview somebody," I said, "charge the whole day off to the paper."

"Don't think I won't."

GROOMED, AUSTERE, ULTIMATELY GRIM.

Military installations. Other worldly, other dimensional. *Do not attempt to adjust the picture. We are controlling transmission. We will control the horizontal, we will control the vertical.* I'd visited as a girl, with my father, a number of bases and posts, in his capacities, both as a newspaperman, and a Naval, later Army Reserve officer. I recalled Fort Bragg, N.C., in particular. I was eleven or so, my father depositing me for safekeeping in a canteen at the hospital, eating a Popsicle, reading a book, while he ran out to interview President Truman, visiting wounded from Korea. I sat cross-legged, in a dress, under some counter, where I'd gotten myself out of the way, and when I glimpsed up from under, I accidentally saw beneath the blue robe of a patient, a man on crutches, saw the stump of his above-the-knee-amputated leg.

Last year, on my Klan case, I'd seen men shot, beaten, blown up.

Yet my most seared-in memory remains that Korea soldier's thigh stump.

The Memphis Veteran's Day ceremonies were outdoors in forty-degree weather. We sat in bleachers, the snow having at least stopped. There were speeches, from a podium flanked by the American and Tennessee flags, by the mayor, a congressman, a fat man from the VFW, and the head of an American Legion Post.

It was the fiftieth anniversary of the end of World War I, for which an Army brass band played, "Over There," the George M. Cohan ditty. That got my father grinning ear to ear: he thought *Yankee Doodle Dandy*, with Jimmy Cagney playing Cohen, to be the greatest movie ever made. I huffed, smiling too, smoking a cigarette, more partial, however, to *Casablanca*. Besides the golden anniversary of the armistice ending the war to end all wars, they were also marking the silver anniversary, more or less, of the return stateside, with her aircrew, for a war-bond-selling/morale-boosting tour—in those dark early days of World War II—of the *Memphis Belle*.

My off-color joke notwithstanding, the *Belle* was not some long-in-tooth denizen of a riverboat-dock brothel. She was a Boeing B-17F Flying Fortress.

The plane, on display, served as backdrop for the day's festivities and speechmaking, a hour and twenty freezing minutes into which—my hot cocoa long gone—a bearish, gregarious man with thick hair, bushy mustache, was piped up to the podium by a flurry of, "Off We Go into the Wild Blue Yonder."

Hutcheson was the only name I caught; he wore a blue suit, flashing a red show hanky, and an American Legion cap festooned with medals. He told of being, in 1946, as a veteran B-17 pilot, commissioned by the then-Memphis mayor to lead a team to Altus, Oklahoma, the *Belle* having been discovered there, awaiting the scrap heap. The Air Force would give the city the bomber as a war memorial, as was common then, and Hutcheson's team was dispatched to ferry the airplane "home." They worked on its state of disrepair for several days, he described, and their first test flight went so well, the ex-pilot chuckled: "We just set our course for Tennessee and kept her right on flyin'."

His craggy pinkish face then turned grave.

Speech sober. "On this Veteran's Day it is well we remember the Mighty Eighth's role. That's the 8th Army Air Force, for you civilians out there, maybe there's a dogface, or a swabbie, like ol' Charlie Russell, I see out there, who need enlight'nin'—"

I twisted.

Surprised.

"You know him?"

My father said, "We've…met."

"It is well we remember the Mighty Eighth's role," he went on, "in winning the Allied victory over Nazi Germany. FDR famously quipped Hitler built a fortress around Europe, but forgot to put a roof on it! It broke the back of the Luftwaffe. With the British Bomber Command, it created a second front, long before Normandy. Crippled vital enemy war industries. However"—he rearranged, settling his weight on his hands, grasping the podium—"significant though these triumphs were, they do not fully account for the Eighth being one of the most famous organizations in the history of warfare. For military greatness is not simply measured by victories. But, by the capacity to sustain great losses, yet return to battle. Here too, the Eighth was tested, and not found lacking. Never turned back by enemy action." He shook a finger in the air. "Never. And no greater was that testing than during the combat career of this grande ol' dame, behind me, the *Memphis Belle*."

Scattered applause.

The band struck up the "Nothing can stop the U.S. Air Force!" stanza of "Wild Blue Yonder." The old plane stood on a concrete pedestal behind chain-link fencing strung with barbed wire. Its windows and glass nose were translucently cloudy, its olive-drab paint faded. "The *Belle* flew twenty-five sorties," Hutcheson resumed, "between November 1942 and May 1943.

Before the rise of the long-range escort fighter. The *Belle* and her sisters defended their honor against the Luftwaffe's marauding, raping, Focke-Wulfs and Messerschmitts, with only the ruggedness of the B-17, and dogged bravery, and supreme determination of her crews to draw upon. Now," he said, and paused, swallowed, "the *Belle* here, always brought her crew home, but during that period she saw action, many were not so fortunate. Typical losses: *fifteen percent* of the attacking force. One of every seven Americans stumbling out of bed in the chill dawn of England, for a mission over Hitler's Europe in early 1943, failed to return. By the Kraut surrender, in that three-year air war, 79,265 American fliers were killed in action."

He paused.

Moment of silence.

True emotion.

I was mesmerized.

"Now, don't misunderstand, nor misquote me—Charlie, Charlie I'm talking to you, our representative here from the liberal press..."

"This guy," I said, "is a real comedian."

"Don't know the half of it," my father said, Hutcheson going on at length, now comparing Vietnam to World War II, calling the hippies outside, "those shaggy Bolsheviks at the gate," slamming their opposition to the war. The upshot being—unbelievably—a numerical comparison of American military dead, across all branches, in Vietnam since 1961, to that not-quite eighty thousand figure he'd quoted for just the air war, just in Europe, in World War II.

The math working out to the Vietnam "score" being less than two-fifths the World War II one.

It was all reminding me far too much of those goddamned nightly news body counts. "I see his point," I told my father, leaning close, "but surely..."

"There's a more sensitive way," he said, "to couch it?"

"Yeah."

"Buzz Hutcheson ain't no charm-school graduate."

"Buzz?"

"His nickname. *Don't* you know who that is?"

"No," I said glimpsing. "Should I?"

"R. J. Hutcheson…?"

I stared, and he added, "Hutcheson Ford-Mercury."

"The guy on TV? That crazy guy? In Nashville?"

"He's the biggest car dealer in Tennessee, and hence one of the paper's biggest advertisers. That's mostly how I know him"—he shrugged—"but I run into him, state-level Legion functions, Boy's State program. Plus," he added, "he's got more money'n you can shake a stick at. Might run for governor in 1970."

A woman in her mid-forties, in a cranberry-red coat with a mink collar, was coaxed up from the front row of seats by Hutcheson, and began talking up protection and restoration. Displayed outdoors for eighteen years now, the Flying Fortress was on a downhill slide, she lamented, pacing one end of the speaker's platform to the other, dome hat matching the pretty red of her coat. Without a lot of funds raised, the *Belle* risked decaying from war memorial to eyesore, helped along by vandalism, weather, lack of public notice. Redcoat's name was Margaret Polk. She was, in fact, the real "Memphis Belle"—ex-fiancée of the bomber's wartime pilot, the woman who'd inspired the plane's nickname and cheesecake nose art.

When the end came at last we were all invited forward to tour the B-17.

"Let's go," I told my father.

"Wait a minute," Charlie Russell said, sheepish.

I dropped back on my rump, which was fairly numb, by the way. "What?"

"We don't have to."

"Said you wanted to see her."

I was smiling, tugging his arm.

"Said you were looking forward to it."

"It's okay. You're cold, punkin. The speeches were overly verbose. I should've known that would be the case, considering all the politicians, and wannabe politicians, involved."

"I want to see the plane, daddy."

"Okay, but, look, before we go…"

"What?"

"I'm sorry," he said, "but, there was an ulterior motive for inviting you."

"Yeeez?" I said, deep-voiced.

"Buzz called me."

"The crazy car dealer."

"Heard you were a detective. Wants to meet you."

"Okay," I said, "let's go meet him."

"Not so fast…"

He sighed. "Dunno if I want you involved in one of his flaky schemes."

I shrugged, swiping my hair back, gloved fingers. "Such as?"

"I don't know what it's about."

"We should go find out," I said. "And, if it's a legitimate job, it's my decision, daddy—*my choice*—let's be clear."

"Okay."

"Why'm I just now hearing this?"

"Guess," he sighed, "wanted you to come, 'cause you wanted to spend time with your old man, not 'cause of some rich Memphis snake-oil salesman."

He stared off, sadly.

Then back.

"Silly, I know."

"Well, it's not silly, and now you know the answer, so let's go meet my prospective new"—my eyebrows bounced—"rich, client." And I admit, I had dollar signs before my eyes. There were no books how to make it as a private detective. Actually there was one, *The Story Behind Private Investigation*, published by some guy in California, ten years ago. It was nuts and bolts, but nothing on how to make a living, the business side, *especially as a divorced woman!* Guess I'd write my own book someday. Had a feeling, though, if there were some secret to success as a female private eye it involved getting my foot in the door with some rich kook, with power, and powerful friends, who might be about to get more power, and more friends.

Like R. J. "Buzz" Hutcheson."

CHAPTER 5

O N TELEVISION, HUTCHESON, THE CAR dealer, dressed like Davy Crockett, with an obvious toy flintlock, in these outlandish, clownish car advertisements seen from one end of Tennessee to the other, mostly late at night. Crossing spongy brown turf that day in Memphis, pocketbook under an elbow, my thumb hooked on the strap, I approached Hutcheson, alongside my father, as a verbal fisticuff was heating up—not about Vietnam—about flyboys having had it easy in World War II compared to ground-pounders. The car dealer was haranguing a Battle of the Bulge vet, leaning on a cane, missing an arm, an eye, and evidently most of his hearing, all from a single German shell—they called it an eighty-eight—ricocheting around inside his Sherman tank. I wouldn't have the audacity to compare dangers with a guy like that, but Hutcheson wasn't pulling any punches, cataloging the heroics and hardships of bombing Germany. Railing about flak, fighters, the SS, enraged civilians, anoxia, mid-air collisions, malfunctions, lack of fuel. "Least on the ground," he bellowed, "you fellers got medical attention. The air, might take hours, get back to base, fatal hours. No fifty-below on the ground, was it? No worries about enough oxygen, keep you alive. You hunkered down in foxholes, didn' ya? No place to hide up there."

Wasn't sure the vet with the cane wasn't going to start waling on Hutcheson with it. But before it came to that my father, the navy guy, and lawyer, interposed himself.

"Gentlemen, gentlemen…"

Luckily, both didn't turn on him.

Eventually we were introduced. Hutcheson, taller than my father, outweighing him by twenty pounds, thanked me for coming. Told me how *enchanted*—that was the word he used—he was to meet me. Then he said, bending to my ear, "Don't want to talk here, operational security, loose lips and all that."

My father, his hands on his hips, rolled his eyes.

"Forgodsakes, Buzz, World War II is over."

"Less go to over to my house."

His heavy hanging face bounced between us.

"We kin have drinks and talk."

"Listen here, I—"

I interrupted. "That's fine, Mr. Hutcheson."

"Good, good. Lemme just wrap up couple things here."

"I want," I said, gently biting, releasing my lower lip, "my B-17 tour first."

Memphis Belle receives title of official airplane of
Tennessee
—Headline in *The Tennessean*, 2017

CHAPTER 6

NOT LONG AFTER, WE WERE ensconced in the game room of Buzz Hutcheson's white-trimmed brick Colonial off Quince Road in East Memphis. In the center was a pocket billiards table. There was a two-horned rhinoceros head mounted on one wall, opposite a tall rack of pool cues. Two thick oxblood leather chairs faced a fireplace at the far end. On the grate a fire crackled and burned putting forth delicious heat, which I absorbed in great gratitude, chilled to the bone as I had become at the armory. My father and I were smoking, he his Pall Malls, myself Kents, in the deep chairs, making use of separate jade ashtrays.

Hutcheson held court from behind a bar with a brass foot rail, to the right of the hearth. His petite tight-faced wife, named Lillybet, had greeted us. She was a blonde, hair combed straight back from her forehead, with a small perplexed mouth, and vivid crimson lipstick. Her maroon dress was wool crepe, plain, except for bright buttons, and tiny loops for trim. Wearing good perfume, she offered me use of an elegant powder room, off the entrance hall, then ushered me back to the game room where the men were settling. "Thank you, duckie," Hutcheson said as she left us, turning with a swirl of her skirt to quietly bring shut the pocket doors, at the end of the ivory-white room opposite the fire, then tap away on very high heels. "Howza'bout a martini?" our host announced, clapping, rubbing big paws in circles. "I'm famous for my martinis."

"You're *famous*," my father said, through clouds of Pall Mall smoke, "for being a fat man in a coonskin cap and fringe jacket, cocking a toy rifle." Hutcheson, snorting, shook a thick index finger. "That get up, Charlie, sells more cars in this, the *City of Churches*, than me gettin' all liquored up on TV would."

"Probably," my father said. "Except it's obvious to most of us, you're pretty damn liquored up before you ever make those commercials."

"You try hawkin' cars sober"—Hutcheson belly laughing, whamming the bar top, open-palmed—"with a raccoon on *your* head."

My father chuckled politely. He had nothing against drinking, only lack of dignity. "No martini for me, Buzz," he finally said, smoothing back the tuft of silver atop his otherwise bald dome. "Have a Scotch and soda, though, if you don't mind."

"Comin' up. All I got's Chivas."

My father huffed.

"I'll make do, thank you."

I turned from my father.

"You may make me a martini, sir."

"Why Charlie," he said, eyes giddy, "you've raised a young lady of sophistication, in spite of yourself."

"Or of iron stomach. Know what Humphrey Bogart said don'tcha, punkin?"

"Here's lookin' at you, kid?"

"Besides that. On his death bed he's s'posed to have said: 'Never should've switched from Scotch to martinis.'"

"Oh, well, then, nothing to worry about, daddy: I still drink plenty of Scotch."

Hutcheson roared.

"Gotchaself a real pistol there, Charlie. For a girl."

Flinching, I felt the color drain from my face.

Why always the qualifier?

For a girl.

Why not just a pistol?

Hutcheson's hair, center parted, and his eyebrows and mustache were all thick and shaggy, black almost, highlighted with gunmetal. He had a broad bulbous nose, heavy jowls, and deep furrows to the corners of his mouth. He fixed our drinks, a highball for my father, then assembled our martinis. A lot of ice in a silver penguin shaker, cold Gordon's gin, French vermouth, several dashes of bitters. He served them in deep champagne goblets, with a green olive in each, on little red skewers. "To success!" he toasted.

"Success," my father and I repeated.

We all drank.

It was a good martini.

I exhaled. "Success of what, sir?"

"All things." He was easing up onto a padded stool, before the bar, twisting his dripping cold glass by the stem.

"We have a possible job to discuss, I believe?"

There was a shuddering nod, then a look at my father.

"Direct, ain't she?"

"You have no idea."

He stood, carrying his martini, jangling change in his pocket, loudly slurping from his glass, pacing about the billiards table heavily. At the far end he stopped, facing us, stance wide.

"An associate of mine was recently killed."

My eyes narrowed. "Killed how?"

"Single vehicle car crash. Mississippi. Near Corinth."

He drained his glass and returned to the bar, pouring a refill out of the penguin. I hoped he wasn't going to have another drink after each sentence. "Cops say he was drunk," Hutcheson resumed, pacing again, "veered off the road, middle of the night, slammed into a billboard support head on."

"Ouch," my father said.

"Been known to happen," I added.

"Sure," Hutcheson said. "And no doubt, Ralph, *was* one to snort down a few too many shooters." As if punctuating that, he gulped from his own, second, martini. "But—he was a damn good pilot. Ralph Butterworth. One of my kids in the 358th."

I glimpsed my father, then Hutcheson again. "My old squadron," he explained. "I was squadron commander. I was 'The Old Man' at age twenty-six. That's how it was in the Air Corps."

"Flew your first combat in the Philippines, right, Buzz?"

He said he had.

I gave my father a look. Don't encourage this man off track, I wanted to say.

"So," I said, "Ralph Butterworth, who you served with, was a B-17 pilot?"

"Yes. Speaking of martinis"—Hutcheson lithely indicated his—"Ralph nicknamed his ship *Martini Jeanie*. Later when he transitioned to fighters—night fighters, specifically—he named his P-61, *Nightcap*."

"Sounds like a man," my father said, "who'd hoist a few."

"My point was going to be," Hutcheson pressed, "Ralph was too good a pilot. Still is...*was*... Find it hard to believe, drinker or not, he'd be behind the controls, so impaired, he couldn't handle himself."

"We're talking about a car, Buzz," my father said, "not a plane."

"Don't think it would matter."

"Think again."

Through my sweater, pinching a bra strap, I asked:

"What do you want from me, Mr. Hutcheson?"

"Call me, Buzz, my dear." He looked at his drink, twirling it, then heavily back down on me. "I wanna know if Ralph Butterworth had help running into that pole. I wanna know, if he was murdered."

"Now just a damn minute, Buzz."

Snapped my head.

"Hold on, daddy. Go on, sir. Why *might* he have been murdered?"

"He called me—full day before the accident—saying he'd be driving through the night, had some business to take care of, then wanted to drive up and see me, right away, then he had to get back to his family. Sounded shook up. Said it'd be 'bout midnight, when he reached Memphis, begged me to see him anyway, despite the hour. Said somebody had sabotaged his airplane, his personal plane. Flies for a charter service. Said somebody tampered with the altimeter. That he'd barely managed to bring it in safe."

"You believe him?" I asked.

He shrugged.

"Said he'd bring proof."

"What kind of proof?"

"Dunno."

"Where was he driving from?"

"Dunno."

"But," I said, "he wanted to drive *up* to see you? His exact wording? *Up?*"

He thought, gazing at the light fixture over the billiards table.

"Yes, that's *exactly* what he said."

I nodded, exhaling. "Where did he call from?"

"Wouldn't say. Said the phone might be tapped. Operational security."

Hutcheson's big furrowed face traveled to my father.

"I had the same reaction you did, Charlie. *Operational security—who's he kidding?* But then, Butterworth never made it."

"You heard nothing else?" I said.

He wagged his head. "Stayed up till three. Fig'red he got tired, pulled off. Next morning, I hung round till noon, then called his home in Pennsylvania. Got one of his kids, said he'd died in an accident, told me where. Then the wife grabbed the phone, sobbing, angry, yelled at me…"

Voice trailing off.

"Yes?" I prodded.

"Hadn't I done enough? she cried."

He sucked dry his second martini.

Poured another, omitting the olive. "Anyway, I'm askin' myself, by this time, was he maybe really into something? And…"

I nodded him on.

"To contradict Mrs. Butterworth, I began to think…maybe…I hadn' done enough…"

I filled full, then emptied my lungs.

"What did you do next?"

"Called the sheriff in Corinth. They asked was I family. Couldn't discuss details 'cept with family. I pressed to know, was there an investigation? Was told, no. Single vehicle, alcohol thought to be involved. Open and shut. Deputy then added, he'd told me too much already."

"Did you," I asked, sipping gin, "pursue your concerns?"

"Not really. Not yet anyway."

He stared down the fathomless depths of his glass.

"That's what I'm hiring you for."

"Buzz. This is my daughter, not one of your service mechanics, or used-car salesmen."

"Daddy. It's okay. It's what I do."

I twisted up, hooking back my hair. "How long ago was this?"

"Accident happened 12:25 A.M.," he said, "Thursday morning, week ago."

"Halloween," I said.

"Yes."

"Why wait, if you were that concerned?"

"That's a legitimate question."

He gave a sigh, harshly.

"Thanks," I said, and ate my olive off its little skewer.

Waiting for my legitimate answer.

"I wanted to wash my hands of it."

"Uh huh."

"Sure, we were comrades in arms."

Then he half-yelled.

Spreading arms.

"Quarter century ago, and not as if we were best buddies."

"I understand."

"Hell, I was his commanding officer. We'd run into each other, one or two reunions over the years, then he calls me up out of the blue asking for money."

I bent my head.

"Financial troubles?"

"Nothin' like that. To finance a project. I've got money. I like to be generous, and he was enthusiastic. I went along. But he kept wanting more. I cut him off. Hell, I'm ashamed to say, when he didn't show that night, my first thought was: *good riddance!* Guess, the honest answer to your question, young lady, is, I feel guilty. Gnawing at me. Didn't help, his wife, makin' me feel like dogshit."

"You didn't catch her," I said, "on her best day."

"Sure," he said quietly, lifting and dropping his brows.

I finished my drink.

"Buzz."

It was my father.

On his feet, hands jammed in his pockets.

"Quit beating round the goddamn bush. What kind of project? What the hell is this?"

I flickered hazel eyes to my father, then back to Hutcheson.

"Perhaps," I said, "you *should* start at the beginning, sir."

"Sure. Refills?"

My father accepted.

I shook my head, and took a pad and pen out—"Just like a reporter," my father quipped, proudly—and I smiled over my shoulder, and waited, legs crossed, pinching my slacks' plaid twill crease, for a whole new batch of martinis to be shaken in the penguin. I used the time to get the particulars jotted down. "You said his name was Ralph?"

"Yes. Last name, Butterworth. Like it sounds."

I wrote that boldly, underlined it. He lived in Pennsylvania. Beaver Falls. He was a bomber pilot in the war, and after helped run a commercial pilot service, charter operation. "But, besides flying," Hutcheson explained, pacing beneath the rhinoceros head by then, a hand pocketed, the other waving his new drink, "he was a writer, and historian. Published several books, numerous articles."

"On?" I asked.

"Aviation. Wartime Germany." He came around us to the fireplace, taking a book off the mantle. "Here's one. He presented it to me, autographed, one of those squadron reunions—fact, he was the historian of the 303rd Bomb Group Association, sort of our alumni club—anyway, I got this from upstairs, thinking you might wanna see it."

"Yes."

I flipped through it, while Hutcheson added a log to the fire, getting it roaring again with a poker wielded vigorously. The book was titled, *Adolf and Eva*.

"I'd like to borrow this."

"Thought you might." I passed it to my father. Back on his feet, I saw Hutcheson reach another book from the mantle, a small paperback. "I'm told," Hutcheson said, "that the stuff, like that"—indicating the *Adolf and Eva* hardcover—"which he published under his own name, is considered quite good, historically authoritative."

"But?"

"But—he published this as well, under a pseudonym." He waggled the paperback at me, handed it off. Copyright was 1966, the book called: *Flying Saucers–Grave Affair*. Subtitled: *Powerful New Evidence That They are Real!!!!!!!!!!* Authored by, according to the cover, a Frank Williams. Thumbing to the ABOUT THE AUTHOR blurb, I read that Frank Williams was a prolific author—no details provided along those lines—an aviator, decorated war vet. I huffed, grinning, seeing amongst his bona fides, TV appearances on Art Linkletter, *The Mike Douglas Show*, and *The Alan Burke Show*. The latter in particular was known for its steady flow of crackpots submitting to personal attacks from the acerbic host. I shut the paperback and, as I had with the other book, said I'd like to borrow it, and handed it off to my father. Who wouldn't, I knew, give a book like that the time of day. "How do you know this Frank Williams," I asked, "is Ralph Butterworth?"

"He told me."

Shrugging, Hutcheson was back, seated, at the bar, his again-refurbished drink held by the rim. "Brought me that, when he came to me, first time, asking for financing."

"Believe in flying saucers, Buzz?" my father asked.

"Course not."

"Why then," I said, "would he believe *this book* would induce you to give him money? When he wouldn't even claim it himself, under his own name."

Hutcheson cleared his throat. "Ralph Butterworth's next legitimate book," he said, "was supposed to be a paperback about Nazi secret weapons. Like V-2 rockets, jet fighters, rocket planes. That kind of thing. Part of a series, and Ballantine, think it was, paid him an advance, but he got bogged down, off on this tangent, missed his deadline. They wouldn't give him no more money, and killed the deal. That's when he came to me, wanting me to bankroll his research. Said he'd self-publish if he had to."

"When was this?" I asked.

He shrugged. "Early this year."

"Research on what?"

"Foo fighters."

CHAPTER 7

S TARTING IN LATE '44, ACCORDING to Buzz Hutcheson, all through that winter into early '45, there had been a rash of sightings, by allied aircrews over German territory, of ball-shaped, spherical aircraft, glowing orange and red. Some described them as fireballs. The nickname *foo-fighters* stuck, *feu*, being French for *fire*. Butterworth, in fact, had been one of the pilots reporting them, when he flew P-61 Black Widows. He'd had a spook with him—an intelligence officer, that is—a corroborating witness. Butterworth had recently tracked that man down to interview him for his planned book. I asked what they were, these, foo-fighters. "Nobody knows," Hutcheson acknowledged. "Some believe they were some super-high-tech Nazi fighter, flying saucer or something. Dunno if I believe that, but it's a lingering mystery, one that interested Ralph, and me, I admit, once we got to talking."

"Which explains you giving him the money," I said.

He nodded.

"And why," I added, askance at my father, "a wacky book on flying saucers, these foo-fighters thought to perhaps be flying saucers, was ironically, a credential of sorts."

"Kept spiraling though," Hutcheson resumed, disgustedly. "Kept telling me less and less, wanting more and more. What was I s'posed to do? Last time he called—well, next to the last time—I pulled the plug. Wanna know the last straw, what he wanted?" He stormed forward, coiled with contained anger. "Wanted me to finance him an excursion to Buenos Aires, forcrissakes. Wanna know why?"

"Sure," I said.

"To look for Martin *goddamn* Bormann!"

Hutcheson stalked away, floor creaking, snapping underfoot, to the far end. "The Nazi?" My father exclaimed, pushing down on one padded arm, pivoting in the leather chair.

"Who?" I asked, looking from one man to the other. "I've heard the name, I think."

My father rattled his head, as if this were all completely nuts, saying:

"Hitler's second in command."

"As I understand it," Hutcheson added, heavy-leaning on the heels of his hands, end of the pool table. "Bormann either died at the end of the war, or escaped, and is alive and well in South America. Well, if Ralph Butterworth wanted to be the American Simon Wiesenthal, fine, more power to him. He could hunt all the Nazis he wanted, but not on my dole. That was latter half of September, thereabout. The rest," he said, flinging ape arms, "much as I know, you know. He called me, panicked, to arrange our meeting, day before the accident."

"And never made it," I said.

"No."

"Doesn't sound like you're to blame."

"Thanks for that," he said, diverting his gaze, propping a hand on a hip.

"Okay," I said, with a sigh, "you want me to find out what happened."

"Yes."

"Buzz," my father cut in. "You call the wife back? Call the sheriffs, or highway patrol in Mississippi back?"

"No."

"Why in hell not?"

"Daddy."

"Because that's what I pay people for, goddamnit. I got businesses to run, and..." Hutcheson sighed. "Look, I don't got the foggiest idea what kinda shit—pardon my language, ma'am—Butterworth got into. Till I do, there are reasons, important reasons, I must stay above it. Fact, I need to know, case there's already a threat of any of it blowing back."

I said:

"The gubernatorial race."

Jolted, like with a little electric shock, he turned, staring out one eye.

Then grinned out one side of his mouth.

"Why, might you say that, little lady?"

"My father told me."

He nodded. Short jerky movements. Rubbing the back of his thick neck, looking at his glass. "All right, that's it, lot of it, anyway."

Then, quietly:

"Don't look at me like that."

"I'm not looking at you in any way, sir."

"I *do* want to know about Butterworth."

"But," my father excoriated, "you don't want to risk getting dirty to do it. You'd rather my daughter—" I was up, shoulders back, eyes level on Hutcheson. "S'okay Daddy." Then to Hutcheson: "I suppose, I should start with the wife."

"You'll help?" he said, vulnerably.

"For one hundred dollars a day, plus expenses," I said. "Five days in advance, refundable if I don't put in that much time."

"Deal."

"Got yourself a detective."

"Good. I've prepared a file. I'll get it when I get your retainer check. A check, I assume, is acceptable?"

"A check would be lovely."

"If I were you," he added, "I'd get hold of his pilot's logbook."

"Okay." I jotted a note about that.

"He's been flying one end of the country to the other, on these investigations, I was paying for: the logbook ought have all that in it, even if there's no other record. A good pilot, a professional, would never fudge his logbook. Oh, just remembered, one other thing he said, during that last call, when I asked where he was, that absolutely made no sense."

"Yes?"

"Said he would coming to me from *Peenemünde*. Said it twice.

All the way from Peenemünde, Colonel, Peenemünde. Then, he said, *Auf wiedersehen*."

"Where's Peenemünde?" I said. "Mississippi?"

My father shrugged.

"Hardly," Hutcheson said. "Germany, Baltic coast island we hit during the war."

Then, pausing a beat:

"Secret German rocket facility."

CHAPTER 8

HUTCHESON SERVED TWO MORE MARTINIS out of the penguin, gave one to me, and poured my father another generous dram of Chivas Regal. "Drink up," he said, excusing himself, cocktail in hand, to get my check and the file he'd prepared. If he was drunk, on his sixth Martini, he wasn't showing it. Not much. While we waited, my father and I shot pool. We weren't very good. The check Hutcheson handed me, upon returning, was written out in bombastic blue fountain pen for $875.

Blinking, I said, "This is too much."

"Decided to pay you $125 a day, and a full week's retainer."

"That isn't necessary."

"Call it incentive. I'm a businessman. I don't make my living, which is a very good living, as I'm sure you know, paying people more than, or even as much as they're worth. But you, my dear, are yet to prove to me you're not worth that and more." He shrugged. "Perhaps you'll work all the harder to show me you are."

I began to fold it, put it in the zippered inside pocket of my purse.

"If you're sure?"

"Besides, wouldn' want your ol' pappy thinking I'm taking advantage. Making you deal with my dirt for minimum wage. Nor, for that matter, do I *want any of that dirt*," he added firmly,

47

"bein' aired out, in the *Tennessean,* or *Commercial Appeal,* or any other news rag." I assured him, looking him in the eye, all *our* dealings would be confidential. "What does our esteemed representative," Hutcheson said, rotating theatrically to my father, "of the Fourth Estate say?"

My father rose, I thought, with a bit of swagger. "You invited me here, Buzz. Spoke freely in front of me with no preconditions. You wanted guarantees from the press, you shouldn't have."

Hutcheson lifted his drink.

"Touché."

"That aside," my father said, me tossing a proud grin his way, "unless and until a legitimate story comes out of this, I won't say anything. My word. And if I do need to print something, I won't blindside you with it."

"Fair enough."

I told him I'd mail him a contract and receipt, adding with a small scowl at my father, I could have brought all the necessary paperwork, had I known they might be needed. "I'm sure," Hutcheson said, "we can all trust one other."

A grin pulled across his bearish face.

"Cheat me, and I'll write a letter to the editor about it."

"Hilarious, Buzz," commented my father.

"One other thing…"

He paced, grazing thick fingertips the length of the billiards table.

"My contribution to all this, completely, nothing Ralph said."

"Go on," I said.

"As a former pilot, I pay attention to these things. And, as an auto dealer, I stay abreast of *that* industry."

"Of course," I encouraged.

"Heard of Walter Reuther?"

"No," I said.

"Labor union leader," my father said, grimacing. "UAW president."

"Yes," said Hutcheson.

"A socialist. Democratic Party figure. Johnson crony."

"Yes."

"And," my father added.

Interest, more than he'd displayed the whole time, alighting his face.

"He was in a plane crash last month."

"Give that man a *cee-gar.*"

"Dulles Airport," my father added.

"Right. And the cause…?"

I looked at my father, shaking his head, and back at my new client.

"*Altimeter* malfunction."

"Same thing," I said, "Ralph Butterworth claimed."

BEFORE HEADING BACK TO NASHVILLE, my father treated me to what he claimed to be the best pork-barbeque sandwiches in Memphis—quick to add, the Beacon Drive-In, in Spartanburg, S.C., might be better, which he'd learned about doing Army Reserve summer camp at Fort Bragg with another newspaper editor/reserve officer, a South Carolina man, who'd attended college in Spartanburg. The two had a friendly debate going over Carolina-style mustard-based sauces versus Tennessee-style tomato-based ones. Driving back we were quiet, only stations between Memphis and Jackson that would tune in being country-western, which my father despised. I'd become a lukewarm fan through my association with Pauline Prescott. We got a laugh out of "Harper Valley P.T.A." He liked Eddy Arnold's, "Then You Can Tell Me Goodbye." When the station faded to static, my father announced:

"Got a damned-good mind to call Buzz up, tell him I don't want you touching any of this with a ten-foot pole."

"Oh no you won't," I said, unfolding out of my gin-and-barbeque-induced half-stupor.

"You're my daughter."

"That's nothing to do with anything."

"Hell it isn't. Look, punkin, if there *is* anything to this, and I have my doubts, but if there is, it's dangerous."

"So?"

"So, he—and you—should let the police handle it."

I snorted, smirking.

My father was a huge let-the-system-handle-it guy. "The point *is*, daddy, they won't. Even if they aren't corrupt, or incompetent, they're busy. This one's wrapped up as far as they're concerned. One more out of fifty thousand motor-vehicle deaths per year. Plus, alcohol was involved. Plus, Butterworth was an out-of-state stranger—*a Yankee to boot!* That makes a difference to some, and *you* know it does. Lastly, thank God, he didn't take anybody else with him. There's nobody else to answer to."

He looked over.

Rearranging his grasp on the wheel.

Gave a nod. "I see your point."

I smiled. "Thank you."

Those words meant a lot, coming from my father.

"So, then," he said. "Why you?"

"Why not?"

"Don't give me that look. I'm not Fred. I don't object to you, any woman, working any job you want, that you're qualified for. I just don't happen to think you're qualified for this." His hands on the wheel shrugged. "Nor would I be."

"Because it's dangerous."

"Yes."

"What was my Klan case? I got shot."

"Methinks, you're making my point for me, punkin."

"I caught a killer, helped the FBI, and I'm still here to talk about it."

"You were dragged into that by your loyalty to and desire to help a friend, maybe by some pangs of white guilt. You were also feeling stifled by Fred. You needed an excuse you could justify, to yourself, and Fred, to pry yourself out of that house, out of the homemaker trap."

I stared a few seconds.

Shaking my head slightly.

Surprised how much he understood. "Go back to political science, daddy." I looked away, not giving him the satisfaction of knowing how right he was. "Pop psychology isn't your forte."

"But I'm right."

"Fine, you're right."

"But here"—I could tell he was picking words carefully, so as not to rile me—"you have not got any loyalties, not to me, *certainly* not to Buzz Hutcheson. Nor is there anything for you to prove, nor escape from. You're out of your marriage. You have your own place, to come and go from as you please. Just asking you to settle down. Get into a routine." We were coming out of Jackson, a highway sign indicating the CASEY JONES HOME AND RAILROAD MUSEUM.

I sighed, studying my manicure, pad of my thumb running across the other nails.

"Sounds like you're advising boredom."

"Routine doesn't have to be boring."

"Here we go again, the Dr. Joyce Brothers act. Okay, message received and understood." I faced his way in my seat, legs folding under me. I rubbed the gold-plaid at my knee. "But you're wrong," I said, "about a few things."

"Such as?"

"Me having no loyalty to Buzz Hutcheson. I didn't, but I do now. He's my client. He asked for my help, which I appreciated, felt flattered, and freely agreed to give. At this point, right or wrong, I need a lot better reason than my daddy wants me to, to back out. Need a better reason for him, and for me. And, if you'll recall, we've had this conversation before."

He nodded, acquiescingly.

"Like it or not, I'm in the investigations business. It wouldn't be good for business, would it, for me to start getting too picky, too soon, about what jobs to take? Not if I want a dog's chance of making a living, staying current on that shiny-new mortgage of mine. On the other hand, could be very good for business if I do a good job for a man, who has very deep pockets, and tentacles all over the state, and might run for governor.

"Okay," he said.

"And lastly…"

"Yes?"

"*So it's dangerous?* Plenty of parents are sending kids, everyday, to Vietnam to be slaughtered. *That's* dangerous."

"Now, that is different, and you know it."

"Why?"

"Don't be ridiculous. Plenty of reasons, other than the obvious fact, that those are *sons* being drafted, not *daughters*."

I straightened.

Jutted my chin, tilted my head: "I'll have you know, daddy, I know for a fact, I read an article, there are over six hundred American military *women* in Vietnam this very minute."

I poked him in the arm.

I was a little drunk.

He looked at me:

"Nurses, every one, I'll wager."

"So?"

CHAPTER 9

A T HOME THAT EVENING, SMOKING AND quaffing Sanka, I typed up, on the used Smith Corona electric I'd bought with my birthday money, a summary of Buzz Hutcheson's account of Ralph Butterworth's death, and the ex-bomber pilot's activities leading thereto. This included what Hutcheson had gathered from the sheriff's department in Mississippi, and the remaining contents of the file he'd prepared me, all pretty thin. Lighting up another Kent and exhaling twin smoke streams, letting the cigarette sag out one corner of my mouth, I completed my summary by typing two entries:

--Peenemunde?

--Plane crash/altimeter. . .

I looked up Peenemünde. The location, cryptically, Butterworth told Hutcheson he would be driving to Memphis from. My 1966 *World Book Encyclopedia* had nothing. I did find it, however, the second place I looked, a single index entry in my *Hammond's New World Atlas*, hauled up from the lower shelf of the built-in bookcase in my living room. It was, in fact, a town or village, so insignificant these days as not to warrant any population notation, at the tip of an island on the Baltic coast of what was currently communist East Germany.

This meshed with what I'd been told—that Peenemünde was in Germany, a place bombed during the war—reference to which, by Butterworth, made no sense to Hutcheson, nor of course, did it make any to me. My research further confirmed there being no other locale by that name, in say, the United States, Butterworth might more plausibly have been driving from that night. No place name was even close, in any state within a rational same-day drive of Memphis, focusing mostly on points south, since he'd told Hutcheson he would be driving *up*—and, naturally, since the accident had occurred south of Memphis, in Mississippi.

I started a file, opened an expense record, and noted my time so far. I prepared R. J. Hutcheson's contract and receipt, placing their carbons in my file, and sealing the originals in an envelope, which I addressed and stamped. For my lovely fat retainer check, I greedily filled out a bank deposit slip.

I WAS UP EARLY TUESDAY, showered, dressed, and after two mugs of coffee and some eggs I placed two long-distance phone calls. First to the Alcorn County sheriff's office in Mississippi. I got myself transferred to the sheriff's secretary, who penciled me in for an early-afternoon appointment, warning me she could make no promises. I thanked her, and asked directions. I made my second call, asking a favor of the party on the other end of the line, and while I awaited a callback on that, I studied the road map spread across my kitchen table. I also cleaned the dishes, unplugged the percolator, and managed to get the map folded back—eventually setting off in my gold 1967 Chevy Impala SS, which I'd won in the divorce.

Heading out of town, I mailed Hutcheson's contract, got gas, and deposited my retainer check, keeping out $50 for expenses. For the second morning in a row, as with my father Monday, I followed I-40 west out of Nashville. That day, however, I exited south onto Route 22 to Lexington, Milledgeville, Adamsville, passed the Shiloh battlefield, and at last crossed the state line in a region of tall pinewoods, and loamy farmland. Top news on the radio involved the British-Rhodesia talks and the racist African country's raising of a new flag, replacing the Union Jack. When I turned south onto Highway 45, small hills had church steeples peeping up out of them, and I soon entered Corinth, Mississippi—pop. 11,453—amidst a thirty-eight-degree drizzle. I got a burger and a Coke at a downtown lunch counter, and by one o'clock I was cooling my heels in a corridor of the Alcorn County Courthouse, waiting for the sheriff to make time for me.

I was smoking a cigarette, using a tall brass ashtray by the chair, browsing a six-month-old *Look* magazine. Nelson Rockefeller's face was on the cover. There was also, I noted on the cover, unrelated I assumed to Rockefeller, the headline: FLYING SAUCER FIASCO: THE HALF-MILLION-DOLLAR COVER-UP ON WHETHER UFO'S REALLY EXIST. I was dressed to dazzle any small-town sheriff, in a knit scarlet-red jacket dress, with three pairs of round gold buttons, double-breasted, down the front, brown gloves, brown Merri-Mocs, and a bone-beige snap-brim hat. The hat brim was flipped up in back and on the left, rakishly downsloped in front and on the right. A Coco Chanel version of Sam Spade, classy and fabulous. I had only to wait twenty minutes before Sheriff Grady Bingham—mid-fifties, dark-haired, slender—could resist my allure no longer.

He had a beard shadow, long tapering nose, looking a lot like Hank Kimball on *Green Acres*, though Bingham seemed as proud and no-nonsense, as the Kimball character was goofy. He was an honest, effective, professional lawman, with a large well-worn Bible atop his desk. The Bible was my observation, the rest was according to the new Negro sheriff of Lavonia County, Alabama.

By happy coincidence, the men had had prior dealings. The Lavonia sheriff, named Patton, had been my second long-distance call of the morning. I'd asked Patton to phone Bingham up, sheriff to sheriff, and vouch for me. Patton and I had never actually met, but he knew me by reputation, from my investigation into the Klan's "Lavonia Massacre"—not to mention the man he'd replaced as sheriff practically died in my arms, shot through the head by Klansmen.

Bingham was polite, though he could clearly be quick-tempered. He told me he simply could not hand over their file on Ralph Butterworth's car crash. He did agree, however, purely as a favor to Sheriff Patton, to review it on his desk in front of me, answering some of my questions. The coroner, he assured me, found no evidence of foul play. "Toxicology testing?" I asked.

"General rule to run a blood alcohol, on all medicolegal autopsies." He flipped some pages, then found something, filling his lungs, exhaling slowly. "Came back...point-three-one-zero."

I whistled through pursed lips.

"Yes," he said, raking the record with a judgmental eye.

"Is it possible," I asked, "for a man to operate a motor vehicle, for whatever distance Butterworth did, *that* drunk?"

He leaned back, rubbing down the sides of his mouth. "Possible," he said, after some thought on the matter. "No skid marks, no evidence he tried to brake, suggesting he was unconscious at the point of impact. But, he didn't have to have started out with so high a BAT. Could have risen after he was already on the road, to the point he became stuporous. Either due to ongoing drinking, or delayed absorption into the bloodstream, from the gut, of earlier drinking."

I nodded.

"Or both," I said.

"Or both." He rocked forward, reading some more from the brown file. "My deputy's report describes the deceased as reeking of alcohol, and a whiskey bottle was found at the scene. Empty."

"Implying," I said, tugging an earring, "he was drinking in the car."

"We believe so."

"What kind?"

"Of whiskey?"

"Yes."

He checked. "Not specified."

I nodded. "No indications of assault, or restraints? Rope burns, for example?"

He daggered me with a hard eye, plugged a cigarette in his mouth. "Told you already, Ms. Russell: No. Foul. Play."

"Yes, sir."

He was lighting up, as I added, demurely: "Don't take offense, Sheriff—I'm certain you would be at least as thorough in my shoes—but are you answering my questions, from *personal* knowledge, or strictly from consulting others' reports?"

He slammed shut the file.

Eyes narrowed. Spots of red coming out on his cheeks. My mother said you can catch more flies with honey than vinegar. Regrettably my questioning of Bingham was slipping into vinegar territory. "I think I do take offense."

Yep.

"Sorry about that, sir. Surely you can empathize with my duty as an investigator—not a police investigator, nor even a man—nevertheless, I am being paid, by a client under contract, to gather information. Is it not part and parcel of that work to rate the quality, the strength of the information collected?"

He was quiet.

Squinting.

Smoking.

I fingered the red hem of my skirt.

My heart thudding a little.

"Yes," he said, after a moment, "I am telling you what's in the reports—reports written by Chief Deputy Mills, and Doc Jones, both men I've known and worked with for years."

"Of course," I said, and gave a smile. "Thank you."

"I don't go out, Ms. Russell, for every middle-of-the-night, drunk-driving accident in the county."

"I understand."

He stared at me awhile longer, finally exhaling, nodding to himself. "Okay, my apologies, ma'am. I'm forgetting Sheriff Patton did ask that I extend you every professional courtesy. Apparently you made quite'n impression on them, over there, last year."

"They didn't cotton to me in the beginning either," I said.

Half-shrugging.

"Suppose I'm an acquired taste."

"All right," Bingham said, reading back into the file. "There was one odd thing surrounding this incident. I may as well pass it along, in deference to Sheriff Patton's request."

I lifted my head.

Cocked an ear.

"The wife," he said, "Myrle C. Butterworth…"

"Yes, sir."

"Down from Pennsylvania, collecting her husband's corpse,

and effects, made a big stink about a missing attaché case. My men didn't find it at the scene, night of the accident, nor later, after she raised the issue. We asked the tow-truck driver about it. Claimed it was damaged beyond repair, and he discarded it."

"That proper procedure?"

"No. Definitely not. We made an effort at recovery, but the refuse at the garage'd been hauled off by then."

"Contents?"

"Mrs. Butterworth said there should have been a typed book manuscript in it, together with some files, and a notebook. Driver said he found the case broken open and empty, thrown clear of the wreck. My guess is—apparently, it was a very nice leather case—my guess, the driver thought he could fix it up, use it, or sell it, but I can't prove it was anything but an oversight. We apologized to Mrs. Butterworth. Deputy Mills assured her, and me, there was no case when he did his initial investigation. He felt real bad. It was him who went and tracked down the tow-truck driver, questioned him, gave him a stern talking to about removing evidence. But, like I said, no recovery was possible by then."

"Who's this tow-truck driver?"

He consulted the file.

"Newel McClanahan."

He spelled it.

"You have an address?" I asked, up from my steno pad.

"Workplace…Selmer Midtown Gulf."

My eyes flicked.

"Selmer?" I brushed my bangs. "Selmer, Tennessee?"

"Yes. Just over the line."

"I know *where* it is. Why didn't your deputy call a local wrecker service?"

"Would have. It was McClanahan, actually, who happened upon the accident, radioed it to our dispatcher."

"So…" I gave that some brief thought. "He had unfettered access to the scene, before any official presence."

"I see where you're going," Bingham said, folding shut the file. "But, he denied tampering with anything, beyond checking the driver for a pulse. That's in Deputy Mills' report."

"Except, now we know, you say he admitted, he did tamper

with something."

"And we talked to him about that, and have no basis for doubting his story. We only even have the wife's claim, there was anything in the case."

"Seems unlikely, doesn't it, traveling with an empty case?"

"It's possible. Maybe he planned to put something in it."

"But not likely."

"No," he said, in a sharp tone. "Look, Ms. Russell, I'm not trying to pick a fight here. A mistake was made. We owned up to it. There was no reason, until it was too late to rectify anything, to believe anything was missing. And there's still no reason to link a missing briefcase to the cause of the accident, the latter being our primary concern."

"No reason not to either," I said, "if you don't know what was in the case."

"Ms. Russell…" Red flushing again to his cheeks.

"Sorry," I said, softly, lifting my hands.

He crossed his arms, leaning back, and waited.

"Do we know," I asked, "what McClanahan was doing down here?"

"Said he was going home from Tippah County. From a cockfight."

"Charming. Where's that?"

He gave a sideways toss of chin.

"One county west."

"That," I said, "is very convenient."

He squinted.

Laced fingers.

"How so?"

I shrugged. "Outside your jurisdiction, so Deputy Mills wouldn't much care about learning of an illegal cockfight, and if the law did ask questions—well—might not get such straight answers, right?"

"Could be right," he said. "But it was, and is, a plausible story, and we had no reason to treat him as anything other than a good Samaritan. Still don't. Not really."

I nodded, and asked where the wreck ended up. I was given directions to a salvage yard off U.S. 45 south of town. I asked if Chief Deputy Mills were available. He wasn't. At least, he wasn't being made available to me. That was fairly clear. "Very well, Sheriff," I said, stuffing my pad and pen away, snapping shut my bag. "Would you, then, ask Deputy Mills for me, if he remembers the brand of the whiskey bottle they found?"

"Sure." He nodded.

"Thank you." I stood, and he gallantly followed suit, chair wheeling back. I hung the strap of my bag off one shoulder. "My office number in Nashville is on my card. Call anytime and if I'm not there there's an Ansafone. One more favor, Sheriff? Phone your opposite number up in Selmer? I'd like to see him, ask about Newel McClanahan."

"Suit yourself. Here, just give'm this…"

Bingham took out a sheet of official stationary, laid it down, and wrote large in black felt-tip:

> *Buford—*
> *Please take care of this*
> *young lady for me.*
> *Grady*

CHAPTER 10

I FOUND GARRETT'S 512 AUTO Salvage down a side road where Bingham said I would and gave what was left of Ralph Butterworth's '66 Olds Starfire the once-over. Not that I was an expert but it seemed to show all the expected mangling of having flown off the road, crashed through a fence, and slammed head-on into the thick wooden stanchion of a billboard advertising Viceroy cigarettes. Blood was dried on the steering wheel and seat; a dent was in the shattered windshield, outwardly directed, size and shape of the top of a man's cranium. Blood and hair were embedded in that. The crash did not appear survivable to me, even if Butterworth had been wearing his safety belt. I was guessing he hadn't, judging from the windshield, and the driver's seat belt remaining intact. Not sliced through by police, or mortuary people, extracting the victim.

Which made me recall something Buzz Hutcheson said.

How Butterworth, a pilot, would not have driven drunk.

Well, according to the coroner, he wasn't just drunk, he was three-times drunk.

Anyway, along those same lines:

Would a pilot drive without buckling up?

To assume it could never happen seemed as absurd to me as assuming the drunk driving couldn't happen. Nevertheless, I jotted a reminder to ask the wife. Right under my note to ask her what brand, or brands, of whiskey her husband frequented. These were questions no one had asked, which seemed as good a definition of my role in all this, as any—to identify and ask questions that hadn't been. I looked at John Tyree, a tall, slim Negro in faded green coveralls, who'd driven me out onto the savage lot, amongst the decomposing carcasses of old automobiles, in grotesque designs, and lumpy piles of rusted parts. He had loaned me a pair of brown rubber boots to use walking in the mud. I thanked him, and asked if he'd noticed anything strange about the wrecked Oldsmobile, Tyree being a man I assumed would have seen a lot of totaled cars in his junkyard career. He said, "No, ma'am."

I nodded.

Turning back to the car.

The rolled-down driver's window struck me odd.

Rolled down, not shattered.

Not broken out by would-be rescuers. I even double-checked, shoved open the driver's door, with a metallic shriek, and rotated the handle.

Mechanism still worked.

The window rose, glass intact, went back down.

I asked John Tyree about it and his eyes nearly bugged out on the ground. He began swearing up and down, frightfully, that not he nor anybody at the salvage yard would've done it. I told him, calm down, I was just asking. His reaction, I guessed, had something to do with me having led him believe I was, in fact, a police detective from Nashville. I hadn't lied, mind you, but I hadn't been totally specific either about what kind of detective I was, when I showed up, identifying myself and what I wanted. I finished, snapping 35-millimeter photos of the driver's compartment from several angles. I wasn't a great photographer, but I was taking lessons from one at *The Tennessean*, a bearded fellow my father had bought me the camera off of, who was counting on a dinner date sometime, as payment for my lessons. The camera was a well-worn Nikon "F"—popular, I was told, with combat photojournalists in Vietnam.

Window rolled down, hmmm…

How cold had it been that night? I wondered, gunning the Impala twenty-two miles north to Selmer, Tennessee. Close to four o'clock, hoping to catch the McNairy County sheriff in his office, and not have to spend the night, or drive two and a half hours back over here again. Nevertheless, when I spotted a public library, I wheeled in, spewing road gravel, and left my engine running as I literally ran up the steps inside. I found a newspaper reporting a low in the area, the night of 30 October—of twenty-five degrees.

Huh...

Butterworth was a Yankee.

Yankees tolerated cold better than we did.

But:

Driver's window completely lowered...

Highway speeds...

Below-freezing weather...

Did not compute.

Of course, if half-stuporously drunk, fighting to stay awake, desperate to make it to Memphis...

I shrugged elaborately.

Perhaps such a man, I thought, backing out, heading on, would drive with the window down.

SHERIFF BUFORD PUSSER WAS DOWNSTAIRS in his office at the courthouse in Selmer. Cinderblock walls, electric heat, cheap flowery drapes back of the sheriff's desk. At his right hand was a large black ashtray brimming over with butts and ashes, alongside a crumbled pack of Salems. When the sheriff stood smiling, to greet me, holding my business card by the edges, I saw a dapper-dressed gentle giant, a foot taller than me, and twenty pounds heavier than my beefy ex-husband. Pusser wore a crew cut, a suit and crisscross-patterned tie, and a pinkie ring sporting several diamonds. Those diamonds, I later learned, originated from rings belonging to Pusser's murdered wife. Holstered butt first on the man's alligator belt was a .41 Magnum revolver. I made myself not fix my gaze too hard on his face, scarred badly about the mouth and jaw. The left eye drooped. Then with a blink, and a thump in my chest, I remembered. Front-page news.

Perhaps a year ago. Assailants had raked Sheriff Pusser's car with gunfire on a rural dark road, when he went out on a call, killing Pusser's wife who'd gone along for the ride, and blasting his jaw apart. Governor Ellington had offered a reward.

He gave me a light and I told him what I wanted, crossing my legs, tugging my red knit skirt. A big-bellied deputy, with a trooper hat on, stood by, listening. I wanted to know anything Pusser could tell me about tow-truck operator and cockfight-fan Newel McClanahan. Something, I thought, passed between the two lawmen. "Ain't that that ornery cuss," Pusser said off to the side, "gave W.T. trouble last year, the White Iris?"

"Think so, Buford."

Pusser eyed me. "W.T. is one of our finest deputies. Also happens to be black."

I nodded.

"McClanahan doesn't prefer the races to mingle, and the drunker he is, more he lets his opinions be known."

"He's a bigot," I said.

"He is that."

"Klan?" I asked.

The deputy, whose name was Pluck, opined, "Don't know as the Klan would have him, ma'am."

I twisted my mouth, imagining what kind of man the Klan *wouldn't* have, given my experience. "Is he somebody," I asked, "might tamper with evidence at, or outright loot, an accident scene?"

"If his hangout is the White Iris," Pusser replied thoughtfully, pressing fingertips of his big hands in front of him, "without bein' robbed, cheated, or beaten, then he's likely an associate of Towhead White's. Which would make just about any illegal enterprise a possibility."

"Towhead? White?"

I wrote that down.

"Carl Douglas 'Towhead' White," Pusser snarled, obvious disdain there, bordering on bare-naked hatred. "Fancies himself the Al Capone of the South—real bad man, ruthless gangster. Don't you even think of messing with him."

"Ookay."

My eyes bobbled some. I'd been known to ignore advice of that ilk. Somehow, though, coming from Pusser, I took it to heart. Much later I learned he suspected White of having masterminded, from Federal prison, mind you, the Dixie Mafia ambush that had murdered Pusser's wife, and shot up the sheriff's face.

The Dixie Mafia…

I had my own history with them.

Anyway, as I say, I later learned, Pusser had sworn vengeance for that attack, Pauline Pusser's death. Part of a blood feud between the men, Pusser and White, ever since Pusser shot and killed White's lover, one Louise Hathcock, in the line of duty, in a violent 1966 shootout at a motel on the "state line."

"Like to talk to McClanahan," I told Pusser and Pluck.

They just looked at each other.

"He gave Alcorn County," I said, "a Selmer Gulf station as his workplace. If he's not there, might I find him at this, White Iris?"

"Possible," Pusser said, nodding, bopping the pads of his thumbs. "But you ain't going to the state line alone, ma'am."

I curled a brow.

"*Oh?*"

"C'mon, Peatie'n'I'll take you. Good to flash the badge down there every few days, kick some tires, remind'em we're here." And before I could think, Pusser was up and out the door. I was scrambling in pursuit, Pluck holding the door for me, grinning. We tore out in Pusser's Olds Toronado, me beside Pusser in front and Deputy Pluck in back. Besides our revolvers—mine was in my pocketbook—there was a shotgun in the car, plus an M-16. We spun in at the Gulf station, McClanahan's tow truck nowhere we could see. Pusser shouted inside over the Toronado's growling V-8. The owner stumped out saying, "Swear, Sheriff, I ain't seen Newel more'n a week. You see'm, tell'm he's fired."

"I will."

And Pusser drove us wide open, close to a hundred miles per hour, me shifting anxiously, tightening my safety belt, Plunk fumbling with his wide-brim hat in back, down Highway 45 to the state-line area, ten or twelve miles covered in eight minutes flat, while Pusser told me of that notorious stretch of border, seedy motels, brothels, illegal casinos, raucous taverns, a hoodlum haven known across the South. Pusser whipped the

Toronado off the highway at the White Iris, a low one-story dive with a rooftop neon sign. We lurched to a stop and he was out, ordering Pluck to keep me in the car if he had to use handcuffs. "Buford," the man shouted, "you ain't goin' inside there alone?"

The sheriff returned.

Reached in to snatch his nightstick off the floorboard. "Good point, Peatie." And set off again, smacking the stick in his beefy hand. In under five minutes he was back, heading us north towards town again. Newel McClanahan, he'd learned, was suddenly off on vacation, Panama City, they said. No one knew when he was expected back. "But," Pusser went on, "he'd said sayonara to all the regulars, buyin' a round of illegal Old Charter whiskey—we're a dry county, you know—peeling bills off a thick a wad of cash."

"Where'd he get that?" I asked, blinking.

"Shootin' dice, they say, at the Shamrock."

"Believe that?"

He looked over, with that damaged smile.

"Nope."

I thought about that, rubbing my temples, staring from the speeding car. By the time we got back to the courthouse it was after sunset and freezing. Pusser offered to phone his friends up, Joe and Juanita, and book me a room at the Old Home Motel, Main Street in Adamsville. He could guarantee my safety there. I thanked him, smiling, saying I was sure I would be fine driving back to Nashville. Wasn't that late, and I was an old hand with Tennessee back roads at night, having worked many a late shift, in my RN days, at rural hospitals. "Can I assume then, you're carryin'?"

"Mean a gun," I said. "Yes."

"Something'll do damage? Not some ladies' pea-shooter?"

"Smith & Wesson .38 okay?" I smirked.

"That'll do. I'll run McClanahan through NCIC, letcha know anything pops up." Pusser was walking me, towering over me, to my car. "I'll query the Panama City police chief, ask to be notified if he surfaces. For now that's all I can do."

"You've gone above and beyond, Sheriff." I pivoted when we got to the Impala, gazing up. I might've been smitten. He reminded me, I think, of Fred, size-wise, anyway. Pusser's suit jacket was a size 54, at least, extra long. We shook hands, and as he closed my car door, I said, grinning, coquettishly perhaps: "You have my number, call night or day, if you get anything."

He said it'd be his pleasure.

AND THAT, GENTLE READER, WAS my adventure with Buford Pusser, big stick and all, who would be dead in six years, and internationally famous after a *60 Minutes* interview the following year, and the *Walking Tall* movies of the 70s. Me, I recall him fondly as a wonderful, and despite the surgeries, handsome gentleman, who fancied fast cars. To this day, I have his business card tucked away in a drawer somewhere, a prized memento, I ANSWER ALL CALLS printed on it.

CHAPTER 11

MY DRIVEWAY WAS SIFTED OVER with oak leaves when I pulled in at home just after eight o'clock that night. I let myself in through the kitchen, having kept that light on, and the one on the side porch. I changed into powder-blue flannel pajamas and knotted closed a fleece robe with floral embroidery. Then I began playing a stack of albums I already had on the stereo: Brenda Lee, Julie London, Tom Jones, Tony Bennett, and Marianne Faithfull. I ate a ham-salad sandwich, and fixed myself a Dewar's and water, and spread an American Oil Company roadmap of the southeast across my dining table. I leaned on the heels of my hands, overlooking the map like I was General Eisenhower or something. I focused on Highway 72, the route Ralph Butterworth was traveling, west toward Memphis, when he drove off into a billboard piling. *Where the hell had he been coming from?* was what I wanted to know, rubbing under my breasts, glad to have shed the underwires for the day. Then I threaded my hair behind an ear, extrapolating backwards on the map...

Florence, Muscle Shoals, Decatur.

From there...

I-65?

If so, he could have come from the north, Nashville, or the south, Birmingham.

Or...if one kept backtracking along 72: Huntsville came next,

431 to Gadsden, perhaps from there to Atlanta. Or U.S. 72 curled back up into Tennessee to Chattanooga. I blew air through puffed cheeks. Paced, orbiting the table, swirling my Scotch, mouthing Julie London singing "Fly Me to the Moon." I had no flipping idea, let's face it, where Butterworth might have been driving from—might as well have *been* the moon—to get to my client that night, carrying proof somebody tried to kill him with a faulty altimeter in that earlier near-plane crash. I stopped swirling Scotch, still padding about in blue corduroy slippers, rabbit fur at the ankles.

I swallowed some, ice tickling.

Then halted.

Might that proof, about the plane crash, the nature of which we didn't know, fit in a briefcase, like the one allegedly damaged in the wreck, and disposed of—perhaps carelessly, perhaps deliberately—by Newel McClanahan, a known, or at least suspected, associate of notorious criminals?

I nodded.

Contorted my lips.

Coincidence? Newel coming into money shooting dice? *Coincidence?* Him suddenly lighting out on vacation, out of state?

I hated coincidences.

More to the point, I distrusted them.

I did, however, like very much my theory of the tampered-with altimeter having been inside that missing case. Along with a book manuscript, if Butterworth's wife had been right about that. A book manuscript that started out being about foo-fighters, perhaps German rocketry, considering the cryptic reference to Peenemünde on the phone, but then somehow lead Butterworth to wanting to go to South America on a Nazi hunt. Anyway, I might be crazy, but I liked the whole notion of Newell McClanahan being paid that wad of cash to help stage a car crash, and remove the briefcase from the scene, containing the altimeter, and the manuscript Butterworth told Hutcheson he'd self-publish if he had to—and whoever might've paid McClanahan to do all that, might also have asked him to disappear for a while, go on a trip, right?

And if half what Pusser told me about the criminality of that state-line area were true, didn't seem too much of a stretch to believe the dive bars around there would be fertile ground for somebody looking to recruit a tow-truck driver willing to take part in such a scheme for enough money.

I liked all of that.

I liked the notion of a million bucks, too, or of Dean Martin sweeping me off my feet. Unfortunately liking something, didn't necessarily make it so.

My new abode was a circa-1912 ivy-covered bungalow with a white picket fence out front on Grantland, in Waverly-Belmont. I adored it. It was all mine—mine, that is, and Commerce Union Bank's, and there was the fact I had to ask my father to cosign for me, the man at the bank not having felt a divorcée free-lance private eye to be creditworthy. At one point, I was told, in order to get my small first mortgage loan, I might be asked, since I was a woman under forty, and had been married, to produce proof I'd been sterilized!

For my father's part, he'd tried like the dickens to talk me out of that particular house. Preaching property values. The neighborhood, once quite fashionable, was in a state of decline. Middle-class Nashvillians moving in droves to more outlying suburbs. Worst of all, an interstate would soon be under construction three blocks behind me, cutting the neighborhood in half, resulting in the demolition of many gorgeous late 19th and early 20th century homes, many others falling into disrepair.

All this meant—lest you think me impractical—I got the place for a steal. The payments I would be able manage comfortably on the alimony checks from Fred, which meant I'd have a roof over my head, without going back to full-time nursing, even if the detective business tanked. I wasn't worried about Fred paying, by the way. He *still* worshipped me, though God knew why. I'd even had my lawyer—much as this rubbed against *his* grain—insist upon *less* alimony than Fred wanted to pony up.

WEDNESDAY MORNING I PACKED SOME. When I thought it late enough, I placed a person-to-person long-distance call to Myrle Butterworth in Beaver Falls, Pennsylvania. I told her who I was, offered my condolences for Ralph Butterworth's death, and asked if I could fly up and talk to her. Perhaps examine her husband's effects, his papers. She was hostile initially, which I'd expected, given Buzz Hutcheson's experience. I figured, though, woman to woman, I might get somewhere, when a two-hundred-pound blunderbuss, who dressed like a fat Davy Crockett to sell cars on TV, might hit a roadblock. Switching on all my girlish charm, and diplomacy, and nice-Nancy-nurse milk of human kindness, I seemingly managed to convince her all we were after was the truth. Actually, the convincing was easier than I'd expected, and it stunned me a little that, rather than sounding persuaded I might be of some benefit to her husband's legacy, and hence to her and her children, she sounded to me, more...?

Angrily ambivalent...?

As if, in the end, she didn't really care one way or another what the hell I did.

At least she'd agreed to a visit. I told her, if I could get a flight up that evening, I would see her in the morning.

"Nine o'clock at your house?"

Curtly, she said fine. I confirmed the address but didn't ask directions, figuring the shorter time we were on the line together, the less chance she'd have to change her mind. For similar reasons I gave her no number to call me back on. Sure, she could call information, but I figured she'd take the path of least resistance and just let me come. When they were open, I drove up to Keaton Travel Bureau downtown, and had Flossie Keaton book me an Allegheny flight to Greater Pittsburgh Airport, and a Hertz rent-a-car at that end. The flight left Berry Field at 3:05 that afternoon. A message had been left on the Ansafone while I was out. It was Sheriff Bingham telling me the bottle they'd found in the wreckage of Ralph Butterworth's car was Canadian Club. After jotting that down, adding it to my file, I called my father and mother. I told both I'd be out of town a couple days, not to worry, then I finished packing, wondering just how just cold it might be in Pittsburgh in November.

CHAPTER 12

THIRTY-SIX AND RAINING WAS my Pittsburgh weather answer upon arriving at 5:52 P.M. EST. I swiveled some heads, if I do say so, pecking high heels, strong legged, quick-footed, within the big terminal of cantilevered concrete and steel and glass. Spotting the HERTZ sign I veered across an age-of-exploration-type compass laid into the lobby floor in green-and-yellow terrazzo. My rental was a two-door red Dodge Coronet, which I drove to a Howard Johnson's opposite the airport on Route 60, the highway I'd take up to Beaver Falls next morning. I got checked in and went to the restaurant and had a sandwich and pistachio ice cream. Returning to my room, after a drink in the lounge, I could make out, in the east, a creepy red glow across the sky, cast by the flames of Pittsburgh's steel furnaces. My father called it the most shockingly ugly and filthy city in the world. I cranked up the heat in the room, hunkered under blankets, and read myself to sleep.

Virginia Woolf.

A Room of One's Own.

Beaver Falls was a burg of 16,000 halfway to Youngstown, a twenty-five-mile drive for me, on a clear crisp Thursday. I still didn't call for directions, still fearing she'd try to weasel out. It was easier to hang up on somebody than boot them off your front porch. Getting into town, I noted a billboard congratulating local-boy-made-good Joseph W. Namath. Joe, that is, who was, if you asked me, the sexiest quarterback in the AFL these days. At the lower end of Seventh Avenue there was a gas station with a map on the wall. The attendant told me how to get to the address I wanted, in an old residential neighborhood rising above the rest of town at the north end of Seventh, called College Hill, near Geneva College. The home, when I got there, was a large stone two-story Dutch Colonial, with casement windows, dormers, a carport/utility-room addition off one side. There were leaves raked into piles on the lawn. Having gotten there early, I drove on and meandered, sightseeing churches, the Reformed Presbyterian campus, and an adorable Old English-style fire station. At exactly nine, I parked in the driveway of the house, trailed breath fog to the steps, and trotted up and rang the bell.

Myrle Butterworth greeted me politely, if not pleasantly. I slipped off my gloves and we shook hands, me repeating my condolences. The house felt wonderful coming in out of the cold morning. She was slim, mid-forties, hair a dyed russet-red bouffant. She had good features, tasteful makeup, would have been quite a pretty young woman in her day. She retained an admirable figure, I thought, for a mother of four. She wore gray with tiny silver buttons. The collar white, a bow at the neck, wide white cuffs. A Puritan sort-of look. She smelled of Faberge. She hung up my shearling car coat and wool-knit beret, while I rubbed the freezing industrial north from my arms and shoulders. I wore beige cashmere, a turtleneck that fit me well, a brown-and-white tweed skirt with a front pleat, and brown leather shoes, with big gold buckles. I paced the living room, soft thick-pile carpet, sliding hands in my pockets, scanning school pictures of the children, all attractive, straight-toothed, perfect, spaced from about eight to college age. The house smelled of Murphy Oil. She offered me coffee.

"Thank you," I told her, twisting.

"Cream and sugar?"

"Please."

Once we had settled and I had shown her my PI's license, I asked her, gentle as a rose petal, narrowing one eye: "What do you know, ma'am, about your husband's last trip south?"

"Ralph *said* he was *just* going to see this old squadron

commander of his…Colonel Hutcheson, was it?"

I nodded.

She was at one end of a carved walnut settee. I was opposite, one stocking-clad leg folded over the other, in a high-backed easy chair with claw-and-ball feet and rose-and-beige damask upholstery. Beside me was a mahogany table inlaid with brass. "One last time," she added, distractedly, "then he would be out of it."

"His book project?"

"Yes."

I sipped some coffee, ran the tip of my tongue around my lips.

"Doesn't sound," I said gingerly, "like you believe he was just going to see Colonel Hutcheson."

She huffed acridly.

I waited, over the brim of my fine-china cup, until further elaboration seemed not forthcoming, and I said: "My client believed there *was* another stop, that Mr. Butterworth would be driving to Memphis—late—from there, wherever that was, for their meeting."

"*Oh,*" she practically burst. "There was another stop, all right!"

Very theatrical.

"Do you know where?" I gave a small urgent shrug, one-shouldered.

Adding, "No one else seems to, not Colonel Hutcheson, not the Mississippi authorities…"

"I certainly do *not* know," she seethed, teeth gritted, "and do not *want* to know."

The corners of my mouth tugged, and she rearranged gracelessly, with quick, jerky motions, uncrossing her legs, recrossing them. I placed my coffee on its saucer, on the occasional table, and studied her, breathing quietly. "Pardon me, Mrs. Butterworth," I said after a time, "I cannot imagine what you're going through. But your answers seem…strange, to me. Angry, more than grieved, if I may say."

"I have cause, don't I?"

"Do you? You seem to know something I don't, and seem to be dancing around it."

Her reply came out low and guttural:

"Oh, don't you know?"

I bent my head, squinting.

"Ma'am?"

"The affair? Don't you know about it? Isn't that really"—*reee-aaally*—"why you're here?"

I blinked.

"Affair?"

"I rather thought…Well, being a private detective…" She sighed. "Don't you people…"

"*Us* people?"

My eyes flashed.

"Well…"

She plucked her gray dress, then stopped, cleared her throat.

"You thrive on…on seamy material like that, don't you?"

Deflecting onto a gilt-framed painting, a green country scene, a little Dutch girl and a windmill, I filled my lungs and emptied them through my nostrils, facing her back. "Ma'am, I assure you, I have no idea what you're talking about. I told you my agenda. To learn if your husband's death, was the drunk-driving accident the Mississippi authorities ruled it. Or was there more to it. Now, if there was an affair—"

"Not much doubt about that."

"*If there was an affair*, then I am doubly sorry for your pain. *But* I assure you it isn't anything I have knowledge of, nor my client, at least as far as he told me, and I'm reasonably confident, though Lord knows I've been fooled before, he was open and above board with me, as far as his dealings with your husband. Now, I'll swear to that, on as many Bibles as you want me to. Okay? I'll let you take me around to that pious college around the corner, bet we can find quite a stack of them there."

She looked at me, blinking back tears.

Yet a tiny smirk shone through. "Okay," she managed.

"However," I went on, evenly, unfolding my legs slowly, and bending slightly towards her at the waist, "if there is reason to believe there was an affair, then you are correct in so far as it is the kind of information I must have, if I'm going to make heads or tails of my case. So, please, Mrs. Butterworth, tell me what you know."

"About the affair?"

"To start," I said.

"It came…like a bolt out of the blue, complete shock."

"I'm sure."

My knees were together, my hands cupped loosely over them. She was quiet, like she wanted to cry, but had already cried out all the tears she had.

"How," I asked, "did you find out?"

"Pictures, photos, that is, in the mail." Her eyes did a lot of blinking and arching. "Day of the funeral."

"Ouch," I said, softly.

"Indeed."

"Any letter? Blackmail demand?"

She shook her head. "No."

Then, suddenly, she looked up. She pointed the tip of her chin at me, eyed me squarely for the first time, and quite hard. "I assumed," she said, with a quivered voice that sent chills down my spine, "that was what you were coming for."

My eyes flickered to my lap.

Up again.

"No."

A shake of my head.

"I'm sorry then," she said, "for selling you short. But, surely, you can see…"

"I can," I said, nodding.

Then, carefully, added:

"May I see them?"

Myrle Butterworth nodded once, squeezing her laced-together fingers, knuckles white, and went to an antique half-moon sideboard, and pulled out the top drawer by its brass handles. She removed a manila envelope, reclosing the drawer, and carried it to where I was sitting, holding it level, well out in front of herself, as if it reeked. I took it, thanking her. It was addressed with block lettering, black magic marker, that might've been a woman's hand. I sniffed it. That told me nothing. "No return address," I commented. "Postmarked Cincinnati." I lifted my eyes across. "Your husband know anybody in Cincinnati?"

"Apparently."

"Anybody you knew of?"

"He knew people all over. It was a joke with our kids." She huffed daintily, gave what might've been a fleeting smile of reminiscence. "You couldn't go anywhere," she elaborated, "with Popsie, without him running into some old war buddy, or flying buddy, or somebody he'd interviewed."

I opened the torn flap of the envelope and withdrew a stack of—I counted—six 8 x 10 black-and-white glossies. Shot by a skilled photographer, with a good camera. Not some sleazy Sam Spade wannabe, crawling through shrubbery, shooting through a window, through a screen, or curtains. From seeming close range, as well, at a high angle. Like the photographer was in the room, in the open, snapping from say the foot of the bed, on the left. I scrunched eyebrows, and pursed my lips to one side, having a lot of trouble imagining, how would I ever get shots like these, if I wanted to. *In flagrante delicto.* Zoom lens? From what vantage? A camera could be mounted, say, high on a wall, concealed even. Either way—human photographer, or remotely, or automatically triggered—the whole thing, to me, screamed set up.

I looked at the wife, exhaling.

Showing sympathy by not speaking immediately. Then:

"I've never laid eyes on Mr. Butterworth, ma'am, or a picture of him. This is him?"

"Him all right. Don't think I know my own husband, of twenty-two years?"

"Sorry."

She exhaled suddenly. "Had to ask, I suppose."

"Yes."

"There's the face, of course; no question it's him. But there's also that birthmark, upper back."

"Very well."

We were quiet while I studied further what we had here. Butterworth was naked except for socks, and a wristwatch, in a comfortable, clean-looking bed, white wrought-iron scrollwork, embraced in various positions and manners by a woman. She wore a black with silver sparkle, sheer, lace baby-doll nightie, ruffled at the top, and fringed at the hem. There was a matching panty so brief it would pass for a G-string. I could only imagine what someone like Myrle Butterworth might have thought, how she'd react, first opening, laying eyes upon—*this*. I tried to learn what I could from the photographed woman. The hairstyle was dark, probably black, Cleopatra pageboy, but curly on top. Might be a wig. Her mouth was large and toothy, the barest underbite. The face was not narrow, though I could tell little else of it—she was hardly mugging for the camera, first of all, though more importantly, she wore a black carnival mask, embellished with sequins, beads, and feathers. It had been Halloween, assuming these were shot the night Butterworth died. So, perhaps the mask was not so oddly out of place.

Otherwise, what of the woman? There *was* something…something enigmatically different. She was Caucasian, certainly, round-shouldered, with prominent, pointed breasts, perhaps medium height, perhaps my height, but if so she'd be twenty-five pounds heavier than me.

Much of it in the extremities.

Much of *that* muscle.

I wasn't perceiving a classically beautiful woman.

Not of the modern Miss America ilk, anyway.

She seemed rather, to me…

Valkyrien?

Oh, and there was an oddly placed tan line, like the pale buttocks of the little girl in the Coppertone ads, except this was on the left upper arm, above the elbow, extending to a couple of inches below the armpit. Seemed to circle the arm, like a…a bandage, or band worn on the arm, while she sunned herself somewhere—somewhere a lot warmer, by the way, than anyplace between here and Tennessee, at present.

As for Butterworth:

His eyes were closed or bleary in every photo showing his face.

I shuffled through a second time, more deliberately. Once I had, it was clear, to me, that while all this was incriminating and scandalous—and indefensible to a wife—there was, nevertheless, no direct photographic evidence of this man being actively amorous with the woman. No puckered lips chasing hers, no lustful hands grasping shoulders, or any other jutting anatomy. I wouldn't even swear, from these images, he was awake—much less, sober enough for sex.

I kept that analysis to myself.

Anything along those lines to Mrs. Butterworth, with me knowing no more than I did, would seem to her a whitewash, a shallow mollification, which might get me perceived as unfriendly, unworthy of cooperation, every bit as readily as if I really were delivering blackmail demands.

At best, she might dismiss me as naïve.

That was one thing I wasn't.

I exhaled, wanting her to have no reason to consider me anything but her best friend.

"I gather you have no idea who this girl is?"

"No." Her tone, a blunt instrument.

"Shown these to anybody?"

"Like who? Our children?"

"Anybody?" I said levelly.

"No."

I nodded, returning the stack inside the envelope, closing the flap.

"May I borrow these?" I asked.

"Burn them to a crisp for all I care."

I nodded thoughtfully at that, then propped the envelope next to my pocketbook, beside the chair. I picked up my coffee, and held it two-handed by the brim. "To your knowledge," I began before swallowing some, "had your husband ever had an affair? Any suspicions, before the photos arrived?"

"Absolutely not. I thought we had the perfect marriage. Till the last year."

"What changed?"

"This…obsession…I think it's fair to call it that…with his latest book. That damnable book. Never home. When he was, he was secretive, short. I mean, Ralph always traveled as part of his work, the flying and the writing, but never as much as this past year. Suppose it's possible, now"—she indicated the envelope, flung her arm—"he could've had them all over the country, one in every city."

"But, beyond the arrival of these pictures, you have had no real suspicions, correct?"

"Correct. The only other women we ever talked about were—"

She began suddenly to sob.

"Excuse me—"

She bolted out. Returning shortly, dabbing her eyes with pink Kleenex.

I heard the furnace cycling on in the warm house.

When she'd settled, I prodded:

"Only other women you talked about were...?"

"The English girls the pilots dated, danced with, fooled around with."

"During the Second World War."

"Yes."

"He was one?" I said.

"Yes. But you see, we weren't married then, we'd planned on it, when he shipped out, but we decided not to make it official, see how we both felt after the war."

"Sensible."

"Don't know why I'm telling you this—I always scolded the vulgarity when he'd get drunk at a party, start telling war stories—but, do you know what the American pilots called the silver wings pinned on their chests?"

My head shook.

"Leg-spreader wings."

I huffed a small huff.

"Sorry, if I'm offending you."

I nodded. "I'll survive."

"Anyway, Ralph came back, told me all about his English girlfriends—there were many—and said if I'd still have him, he wanted to marry me. We got married."

I nodded, smiled.

Thought, snatchingly, about my own, fresh divorce, failed marriage. I asked her, next, stuffing all that out of my mind, fingering my hair, to try to assume for the moment she had never received those explosive photos in the mail, and try to answer my opening question from that perspective. She said she'd try. What did she know about her husband's final trip? "Not much," she replied. "Very secretive. But I did think it quite odd, actually."

"Odd?"

"Him driving the car."

"He would usually *fly?*"

"Ralph was a man," she said, "who'd fly himself from here to Youngstown. This was all the way to Tennessee. He told me, he had no choice, the plane was being worked on."

"I can probably answer some of that, Mrs. Butterworth."

"Please, Myrle. I feel badly, how I treated you, at the beginning"—she glimpsed my card—"Sherry, is it?"

"Yes. Your reaction was quite understandable, under the circumstances."

"Kind of you. What were you saying?"

"One of the things Mr. Butterworth told Colonel Hutcheson," I said, "was his plane had been tampered with—sabotaged, he believed—an altimeter problem, said he'd barely managed to land it safely."

"He didn't tell me anything about that," she said, looking away. "Must've been the charter to Akron. Night flight, Saturday before he died. He was supposed to return that night, then fly back for the clients Sunday afternoon. But, he called me up, said they had invited him to dinner, wanted a night on the town in Akron."

"Would he normally have told you?" I asked. "Or would he cover up a, say, near miss, a near crash, so you wouldn't worry?"

"I'm a pilot's wife."

She rose up in her chair, to emphasize those words. High chin. Shoulders back.

Then she swallowed, gaze wavering.

"*Was* a pilot's wife."

"Go on."

"I knew there were risks. We had an agreement from the first. He'd have told me anything outside the routine, a mechanical failure or something. It's that kind of honesty, trust that he'll tell you things like that, that helps you deal with the fear, you know?"

I nodded.

"So," I said, "you have no idea what kind of proof, of sabotage, he might've been bringing Colonel Hutcheson?"

"No."

CHAPTER 13

I ASKED MYRLE BUTTERWORTH WHAT whiskey her late husband would have drunk on the road. "None," she told me, without hesitation. "Gilbey's gin was all he ever drank anymore."

"Never Bourbon, Scotch?"

"Hardly ever." She shrugged. "Kept it around for guests."

"Wouldn't have traveled with it?"

She pursed ruby-red lips, giving her head a shake. "No."

"What kind of a drinker was he?"

"I don't understand."

"Forgive me, but it's important," I said, swallowing. "Would he ever be a sloppy drinker, take the bottle by the neck, say, quaff it down straight?"

"No, never."

She seemed definite, adding: "Don't misunderstand, my husband could drink with the best of them, but he was precise. With, I guess you'd say, the discipline of a pilot."

I nodded.

"Go on with that."

"Well, he would never drink within eight hours of flying. And he liked to mix cocktails: martinis, gin rickeys, gin sours, gimlets, pink gins—brought that one back from the war, from Britain—and Ralph was a purist about recipes, types of glassware. A martini had to be six-to-one. Fact, you asked about whiskeys…"

"Yes, ma'am."

"If he ever had whiskey it would be mixed in a cocktail: a manhattan, an old-fashioned."

"Never out of the bottle."

"Nooo..." Shaking her head.

"They found an empty bottle of Canadian Club in his car," I said.

I saw Myrle Butterworth react with a spastic twist of head.

A narrowing of eyes.

"They tell you that?" I said.

"No," she said. "Told me he'd been drinking, that that was felt to be the cause of the accident. That and exhaustion, considering the late hour."

"It surprise you," I asked, "he would drink and drive?"

She shrugged mildly. "I would never call Ralph an irresponsible driver, but he wasn't as obsessively careful behind the wheel of a car as he would be behind the control of an airplane, if that's what you mean."

"That's *exactly* what I mean."

Then I told her: "His blood-alcohol was three times the legal upper limit."

She stiffened.

"Oh...my."

"They didn't tell you that?"

"No."

"Probably wanted to spare you."

She breathed deep. "No doubt."

"Does *that* surprise you? He would be *that* drunk?"

"Yes. Most definitely."

Her face looked like it smelled a rat.

As did I.

Then the look was erased: she stood from the sofa, and began to orbit the room, long slender fingers lacing before her. I turned my head one way, then the other, following her all around. When she got to the archway out to the foyer, she stopped, facing me, knotting her arms. "Of course, until I got those dis-*gusting* pictures in the mail, I would not have questioned his fidelity to me, either. So perhaps I didn't know Ralph as well as I thought I did. Knowing, now, he was down there visiting that…that jezebel, guess that throws all one's old assumptions out the window, doesn't it?"

I sighed.

Deciding I had nothing to add to that. I asked if she knew what had been in the missing briefcase. She said, his manuscript. "That book. That damned book." She had seen him put it in there. Some other routine items, nothing that would be, to her thinking, evidence about the Akron almost-crash. I asked if her husband had had an office somewhere, or had he done his writing and research from home. "Home," she said, thumbnail between her front teeth. "I suppose you need to see his study?"

"If I may. Try not to make too big a mess."

THERE WAS A LARGE BASEMENT down a staircase through a door off the foyer. Half of it was laundry room. The hot-water heater was down there, the washer and dryer, and a big deep wash basin, I envied. There was an ironing board. I smelled Downey fabric softener. The walls were cinderblock. I followed Myrle around under the stairs, amongst some old furniture and boxes, some labeled in magic marker, XMAS DECOR'NS, to a solid door, secured with a shiny new deadbolt. She had the keys and we entered Butterworth's study, comprising the remaining half of the basement.

Walnut paneling, gold pile carpet, acoustical ceiling tiles. There was a small elongated window high up near the ceiling at the far end, filtering in daylight. On the right, one entire wall was books, floor to ceiling, on hand-built shelving. Opposite the book wall was a large sectional executive desk with a lot of carved details. The hardware was brass, the finish cherry-wood. A big beige Remington manual typewriter sat on part of the desktop, which was also piled deep with the usual desk stuff, including a portrait of Mrs. Butterworth, a desk lighter, a fancy ashtray the size of a swimming pool, a selection of pipes of various shapes surrounding the edge. My father smoked a pipe, sometimes. I liked it when he did. I inhaled, pleased by the scent of tobacco at Ralph Butterworth's desk.

There was a corner cabinet with a tooled leather top on the left as one entered. There was a tray on top of it holding a large ice bucket, ice tongs, a jigger, and cocktail shaker. Inside the cabinet were cocktail glasses, a half-full bottle of Gilbey's, some dry vermouth, and bitters. No whiskey, Canadian Club or otherwise. Shutting the cabinet, I straightened and rotated, Myrle waiting in the doorway. The paneled walls, not covered by books, were covered with framed photos, aviation and military subjects, mostly. One, prominently placed behind the desk, catching my eye, was a close-up of the nose of a parked B-17, same type Buzz Hutcheson had escorted me through that day in Memphis. The old picture, from the war, had five men in flying gear posed beneath one of the bomber's large three-bladed propellers. A young Ralph Butterworth, Myrle confirmed, was in the center, with captain's bars gleaming, leather bomber jacket half-zipped, floppy officer's cap rakishly cocked, off to one side. Painted on the Flying Fortress, below a window with a vented machine-gun barrel poking out, was the plane's nickname, *Martini Jeanie*. Below the cockpit windshield, further back, was the kind of risqué nose art for which, I'd been told, B-17s were famous. This masterpiece was a nude Rita Hayworth-type, reclined inside a giant cocktail glass: her arms tucked behind her knees, thighs hugged up against her amble bosom, legs scissoring.

Very cheesecake.

Myrle gave me some keys to desk drawers, and three steel file cabinets, and said she'd be in the kitchen. She offered to bring me down more coffee, which I accepted. Walking out, she rotated back. Announcing with a sigh, colored with anger, and a swipe of her arm: "You have the run of the place, Sherry; I got all our bills and tax records out already. Upstairs. Will you need those?"

"I shouldn't think so." I asked, though, for a recent snapshot of her husband, I could borrow. She said she'd find one and I heard her rapidly take the stairs back up to the foyer. I got started, scouring for potential hiding places, places one might conceal contraband—you know, photographic negatives, a claim ticket, an airport locker key. I didn't know what I was looking for, or really expecting to find anything, but I figured if I did, it was important, and I doubted I'd be back. I looked under and behind drawers, for something taped, behind pictures on the walls, inside the typewriter, underneath the tray on top of the bar cabinet, inside the cabinet, under shelves. I studied the edge of the carpet. I climbed a step ladder, fingering along the sill of the window, finding dust, which got up my nose, making me sneeze. I couldn't lift the typewriter to see underneath it. Looking up, I saw no sign of ceiling tiles being removed and replaced. I got the ladder again, checked the bowl of the light fixture, full of dust, and brittle dead bugs. Toilet tanks were great hiding places, but the basement toilet was inside a bomb shelter out in the laundry area. I figured if Ralph Butterworth did hide something down here, he'd take advantage of that new Craftsman lock on the study door. So, I didn't bother with the toilet. I checked his tobacco pouch, the bottom of the big ashtray. I waited for Myrle to bring my coffee, and the photo she was lending me, and to leave me on my own again, to get the tiny screwdriver set from my pocketbook. I used it to get looks behind the light-switch plates, inside electrical outlets, and lastly inside the telephone. Books were an excellent stash, even could be hollowed out to conceal relatively large objects. Butterworth's library, though, was far to large for me to check. I fanned the pages of a Bible, and a *Webster's New World Dictionary*, and let that be that.

I sat in the mahogany desk chair, rotated and used Butterworth's desk lighter to fire up a cigarette, before starting a more standard search of the desk and file cabinets. After two hours, three cups of perked coffee, and a half-pack of Kents, I'd found little. What was there, and not difficult to find, was a file of bare-bones research material and a barely started typewritten manuscript titled, *German Secret Weapons: Futuristic Tools of the Nazi War Machine.* I skimmed a contract signed with Ballantine Books, referencing that title, specifying a $2000 advance, and a later letter, dated 1/8/68, killing the project, citing repeated missed deadlines. There was nothing in any of that I hadn't been told already. There was nothing in the office, I could find, suggesting what he had been doing instead, flying his plane all over the place, rather than writing what was to be part of a series called *Ballantine's Visual History of World War II.* I found no current pilot's logbook either, only a stack of old ones rubber-banded together, in one of the deep desk drawers.

I found no evidence of an affair:

No cache of love letters.

No birthday cards from a woman not his wife.

No receipts for jewelry, restaurants, flowers.

Only two things stuck me of any possible significance. There was a file folder atop the desk, obviously rifled through quickly, then left disarrayed. Mostly it contained photos, some strewn or allowed to spill over the edge to the floor, left where they dropped. All part of Butterworth's volunteer work as the 303rd Bomb Group Association historian. Except this particular treatment of these no-doubt precious archives seemed quite shoddy, to me, for a man otherwise compulsorily neat, a thorough filer, and record-keeper. For instance, there was a thick folder in one of the cabinets where he'd compiled case studies and war-crimes trial outcomes on cases where 303rd crewmen had been murdered by Germans on the ground, after parachuting from stricken Flying Fortresses.

The file on the desk, some of which had spilled—the setup suggesting to me there was something special about it, Butterworth having torn through it looking for something, just before leaving on his last, fatal, trip—contained group photos of various unit personnel with typewritten captions stapled or paper-clipped to each. Captions like: **303rd S-2 Intelligence Personnel, 303rd Operations Personnel, 27Feb45, 360th Squadron Operations, 5Feb44, 358th BS Operations Staff, 444th Sub Depot Officers, 303rd Station Hospital…**

And so on.

If anything was missing, I had no way of knowing. Mrs. Butterworth likely wouldn't either. I did ask her, waving a sample war photo in one hand, fixing a bra strap with the other, when she brought me down more coffee, plus a warm home-baked oatmeal cookie. I asked if Mr. Butterworth had said anything about any of this, indicating the photo files, something he had discovered, a face recognized?

No, she said, adding Ralph hadn't discussed his work, not the last year. I nodded. She went off, and I dug back in, taking a drag off my cigarette. My only other finding in Butterworth's study remotely rising to the level of being a clue, was a small yellow legal pad by the phone, with impressions left by what had been jotted on the last sheet to have been torn off.

I found a #2 pencil, sharpened it, and lightly skimmed the

side of the lead to and fro over the notepad.

Raising a ghost image of Ralph Butterworth's last notation. It said:

—DASCH
—MAPLE HILL CMTRY
—W—1:00

I exhaled smoke from my nostrils slowly.

A shudder worming through me, as if the man were speaking to me from the grave. I carefully tore the yellow sheet off, tucked it away with the meager notes I'd made, and put all that in my pocketbook. I stubbed out my cigarette. Nothing else seemed worthy of taking. I clicked off all the lights, closed the door, and stopped off to use the toilet in the bomb shelter, after which I flushed and checked the tank and under the lid, to satisfy my own compulsive nature. Nothing hidden there either. I trotted up to the foyer, finding Myrle where she'd said she'd be, in the kitchen, wearing a princess-style, floral-print apron, working with a shoulder roast, starting it to marinade. A pressure cooker stood out on the counter. The wallpaper was pink gingham, cabinets pearl blue, curtains and valances white and ruffled, with embroidered eyelets. I asked if she knew who or what *Dasch* was. Where Maple Hill Cemetery might be. I got a "No" on both counts. I asked if her husband used his safety belt when driving. She looked over her shoulder, saying he did— usually—not always. I asked if he made a peculiar habit of driving with the window rolled down on cold nights. Her answer to that, a perplexed, "No." Lastly, I wanted to know if there was any other place her husband might've kept important papers.

"Something he wanted to protect," I added, "perhaps kept secret?"

She turned a fatigued, vaguely savage face, upon me.

"From me?" she burst, wiping hands, back and front, on the apron. "That what you mean?"

"No. Not exactly what I mean. From anyone. Something, say, dangerous, to him, to you, the children, if it were known he knew."

"He was doing historical research," she grimaced. "What

could be dangerous?"

"Probably nothing; I'm just asking." I pocketed my hands in my skirt.

Gave an easy shrug.

"Brainstorming."

Pacing, Myrle thought, wrung her hands, then relaxed back against a built-in double oven. Then, exhaling harshly, she lifted her gaze, flipped a hand my way, as if tossing off a thought. "We have a safe deposit box at the bank—that the kind of thing you mean?"

"Could be," I said. "Have you been in it since he died?"

"No. No need. I had a copy of our will, and our agent handled the life insurance."

"I...hate to impose upon you, like this, Myrle," I said and ran my tongue along my lower lip, "but can we go visit the bank, open up that box?"

She read her watch.

Stared at the linoleum some.

"They're two minutes away," she finally said, looking up. "Reopen at one o'clock, after lunch. I don't mind going, provided we're back for my two youngest getting home from school."

I smiled.

"Doesn't sound like a problem."

"Care for a sandwich, while we wait, some soup?"

CHAPTER 14

W E RODE TO THE BANK in Myrle's station wagon, arriving just as they reopened for the afternoon. There was a marquee beneath the big CNB, COLLEGE HILL OFFICE sign flashing between the time and 40°F. The glass door said: *Friendly Banking Service*. We had our dealings with the branch manager, a prissy fat man named Duncan, with greenish eyes, in a gray suit, who asked if we also wanted to access the second box.

Myrle's eyes burst at me.

My brows lifted right back. And simultaneously, as if by some servomechanism, both of us rotated looks onto Duncan. He stroked a pencil-line mustache, center outward, with thumb and forefinger. "I wasn't aware," Myrle scolded, "of any second box." Duncan cleared his throat. Gave one abrupt nod, making the fat of his neck bulge above his white shirt collar. "My apologies, Mrs. Butterworth, I...I naturally assumed you knew."

"Naturally."

"Mr. Butterworth left the key in my possession," he said, "with instructions to give it to you if anything..." More throat clearing, twinkling eyes twitching. "If, I'm sorry"—he sighed—"if anything happened to him. Naturally, I didn't think anything would, at the time."

"Naturally," she repeated and rose up, leaning across the desk into the man's pinkish, roundish face. "Why am I only

90

now—my husband's been dead two weeks—*hearing* of this?"

"I...was out of town when...when it happened, sorry, and...I only recently heard. I was planning to call."

"We'll save the bank that dime," she said, straightening.

Adding: "Yes, we are *very* interested in that *second* box."

Duncan offered us chairs in the lobby and scurried off. The first box, the one Myrle Butterworth knew about, was spectacularly uninteresting, for my purposes: insurance papers, copy of the couple's will, some cash, savings bonds for the kids' college, proof sets of U.S. coins, titles on cars, a boat. The second box was one of those king-sized ones, largest the bank offered.

When we swung open the steel lid, inside the private cubicle Duncan provided us, it was clear there was well over a thousand pages of material, both of us glaring in awe. I let Myrle have first crack. Maybe Ralph had written the great American novel, and it needed a lot of editing. But it wasn't a few seconds before she cast a sour look my way over her bony shoulder. "I think this is what you came for, Ms. Russell."

We exchanged places.

She entwined her arms and bumped a deltoid miserably against the cinderblock wall, staring askance. I dug down a few different levels, lifting out pages, putting them back, like a mine engineer core-sampling different depths, seeing what the prospects were. Some of it was about UFOs. A lot of interview transcripts. I think I glimpsed something mentioning *King Solomon's treasure?* Surely not. Some of it was about Nazis, reminding me of Buzz Hutcheson saying he'd refused to bankroll a trip Butterworth wanted to make to South America, to hunt Martin Bormann.

I exhaled, facing Myrle. "May I take this back to my motel, sift through it?" I shrugged. "See if it means...*anything?*"

"Take it," she told me, sternly. "Take it back to Tennessee. If it doesn't involve our personal finances, and such, I don't really give a damn. My husband cheated on me, Ms. Russell. I don't care about any of this, whatever the hell it is."

"Very well," I said.

Duncan gave us a sturdy box for all those papers, and rolled it out for us, on a dolly. Myrle was silent driving us back to her house. Finding all that, I guess, hidden away from her by her husband, whatever his motives, had rekindled her bitterness. I heaved the slot-handled box into the trunk of my rented Dodge, when we got back, suffering only a very small hernia. "Oh," I asked Myrle, after slamming the trunk, swiping off the palms of my gloved hands, "do you know where Mr. Butterworth kept his pilot's logbook?"

She shrugged as if she didn't care.

"It's important."

"If not in the plane," she said, "there was an office he shared with other pilots, out at the airport."

I nodded. "One last favor, then..."

She barked: "I'm really about—"

Shaking her head.

She stopped herself.

Rubbed over her right eye, deep like she had a sick headache. My welcome clearly wearing thin. "Two favors, actually," I ventured, after a pause, adjusting the chain handles of my bag in the crook of my elbow. "First, might I use your powder room, before I take off?"

Dropping her hand, she threw off some *Of course, where are my manners?* gestures, and led me through the carport, and utility room, up a couple of steps into the breakfast room. My bladder really wasn't full, but I figured that wasn't the kind of request most women would refuse another. It got my foot, literally, in the door, to ask my real favor. "And, uh," I said, leaning out the frilly half-bath, calling back into the kitchen, "would you be even more of a dear, and call someone at airport, give your consent for me to search Mr. Butterworth's plane, and his desk, in that office you mentioned?"

Blandly, she agreed.

CHAPTER 15

I STEERED AWAY FEELING LIKE I was leaving behind a shell. The life force, or whatever, depleted out of Myrle Butterworth, discovering her perfect husband had apparently cheated on her, their perfect life. I thumbed the dashboard lighter. When it popped, I got a cigarette going, and blew the smoke, sighingly. I found myself suddenly wanting very much to prove he hadn't, that Ralph Butterworth had not, after all, betrayed his marriage vows with a strangely built woman in a carnival mask, the photographic evidence notwithstanding. The man could not be resurrected, but perhaps Myrle Butterworth's fond memories of him, of the marriage, could be. I wasn't hopeful, given my own experiences. Divorce cases I'd worked. My father having cheated on my mother. My first fiancé and the Harvey's salesgirl.

Anyway, felt to me like I was working for her, for Myrle Butterworth's piece of mind. Not for Colonel Buzz Hutcheson, for his guilt, for his ambitions to be Tennessee governor.

But it was nice.

Him being willing to pay the freight and all.

BEAVER COUNTY AIRPORT SAT IN the fork of two highways four miles outside town towards Ohio. I found the commercial charter operation Butterworth had worked for—Beaver Valley Aviation—occupying the last of a row of long corrugated-metal hangers on the east side of the airport. I drove to the end of the building nearest the runway, saw a glass door where a sign said office, and I parked. The man Myrle Butterworth had talked to, named Hennepin, was inside behind a plastic-topped counter. I gave him my card. "Ookay," he said, voice of a bass tenor, looking up from it, doffing his aviator glasses. "Myrle said give you whatever you wanted."

He was a sturdy, deliberate man in his fifties, with a craggy face, which had been windblown and sunbaked a lot in its life. The eyes out from behind the glasses were keen and azure blue, and put a fair investment of effort into assessing the tight fit of my beige turtleneck. He had a mane of pewter-gray hair, and wore a sage-green nylon military-style flight jacket, elastic ribbing at the wrists and waist. He called me "Buttercup" and asked how he could help, bending an ear close, to hear better, as if he spent a lot of time around loud engines.

For starters, I said, information about Ralph Butterworth's last charter.

Purpose of the trip, if he knew.

He said he did.

The clients were two liberal-arts eggheads from the college, flying up for a symposium at Akron University, all about, he said with hilarity, "American poets showing the influence of T. S. Eliot's style."

I threw my head up.

"What?"

He roared a great belly laugh, which was followed by us exchanging quips over the likely boredom-level of this symposium. Unfortunately Hennepin's anecdote blew my theory out of the water—that maybe Butterworth had been flying some union officials, maybe some conclave between oil or steel people from Pennsylvania, and Akron rubber people. My brilliant idea being, if the same tampering was, in fact, done to their plane that was done to Reuther's, the UAW president's, before his Dulles Airport crash a month ago, might be some generalized anti-organized-labor shenanigans going on. And if the targets of Butterworth's altimeter tampering, and near-crash, were his passengers, not Butterworth, then his days-later fatal car crash, in another state, might simply be an interesting, unrelated, coincidence. Butterworth's panicked call and planned midnight visit to my client, product of an overly exuberant imagination. Or paranoia.

I liked my theory.

Hated having to ball it up and deep-six it.

But I did.

"They left here," I said, "late afternoon, Saturday, twenty-six October."

"Yes," Hennepin said, in his deep tone.

"It being a short flight, Butterworth was supposed to return, then fly back the next day to pick up his charges."

"Yes."

"But a problem kept him in Akron overnight."

"That's true."

"Mrs. Butterworth knew nothing about this—her husband kept it from her—but I have another source telling me there was a near-crash on landing in Akron caused by an altimeter malfunction."

Hennepin's jaw muscles bulged.

Relaxed.

"Indeed."

"What can you tell me?"

"Instrument failure. It happens."

Tone sharp, voice clipped.

No more checking out my figure.

Fully focused, defensively so, upon my face. "Fortunately Ralph had eyes like an eagle. He was on approach, realized he was closer than he should have been, scudding some streetlights in a neighborhood he was over. He pulled the nose up, before snagging any treetops."

"Close call. What did he do?"

"Told the tower he thought he had a bad altimeter, declared an emergency. They cleared traffic, and he landed by instinct. And that, if I may add young lady, took a superb pilot, like Ralph Butterworth, rest his soul."

"I can see that."

"Flying the gauges, altimeter reading two-hundred-feet off, still everyone walked away. Not to mention Ralph even brought the airplane through still flyable."

"That plane was flown back Sunday?"

"After the Akron mechanics installed a new altimeter, yes. And Ralph flew a solo test flight before letting his passengers anywhere close."

I squinted, bent my head.

"Don't the Feds investigate these things?"

Mention of Feds got Hennepin's jaws straining again. "Civil Aeronautics Board, till a year ago, investigated aviation accidents. Now it's this new NTSB they got. But, there was no accident." He shrugged. "Ralph brought her in, when and where he was supposed to, no injuries, no substantial damage. No accident, so, no investigation."

"There was," I said, "a dangerous malfunction."

"If we made a literal federal case of every mechanical failure that might lead to a crash, I couldn't keep this business flying. That's why we have professionals, Ms. Russell, men like Ralph Butterworth, who take proper actions, whose highest duty, is to take proper, necessary actions, when the—well, you know—the *waste* hits the fan."

I nodded.

"When he returned, you talked?"

"First order of business."

"About the incident?"

"Yes."

"To what, did he attribute it?"

"Random instrument failure. Dumb luck."

"Nobody's fault?" I said.

"Nope."

"No negligence? No malice aforethought?"

"That was Ralph's assessment."

"He's dead now."

"Not from a plane crash."

"You buy that?" I asked. "Random instrument failure? Dumb luck?"

"I don't work with pilots whose judgment and word I don't trust."

I exhaled, swiping my hair back.

"What happened," I asked, "to the faulty altimeter?"

"Ralph brought it back."

"What was done with it?"

"Vince Petrolino disassembled it, in the shop."

I wrote *PETROLINO* on my pad.

"My chief mechanic."

"I'd like to talk to him."

"Sound like you, Ms. Russell, think we're hiding something."

"No, sir. Just doing my job, asking questions of as many people as I can, who might know something I need to know. And right now, frankly, I don't even know what I need to know. I'm poking around, to see if the Akron incident had anything at all to do with Butterworth's auto-accident death, down south, less than a week later."

Hennepin shrugged with his eyes.

"Ask me, I'd say no."

"Probably right," I said. "May I see Mr. Petrolino?"

CHAPTER 16

AFTER A BRIEF CHECK, WHICH came to naught, of Butterworth's personal effects removed, boxed up, from that office he'd shared with the other pilots, Hennepin led me back into the tool-and-equipment-crammed main hanger, through several connected maintenance bays, some with sliding doors open to the outside, others not. He zipped his jacket higher; I wrapped up in my shearling coat, gloved hands dug in my pockets. There were hoists and chains, parts on steel shelving, and grease, lots of grease, thick grease. There were single- and twin-engine civil aircraft parked in some of the bays. I saw two employees, both mechanics, doing maintenance on different aircraft, separate bays. The first was taller, younger, reddish hair, short and straight, up a ladder wearing black lace-up boots I only noticed because they were spit-shined to an improbably high gloss. "How are you, Colonel Hennepin?" he said from atop the ladder as we threaded through. Adding: "Good day, miss."

"Fine, Bobby, just fine. In early, ain't you?" Pulling back his knit cuff, consulting a heavy aviator's wristwatch. "Got to get the work done, sir. You have a nice day." Hennepin grunted, not looking back. Irritated, you ask me, by the younger man's obsequiousness. The second man we encountered was Petrolino, olive complexion, deftly spinning a ratchet wrench on a Piper Cherokee with the engine cowling off, a lot of brightly colored wiring dangling out like a hemorrhage. "Hey, Chief," Hennepin called up, as we approached, in his baritone.

"Yo!"

"Interrupt you a moment?"

He waved the other man down.

Engine hummings and growlings came from outside.

Blurred and indistinct.

Interspersed with silence.

Bouncing when he landed, Vince Petrolino was five-eight, about 165 pounds, with eagerly smiling brown eyes, flat ears, and a handsome head of thick black hair. He wore faded navy coveralls, and a Pittsburgh Pirates baseball cap, removed with a flourish, once he saw a lady was present. Fortyish, he had a tattoo where his cuffs were rolled back. It said *Lucille*. He wiped oil off his hands onto a rag that had had a lot of that done on it, before shaking mine gingerly, fingertips only, as if he might shatter me. "This pretty young thing," Hennepin said, hands tucked down back pockets, overlooking us both, "is a detective looking into Ralph Butterworth's death." Petrolino was nodding spastically, neck on a heavy spring, back and forth between us. "She'd like to ask you some questions, then look over the Cessna. Myrle Butterworth gave her permission, so, anything Ms. Russell wants, she gets."

"Count on it, boss."

Hennepin excused himself, leaving Petrolino studying me happily, intriguedly, bending back for perspective. "Detective?" he said. "Mean like, an insurance investigator?"

"Something like that," I said.

And after checking, making double sure Hennepin was gone, I added:

"I'm not going to tell your boss anything."

Something moved behind his eyes, and he pulled a toothpick from behind an ear.

Started chewing it, squinting, an askance look.

"Not gonna tell my boss *what?*"

"Everything you know about the altimeter pulled out of Butterworth's plane in Akron. He believed it was sabotaged, deliberately, to read falsely high, for the purpose of causing a crash. I think he based that belief on *your* examination. And he convinced you to keep that information under your hat—in effect, lie to your boss."

I paused.

Filled, emptied my lungs.

"How'm I doing?"

"So far..." He took the toothpick out, shook it at me, then bit back down on it.

"You battin'em outta the park, lady."

"Thanks for being honest."

"Honest..."

He huffed. "Hell, couldn't be happier. 'Bout time somebody looked into this. Little surprised they sent a dame, but"—quick shrug of stocky shoulders—"the times..."

"Yeah," I said. "They're a changing. Actually though, what I was hired to look into was Butterworth's car accident. But, I got to thinking, anybody who could engineer a near plane crash, might could do the same thing to a car. And maybe that time succeed."

"Yeah." He was nodding. "Pretty smart thinkin'."

"For a dame."

He grinned huge.

"Sorry 'bout dat."

"Where's that altimeter?" I asked.

"Search me. Mr. Butterworth took it."

"Assume you haven't talked to the police, or FAA?"

"Said he'd take care of it."

"Butterworth?"

"Yeah. But I ain't heard nothin' more, till now."

"How would this be done, the sabotage? Explain it to me in words I'll understand."

"Step into my office..."

With a gallant sweep of Popeye-muscled arm, he escorted me to a workbench, along a back wall, everything oily and metallic smelling. There was a tattered *Playboy* centerfold up on the wall behind, like it'd been there several years, a poufy blonde, iridescent aquamarine eyes, with bigger boobs than Pauline Prescott's. She wore lacey panties and was propped against a hi-fi set. Miss October, of whatever year. "Oh, sorry," Petrolino said, sheepishly. "Meet Rosemarie, kinna our mascot, round here."

"What makes you think, sir, I don't see the same thing everyday in the mirror?"

He laughed, "Hah!"

Pointing, saying, "You know, I like you."

"Thanks." No part of the bench top was tidy enough to set my pocketbook on, so I used the floor, and hoisted onto a metal stool, after wiping it, feeling for grease. Swiping my hair, and crossing my legs, I kept my back to Rosemarie. Might make me self-conscious. Petrolino took the other stool, starting to explain, "Ya see, an aneroid altimeter don't really measure height in feet."

"It doesn't?" I said, big-hazel-eyed.

"No, ma'am. Basically it's a barometer, see. Measures air pressure, like the weatherman on TV talks about."

"Okay," I said, enraptured. "Go on."

"Higher you go, lower the pressure, and it drops at a...what do you call?...*predictable* rate, so each altitude has a specific barometric pressure."

"I see."

"The instrument reads the pressure, but the dial don't show the pressure, see. It shows the feet above sea level going with that pressure. But, here's the trick. Barometric pressure ain't always the same, is it?"

"No," I said, "it isn't."

"Mean, that's what the weatherman tells us every night on the eleven-o'clock news, right?" He took on an animated announcer's voice. "The barometer today was thirty-point-oh-six, or whateveh. More important, elevation above sea level of every airport is different, right? Here, for example, we're 1253 feet. Go to Denver, a mile up, right—5280 feet, or whateveh. So we can't just fly around, assuming the altimeter is automatically going to read zero when the airplane's wheels touch down, right? You gotta set—we call it calibrate—you gotta calibrate the instrument to read zero at the barometric pressure at ground level for the runway you wanna land on. Here, at this airport, that would be the, current, barometric pressure at 1253 feet above mean sea level, see."

"I do," I said. "Was Butterworth's altimeter calibrated wrong?"

"Close, but no cigar. Actually, yes, but it's more complicated. The instrument, see, had to appear to be functioning normal on the ground before takeoff, but fail at altitude, when, say, the elevation of the Akron airport was dialed in." The chewed toothpick was pointed at me again. "Here's the real innerestin' thing—the altimeter Mr. Butterworth brought back from Akron, the Akron crew yanked outta that Cessna, ain't the instrument I installed six months ago."

I curled a brow.

No longer faking fascination. "How do you know?"

"Got maintenance records, see. They show the model number, date of manufacture of the instrument I installed. All that etched into the outside of the case. But the instrument coming back from Akron had no identifying data on it. An untraceable altimeter"—he straightened, indignantly, lifted his beak nose—"switched out for my original."

"A substitute," I said, "tampered with, somehow, to fail in flight."

"Not just *somehow*—I *know* how."

Petrolino flashed that toothy eager grin.

"Pray, tell," I said, shifting on the stool. Recrossing my legs. The other mechanic, I suddenly spied, the lanky, reddish-haired one, who Hennepin called Bobby, wearing a hunting cap with the ear flaps up, was taking a smoke break, languidly outside on the tarmac. Casually halting just in front of the bay Petrolino and I were in, lighting up, cupping a hand over the flame of his lighter. Then he stood out there, puffing in the chilly breeze, glimpsing Petrolino and me, running a thumbnail along his jawline. Taking in my gams, I assumed, for which I'm famous.

Petrolino, explaining the sabotage, drew my attention back.

"...I get the instrument from Mr. Butterworth, see, " he was saying, "and I notice immediately somethin' rattlin' inside the case. Well, these are precision instruments—things don't just rattle around, ya know. I open up the case. What was rattlin' was one of the set screws out of the rocking shaft, and that, see, would permit the calibration arm assembly to be all loosey-goosey in the shaft. Mr. Butterworth asked me to check it out. I did. Called a technician at Barfield."

"Barfield?"

"Barfield Instruments. He tole me an instrument like that with a loose set screw, exposed say to ten thousand feet, on descent would indicate high by 225, maybe 250 feet."

I nodded.

"Couldn't," I said, "a set screw work its way out, by accident?"

"Sureh," Petrolino said, winking. Tapping his own temple. "But that ain't what happened, see. I got me one of them jeweler's loupes, ya know, powerful magnifier."

"Uh huh."

"And looked *reeeal* close at the threading on the set screw."

"And?"

"Nothin'."

"Nothing?"

"Nothin' worn out, nothin' damaged."

"Okay."

"But when I look at the screw hole in the rocking shaft, guess what?"

I curled a brow.

"What?"

"Guess."

"*Mr. Petrolino....!*" I snarled.

"Sorry. Been drilled out."

"Drilled out?"

"Like with a high-speed drill bit."

"Wow," I said numbly.

Leaned back, clutching my knee. Then, glimpsing outside, I didn't see the other mechanic anymore. I shrugged, lightly. Probably *had* just been on a smoke break, sneaking another ogle at the girl he'd seen hanging with his boss. "Do me a favor, Chief," I said, when I came back into Petrolino's big pleasant face. "Want to help me figure out what happened to Mr. Butterworth?"

"Sureh," he said.

"Write all that up, better yet, type it up."

"Okay."

"All those details, make sketches, include the name and number of the technician at—Barfield, was it? When you have all that, get it signed before a notary, and mail it to me at this address." I shoved him my card, with the Nashville P.O. Box on it, I used for business mail. "Okay?"

He took the card by the corner, looked at it.

Looked at me, grinning.

"Sureh."

CHAPTER 17

VINCE PETROLINO TOOK ME OUT onto the apron to the white, red, and black Cessna 172 Skyhawk flown previously by Ralph Butterworth, parked on the ramp, twenty yards from the Beaver Valley Aviation building. It was lashed down with ropes against a blustery wind-chill. A gleaming white Lear Jet was taxiing out, emitting an engine whine stabbing to the ears, the atmosphere back of the exhaust nozzles opaque, distorted by immense heat. The chief unlocked the Cessna's cockpit, then baggage compartment, and once the Lear Jet leapt off the runway, so we could hear ourselves think, he asked if I needed him to stay. I said I'd be fine, he could get back to his work, and in short order, I found what I wanted:

Butterworth's flight logbook.

Pocket, back of the pilot's seat.

I tucked that inside my purse and continued searching, giving it a few minutes, but found nothing else of interest, at least nothing striking me so. When I pulled my head out, however, of the baggage compartment behind the cockpit, straightening, smoothing wind-mussed hair, I was jolted by the sight of that mechanic again, Bobby, in the hunting cap and glossy boots. He really was starting to ruffle my feathers, especially now, because I couldn't put this off to any kind of innocent girl-watching. Because he couldn't see me at the moment: his back was to me. He was outside the B.V. Aviation office, a flapping paper in hand, a nub of yellow pencil, copying the license number down off my Hertz rent-a-car, concentrating on it, like it was a trigonometry problem.

When he was finished, he gave a furtive glance over his shoulder—did a double take, seeing me set off towards him in my tweed skirt and leather pumps.

He slinked away, hands digging into coverall pockets. I watched him hurry, disappearing around the side of the white-metal hanger, into a maintenance bay. I followed, sped my pace, my heart knocking, boobs jouncing. But by the time I reached the bays, peering inside each, bending and twisting, no Bobby was to be found. I shook my head, exhaling. Vanished into a restroom or storeroom or something, nowhere near the plane whose engine he'd been tinkering with, when he'd first spoken to Hennepin and me.

Thinking back, I knew it to be entirely possible Spit-Shine Bobby had overheard—*been making the deliberate effort to overhear?*—my talk with Vince Petrolino, about the missing, tampered-with altimeter. I found Petrolino back in that same oil-smelling maintenance bay, working on that same Piper Cherokee. I gave a nod to Rosemarie's enormous mammaries, asking, oh by the way, if he'd spoken to anyone else, other than Butterworth, and the guy at Barfield Instruments, about the proof he'd found of deliberate, sophisticated sabotage—effectively, of attempted murder.

No, no one, he swore.

I spread my coat and racked my hands on my hips, working on deciding what was best to do now. I rubbed the middle of my forehead, sighing. Bobby was either a potentially important piece in the strewn-over-the-table-still jigsaw puzzle of my case, or he was a sex pervert.

Either way, I ought to learn more. I asked Petrolino about him, making it sound routine, no big deal. "Kaplan," he told me, leaning on hirsute arms, down-looking from up his ladder. "Bobby Kaplan. Night mechanic. Part time. Works to nine. Airport closes then, during the week."

"Would he ever stay here," I asked, head back, my eyes up and shaded against bright work lights, "past airport closing time?"

"Sure. That just means no flights in- or outbound, runway lights off. But"—he shrugged—"we needed a plane readied for morning…"

So," I said, "Kaplan would have had access to Ralph Butterworth's plane, could've done work on it, late, with few people, or maybe no one, around. That right?"

The chief shrugged again, socket wrench drooping from one hand.

"S'pose that's true," he said.

Then raked thick black hair, and looked at me sideways, narrowing an eye.

"You got suspicions?"

"Do you know if he worked the night of Friday October twenty-fifth?"

"Night before Butterworth's mishap. Prob'ly. Always takes weekend shifts—kind of a loner, I gather. No sweetheart. But we like that, a man likin' to work weekends, I mean, not the no-girl-friend thing. Some mechanics go off on benders from six o'clock Friday, on."

"Thanks for the tip," I said. "I'll avoid flying first-thing Mondays."

"That's the size of it. Anyway, check the office: Colonel Hennepin's got the time sheets for that Friday."

"I will, thanks. Kaplan been here long?"

"Two, three months."

"Where'd he come from?"

"Walked in with a résumé. Been a machinist for an air-brake manufacturer, but got'na fracas with his supervisor, an' up and quit before they could fire him."

"Fracas? Words, or fisticuffs?"

Petrolino huffed.

"Fisticuffs."

"Make a habit," I said, "of hiring men, who trade blows with their bosses?"

"He was straight with us 'bout it. Showed us his honorable discharge from the Air Force. That's where he trained to be a mechanic. Did a tour in 'Nam. Those are good 'nough credentials for most guys round here. Most of us are ex-military, like Colonel Hennepin"—he gestured—"*your* Mr. Butterworth."

I nodded.

"Get in any fistfights here?"

"Nope. Kept his nose clean. Shows up, on time, sober, not high on dope. Counts for somethin' these days. Look…" Petrolino dropped the socket wrench, banging onto a tray of tools, and climbed down, coming round close in front of me, stern. "Level with me, Miss." He was wiping his hands again with the oily rag. "Anything you know, I need to. I'm responsible for these airplanes, keepin'em in excellent working order. That's a responsibility I take very seriously, life-and-death responsibility."

I swallowed. "I know."

"Do you?"

He said it with a bark, giving me a jolt.

"*Yes.* Used to be a nurse. I understand."

"Awright. You understand if anybody's sabotaging aircraft, or just being sloppy, I need to know, or people—"

"Could die. I get it. But nobody was being sloppy, were they, Mr. Petrolino, when they drilled out a set-screw hole in an unmarked altimeter, and installed it in Butterworth's Cessna? That's sounds very deliberate, doesn't it? Could *Kaplan* do that?"

He bent back his head.

Thrust his jaw.

Rocked it side to side. "Could've switched out the instrument," he said at last, "lot of us could, but I…doubt he's got the skills to rig an altimeter, way that one was."

"Could anybody in this company, this airport do that?"

He grimaced.

"Doubt it."

"You? You figured it out."

"I checked out a rattle and made a phone call, ma'am. Working on the guts of an aircraft instrument is like…it's like watchmaking. But you changed the subject on me. Do you or do you not, Miss Detective, consider Bobby Kaplan a suspect?"

"When I was out at the Cessna," I said, "I saw him copying down my license-plate number."

"Huh," he grunted.

"When we were talking, I spotted him looking at us."

Then I shrugged.

"Looking at *me*, perhaps. Or Rosemarie."

He snorted a lascivious chuckle. The toothy grin returning, playful eyes. "I said Bobby had no steady girl. Didn't say he was no homo."

"Understood…" Nodding, feigning embarrassment.

"Wa'me talk to him? Tell him not to stare so much at the merchandise?"

"No, I don't."

"Okay."

"I mean it. Don't go all paternal on me. I'll deal with him."

"Oookay."

"Mr. Petrolino," I said, "I do understand your position, but none of what we just talked about is enough for me to accuse a man of attempted murder, nor for me to suggest you fire him, when, as far as you know he's a reliable, disciplined worker."

He sighed.

Agreeingly.

"Just call the number on my card—collect—if anything seems strange with him, or he disappears, or if there's another incident."

"Okay," he said, "but this deal cuts both ways."

He waggled two fingers between us.

"Okay," I said. "Deal."

CHAPTER 18

BOBBY KAPLAN HAD WORKED THAT Friday night.
I got his address from Hennepin, embellishing the truth about how I was piecing together a timetable of Ralph Butterworth's last week, and outright lied I had reason to believe Butterworth had come to the airport late the night before the Akron charter. I said I might want to talk to Bobby Kaplan the next morning, before my flight back to Nashville, since Kaplan might have seen Butterworth, but unfortunately I didn't have time to talk to him right then because I was late for an interview with one of the Butterworths' neighbors—unbeknownst to, I winked, Myrle Butterworth. The whole neighbor-thing was a lie too—all of it a bamboozle to get Kaplan's address out of his boss, after which I asked Hennepin not to say anything to Kaplan. Best if he weren't prepared, I preferred spontaneity from my interviewees.

He agreed.

The address was a dozen miles away in East Liverpool, Ohio. I traced the curl of the Ohio River to the state line, whereupon a city-limits sign boasted East Liverpool to be the *Pottery Center of America*, pop. 22,306. As in Beaver Falls, I stopped for directions at a filling station. A derelict roofing-tile manufacturer bordered the scabby neighborhood. I had seen steel-fabricating concerns, and knew there was strip-mining in the area, a manifestly evil, vicious process, defacing the countryside. Below the railroad tracks, near the river, 1644B East Fifty-Fourth Street, it turned out, was a dried-out brown duplex on a dried-out brown lot. It was past four o'clock in the afternoon. The attendant at the filling station told me be careful, it wasn't the best neighborhood. The advice seemed sound. I didn't like being there, and I would like it less in the dark.

Why *was* I?

I wasn't the vainest woman in the world, but if I lighted out, as a matter of policy, after every man who gave me the eye, besides being certifiable, I'd also probably have gotten myself into far more trouble than I had in my life—a life in which the amount of trouble I had managed to get into, was not trivial.

Anyway, him jotting down my license number, then disappearing, was beyond suspicious. There might be an explanation having nothing to do with Ralph Butterworth. Maybe he was B. V. Aviation's parking-lot monitor. Maybe he thought he could learn my address from the tag number, and was East Liverpool's answer to the Boston Strangler, planning to gain access to my home posing as a workman, leaving me stripped, bound, raped and strangled, by an item of my own clothing, a pair of my own stockings perhaps, tied into a bow under my chin.

I felt safe enough from that, the rent-a-car not likely to lead him to the Howard Johnson's, and anyway, I was leaving for Nashville the following morning. Still, if I heard about a string of sex murders up here, I'd sure as heck call my FBI acquaintance, Special Agent Legate, with a big fat tip about Bobby Kaplan.

My main issues, of course, with Kaplan involved his aircraft-mechanical skills, coupled with his access, unobserved, to Ralph Butterworth's Cessna the night prior to Akron.

I was rubbing my shoulder, shrugging, surveying the dreary duplex from the warmth of my idling Dodge Coronet.

Plenty of mechanics, no doubt, worked at that airport. The culprit didn't have to work for the same outfit Butterworth did. Perhaps my trek out to East Liverpool, Middle America, *was* a long shot. I'd taken them before, though, and this one seemed worth it, as long as I was up here—and assuming Vince Petrolino wasn't completely full of hot air and that altimeter really had been tampered with, in so sophisticated a manner.

Given all of that, it was hard to ignore the altimeter as a potential clue in explaining Butterworth's death. Turning his Mississippi drunk-driving crash from tragic accident:

To diabolical murder.

Kaplan might've had no part in any of that, but I didn't have a better candidate at the moment. And, all other things being equal:

He gave me the willies.

To use a technical investigator's term.

His eyes were like a crazed Jehovah's Witness's. Might've been merely sexual, but I had an eerie feeling of there being something more behind it. *Woman's intuition?* Perhaps, curling a brow, a corner of my mouth, as I climbed from the car, curbside, in front of the address, weather close to freezing. I buttoned my coat, then cradled in the crook of my left arm a clipboard, on which I'd clamped an official-appearing blank form. Bracing myself, I breathed deep.

Exhaled a lot of breath fog.

The form was an application for life membership in the RCA Victor Record Club.

Any four albums for 99¢.

Stereo or regular hi-fi.

Double discounts on Tijuana Brass, Al Hirt, Bill Cosby, Ferrante & Teicher, Peter, Paul & Mary, Sonny & Cher, The Supremes, Henry Mancini, Brigit Nilsson, Ramsey Lewis, Segovia. Who could pass it up? From the street, I went along the cracked walk, up some steps onto the porch, with a Bic pen poised to fill in the blanks on my clipboard. The bell didn't work. I rapped on the margin of the screen door. From the other half of the duplex, a window curtain was drawn aside, a peering face pressed close to the glass, an old woman's face, a flurry of white hair. I backed up from the door, on my two-inch heels. Waved at the old girl, a flutter of fingers. The curtain fell.

No one answered at 1644B.

Not that I'd expected anyone to, but I had to appear to have expected it. Bobby Kaplan was at work, and said to be a loner. I wasn't expecting a wife, or live-in girlfriend. You never know, though, what to expect in detective work. Sometimes you don't know a clue if it springs up like a claymore mine, blowing up in your face.

Others are right out in the open, minding their own business.

There was a bullet hole in the window of 1644B next to the door with several spider fissures in the glass radiating from the center, Scotch-taped over from the inside, a big translucent X. Two more bullet holes were in the stucco. Feeling my heart, I yanked at the screen. It wasn't hooked. I tried the knob. The inner door was locked. There were two bullet holes in it, which had been puttied over.

A placard thumbtacked into the door read:

WHITE MAN FIGHT
SMASH THE BLACK REVOLUTION

Not again... I groaned, slapping my beret. Old Nosy, in 1644A opened her door, shuffling half out onto her porch. She was stooped over and bundled against the cold. She'd be a wisp of a thing under her shapeless dress that might've been calico many moons ago. Over that she'd wrapped herself in a man's gray cardigan. She was wearing fuzzy slippers and argyle socks. A voice dragged up out of her throat saying he wasn't there—Kaplan, I guessed—then it asked what I wanted. I clipped down steps and crossed the dead lawn, carefully, to the foot of her porch. "I'm from the power company," I said, looking up, "taking a...a utilization survey. Do you know when Mr. Kaplan will be home?"

"Late."

"I see. My bad luck. Perhaps you can help: do you know Mr. Kaplan?"

"Some. I'm the landlady."

"Oh," I said happily. "Mrs....?"

"Croxall."

I nodded.

"Keeps to himself, mostly," she tattled on, "but he's a polite helpful boy. Respectful. Pays his rent on time."

I pointed over. "Those are bullet holes."

"There's a war on, you know."

My nod came with a very slow upstroke. "My Henry's one of our doughboys over there," Mrs. Croxall added. "Got gassed

113

though, in the trenches. Shipping him home any day now."

"We...appreciate his sacrifice," I said.

"Bobby's in the army, too, you know."

"Really," I said. "Bobby Kaplan?"

"Yes. Having another of our boys right next door makes me not miss Henry so much."

"I'm sure it's a comfort. How do you know, ma'am, Mr. Kaplan is in the army?"

"I see him going out in uniform."

"Every day?"

"No..."

She thought about this.

"Not every day. Once or twice a week, I might say."

"What kind of uniform?"

"Oh I dunno uniforms, and I don't see that well."

"Is it like your Henry's uniform?"

"No."

"What color?"

"Brown, I'd say. Light brown. Tan."

"Boots?"

"Black, very tall and shiny."

She smiled, as if proud, actually straightening her spine out a lot. I shook my head, staring off, trying to figure it. Wisps of mist sailed off, with my breathing. Kaplan could be in the Army Reserves, National Guard. Then again, Petrolino told me he had applied for his airport job, bolstered by his honorable discharge from the Air Force. Why then was he in uniform now? Maybe he was a scoutmaster, or something. "Oh," the landlady perked up, and I twisted back up at her. "Just remembered, he gave me a pamphlet once, when I commented how handsome he was."

"Handsome in uniform?"

"Yes."

"What was it about?"

"Oh I didn't read it; I don't see too good to read you know."

"Yes, ma'am."

"But I kept it. Somewhere. Would you like to see it?"

"Very much."

She invited me in out of the cold, and I thanked her, stepping through into her living room, letting my eyes roam. I put a hand

114

back to catch the screen, keep it from banging, then pushed the front door shut, feeling the latch snick. Felt like ninety degrees in there. I opened my coat, and pulled off my gloves. Place smelled of dust, and cat-litter boxes needing cleaning. I waited while she shuffled to the back part of the house, through a connecting dining room, and kitchen beyond. I surveyed, tapping my front teeth with the blue cap of my pen. On the right, off the living room, was a bedroom. In the living room, a black-and-white nineteen-inch TV, with a vertical-hold problem, sat on a cart, in a corner, with rabbit ears, droning on, flickering. There was faded overstuffed furniture, a wooden rocker, frayed lamps. Two long-haired contributors to the cat-litter smell were on the furniture looking unhappily at me. Had a feeling there were others. I heard various drawers opening and slamming, from the back, replaced by slow shuffling again as the old woman came back, grinned at me triumphantly. She gave me a cheaply printed trifold flyer for something called the OHIO WHITE NATIONALIST LEAGUE.

I opened it.

A big swastika headed a gamy piece of anti-Semitic hate literature.

I looked at the woman.

"Tell me more about this uniform. Any emblem? On the sleeve? You know, like, sergeant's stripes?"

"Oh, well…" She thought with her tongue and lips.

"There is a very attractive band, left arm, I believe."

"What color?"

"A striking crimson." Her eyes glittered.

"With a white circle?" I said.

"Yes."

"With that in the middle?"

I showed her the swastika.

Tapped the center of it on the paper with my pink manicured nail

"Why…why, yes, now you mention it."

She said this as naively innocent as a newborn lamb.

"Say…" I was stuck by a notion. "You're the landlady."

"Yes."

"You have a key to next door, right?"

"Yes."

I gritted my teeth. "Mrs. Croxall, could you let me in, just for a couple of minutes, no more?" I scrunched my face up pleadingly. "Promise not to disturb anything. It's getting dark, and I like being home before dark, but I need to get one more survey done or my boss at the company will kill me. All I need is…is to count the number of…electrical appliances, and document the voltage of their…uh, plugs."

Smooth, Sherry.

Didn't grow up reading Nancy Drew for nothing. Fortunately, for me, I could've told this ol' bird I was Secret Squirrel. "Oh, I guess there's no harm," she eventually wheezed. "You're such a polite young lady, and you certainly don't want to be out after dark."

"No, ma'am," I said, "not the way the world is today." She got me a key, which I promised to bring back. I crossed over to 1644B, carrying my clipboard, and let myself inside. It was a mirror image of the old lady's place, front bedroom on the left as I entered. The window blinds were closed, so I had to cut on a light to see.

Don't know what I was expecting.

Not this.

Firstly, the place was spic and span, the only smell… Thought it might be gun oil, and oh yes—the highly polished boots—there was a scent of Kiwi wax. The living room was nothing like Old Nosy's. Middle of the floor sat an exercise bench with a selection of racked and stacked barbells and dumbbells, plates for each going up to twenty-five pounds. There was a single armchair with vinyl upholstery, a step table with a lamp, next to that. No TV, only a large clean cabinet radio, which might've been twenty years old, and a Silvertone portable phonograph. That and some record albums were on heavy-gauge steel shelves in black enamel, with brass legs, arrayed on both sides of the bedroom door. Atop one of those was a seven-band Hallicrafters radio receiver. Most of the remaining shelving housed books, mostly military history, back to the Romans and Greeks. There was an *American Heritage Picture History of World War II*, and volumes, too, on World War I, even Napoleon. My heels knocked, echoing, the furnishings sparse, utilitarian. Little cushioning to absorb sound. The floors were hardwood, waxed to a very high gloss, except for a rug where the exercise bench sat.

Pinned-up maps, domestic and world, covered the walls. The bedroom contained a twin bed made up with a wool army blanket you could bounce a dime off. There was a bureau, a full-length mirror, a beige baked-on-enamel wardrobe cabinet, a footlocker with Kaplan's name stenciled on the lid, and a tin wastebasket. The bureau and wardrobe contained a working-man's clothing, of the usual ilk, and not a great deal of it. The uniforms the old lady mentioned weren't there. The footlocker was padlocked. There was a small closet in the back corner. That's where two sharply-creased, starched-like-cardboard complete uniforms were hung, of the type the landlady described. Back of the closet stood a pump-action shotgun and an M-1 Carbine military rifle. I shut the closet, went into a tiny bathroom, which told me nothing. There was a door between the sink and toilet leading, I guessed, to the back bedroom. It was locked tight. There would be another way in via the kitchen.

I went back along through the living room, picking up the pace, knowing any minute Old Nosy might come alooking. The dining room served Kaplan as both a place to eat and an office. There was a table and one chair, a black telephone on the table. A neat stack of bills and letters, a selection of pens and pencils standing in a coffee mug. No ashtray. No ashtray or cigarettes anywhere in the house as far as I'd seen. Yet I'd seen him light up outside the hanger at the airport. I shrugged over that, about to move to the kitchen. Letting my eyes scud over a spiral notepad, arranged perfectly straight alongside the telephone, when something flexed my subconscious brain. My head snapped back to what was written on the notepad, bringing my body with it.

It was in pencil, in a not very sophisticated hand:

Cherie Russell
Nashville
Private eye!!!
Butterworth

0900 Th!

For a moment I stood blinking as though I hadn't read anything at all and was waiting for that to change. Then a slow shudder ran along my spine, and passed over my whole body. I breathed deeply to calm my heart, my suspicions about Bobby Kaplan borne out in spades, more than I could ever have imagined.

That was me, of course, the French spelling of my given name. Someone had phoned Kaplan, given him my name, how he thought it was spelled, where I came from, my profession, and that I had arranged to go to the Butterworth house in Beaver Falls, nine that morning. Whoever had called, wanted what? Kaplan at the airport, looking out for me, case I made my way there from the house? I remembered Hennepin being surprised, Kaplan being there so early. Now we knew why: it was spy-on-Cherie-from-Nashville day. The only person who knew all of that info, scribbled on that pad—that I knew of, besides me—was Myrle Butterworth.

Either she had told someone...

Possible, I shrugged, with mouth and brow.

Innocently, or not, or...

Her phone was tapped.

Ralph Butterworth had told Buzz Hutcheson his concerns about electronic surveillance, the whole operational-security mantra. Maybe he wasn't totally paranoid. Spelling my name *Cherie* meant they'd only heard it spoken, not written, not printed. That supported the interception of my phone call with Myrle Butterworth as the source of Kaplan's information. Of course, she still could have told someone. She hadn't seen my name in print either, prior to being handed my card, by me, that morning.

I made myself move on to the kitchen, surprised Old Nosy wasn't rousting me already. I switched on a light. No dirty dishes, no pots on the stove. Bobby Kaplan, loner or not, kept his house in good order. Military order. I couldn't claim my kitchen to be as scrubbed and polished. A door opened from the kitchen into the back bedroom, as I knew it would from what I'd seen in the other half of the duplex. This one wasn't locked.

Squealing it open, I stepped through, slow and precise, ranging the room with my eyes, in wonder.

Black walls.

I found a light switch.

There were red candles, half burned, in dime-store holders.

The walls were adorned with American and Nazi flags and adjoining portraits in cheap frames of Adolf Hitler and George Washington. On a small table that was draped in red, below the two portraits, was displayed a book on an easel-like stand, like a Holy Joe might display a Bible. Except this wasn't a Bible; it was a secondhand-bookstore copy of:

Mein Kampf.

A second book was propped on a stand as well, side by side with Hitler's manifesto. Half surprised me, anything getting co-equal status with that, so I picked it up.

Leafed through it.

Crudely bound and printed, it was a self-published autobiography of George Lincoln Rockwell. Tucked between some pages was an 8/26/67—last year—newspaper clipping.

Headlined, AMERICAN NAZI SLAIN.

George Lincoln Rockwell.

Führer of the American Nazi Party.

Shot to death in his car outside a Virginia laundromat.

Title of Rockwell's autobiography:

This Time the World.

CHAPTER 19

I DROVE THROUGH A TIP of West Virginia twenty-five miles back to the Howard Johnson's in Pennsylvania. Blood orange glowed in my mirrors from the setting sun. I was bushed, and incredulous over finding myself in West Virginia, and out of cigarettes to boot. News on the radio said the U.S. and South Vietnamese had repulsed an attack by Communists near Cambodia, leaving 287 enemy dead, ending the lull following LBJ's halting of the bombing, two weeks ago. Tricky Dick had a "secret plan," supposedly, to end the war.

Believe that when I saw it.

A Yankee, it occurred to me, might be more likely than a southerner to assume *Sherry* was spelled *Cherie*.

What that got me, even if true, I hadn't the foggiest.

In other news: the Soviets beat us to the moon.

Again.

A probe named, believe it or not, Zond 6 had circled the moon, that "moist star upon whose influence Neptune's empire stands," and was heading back now, carrying turtles, or something. We can send a turtle to the moon, but we can't stop beating each other's brains out in Vietnam. At the bar, in the cocktail lounge of my motel, I drank two Scotches, smoked five cigarettes, and ordered a hamburger, fries, and coleslaw. A total stranger in a Nehru jacket wanted to buy me a drink. I was more rude to him than I should have been. Needed to work on that, I thought, now that I'm officially divorced, blowing smoke through pursed lips. I walked a Sanka in a Styrofoam cup back to my room. Bobby Kaplan didn't jump me in ambush, nor the guy in the Nehru jacket. A new show called *Hawaii Five-O* was on. I watched it, drinking the coffee, after shucking my bra off, sitting cross-legged on the bed. I had a fifth of Dewar's in my suitcase. I drank one during *That Girl*, then took a scalding shower, shaving my legs and such, and had another watching Dean Martin, guests: Lainie Kazan, Minnie Pearl, David Janssen.

Dino sang "Oh, You Beautiful Doll" just to me.

Appropriately then he and Lainie dueted, "Show Me the Way to Go Home." Which I did the next morning. I had breakfast, borrowed a roll of strapping tape from the front desk, which I used to secure my box full of Ralph Butterworth's bizarre research for the flight home. Then I packed, made two telephone calls, and checked out, charging $40.37 to my BankAmericard, noting the amount in my expense book, clipping the receipt inside. The phone calls were first to Myrle Butterworth. Had she told anyone about my planned visit after my initial contact Wednesday morning? My name? Who I was? When I was expected? She said no, not even her children. "I hadn't wanted to upset them," she added, and I thanked her for all she had done, and repeated my condolences.

When I hung up, I kept the receiver tucked between my ear and shoulder, checked the time by my wristwatch, and was already swiping through the Pittsburgh Yellow Pages. Not much time to spare to make my flight, but I was hoping to get the ball rolling on something. Under DETECTIVES I found a listing for a man named Bernard B. Petrosky, Blaw-Knox Building, Wood and Oliver downtown.

His quarter-page ad gave eight separate security services: one being, electronic bug detection. I rotary-dialed his number and reached a gravel-voiced secretary. I told her who I was. She put me on hold, and a minute later connected me to Petrosky, a man speaking with an eastern European accent, Polish, or Hungarian, or something. I repeated who I was, told him I was investigating a suspicious death and, though I was on my way out of town, I wanted to subcontract out an electronic security job. Go on, he urged. I wanted to know if Myrle Butterworth's phone line was tapped, and if possible by whom. I did not want her knowing about the check. I read him the Beaver Falls address and the telephone number there. No, I didn't need the bug removed, just confirmation whether there was one. I said I'd be happy to wire him his fee before he passed his report along. He said those arrangements would be fine, he could do all of that, no problem, but he needed confirmation I was who I said I was, before he could accept such a job over the phone.

That due diligence, in fact, bolstered my own confidence in reverse, having simply picked the man out of the phonebook. He was sounding reputable and professional. I told him he could check my private investigator's license with the Metropolitan Nashville District Attorney's Office. I did not give him the name or number of the secretary I was friends with there, figuring a man like Petrosky, if reputable, would trust better information he'd dug up himself, with a little effort, over anything spoon fed him. I assumed I was right when he asked me no more questions, just agreed to our arrangements, and asked how to reach me when he had something.

NASHVILLE WAS A DRIZZLY SIXTY-six degrees when my Convair turboprop landed at Berry Field. I tipped the sky cap two dollars who helped me with my suitcase, train case, and that three-ton box containing what I had taken to calling "The Butterworth Papers." I bought groceries at H. G. Hill on the way from the airport, and put them away, then unpacked. I changed into some brown corduroy capris, and a knit shirt in sky blue, and walked next door to pick up the mail. I paid some bills, balanced my checkbook. I heated a can of soup and ate at my desk, starting to type up three sets of investigative notes. I filed separate reports on: (1) my visit with Myrle Butterworth, (2) my drive out to Beaver County Airport, separate pages relating my talks with Hennepin and Petrolino, and my search of the Cessna, registration N52140. And lastly (3) my trip to East Liverpool. What I'd discovered in Bobby Kaplan's home, and documenting the landlady had let me in with permission. I figured if that were any violation of her lease agreement with Kaplan, it was her problem, not mine. I phoned my client, Buzz Hutcheson. It was late on a Friday but he was at his flagship car dealership in

Memphis. I had little trouble getting through, once I gave my name to the fluffy-voiced PBX operator. "I'm back," I told him. "I talked to Mrs. Butterworth, and a couple of people who worked with Butterworth at the airport. I got the logbook, as you suggested." I told him about the photos mailed to Butterworth's wife, that there might be marital infidelity involved, but I had my doubts, and why. "Okay," he said, and waited for more. I told him about the altimeter, that a mechanic named Kaplan, who could've been involved with the tampering, had acted suspiciously at the airport, and turned out to be tied in with, it seemed, the American Nazi Party.

"Butterworth," he said, "was researching Nazi secret weapons."

"True and maybe there is a connection. I don't know enough to say. But what I *do* know of these guys, the American Nazis, is that they're very low-rent bigots. Klansmen without robes, and fewer religious scruples. I don't know how plugged in they would be to real ex-World War II Nazis, if you see my point."

"But it is a possibility."

"Sure," I said. "One of the main reasons I'm calling, Mr. Hutcheson, is Kaplan *knew* I was there and why, *knew* I would be visiting Butterworth's wife. There was evidence of that at the duplex."

"I didn't tell anybody."

"You didn't know as much about my trip as he did."

"I see."

"Somebody called him," I said, "told him to spy on me. I think it's important we know who that is, and how they got their information. That seems key to figuring this all out."

"I agree."

"Good," I said, "because I hired a man up there to find if Butterworth's house was bugged. One of us will need to pay him." Hutcheson said he'd cover it, to let him know. I fluttered my lashes with relief. I hadn't really thought you could hire a Pittsburgh private detective on a Nashville private detective's wages. I thanked him, and said I'd stay in touch. He said it sounded like I was doing a crackerjack job.

I grinned.

Didn't even add:

For a girl.

I had my first Scotch of the day finishing those reports, then put on a stack of records—Dean Martin, Peggy Lee, *Brazilliance*—and cranked up the volume to hear the music from the back, where I soaked in a bath. Alone, in my own house, snug as a bug in a rug. After that, I put my feet up, wearing paisley cullotte pajamas, and had two more drinks, reading, starting with *The Confessions of Nat Turner*, though after a minute, I put that down, vacillatingly, on the side table, and got *Orlando* from the nightstand drawer, and read that instead.

For it was this mixture in her of man and woman, one being uppermost and then the other, that often gave her conduct an unexpected turn. The curious of her own sex would argue how, for example, if Orlando was a woman, did she never take more than ten minutes to dress…? She could drink with the best and liked games of hazard. She rode well and drove six horses at a gallop over London Bridge. Yet again, though bold and active as a man, it was remarked that the sight of another in danger brought on the most womanly palpitations. She would burst into tears on slight provocation…

—Virginia Woolf, *Orlando: A Biography*

CHAPTER 20

S ATURDAY I SLEPT TILL NINE, and after some bacon, eggs and grits, and reading the paper, and working the crossword, I completed the hernia I'd started in Pennsylvania, hauling Butterworth's papers in from the car. I threw open some windows—supposed to warm up that day—and carried my third giant mug of coffee into my office, and clapped Butterworth's logbook onto my desk blotter for later. I shoved up my sweater sleeves, slashed the strapping tape on the box with a steak knife and by one-thirty, I had the contents—a hodgepodge of formal typed transcripts of interviews, news clippings, letters, documents (some disturbingly official looking), handwritten notes on scrap paper, typed memos of record—all separated and organized into nine categories, covering a card table in my office, my cedar chest in the bedroom, and much of my dining table.

Mostly I'd sorted by geography, with a miscellaneous category for letters, notations, a photo, and reports that didn't seem, at first glance, tied to any one stopover in Butterworth's odyssey, zigzagging all over heck and back for the past year and a half, working on, whatever it was he was up to. Next I took a stupendously well-deserved, not to mention, insanity-avoiding break from shuffling papers, and opened up the man's pilot's logbook.

I paced into the kitchen with it, leafing pages. I put it on my breakfast table, brushed back my bangs, and made a sandwich with egg salad, lettuce, and extra mayonnaise. I sliced it diagonally and arranged it, on one my grandmother's Desert Rose china plates, with a small pile of Ruffles. I licked my thumb off, got a bottle of Coke from the fridge, popped the cap, and took everything to the table and sat, one leg folded under me. I was wearing a white tank top, and Wrangler jeans. I ate and studied the logbook, from back to front, most to least recent. It had a worn black cover and entries beginning with December 1966, which was the point he would have filled up one of those others I found in his desk in Beaver Falls, and started using this new book. It said PILOT'S LOGBOOK in gold on the cover with a swoosh. It was about eight inches long and four tall. It was a goldmine—my Rosetta Stone for this mass of papers overrunning my house.

Excluding obvious business charters within the Pittsburgh-Buffalo-Cleveland industrial triangle, there was a trip destination documented in the logbook corresponding to each of my geographic stacks. I love when things make at least a little bit of sense. This prompted me, immediately, to rearrange my stacks based on chronology. He had first gone to Alabama, specifically Huntsville—*Rocket City, U.S.A.*—in March 1967 to interview a NASA official named Arnold Reinhard about the German rocket program in World War II, kick-starting his research for his German secret weapons book. There had been an exchange of letters with Reinhard, describing the book project, Reinhard replying that his schedule was, Butterworth no doubt understood, hectic these days, but he would try to be as generous as he could with his time.

Dr. Reinhard's signature block, ending the letter, gave as his official title:

> Manager
> M.S.F.C. Saturn V Program Office

"Humph," I grunted.
Saturn V.
Saturn Five, that is.
The moon rocket.

In October 1967, Butterworth traveled to Rahway, New Jersey, flying into Linden, outside Newark. This trip, for the purpose of interviewing a man named Drexel he flew with during the war—an army intelligence officer, in fact—in those Black Widow night fighters, Butterworth had transitioned to after his bomber tour. Drexel referred Butterworth to a still-active-duty Air Force intelligence officer in Arizona, at Davis-Monthan Air Force Base. That trip came a couple of months later, before Christmas. In between, in late October, he flew into Orange County Airport in California, and met an engineer with McDonnell Douglas, in Huntington Beach. Moving to 1968, in February, the red, black, and white Cessna touched down in Greenwood, South Carolina. In a town near there, Abbeville, he visited a retired army intel officer on his poultry farm. His name was William H. Sinclair, and the transcript of that interview was actually quite long. Some of it involved Sinclair's accusation that a number of U.S. military intelligence officers had been murdered in Passau, West Germany, in 1946. The house, scene of the massacre, burned to the ground, Sinclair claiming his efforts to avenge his fellow officers had hit a brick wall, the affair declared a security issue, covered up. Compelling reading—I saw why Butterworth wanted to write this book, not the secret-weapon book, but a different book—and Sinclair had tons more to say.

I made myself stop.

Stay on track.

Stay organized.

Too much here for me to get bogged down, at this early stage, with any one of Butterworth's trips and contacts. I needed to skim all this for the barest sense of each trip, then hope to Christ something slapped me in the face, telling me where to focus. Later, in March—this seemed really bizarre—he went to New Orleans, to visit a Tulane medical school professor. He had been a medical officer, involved in liberating Dachau. He told Butterworth a tale about Nazis looting King Solomon's treasure, the "Treasure of the Ages." I blew air out puffed cheeks, reading that, and rocked back in my chair, recalling my father's concern about Buzz Hutcheson dragging me into something completely cuckoo. And also that one of Butterworth's earlier publishing credits had been a seemingly flaky book about UFOs.

A second trip to Huntsville came in mid-September 1968.

That was a year and a half after the first, and only six weeks before Butterworth's death.

He re-interviewed Dr. Arnold Reinhard, this time at the NASA man's home. Also, having failed to be granted an audience with Wernher von Braun, director of the George C. Marshall Space Flight Center—besides being the foremost rocket engineer in the world, as every Tom, Dick, and Harry knew, unless they'd been living under a rock the past decade— Butterworth instead talked to Von Braun's deputy.

One, Erchanbolt Ritter, at his MSFC office.

I put that interview down.

Saving it for later, clawing back up instead the second Reinhard transcript, staring at it as if waiting for it to talk to me. What I was mostly looking at was the bold handwritten notation in the margin:

Dasch??

An actual clue.

This prompted my rise from my desk, padding back to the bedroom, whereupon I re-sorted the yellow legal pad page taken from Butterworth's study in Beaver Falls, onto which I had made the name (if it was a name) *Dasch* appear out of the ether with a pencil rubbing, from the miscellaneous category of papers in the bedroom, to the second Huntsville stack, containing the Reinhard transcript, with the same name or word, Dasch, scribed in the margin.

That same little slip of paper also showed the cryptic:

MAPLE HILL CMTRY

I tapped the end of my pen against my front teeth.
And:

W—1:00

THE LAST ENTRY IN THE logbook prior to Akron, the charter on which Butterworth narrowly escaped death by altimeter, was a flight to Miami. There he interviewed, at the Fontainebleau, an American in the import-export business in Uruguay named John F. Graham. Graham had been attached, post-World War II, to the cultural department of the American embassy in Buenos

Aires, dealing with labor matters. I set that aside, the level of anticipated boredom more than I felt I could stomach for the moment, and began to move around and knead hard at the knot between my neck and left shoulder, arching my spine, and groaning, and twisting my head, as I worked it.

Returning to the table, I took a fortifying breath of oxygen and selected, paging through, one other document produced by the Miami trip: a detailed typed account (though it was not a formal interview transcript) of Butterworth's encounter with a man identified only as "Dr. Schmidt," in his hotel lobby. Like the rest, I read none of this in detail yet—though my roaming eye did snag over that word again.

Dasch.

Which triggered something in my brain.

Sent me pacing the length and breadth of my house a few times, smoking, and thinking—about two trips to Huntsville— tossing my smoking arm out theatrically between puffs, spewing the smoke out pursed lips, turning my head to keep it out of my eyes. Two trips to Huntsville. During the second, the name Dasch—I was assuming, for now, it to be a name—first appeared.

The name figured into the Miami trip as well.

And the last trip. The fatal trip, the one after the altimeter incident, the one Butterworth drove his car on, rather than fly. And because he didn't fly, that trip frustratingly wasn't documented in the logbook.

Destination unknown.

But Dasch factored into that trip too.

Unless I was greatly mistaken.

Why? Because a meeting had been set, with Dasch, for one o'clock Wednesday.

That would be October 30, 1968.

At Maple Hill Cmtry.

Cmtry shorthand, almost certainly, for *Cemetery*.

I got my *Rand McNally Road Atlas* and confirmed Highway 72 through Corinth, Mississippi, where Ralph Butterworth died, was smack along the most direct route between Huntsville and Memphis, to where the deceased was supposed to be driving to meet with my client. I grabbed up the phone, dialed long-distance information.

For Huntsville.

"Number to Maple Hill Cemetery, please," I requested.

The operator gave it to me.

I hung up.

Huntsville.

The last trip.

The fatal trip.

Huntsville.

CHAPTER 21

I T WAS LATE, FOUR O'CLOCK. I leaned over, snubbing out my cigarette. Have to admit I was enraptured, by the work Butterworth had devoted his last year to, last one of his life, which might have cost him his life. It had all so usurped my focus, I hadn't yet stopped to fix myself a drink. I laughed at that, hard, and stood gazing through the front window of my small quiet house, above the cozy inglenook, stretching the muscles some more in my arms and shoulders, and twisting my torso at the waist. I spotted the afternoon paper tossed out there. I fetched the mail from the box on the porch, then bounded down, hoping I wasn't scandalizing the neighbors, going braless far enough to snatch the *Banner* up out of the driveway. Back inside, I locked the door, dropped the mail, and swiped the little green rubber band off the tightly rolled-up newspaper, and checked the headline:

U.S., NATO WARN RUSSIA
WEST BERLIN AID VOWED

Typical Cold War stuff. I left it on the sofa with the mail, and ran a glass of water from the kitchen tap, and sipping from it, decided to dig into, in much greater detail than I had been, Butterworth's material, starting with what I'd sorted into the miscellaneous category—no assigned geography—only because that stack was relatively meager compared to the rest. It was no less interesting, though, and turned out to be comprised of materials with more commonality than I'd thought at first glance. Two items particularly intriguing were:

One, a letter from Vienna, Austria.

Two, an internal FBI document.

The Austria letter was dated September 3, 1968—five and a half weeks ago—addressed from the Jewish Documentation Center, 7 Rudolf Square, Vienna, signed by the famous Nazi hunter, Simon Wiesenthal. A corner of my mouth tugged one-sidedly at that.

I leaned on one elbow, reading, fingertips splayed against my temple. The typewritten letter described what was known about a Nazi war criminal, thought by many to be dead, named Heinz Dieter Friedrich Karl Valdemarr.

Valdemarr had been a civil engineer born in Stettin, Germany, in 1901, a high-ranking officer of the SS in World War II, towards the end of which he was put in charge of the V-2 rocket program.

"Okay," I said, to myself: V-2, secret weapons, made sense Butterworth being interested, for his book. There was more to this guy than rockets, however, as I read down through Wiesenthal's letter—until I finally, at one point, cried out, "My God!"

I rose up in my chair as well, slapping a hand over my open mouth.

That stunned, because according to Wiesenthal, Valdemarr was deputy to the head of the whole concentration-camp system! Chief of something called Amtsgruppe C, which—Wiesenthal claimed—designed and constructed...

Concentration and extermination camps.

Jesus.

Valdemarr oversaw, I read on, the installation at Auschwitz, Maidenek, and Belzec of gas chambers, and crematories. There was more, several pages of it. I saw *Peenemünde* as I skimmed, the wartime German rocket facility Butterworth told Hutcheson he'd be coming from, which we all knew to be impossible.

The long letter ended with a list collected by Wiesenthal of five different accounts of Valdemarr's death in May 1945.

An eight by ten, black-and-white photo was attached. Captioned, **Obergruppenführer Valdemarr, August 1944**, it was a head-and-shoulders shot of a stern man with downturned mouth and close-set eyes. He was in German uniform, SS skull emblem above the bill of the cap, below the eagle of the Reich. Clipped to the Wiesenthal letter was a photostat of Ralph Butterworth's letter to him, requesting this information, and naming a current Pennsylvania Supreme Court justice, a former Nuremberg war-crimes judge, Michael A. Musmanno, as a reference. "Wow," I sighed, setting that carefully, a little quaveringly, aside, taking up the FBI document, a report dated August 1948—twenty years ago—from Special Agent Francis E. Crosby to J. Edgar Hoover himself, regarding Crosby's mission to South America to investigate claims Martin Bormann was alive and well.

Humph...

Bormann...

Big-time World War II Nazi.

The conclusions of the FBI agent's report assessed the "Graham report" to be without substance.

John F. *Graham*, I realized, the import-export man Ralph Butterworth had interviewed in Miami. I added the FBI report to the Miami stack, caving to my obsessive need to impose order upon all this chaos. There were two scribbles from Butterworth on the front page of the FBI document. One was a date. Specifically it said:

**Rec'vd
9/27/68**

The other a question:

Who leaked?

So...

Butterworth did not know where, or from whom, he had gotten that document. Nothing told me even how, just that it had come into his possession on September 26 of this year. I paced, massaging my neck more, pondering things, contemplating my beamed-ceiling living room, its soft peach walls.

He'd attracted attention.

Which meant, I thought, returning to my office, he was doing something worthy of attention—which meant this probably wasn't all UFO and space-alien crazy stuff—the attention coming from someone with access to official U.S. government documents. One in particular, about Martin Bormann, a famous Hitler crony.

Who I hadn't heard of him, prior to taking this case, though my father had.

I looked him up in *World Book*.

Nothing.

Nor on Wiesenthal.

Then an idea struck me.

I checked my watch.

Barely time to get to the library before five, when it closed. I threw a bra on under my tank top, and a windbreaker over that, and got decent shoes on. I grabbed my pocketbook. The Ben West Library was a straight shot up Eighth Avenue two and a half miles. Took me five racing minutes to get there and get parked. I beelined for the card catalog, and by five-thirty I was home, having taken notes on Martin Bormann from *The Encyclopaedia Britannica*, and checked out a 1967 book entitled:

The Murders Among Us:
The Wiesenthal Memoirs.

Its last chapter called:

"Where is Bormann?"

Amongst its concluding thoughts: "Martin Bormann...most probably now living near the frontier of Argentina and Chile...is well protected...can easily submerge in South America...has money...And a network of fanatically devoted helpers." Something else caught my eye, skimming the Bormann chapter. Page 328, that he, Bormann, "would be one of the most important travelers on ODESSA's 'monastery route.'"

ODESSA?

The book had no index.

Its contents though showed another chapter titled, "The

Secrets of Odessa." I found in it a passage where Wiesenthal described interviewing a Nuremberg witness, who asked, "Didn't you ever hear of Odessa?"

A city in Ukraine, Wiesenthal had thought he meant. But the man corrected him impatiently, describing ODESSA as the secret escape organization of the SS underground.

"Humph…"

The Bormann encyclopedia article called him Hitler's closest advisor, after Hess's flight to Britain, in 1941. Okay, I thought. Alongside Himmler, Bormann was the second most powerful man in the Third Reich. He was present in the *Führerbunker* when Hitler and Eva Braun committed suicide.

After which, he disappeared.

I shrugged.

Filed my notes on Bormann.

Put the Wiesenthal book aside for night-table reading.

I padded back to my miscellaneous stack of Butterworth's material, breathing long and deep in and out of my nostrils, and sifted.

I was getting tired.

There was one of those group military photos from the war, like Butterworth had a big file of in his study. This must've been the one he was searching for, recalling how I'd found these archives strewn about, in surprising disarray. This one, the apparently significant one, showed—I counted—twenty-five uniformed men, officers and enlisted, posed for an official photograph outside a Quonset hut. The men's names were on the back. None jumped out at me. The caption stapled to the bottom right edge, on the front, said: **303rd Bombardment Group (H), Intelligence S-2 Personnel.**

I shrugged again.

Didn't seem to be anywhere I could take that at the moment.

I set it aside.

There were handwritten notes about a phone conversation, a man I quickly realized to be Musmanno, the Nuremberg judge named in the letter requesting Wiesenthal's assistance. Those notes mentioned the man Heinz Valdemarr.

That he might be hiding in South America.

With Bormann.

Musmanno added, if anything more were known, about Valdemarr, Wiesenthal (*of the Eichmann case*, Butterworth jotted, underscored) would know it, saying he would write Wiesenthal a letter of introduction for Butterworth. There were brief typewritten notes, documenting overseas phone calls to several Germans. The rocket people were discussed. Yet again, Valdemarr. There was another piece of paper ripped from that small yellow pad on Butterworth's home-office desk.

Same pad I'd lifted the name Dasch from.

Phone number on it to the FBI Birmingham Field Office.

Birmingham.

That struck a chord.

I knew a guy from that office, from my Klan case.

Lastly, a scrap of paper, simply and cryptically read:

HOME PHONE!!!

Didn't know what that meant. Not for sure. But he had expressed concern to Buzz Hutcheson about phone lines being tapped. I had unrelated reasons to believe his home was, in fact, being monitored, still. So—I stubbed out a cigarette—maybe he was worried, getting scared, his home phone was being monitored, his home, perhaps family being watched. This Valdemarr character, shaping up to be a major-league evildoer, judging from the Vienna letter. If he wasn't dead. And it was a name coming up ever more frequently in Butterworth's investigations, as they approached their truncation in a Mississippi drunk-driving accident…

If an accident…

Heinz Valdemarr was mentioned by the Nuremberg judge, leading to the Wiesenthal query. He'd been mentioned in phone conversations with Butterworth's German contacts—sources from other book projects, I guessed. Like the *Adolf and Eva* thing. And I was pretty sure I'd run across the name Valdemarr elsewhere…

Prowling room to room…

Stack to stack…

Eureka!

Found it, Valdemarr's name again.

Both interviews, second Huntsville trip. First, Arnold Reinhard at his home, the interview whose transcript had

Dasch?? scrawled on it. Second, Erchanbolt Ritter. Both these men were top NASA officials working at the Marshall Space Flight Center in Huntsville. Deeply, no doubt, immersed in the current, so-called, Space Race. The race—

MY RINGING PHONE JAGGED IN my head.

Derailing completely—

My train of thought.

"Shit," I said.

It was my mother, being sure I was coming to Sunday dinner.

I, curtly, said I was.

Her brother, the dry cleaning magnate of Murfreesboro was going to be there, with his wife and my cousins. She mentioned perhaps inviting a nice boy interested in meeting me. "No! Absolutely not."

"Now, now, Sherry *Louise…*"

"If I arrive," I blasted, eyes flashing, "and anybody's there but Uncle Irby and Aunt Sue and their brood, I will turn right around, and walk out, I promise, Mama, no questions asked."

"Okay, okay," she said, sighingly, despondently.

I could see the head shaking.

"I'm just worried," she morosed on.

I knew she wouldn't—couldn't—stop.

Knew it!

Heel of my hand crushing into my skull above my left eye.

"A young lady needs a man to get by in this world."

"*What* are you talking about, Mama?" I flung the hand. "You have been divorced from daddy close to twenty years, and you've hardly ever, in all that time, gone out on a date."

"My situation was different."

"How?"

"Your father cheated on me."

"So? What? You in permanent mourning, or something, for your marriage?"

"Are you?" she asked.

"Matter of fact, I'm not. Look, Mama, I'm sorry daddy cheated on you and ruined your marriage, but I am actually quite happy about being divorced."

"Sherry Louise," she huffed, "don't you *dare* say that."

"Why? We weren't compatible, Mama. I'm not mad at Fred, but I am happier without his leash around my neck, and God willing, he'll find some nice traditional—*barefoot*—girl to give him what he wants, which is about six kids."

"He loves you."

"I know."

"He still does. He's told me."

"Mother!" I snapped.

"Okay, okay, I'm done lecturing."

"Good. I'll see you tomorrow. What time? One?"

"You could take me to church?"

"*One?*" I half screamed.

"That's when I told your uncle to come."

I said I'd be there. Stamped the phone down.

Then decided to change, and go out awhile.

CHAPTER 22

I HADN'T PLANNED ON GUSSYING up much, but once I got started, it just sort of happened. There hadn't even been any real plans to go out that evening. It all had something to do with arguing with my mother: shock therapy, or something. *Why not?* It was Saturday, decent weather, I no longer had to keep my nose clean, waiting for my divorce to finalize. I was—to borrow that aphorism of disapproval from my mother—*footloose and fancy free*, so I preened for over an hour, spritzing on even, for the first time since buying it on impulse, some CHRISTIAN DIOR EAU SAUVAGE. Bringing the inside of my wrist close to my nose I found it lemony, jasminey, mossy—bewitchingly dark, I thought, curling a lip, in the mirror.

At almost eight-thirty I parked and locked the car on Union in front of the First American Bank, and strutted east toward the river wearing a navy blue double knit with a scoop neck and long fitted sleeves. I wore a twenty-inch necklace of large gold-metal beads, and a matching ring, and two-and-a-half-inch-long earrings that were gold balls on gold-metal rods. A block over stood the Andy Jackson Hotel where "Queen Pauline" Prescott's husband had once fired a revolver through the door of a sixth-floor luxury room at Skip Talbot and me. I crossed Fourth at the light, a car beeping, driver watching me in my dress, dripping with gold costume jewelry, flouncing along for another half block before going to the right down Printer's Alley.

The street was a bawdy, celebratory mob, amidst which you could not help but be jostled. It was narrow, literally an alley, with much gaudy lighting, Nashville's answer to Bourbon Street, having much the same flavor of drinking, stripping, and cavorting. Overhead a latticework of black-iron fire escapes was bolted onto the backs of buildings once housing the many newspaper and publishing concerns, print shops, that flourished on Fourth and Third Avenues, in the heyday of that industry in Nashville—all of it not too far removed from the Cumberland riverfront, where barges would off-load newsprint, ink, and other supplies. I strode the cracked-concrete length of it, threading my way, nightclub neon signs on either side overlapping in places, smelling cigarettes, tobacco and pot, turning some heads myself, garnering some wolf-whistles. Liking it. Sorry, Mama. Sorry, Fred. Music spilled from the clubs: Jazz, R&B, rock, Printer's Alley being the one area of Nashville where one could go and hear pop music, as an alternative to classical at the symphony, country-western everyplace else.

Fred had been damn lucky to have me for a wife.

He should have figured a way to make it work.

It wasn't as if I hadn't tried.

Nearing the Church Street end of the Alley I went through a door into THE BRASS RAIL STABLES AND CARRIAGE ROOM LOUNGE, occupying a building Andrew Jackson had boarded his horse in, when he was governor, hence the name. I ordered one of their "elegant steaks." I had two martinis—Buzz Hutcheson having turned me onto them—while I waited for food, then switched to Scotch. Liquor-by-the-drink was a year old in Nashville by that point, but truth be told though, you could always get mixed drinks in the Alley, which had been called "The Men's District" at the turn of the century. Even during Prohibition, you could get drinks here. You could get any naughty thing in the Alley. Politicians and judges protected it, and frequented it, and vice cops looked the other way. Printer's Alley was Nashville's dirty little secret. Nightlife in a city that went to bed earlier than most.

I paid for my elegant steak.

I'd had better, but it was fit to eat, and didn't move. I left The Brass Rail and vamped my way back past THE EMBERS with its black-and-gold medieval-shield/crossed-battleaxes logo. EXQUISITE CUISINE. ENTERTAINMENT. DANCING. Smelled good: should've gone for *exquisite* over *elegant*. THE CAROUSEL CLUB. THE CAPTAIN'S TABLE. THE RUSTIC DINNER CLUB. THE VOO DOO ROOM. THE WESTERN ROOM. I knew Skull Shulman, an institution in the Alley, who operated the RAINBOW ROOM, whose strippers danced to live music. High class. I knew the bouncer at THE BLACK POODLE next door. Their music was canned, their sign showing a cartoon frou-frou dog playing the flute. I knew Printer's Alley from my divorce business, the kind of area men gravitated to, getting away from their wives or girlfriends, having a wild time of it. I followed these men into clubs, seeing what shenanigans they were up to, so I could rat them out. I'd never ventured down as a customer, however. And since I was officially divorced, I thought it high time. At least *I* wasn't cheating on anybody.

I went in the Black Poodle:

XXXXXX

EXOTICS

The bouncer I knew assumed I was there on a tail and I let him keep thinking it. He got me a dark booth in back. I ordered a Jack Daniels, rocks, variety being the spice of life. The talk was loud and virile, undercurrent of ice against glass. The room, hazy with smoke, crowded with middle-aged fat businessmen, politicians, visitors from out of town, skinny long-haired college boys from Vanderbilt. All went crazy, leaping up, whistling, whopping and clapping, as the feature attraction was introduced. I quietly, big-eyed over the rim of my glass, swallowed some Jack.

Heaven Lee.

She was Cuban.

She was just getting started then. Ten whole years before Metro's nipple-covering law would cramp her style, the goddess boldly answering back with her famous lace pasties, nudity after all being art. Heaven Lee would become a Nashville icon. Whenever anybody said "exotic dancer" in Nashville, they meant her. A night on the town with Heaven Lee would one day be auctioned off as a fundraising gimmick by the local public TV station.

That was 1980, a hundred years later.

I was forty then, and bid $95.

The winner paid $175.

Their dinner was, by the way, at the Brass Rail; there was a picture documenting it in the paper, and I always thought the guy looked a whole lot happier about everything than did Vianka—that was her real name. I'd seen her act once before, down here, on business, and it was, frankly, why I was down here now. Trying to make sense out of that. She had luscious full lips, a gout of bright-gold blonde hair, cascading over her shoulders, halfway to her waist. Flesh jiggering every which way, she wore a snap-brim hat out of snakeskin, and a lot of pink feathers.

Even before she took her bows, I slapped money for a tip down, lurching out of my booth. I went two doors south to a topless bar called THE JOLLY ROGER. The waitresses there wore G-strings and black pirate hats, and the bartender asked if I had someone with me. I said, "No," and ordered Bourbon, asking for a book of matches. The matchbook was black, a leering Captain Hook-type character on the front, the bar's name, number, and Printer's Alley address on the flip side. It was dark and narrow, candlelit, the candleholders like lanterns off a sailing ship. I fingered my hair, smoked a cigarette. They played calypso music, played it soft. I pride myself on tolerance for alcohol, but I admit I was very drunk by then, and delighted to be so. Otherwise I might bolt rather than do what I must. I sat at the bar nursing drinks, shifting one hip to the other, crossing and re-crossing my legs, the sheer feel of my slip and stockings, gliding together, until past eleven-thirty. That was when a man hoisted onto the stool beside me and planted his meat-slab of a hand on top of my knee. He looked at me and squeezed it, not too roughly. I pretended not to notice, swallowed some of my drink. The hand moved under my blue dress up along my thigh. I let it, stiffening, somewhat.

Thick fingers rubbed through the crotch of my panties.

I exhaled.

Shuddered.

Swallowed.

Looked the man in the eye.

Half his face was shadow.

The rest glowed red in candlelight.

Don't remember much what he looked like, or smelled like, or said. Some braggartism, I...think, about Vandy football.

All-American center...perhaps it was...

Forty-eight team.

Sin was abundant in Nashville, in those days.

In the buckle of the Bible Belt.

Motor courts featured high fences or attached garages where one might hide one's car from prying eyes. The Belle Meade Motel was nicknamed the "No Tell Motel." That was where the All-American took me. Must've lived out that way, down Harding, lawyer, or judge, or Methodist publisher, or something. His car was big, smelling wallowingly of leather. The sex was rough and kind of angry. I do remember him cursing my scars, sneering up at me, asking what the hell happened to me, as he lay all furry and hard-flabby like a bison gone soft while I straddled him bouncing determinedly with him deep inside me, until I began to quake below and gushed out with a wail, and a groan, then with a clapping of flesh I lay upon the sweating, puffing man, catching my own breath, feeling our hearts one against the other beating, his a bass drum, mine a conga. He wasn't Fred. That made me sad, but it was my first time since our last time—September 13, 1967—just before we fell apart. Fourteen months, and you can bet your bippy I wasn't about to let the All-American weasel away.

Don't worry, he got everything he wanted.

I made sure of that.

A few times over.

I awoke Sunday morning naked and sore and with an enormous hangover. I was alone. It took me a bleary minute with the heels of my hands pressed to my temples...to remember where in the hell I was...and why.

I managed.

Oh, and I wasn't totally alone.

The All-American had left me a twenty on the dresser.

Jesus Christ.

Bastard thought I was a hooker. When all I was was a drunk and horny divorcée. I took a hard, hot shower and got dressed. I called a taxi to take me back to my car downtown, trying not to think about what the cabbie would be thinking of me. I left the twenty on the bed for the maid, and the front desk, to take their nickel or whatever out for the local call.

My car was where I'd left it.

Hubcaps and all.

Who said I wasn't living right? I drove out Broadway, down 21st to Pancake Pantry for a stack of—*guess what?*—pancakes, of which they claimed twenty-three varieties. I had mine with a ton of butter and syrup, to settle my stomach. I chugalugged a glass of orange juice, chasing that with a lot of coffee. Bobby Goldsboro was there eating with some people. It was ten-thirty when I got home and peeled back out of my clothes. I took three aspirins and my birth-control pill, brushed my teeth and had a second shower. I made it to my mother's house on a quiet residential street in Murfreesboro, in the rain, by one o'clock as promised. The house was on a large, tree shrouded, autumn-leafed lawn. Murfreesboro was a college town of nearly 20,000, thirty miles southeast of Nashville, at the geographic center of Tennessee. I'd spent part of my childhood and teen years there, and it was where I'd lived with Fred as husband and wife. My whole life was turning out to be one long series of back-and-forth moves between Nashville and Murfreesboro. I kissed Mama. She told me I had bags under my eyes and that a lady needed her beauty sleep. She trotted out no prospective dates, at least, so I deigned to stay. I went in the den, bent down kissing Uncle Irby on the forehead, and we watched football with one of my cousins. Irb asked how my father was. "Good," I told him, nodding, smiling out that side of my mouth. I wore a gray wool sweater with a V-neck and white turtleneck dickey, gray and white tweed pants, and black suede ankle boots. I folded my legs under me on the overstuffed couch, and we drank RC Colas and ate peanuts.

These people were teetotalers. My taste for spirits I'd inherited from my father. My mother served her famous Swiss steak, tough as ever—Uncle Irb's and my eyes met amusedly, as we masticated, cross-table from one another—with lima beans, and baked macaroni and cheese. Most of the conversation, when not obsessing about the dry-cleaning business, revolved about that age-old debate on whether mac'n'cheese should be crispy or creamy. Aunt Sue had made a tray of fudge brownies and my uncle and I retreated with them and mugs of coffee, back to the football games, first chance we got.

There was drizzle, and fifty-something degrees, outside Mama's picture window. My uncle liked to jump out of the Barcalounger and flip between channels every time there was a commercial. Which meant, through the afternoon, we heard play-by-plays and commentaries from Curt Gowdy and Kyle Rote, Jack Buck and Pat Summerall, Lindsey Nelson and Tom Brookshier, and Jim Simpson and Al DeRogatis. Oakland beat the Jets, Dallas beat Washington, Cincinnati beat Miami, the Packers, in post-Lombardi year one, stomped all over that new team from New Orleans. Only one of the games, ironically, turned out even close. The Jets/Raiders—the Jets, led by "Broadway Joe." I told Irby about having just, by coincidence, visited Namath's hometown, and about the billboard I'd seen. Anyway, the Jets led much of the game, until a George Blanda point-after tied it at 29 in the fourth quarter. The Jets then scored a field goal with fifty seconds to go, and led 32 to 29.

Oakland scored two touchdowns in the next forty-two seconds, the last on a two-yard fumble return, and won it, 43 to 32.

Great game, huh?

Problem was, top of the hour, with that fifty seconds remaining, Jets leading, NBC switched to a scheduled made-for-TV version of "Heidi," starring Jean Simmons.

Irby exploded.

Along with the rest of America.

Luckily he didn't kick the picture tube in. That's right: the infamous "Heidi Bowl," and yours truly was at ground zero. I helped Mama clean up after they'd left, and since at no point in the whole visit did we get into a fight, I considered the day stunningly successful. It was an hour drive home for me, and I was exhausted and went to bed without even getting a drink or brushing my teeth, and slept like a dead woman until sunrise woke me about a quarter to seven on Monday.

CHAPTER 23

BESIDES THE FALLOUT FROM THE Heidi Bowl, Edwin Newman reported heavy fighting, Red rocket and mortar attacks, around Da Nang, sit-ins in Czechoslovakia protesting the Soviet invasion—owing to which, Trudeau announced Canada would not, after all, cut its NATO commitment. I watched Hugh Downs interview Shirley Chisholm over my second cup of coffee. By eight o'clock, heavy rain pelting my roof, wind blowing, making the old house rattle and creak, I was dressed, warmly, and getting down to work. I spent a half-hour reshuffling, becoming reacquainted with Butterworth's research. By the time I'd broken it off Saturday evening, I'd concluded two things:

First:

Huntsville was key.

Butterworth had visited twice for sure, probably a third time. The latter to meet a man named Dasch at Maple Hill Cemetery. His last stop, that I could by this point divine, before he died.

Second:

The names *Valdemarr* and *Dasch* were important.

I did not know Dasch from Adam, anything about him, but the name first appeared on the transcript of the second Reinhard interview, during the second Huntsville trip. I did know, on the other hand, that Valdemarr was a Nazi war criminal, who might or might not have died over twenty years ago. Considering

Butterworth, at least with respect to some of his writing, was shaping up to be a crazy conspiracy theorist, maybe—for all I knew—he'd gone off on a ghost hunt, for Nazi phantasms. Perhaps disembodied spirits, those of Heinz Valdemarr, Martin Bormann, hell, why not George Lincoln Rockwell, walked amongst us, plotting a takeover. Don't laugh, I sighed.

Butterworth *was* dead, killed, murdered, on Halloween.

Think me silly, but I'd never been able to separate the dark aspects of Halloween from its playful trick-or-treat side, ever since Halloween '63, the night Alec Longhurst summoned me to his office.

To talk research.

I shook that out of my head.

Ghosts too.

Get serious, Sherry, ol' gal.

There was a third important name, besides Valdemarr and Dasch.

Reinhard.

On both documented Huntsville trips Butterworth interviewed a Nazi…

Pardon me, Freudian slip…

NASA, not Nazi, official named Arnold Reinhard.

Three names, each connected, in Butterworth's research, to Huntsville.

So, I'd start with Huntsville.

It was in the neighborhood. Two hours by car. It bookended Ralph Butterworth's odyssey all over the country, and desire to go to Buenos Aires looking for a notorious Nazi, which my client had nixed. The dead author's research had started and largely ended in Huntsville. I figured, once I'd fleshed out what he'd done and learned there, it might be clearer which of Butterworth's other contacts I should seek out, and re-interview. Hoping not to have to retrace all his travels, literally, from sea to shining sea, and sure Buzz Hutcheson's wallet would prefer I avoid that tactic as well.

Why Huntsville?

Huntsville, Alabama?

I blinked, crossing my arms, creaking back in my chair. I knew what most people did. There was a lot of space-program work there. We were racing the Russians to the moon, wanted to get there before the end of next year, 1969. John F. Kennedy's famous, "We choose to go to the moon," challenge, back in those halcyon days, "by the end of the decade."

That speech drove everything.

Would we be striving so hard, I wondered, had the man not been assassinated?

It was also common knowledge that some of the work was being done by men brought to America from Germany— scientists having worked on Hitler's rocket programs—and the Russians, naturally, had their own collection of German rocketeers. Both rival space programs, both racing to the moon, both dependent on the brain trust of the same defeated enemy.

How screwball was that?

Wernher von Braun.

The household name *everybody* knew.

"Mister Space."

Personification of the Space Age. Heck, I remembered his Walt Disney "Man in Space" TV shows, in the fifties. But there were others, other Germans, probably these men, Reinhard and Ritter, NASA officials Butterworth had interviewed. I was judging of course solely by the Germanic-sounding names. I decided some basic information would help. I went back to my encyclopedia, looking up HUNTSVILLE. My father had bought me cheap this set of *World Books* from *The Tennessean* when they updated their library. I'd stocked and furnished my office over the years in much the same way. My battered gray desk and desk lamp, typewriter stand, file cabinet, all once having served the newsrooms of *The Tennessean* or *Banner*, one.

I found Huntsville's entry.

There were, impressively, for a medium-sized southern city, three full paragraphs devoted to Huntsville. My surprise rooted in having become accustomed, in my life, to the South not being given credit for much, unless it related back to ignorance, bigotry, or poverty.

Anyway, Huntsville:

Population, 72,365.

Quadrupled, this write-up said, since 1950.

Talk about population explosions. Known as *Rocket City,*

U.S.A., one-time capital of Alabama, first incorporated town in Alabama. The U.S. Army had transferred its guided-missile research activities from Ft. Bliss, Texas, to Redstone Arsenal in Huntsville, in 1949. And with it, there was that name, Wernher von Braun, and other scientists, who developed guided missiles, including the Jupiter-C, which launched our first satellite into space in 1958.

In 1960, NASA opened the Marshall Space Flight Center there. I looked up VON BRAUN, WERNHER: born 1912, age twenty took over German army's rocket station, developed V-2, used to bombard London. The article went on to say, "when Hitler took personal control of rocket work, von Braun resigned and was put in jail."

He was director of the Marshall Space Flight Center.

Had become a U.S. citizen in 1955.

The entry said: "see also GUIDED MISSILE."

I did.

And there it was again, turning up like a bad penny, no pun intended:

Peenemünde.

"In World War II," *World Book* said, "Germany made the first successful use of ground-to-ground guided missiles in combat. The Germans built a huge missile-research center in 1937 at Peenemünde on the Baltic Coast. At this center more than 20 types of missiles were developed and tested." I read on, bending closer. Two of these were the V-1 and V-2—*Vergeltungswaffe*—Vengeance Weapons, the V-2 described as "even more terrifying" than the V-1, which had killed thousands in England in '44 and '45. The Huntsville article had cross-referenced REDSTONE ARSENAL. I looked that up: 40,000 acres, near Huntsville, established 1941, named for the red soil. *Humph.* Several Army facilities, including HQ of its missile command, and—*low and behold*—the Marshall Space Flight Center. Which "manages the research and development of high-power rocket boosters."

Then came a jolting in my brain.

I stood, paced, a thumbnail between my front teeth.

That's it!

I understood, suddenly, what Butterworth had meant telling

Buzz Hutcheson he was coming from Peenemünde.

Huntsville…

Was Peenemünde.

Figuratively at least. Both were major centers serving the same function—decades apart, continents apart—that function being, cutting-edge research and development of high-powered military rockets, and now, for NASA, civilian rockets. I stopped in the archway to my dining room, exhaling, hands on my hips, facing my built-in sideboard, beveled glass cabinet doors. Peenemünde was code, perhaps, *Riddle me this Batman*, owing to Butterworth's operational-security concerns, trying to let on to Hutcheson, furtively, that he'd be in Huntsville, that he'd be coming to him *from* Huntsville—*in case anything happened?*

Might've been code.

Might've been an inside joke.

So inside it took us three weeks to figure it out.

Now, being as how I—Sherry Russell, master detective, Sherlock Holmes with C-cups—had already determined by other means, that Huntsville was the place. The place Butterworth had driven from, to his death. The place for me to focus first.

Given that, did my brilliant solving of the Peenemünde riddle, amount to anything?

I pivoted, rubbing my forehead.

Padding through my living room.

There was a cold driving rain outside my picture window, a hunched-up, feathers-fluffed, brightly red cardinal perched on a tree limb, as I paused, peering out, smiling. I turned, and cozied up thoughtfully, in the corner of the inglenook, by my fireplace, hugged a knee to my chest. Wondering if there might be more to Butterworth's Peenemünde metaphor than a location.

Might he have been drawing a connection?

A link between the people themselves, the Germans at Peenemünde in World War II, the Germans at Huntsville today?

Von Braun, for one, had been both places.

No doubt others.

According to Wiesenthal's letter to Butterworth, a heinous Nazi war criminal, Heinz Valdemarr, a key player in the extermination of six million Jews in the Holocaust, had been at Peenemünde.

Was *that* it?

Heinz Valdemarr?

Was he in Huntsville, working for NASA?

Could that be the kind of secret that would get a man killed?

Make him fear for his life, that of his family?

I sprang up, heading back along the hall to my office, spurred by that speculation, and picked up the Huntsville stack to start reading, voraciously, to learn more.

When I did, the small yellow sheet fell out, floating to the floor, upon which Butterworth had jotted the area code and telephone number of the FBI Field Office in Birmingham.

I put down the papers.

Knelt to retrieve the legal-pad sheet, examining it.

I rose and sat, after a moment's consideration, and rolled the chair up to my desk, picking up the telephone.

Shoulder-cradling the receiver, I rotated in Butterworth's FBI number.

I asked the operator, might I speak with Special Agent Alan Legate.

CHAPTER 24

W HOM MAY I SAY IS calling?" I was asked.
"Sue Williams," I told the Birmingham Field
Office, bouncing my brows. "Old friend, from the
Pine Crest Motel." The undercover name Legate assigned me
last year when the FBI hired me to infiltrate a Ku Klux Klan
rally. The Pine Crest was a bug-swarmed motel near Millport,
Alabama, bought lock, stock, and barrel by the FBI, to be used
as a secret base of operations.

Legate's Bostonian brogue came on the line, sounding more
like the late Bobby Kennedy than Bobby Kennedy himself. "I
gaather," he began, and I could visualize horn-rimmed spectacles
being removed, placed aside on his desk blotter, "this is
Nashville's answer to Philip Marlowe? The famously gutsy, ever-
manipulative, private eye, Sherry Nates."

"Actually, it's Russell again. I'm divorced."

"Sorry."

"Had to happen," I said. "By the way, you forgot
voluptuously blonde."

He was tall, thin, a natty dresser, within the bureau's strict
white-collar standards.

I recalled fervent, daggering eyes, Northeast liberal elitism, a
prep-school-history-teacher demeanor.

Alan Legate.

J. Edgar Hoover's golden boy.

"You staawrt rumors about me meeting geerls in motels, the director will fire me, summarily, for moral turpitude."

"You're the most moral man I know, Legate."

"Thank you."

"So straight-arrow you'd follow the rules right off a cliff, you didn't keep a few of us rogues and scoundrels around, to yank you back."

"Perhaps."

I knew he was grinning through the receiver, like some dementedly evil clown. "How might the FBI be of assistance, today, Ms. Russell?"

"I'm on a case," I told him, firing up a cigarette, shaking out the Jolly Roger nightclub match. I explained briefly about the car crash outside Corinth, Mississippi, the death of book author Ralph Butterworth.

"Foul play?" I was asked.

"Local sheriff and coroner say no. Officially, he was heavily intoxicated, drove off the highway into a billboard stanchion." I blew smoke, my elbow on the desk, cigarette smoldering between two crooked fingers. "Maybe he did, maybe didn't. That's what I was hired to find out. Reason I'm calling you is, well, the number I dialed to reach you this morning, I found in the deceased's papers. For some reason he contacted, or considered contacting the FBI, your office specifically."

"Any idea," he asked, "what about?"

"No."

For now, I would keep to myself, the 1948 report leaked to Butterworth, of FBI Agent Francis E. Crosby to Hoover, regarding the mission to South America seeking information on Martin Bormann. "When?" Legate said.

"Last few months, perhaps weeks."

"Hmm," he said.

"Ring any bells?"

"No."

"Ask around the office, if you don't mind." I was affecting a coquettishly pleading lilt. "See if anybody talked to this man, if so, 'bout what?"

"Understaand, I caan't be at liberty to discuss bureau business."

"Just ask, please, for old time's sake. Then decide what, if anything, you can pass along."

"You could, of course, extort this information."

I grinned.

"Using those papers," he said, going on, "Agent Perry gave you."

"I was going to be decent enough not to bring that up. But..."

"I'll ask."

"Thank you."

"Give me your number."

I did, and Butterworth's details.

"Very well. See what I can do. Are you well, Ms. Russell?"

"I am." My eyes flickered about my office, to the tip of my cigarette.

"Leg okay?"

"Good as new."

"I'm glad. Let you know, one way or the another, about this."

"Thank you," I said, and put the handset down softly on its cradle.

Confident I knew enough dirty little secrets about FBI business, that Agent Legate ought to be nicely disposed toward more cooperation with me than with the average private cop, all my feminine wiles aside.

CHAPTER 25

BIOGRAPHICAL INFORMATION FRONTED THE TRANSCRIPTED first interview with Arnold Reinhard at the Marshall Space Flight Center. Clipped to the bio was a photograph, stamped in red on the back, MSFC PUBLIC INFORMATION OFFICE. Turning it back over, I studied Reinhard, an older man, nearly bald, frail-looking, in a suit, holding a foot-and-a-half long model of the second and third stages of the Saturn rocket, the Apollo spacecraft at the tip of it. This display had been detached from an upright, foot-tall model of the Saturn V first stage, standing on a table at his elbow. There was a curtained backdrop. He appeared to be explaining the rocket, probably, I imagined, to the press.

Butterworth's interview had been tape recorded then typed up by a free-lance secretarial service he'd employed. The bio sheet listed Reinhard's birthplace as Stepfershausen, Meiningen, Germany, November 1906. Making the man sixty-two today, I thought, sixty during this first interview. He had one daughter, wife killed during World War II, by British bombs. Reinhard and his daughter came to the United States with Wernher von Braun in 1945, their work moved to Redstone Arsenal—Huntsville—1950.

Project manager, Pershing missile, 1956.

Joined NASA, 1961.

Project director, Saturn V moon rocket, 1963.

The interview began affably with Butterworth thanking Arnold Reinhard for his valuable time. "You may know already, sir, that Dr. von Braun had no time for me, and I certainly understand, with the setbacks, the tragedy, the Apollo program has suffered, you must be under enormous pressure."

This interview, I only then realized, took place in March 1967, two months following the Apollo 1 fire. "I've had my daily blow up," Reinhard replied, "with North American Aviation and the McDonnell Douglas people." Spreading fingers. "I don't have to have another until tomorrow. It will be a pleasant diversion to speak about simpler times, when truly we were doing revolutionary work." Butterworth penciling in, *he smiles*.

"You are project director for the Saturn V—tallest, heaviest, most powerful rocket ever to fly—is that not revolutionary?"

"It will be, when successful at breaking men free of Earth's orbit. That goal is yet to be accomplished. Soon we hope. Regardless, Saturn V exists in a world where large rockets are commonplace. Not true of the A-4 series."

"A-4—early designation for, V-2?"

"*Ja.*"

This went on a few pages, pretty dry and irrelevant, to me. Barebones research for Butterworth's book on German secret weapons of the 1940s, before he'd gone off on his tangent that got the book deal killed, perhaps himself. Arnold Reinhard reminisced about early work on a rocket car, and his inspiration, a 1929 silent film titled, *Frau im Mond* (Butterworth noting, *Woman in the Moon*), in which the basics of rocket travel were presented to a mass audience for the first time, including use of a multi-stage rocket. His first encounter with Wernher von Braun, at a meeting of the *Verein für Raumschiffahrt* (Society for Space Travel), early thirties. Soon after working under von Braun on a German Ordinance Department tasking to develop a rocket-based weapon, the spaceflight society subsequently dissolving in disagreement over whether to support military work. "You know," Reinhard mused, "it could be said our rocket work was a direct offspring of the Treaty of Versailles."

"Treaty ending World War I," commented Butterworth. "How so?"

"The 1919 treaty imposed severe restrictions upon German

conventional weapons. Our armed forces turned to rocketry, not subject to treaty restrictions [he laughs]. No one, naturally, imagining such a thing, in 1918 and '19."

They talked about A-2 and A-3 engines.

Test launches, 1934.

Static testing for the high command, 1936.

Then, 1937…

Peenemünde.

Arnold Reinhard placed in charge, of designing the production plant, at Peenemünde, for the A-4 military rocket. More technical stuff, I skimmed. Finally, after two failures, the first A-4, renamed V-2, was launched along the coast of Pomerania, 3 October 1942, rising to an altitude of fifty miles, falling back to earth in the correct position, 119 miles away. "And with that, Mr. Butterworth," Reinhard trumpeted, "the ballistic-missile age was born!"

Butterworth noting, at that point, he'd pounded his fist off his desk.

The typist then described, from the tape, pauses and sputters.

Butterworth noting, Reinhard had suddenly become racked with emotion. "Doctor? Would you like to take a break, sir? Or, continue another day?"

"No. I must apologize. In fact, this is good. This, I need to get off my chest. I've blocked it a long time. Buried it under the weight of my work."

"Please continue."

"I feel…I traded…the life of my wife…for these weapons."

"Sorry, Doctor?"

"All this—the V-2, right up here to the Saturn V—all of it must succeed for her, otherwise I have failed her, my Helga. Otherwise, her life was a waste, for nothing."

"Please explain."

"When the British got wind of what was up at Peenemünde, and why: the development of unmanned weapons, the V-1, the V-2—I was not involved with the flying-bomb project, that was the Luftwaffe—with which to resume the attack on England…"

"Attack on civilians, you mean? On London?"

"*Ja.* To quote, I believe an American: War is hell."

"Yes. Go on."

"Well, when the British spies figured it out, the RAF Bomber Command dispatched six hundred four-engine heavy bombers to attack us at night. One tiny area. Not an entire city, such as Hamburg or Nuremberg, normally the target of such a force. My wife was killed when an incendiary bomb came through the roof of our shelter. Sparks showered down on the head of our little daughter, burning her hair. Fortunately I was able to extinguish it and get her out, only by the most incredible miracle."

"I'm sorry."

"They hit the housing estate, home to three thousand men, women, children."

"I see."

"The factory survived. The V-2 survived. All but two of our leading scientists survived. The housing estate, it was decimated, seventy to eighty percent destroyed. Bombs also rained down on the foreign laborers' camp. Of 735 total deaths, nearly all were either the laborers—Poles, Russians, Ukrainians, few Frenchmen—or the German workers' families."

"Terrible."

"*Ja.*"

"That was...1943?"

"*Ja.* Night of 17 to 18 August. I remember."

"Of course you do. My condolences."

"I feel, I have to feel, we were spared for some reason. Some greater purpose. All this perhaps."

"Who can know? Who can answer such questions, Dr. Reinhard?"

"Only God, huh?."

"I should tell you, sir, I was a B-17 pilot. I never bombed Peenemünde, but I dropped my fair share of tonnage on Germany and German-occupied Europe."

"But, you're an American."

"Interesting comment."

"You bombed by day."

"Hell of a lot more dangerous."

"You made the effort to limit death and destruction to legitimate military targets."

"That was the idea," Butterworth said. "But we missed plenty."

"Still, big difference between daylight precision bombing, and nighttime saturation bombing, to the populations on the ground. The wives. Little girls. I thank you, for your efforts, for the risks taken."

"We can discuss the relative morality of British and American war efforts all day, Doctor, but don't forget about the Luftwaffe."

"*Ja*."

"The Blitz, Buzz Bombs, your V-2s."

"*Ja, ja*. Well you didn't come here to discuss battle tactics, and I am no expert on them."

"You were saying, your wife dying in that raid, drove you. Inspired you, to this. That's an interesting angle. Tell me more."

"If the British bombers had been on target that night, we might not be here talking, might we? There might never have been an operational V-2. We might not be preparing to send American men to the moon, atop the V-2's great-grandchild."

"The Saturn rocket."

"Or perhaps, they *were* on target."

"What?" asked Butterworth.

"It's silly. [hand swipes the air] I'm rambling."

"Please, ramble."

[He sighs] "It has been speculated, I don't believe this, I can't believe this, the factory was deliberately missed. The all-important wind tunnels, guidance and control buildings—almost untouched."

"To what end?"

A pause.

"So the technology would survive," Reinhard said. "The science would survive. So we would move it—to safety—underground, which we did. The program was delayed, not destroyed."

"England was saved. That was the goal."

"The war was won by you and your allies; we were brought to the U.S. to continue to work on the V-2 at White Sands."

"You're saying Peenemünde was spared so that post-war America could have the V-2?"

"And it's descendants."

"Far fetched," Butterworth said.

"I agree." [flinches a smile] "Yet here we all are."

"All?"

"Me, von Braun, Ritter, many others, many serving the same capacities they did at Peenemünde."

"How many?"

"How many what?"

"How many from Peenemünde are in Huntsville today?"

"Over one hundred."

"That's fantastic," gasped Butterworth.

CHAPTER 26

I LEANED BACKWARD, CHAIR SQUEAKING, swiveling a quarter turn, and gouged out the last cigarette from my pack, which I then crumpled and tossed back over my shoulder into the trash pail.

Lighting up, I sighed:

"Huntsville is Peenemünde."

This was not news to me.

Nor the fact there were wartime German rocket scientists working for NASA. The number might be a revelation—seemed to surprise Butterworth—and that they were basically doing the same jobs today, they had at Peenemünde. Still, was any of it a problem? I didn't see it being so, provided everybody was who they said they were. That, for instance, Heinz Valdemarr wasn't amongst them, concealing his war-criminality behind an alias, and high-priority government work.

There *were* people, I assumed, who'd kill to cover something like that up.

Or it all could be much simpler.

The avenging of a dead wife?

A wife burned to death by incendiary bombs, full view of her rocket-scientist husband and the couple's child. Did Arnold Reinhard believe the conspiracy theory he'd promulgated, about the Peenemünde factory being deliberately missed, the housing areas targeted instead? Even if he didn't, there was the bombing itself. A small target area, many hundreds of attacking planes, black of night, thousands of civilians, women and children in close proximity. Some were bound to be killed, ulterior motives or not.

I blew a hard straight stream of smoke, like from the tail cone of a rocket.

A dead, burned-alive wife.

Decent motive for murder.

Reinhard was struck an emotional blow during that first interview. He'd said it himself: I've blocked it out. Buried it with my work. Traded my wife for these weapons, now the Saturn V. Was that the end of it? Or did that blow fester? Coming to a head, an explosion of rage, or maybe not an explosion, maybe a cold seething of hatred, roused by the second meeting, after a year and a half in mid-September, between the men.

Between Butterworth, a heavy-bomber pilot, and Reinhard, a wartime victim of heavy bombers.

Six weeks after that September meeting, Butterworth was dead.

Hardly an airtight theory.

Six weeks?

Then again, I shrugged, what was six weeks?

Avenging a wife's death after a whole quarter century? Nor might it matter Butterworth hadn't personally been there over Peenemünde that flaming, deafening night. Even Butterworth had acknowledged American daylight-dropped bombs killing and maiming their share of innocent wives and mothers.

If Reinhard had thought things through even that coherently.

If I wasn't creating fantasy.

Deciding to take a break, get some blood pumping, I put on a coat, opened an umbrella and strolled the raw, blustery neighborhood, the rain down to a drizzle. I went two blocks up to Benton where there was a big brick house with columns: Ionian, I thought they were. I took a right, uphill a block, away from the automotive ebb-and-flow on Eighth, to White and made another right where stood a gorgeous Victorian. I was knocked in the back by a chill-wind gust. No I-65 construction noise, owing to the weather. When I got to the first block, Prentice, I headed back down toward Grantland, my street. Past the first deep lot I crossed the outlet of an alley running behind all the houses fronting on both White and Grantland, which included my bungalow. Sometimes on these constitutionals, as my father called them, I would return home by way of the alley, if the lined-up garbage cans weren't too stinky, letting myself in through my backyard.

I decided this day to press ahead down to the corner because when I walked by on Grantland the first time, heading for Benton, there had been a car parked, a man behind the wheel, for no obvious reason, and I wanted to see if it was still there. It had been idling out front of the first house in the next block north of mine, faced the wrong way, such that the man would be easily, but not too obviously, able to observe all the comings and goings from my address.

Me, in other words.

That didn't have to be why he was there, but since I did that sort of thing all the time, following people, watching houses, on my divorce cases, I had a pretty good sense of what surveillance looked like.

It was there.

Hadn't budged.

Blue Renault. Convertible. Wipers going, condensation puffing. Out-of-state plates. Illinois. Man still in the car, reading a paper, or pretending to be. Huge, middle aged, like a professional-football lineman in retirement. I continued to the corner, across Prentice from where he was watching—if he was watching—and I stopped and faced him, staring, lowering my head, interested in what he would do. Didn't appear I was scaring him to death. He met my look, smiled, and waved— *flirtingly?* I took my free hand from my pocket, fluttered in return, then rotated away and trudged off again toward my house. Playing it cool, not looking back, I kept up a steady pace, feeling a knot in my stomach. My ears detected no changes in pitch from the idling engine, meaning he was neither following, nor fleeing in terror. Both of us, in fact, behaving just as if his being there had nothing whatsoever to do with Sherry Russell.

Which of course told me nothing because that's exactly what I would have done, nothing, were our roles reversed and I was staking him out.

He still could have been there for no reason that mattered to me, however. I hunkered back down in my office, uneasily I admit, after perking some fresh coffee, and fixing a sandwich. My doors and windows, I'd double-checked, all securely locked, chained, latched, and I'd keep my revolver close. Just in case. Call me "Paranoid Sherry." By that point, I was digging into the fruits of Butterworth's second Huntsville trip. Arnold Reinhard by then had been named Special Assistant to the Director, Marshall Space Flight Center. Special Assistant, that is, to Wernher von Braun, who had again declined to be interviewed—"tersely" being the word Butterworth applied to this declination. The second Reinhard interview unfolded not at MSFC, but at the rocket scientist's private home, the address noted to be: 7123 Panorama Drive, Huntsville.

This was the transcript upon which the name *Dasch* had been scribbled, with two question marks after it.

I began to read.

Butterworth going straight for the jugular this time—asking about Nazi war criminal Heinz Valdemarr, who was either dead or wasn't, the gist of Reinhard's replies being he had neither seen nor heard from Valdemarr, nor an iota about him, since coming to the United States in late 1945. They had known each other, naturally. Valdemarr, a civil engineer, had built, and eventually become Reinhard's SS boss at Mittelwerk, the underground, better-protected rocket plant, in the Harz Mountains, whose existence derived directly, apparently, from the kick in the pants the British gave the Germans at Peenemünde.

Other questioning ensued.

Questioning that seemed utterly odd to me and to Reinhard.

Involving, for instance:

Nazi gold.

Looted religious artifacts.

Precious stones.

Swiss accounts.

Scientific terms like, *Xerum 525, plasma shock waves.*

Reinhard denied all knowledge of these areas.

Then came the war crimes.

Not Valdemarr's, mind you.

Accusations against Reinhard himself—

And—*My God.*

Wernher von Braun.

Mister Space.

Accusations including the use of slave labor in building the facilities at Peenemünde and Mittelwerk, and in working the assembly lines, atrocities including beatings, and hangings, of prisoners, and the extreme cruelty of the Mittelbau-Dora labor camp, where twenty thousand died, which supplied Mittelwerk its workers. "I built missiles," Arnold Reinhard countered, Butterworth noting a distracted, fatigued calm from the sixty-two-year-old German native. "You advocated," Butterworth pressed, "my sources tell me, for the use of SS prisoners for missile production, you directly managed it."

"Those workers were forced upon us, by the SS!"

"Von Braun was SS, a major, he wore a black uniform, joined the Nazi Party in 1940."

Reinhard knew nothing

The Sergeant Schultz of rocket science.

"What you are saying simply cannot be," he added.

"Why?" Butterworth asked.

"Your President Truman, when he approved bringing us here, to work on your military's guided missiles, eventually your space program, expressly forbade members of the Nazi Party, or participants in their activities, or militarists."

"People lie," Butterworth said. "Expunge records."

"Who is lying sir? Me? Or those countless victims of Hitler's Germany, that terrible war—victims amongst whom I count myself, as you know, sir, at least my wife, my poor Helga—victims who hate, who would strike out by any means, anything, or anyone German."

"You have the audacity, Doctor, to label this racism? Racism against Germans?"

"Yes. Many people—Jews, British, French, Russians, the list goes on, even Germans themselves—have reason, or think they do, to despise Germans, whether or not they were Nazi or SS or Gestapo. Or mere innocent victims."

Reinhard denied everything.

And soon terminated the session.

Ejecting Butterworth from his home.

The second Reinhard interview was thrice valuable to me:

(1) The Dasch scribble.

(2) The vivid picture it painted of the tangent Butterworth's research had gone off on by that point.

And (3), its reinforcement of my conviction that Arnold Reinhard, sixty-two-year-old rocket scientist, counting himself— "my poor Helga"—amongst the war's victims, might well have taken out a husband's revenge, after so many years.

Upon an old bomber pilot.

Named Ralph Butterworth.

CHAPTER 27

ERCHANBOLT RITTER.

Born 1909, Baden-Württemberg. Engineering master's, Dresden Institute of Technology, 1934. Wernher von Braun's deputy from World War II to Apollo. From Peenemunde to Huntsville. Seemed incredible. Again, as with the second Reinhold interview, the Valdemarr card was played right out of the gate. Butterworth having made a notation on the transcript that there had, indeed, been a reaction to hearing the name. As with Reinhard there was talk of Nazi gold and Solomon's treasure and Swiss accounts. Unlike with Reinhard—who'd either stonewalled, or truly knew nothing, or played the pity card—Ritter reacted with what seemed to me, arrogant defensiveness.

Directing Butterworth, at one point, to talk to his own government:

"We all—Nazis, if that's what you want to believe I am, and you red-blooded, apple-pie Americans—we all share a common enemy, don't we?"

"Pardon?"

"Communism, you idiot. The Soviet Union."

"You saying, we used the money—the loot of Europe—to finance the Cold War?"

Handwritten:

Ritter shrugs.

"Never be tolerated," Butterworth countered.

"Vere it known."

"Elaborate."

"There are secret agencies in your government, as in the U.S.S.R., as in all modern states."

"The CIA, you're saying, appropriated the loot of Europe?"

"I am say nothing—except, sir, don't be obtuse."

He pressed Ritter on Valdemarr:

"You never really answered me."

"Nothing to answer," Ritter said. "Died in 1945. Committed suicide, I was told. By cyanide capsule."

"Reports of his death being varied, and mutually exclusive, Herr Ritter. Is he dead? Or, did he simply disappear? Escape to, oh, say, South America, war's end?"

"Pure speculation."

"You're as close to von Braun as anybody, and von Braun refuses to speak to me. Isn't it true, however, that on April 4, 1945, von Braun spoke to Obergruppenführer Valdemarr, to urge a resumption of rocket research, and he responded, in confidence, that he was about to disappear for an indefinite period. And none of you, after that, ever laid eyes upon Valdemarr again?"

"Hardly surprising, Mr. Butterworth. Within little more than a month, the Führer would be dead and Germany would surrender unconditionally. I might add, sir, if you harassed Dr. von Braun with matters of this nature, at such a crucial time in the race to the moon, I think very likely someone in your own government would arrest you."

"You might be right, Herr Ritter. But I'm not talking to von Braun. I'm talking to you, and I've accused you of nothing. Tell me, you called it speculation, Valdemarr being alive and well, in South America?"

"Indeed."

"Is Martin Bormann speculation?"

"He is dead as well."

"No body produced, same as Valdemarr."

"Do you have any idea the confusion, chaos in Germany, in those last days?"

"I do, yes," Butterworth said, "I was there. Strikes me the

perfect environment, for people with enough money, and resources, to disappear."

"And for corpses to be lost, misidentified."

"Chief of the SS secret-weapons empire, a man in Himmler's confidence—moreover, Valdemarr was literally the architect of the concentration camps, builder of the gas chambers, executioner of Mittelbau-Dora—this man disappears without a trace, and no one seems to take much interest. Yet despite no body, unlike Bormann, Valdemarr was never tried in absentia, at Nuremberg."

"What conclusions do you draw from that, Mr. Butterworth?"

"I'm asking the questions."

"I certainly do not know."

"Should my next stop be the director's office, *Cape Kennedy*? Debus, another Peenemünde alumnus, V-2 flight test director. Quite an amazing transplant trick you all pulled off, from Nazi Germany to NASA."

"Your government certainly would have no more tolerance for you irritating Dr. Debus with this nonsense than they would Dr. von Braun."

"According to Simon Wiesenthal, Martin Bormann is alive."

"So?"

"I think Valdemarr is too. I intend to find him."

"Go ask Martin Bormann vhere he is, if you believe the ravings of that vindictive old Jew."

"Perhaps I will."

WEEKS LATER BUTTERWORTH FLEW TO Miami to talk to John F. Graham, armed with an old leaked FBI report dealing with Graham's claims about Martin Bormann living in South America, Argentina to be exact, shielded by a Nazi group banded together in a well-financed conspiracy to build a Fourth Reich upon the ruins of the Third. Far as I knew, Butterworth never knew the source of the leaked document, and nothing I'd come across gave a clue as to how Butterworth came into its possession. All I knew was when—Friday, September 27, 1968—after Huntsville trip #2 and less than a week before Miami.

I read the Graham interview. A staunch opponent of the Nazi-friendly Perón regime at the time, he was fired by the state department in 1946, and subsequently expelled by Argentina. In 1948 he sought out U.S. Supreme Court Justice Robert Jackson, a Nuremberg prosecutor, who asked the Truman Administration for an FBI investigation, which Graham subsequently characterized, to Butterworth, as having been perfunctory. A single agent—whom Graham took an immediate dislike to, the feeling apparently mutual—a mere seven weeks, all spent scrutinizing the credibility of Graham and his Buenos Aires port-authority contact, rather than pursuing Nazis. The FBI, Graham told Butterworth, had failed to pursue the most hated of all Nazi war criminals, Martin Bormann. He gave Butterworth the name of his Buenos Aires informant, a man named Serrino, who in 1948, had been seventy-four years old, making him ninety-four today, if he were alive, Butterworth observed, skeptically.

CHAPTER 28

AN ATTORNEY IN A CHICAGO high-rise took the call just after four on Thursday 3 October.

"Our friend in Pennsylvania," said the voice on the line, "reports Herr Butterworth is again traveling without passengers."

"Destination?"

"Flight plan for Miami."

"Do we know his lodgings?"

"I have arranged a local colleague to tail him from the airport and report."

"Gut," the attorney said.

"I had my secretary call, claiming to be the man's wife. Our operative believes it to be a domestic matter."

"Very well. Notify me when you have the location. Immediately."

"Yes, Kamerad."

The Zyklop put the phone down.

He thumbed through an address book and eventually fixed on a name. He picked up the phone again, calling the number of a Hialeah, Florida gynecologist.

CHAPTER 29

I'D HEARD MY FATHER PHILOSOPHIZE: *If you're going to grab a tiger by its tail, damned well better have a plan to deal with its teeth.* I had the benefit of 20/20 hindsight; I knew Butterworth was dead. But it was seeming to me he'd been injudiciously throwing the names of some pretty dangerous characters around, and it made me wonder if everything boiled down to him grabbing tigers' tails without a plan going forward. Which got me squirming in my own chair about my situation. I put on a hat and coat and went out the back of my house, going north along the alley. It would be dark soon. There were snow flurries. At Prentice, I peered west toward the corner, through cold gray. If the Renault from lunchtime were still there, it was invisible from where I was. I crossed and eased down, with a tingling in the chest, toward Grantland, checking big-eyed both ways along my street when I got to it.

No Renault.

No suspicious characters.

I exhaled breath fog.

Shook my head.

Better safe than sorry. I levered open an ice tray, back toasty warm in my house, and dumped the cubes in a chilled ice bucket. I poured some Dewar's over a couple of the cubes and added water from the tap. Then I put tomato soup in a pot on the stove. While that heated I stood over my desk, swirling my

Scotch, taking sips from it, letting it wash over my tongue, as I looked at the only document remaining unread from Butterworth's Miami trip.

Out of the blue, in his own Miami Beach hotel lobby, the Floridiana, after returning from the Fontainebleau where he'd met with Graham, he was approached by a middle-aged man with a vaguely German accent, in a black golf shirt, carrying a tan narrow-brimmed straw homburg. "Mr. Butterworth?"

"Yes."

"Mr. Ralph Butterworth?"

"Yes."

Dr. Schmidt was the name given, with a short, jerky bow. No card proffered. Butterworth made a point of detailing this, suggesting he didn't entirely trust the man's identity. No formal, recorded and transcribed interview as with the others. Handwritten only—fast, jaggedly nervous hand. "I am told you are a book writer, a researcher of military history. A very good one."

"Thank you," Butterworth said. "But I'm afraid, sir, you have me at a disadvantage."

The men sat at the bar off the lobby, ordered drinks, Butterworth maintaining silence, waiting for Schmidt. "Some friends of mine," he finally said, raising a glass of Port, "told me you were asking questions about certain parties, and I thought I might be able to help."

"Dasch send you?"

"Who?"

"George Dasch."

"Good heavens," Schmidt said, and seemed honestly surprised. "Who is that?"

"Never mind," Butterworth said. "Valdemarr then. Heinz Dieter Friedrich Karl Valdemarr."

"Well, at least now, we are dealing with names we can discuss."

"Here about Bormann too, aren't you?"

"Indeed."

"You're going to help me…*how?*"

"By assuring you both men are dead."

The lid on my soup on the stove began rattling. I crossed

into the kitchen, returning with a little crock of soup and a spoon, and sat at my desk. I picked back up the treads of Butterworth's encounter with Dr. Schmidt. "Really, you are wasting your time," he had said next.

"My time to waste."

He ate the olive from his Gilbey's martini.

"Insolence," Schmidt said. "I remember that about you American flying officers. So much insolence. I was in the Luftwaffe myself [UNLIKELY, ACTS SS]"—*a notation of Butterworth's*—"and met quite a number of you during my time as adjutant to the commandant of Stalag Luft III. Now, sir, I assure you, is not the time for insolence."

"Is it insolent to say no other prominent Nazi has been declared dead, then revived as many times as Martin Bormann? The Jews believe he is alive and greatly admired in South America. All the big Nazis I know—and I do know a few, doctor, from my earlier books—are convinced he's alive. Eichmann told Israeli investigators he was alive."

"Explain, then, why no one has claimed the $25,000 worth of deutschmarks the prosecutor's office in Frankfurt will pay for information leading to Martin Bormann's capture?"

"Forget Bormann," Butterworth said. "Nobody's going to get him. Too well protected, too revered. He's going to die of senility ensconced in some palatial jungle plantation house. Fine. I don't care. You can tell your friends that. I bit off more than I could chew with Bormann. Never should have mentioned him. But you are right: your visit has helped me."

Schmidt squinting, asked, "How so?"

"You and these friends of yours don't care about me and Bormann. He's remote, protected. Besides, there've been so many rumors, legends, *Mission: Impossible* episodes, sensational IS BORMANN DEAD? magazine covers, why should one more crackpot, wasting words, asking more of the same questions, matter to anybody?"

"I don't—"

"It wouldn't," Butterworth snapped, "meaning you're here, not about Bormann, but about Valdemarr."

"Sir—"

"Valdemarr is alive," Butterworth declared. "You coming out

of the woodwork confirms it. Furthermore, if he were with Bormann in South America, under the same protection, it would be the same as with Bormann. Who would care? But they do care, these friends of yours. So, Valdemarr isn't with Bormann. He's vulnerable, isn't he? He's in the States. *Isn't he?*"

"Butterworth, you are being very foolish."

"I've been foolish before."

"Permit me to give you a word of advice."

"I'm listening."

"Drop this inquiry."

"Why?"

"Valdemarr is dead. He died in a shootout with Czech partisans outside Prague on 8 May 1945. Soviet troops found Valdemarr's dairy in the overcoat pocket of a dead man. That diary is today in Moscow, and is considered beyond doubt to be genuine. There is a copy as well in the files of the East German authorities. Don't ask me how I have come by these facts, but you may rest assured they are absolutely accurate."

"How many dozen cases do you suppose there are, Dr. Schmidt, of prominent Nazis putting their own identity papers into the pockets of dead men, hoping this would prove that they, the prominent Nazis, were in fact dead?"

"I am sure, I don't know," Schmidt said tersely. "But, I repeat, you are being very foolish."

"Threatening me, sir?"

"I am merely a messenger; I urge you, however, to not dismiss me."

"Listen here, Schmidt, tell this to *whoever* sent you, *whoever* he is…"

He stared down along his Aryan nose. "Yes."

"I want an interview with former SS Obergruppenführer Heinz Valdemarr."

"An…*interview*…"

"Yes."

"With a dead—"

"Cut the Kraut crap. He's not dead. If I'm wrong, my request shouldn't worry anybody. I want an interview. That's all. His terms. Anyplace. Anytime. I'll submit to being blindfolded, the location of our meeting their secret, if necessary. You acknowledged yourself, Dr. Schmidt, I am an author and researcher of military history. With a good reputation. I am not a cop. I am no Nazi hunter. I am certainly no Jew. I promise—and if I break that promise he's free to call a stop to the interview—no questions about concentration camps, ovens, slave labor, any atrocities. I'm truly interested in only one matter."

Dr. Schmidt canted back his head.

Eyes cold. "What would that be, sir?"

"Advanced weapons research, his, and what became of it."

"I see."

"I'd hoped," he said, "that might ring a...*a bell.*"

CHAPTER 30

THAT WAS THE END OF Butterworth's research. Within four weeks of the Miami trip he would survive one presumed attempt on his life—the altimeter—then die in a single-vehicle car crash in Mississippi, driving to meet my client in Memphis, from a third visit to Huntsville. Nothing had ever come, as far as I could tell, of his request to interview Valdemarr. Interestingly, it was seeming to me Butterworth might have, in those last weeks, been getting back on track, researching World War II secret weapons. Off the Nazi-hunting tangent. Perhaps the matter of Buzz Hutcheson cutting him off, the money teat going dry. That had come in late September, on the heels of the important second Huntsville trip: Hutcheson was asked and refused to finance an excursion to South America.

At that point, it seemed clear, Butterworth had intended to do just what he and Erchanbolt Ritter had bantered about.

He was going to go to South America.

To look for Martin Bormann.

And Heinz Valdemarr.

He changed his mind when Hutcheson cut him off. That made sense. A prolonged international trip would be far more expensive than what he had been doing, not something he could manage without backing, not and still keep his family solvent. He wouldn't even be able to fly his Cessna that far.

Then came the Miami trip.

Why?

Why go there to talk to Graham about Martin Bormann, if he wasn't interested in hunting Nazis anymore? His conversation with the mysterious Dr. Schmidt, minutes after the Graham interview, made clear he'd already decided before Miami it would be folly to go to South America pursuing Martin Bormann. Or maybe he decided that while speaking to Graham. After all, there had not been much in that interview, that I saw, to encourage a South American excursion. At any rate, the Schmidt encounter did demonstrate he was still interested in Valdemarr, all the more so because Valdemarr was tied into secret weapons, and Butterworth was back to writing a book about secret weapons.

But the Schmidt encounter was not planned. It came out of the blue. He went to Miami to talk to Graham, and again, I was asking myself, *Why?*

Okay... John F. Graham was not a source Butterworth developed on his own. I'd seen no reference to him in any of the Butterworth Papers prior to the leaked FBI report, received only days before the Miami trip. *What did that tell me...?* He was spurred by the report to go talk to Graham personally, about an earlier hunt for Bormann in South America, in spite of having already been dissuaded from pursuing his own. *Had he thought Graham might know something about Valdemarr's whereabouts, Valdemarr being a Nazi he was still interested in? Had he thought Graham might give him ammunition to take back to Buzz Hutcheson in a renewed plea for travel money?*

In all likelihood, Butterworth took his precise motivation for going to Miami to his grave. Nobody alive could tell me the answer. But contemplating all of this was highlighting for me one of those coincidences I didn't like. Meaning: I did not accept it as coincidence that within a very short span of time—two to three weeks—Butterworth talked to Erchanbolt Ritter and got jazzed about Nazi hunting in South America, then got turned down for the necessary financing, and bagged the idea, then somehow came into possession of a twenty-year-old FBI report, that at least on some level stirred up his Nazi-hunting juices all over again.

It was almost like somebody with access to government documents had become aware of Butterworth's interest, then flagging interest, in Nazi hunting, and decided to try to rekindle that flame with a cryptic leaked document.

Humph…

His conversation with Dr. Schmidt, the Valdemarr interview request, the assurances, all suggested he was trying to salvage his book about foo fighters and flying bombs, secret weapons of yore. Surely a safer topic than tracking down big-time Nazi war criminals. Those kinds of people had something to protect, things to hide.

Who, on the other hand, could feel threatened by old military secrets from the 1940s, secrets of a defeated enemy, no less, in this day and age of H-bombs, spy satellites, lasers, Polaris-missile submarines—just one of which was said to carry more destructive power than all the weapons used in World War II—not to mention B-52s, and ICBMs in silos tipped with multiple warheads?

If Butterworth had dropped his Nazi hunt, why kill him?

He had said something to Ritter, I recalled all of a sudden, about Valdemarr.

I leafed back through that transcript. Up to then, the only thing I knew about Valdemarr having anything to do with secret weapons—remember: he was a civil engineer, not a rocket scientist. He built concentration camps, installed ovens and gas chambers. But then the SS took over the V-2, the big rocket for attacking London that von Braun and Reinhard had developed, and Himmler put Valdemarr in charge of it, the V-2. But, when Butterworth talked to Erchanbolt Ritter at NASA during the second Huntsville trip, he didn't identify Valdemarr as head of the V-2 program.

He called him… I read the line back aloud, to myself…

"Chief of the SS secret-weapons empire."

Not a single missile project.

Head of an empire.

I drew a five-pointed star in the margin next to that line. Then, when he talked to Dr. Schmidt, in Miami, he referred to Valdemarr's advanced weapons research. *His advanced weapons research.* This had to be information Butterworth developed throughout 1967 and early 1968 flying one end of the country to the other interviewing current and former intelligence men, and an aerospace guy at McDonnell Douglas. I hadn't dug into all that: seemed pretty dense, pretty technical stuff. Over my head. Padding back to my kitchen with my soup bowl and whisky glass, both empty, I wondered if Butterworth had thought Valdemarr might be enough of an information goldmine, that he was worth pursuing to South America, or wherever. Maybe he thought he could write a great book, no publisher would dare turn away, chockful of new insights on cutting-edge research, conducted by brilliant engineers, on rockets and flying bombs and jet fighters, even the A-bomb, all in the service of a doomed regime, as the allies were tightening the noose. I'd make for a fascinating history. Not my cup of tea, mind you, but for people who went in for that sort of thing. I washed my bowl and spoon and put them in the drying rack. I put the leftover tomato soup, still in the pot, with the lid on, in the fridge. I fixed myself another Dewar's.

Swallowing some, I thought:

Wasn't until his talk with Schmidt, if that was his real name—Butterworth believed it to be an alias, meaning, probably wasn't much hope of me tracking the man down—that he had deduced Valdemarr might be in the States, rather than hiding in South America with Martin Bormann like a good little Nazi.

So, if Butterworth had dropped his war-crimes focus, was purely interested in what Valdemarr had to say about innocuous, decades-out-of-date, science and technology, he would still be thinking he had to pursue that search in South America. Okay, that made sense. He could have been off the Nazi-hunt bandwagon, and still gone to Miami—prodded by the leaked document—seeking information about Valdemarr, and justification for funding to go to South America.

Why would Nazis kill Butterworth?

If his only interest was, what amounted to, the ancient history of modern weapons development?

Had to be Nazis. I was, I admit, going on a leap of faith that the car crash and altimeter tampering were linked. Their timing, so close, could be a coincidence, but assuming that got me nowhere. Nor did it pass muster with any instinct I had about such things. So, if there was a link, if the same people, or group, were behind both attempts on Butterworth's life, it had to be

Nazis. They almost had to be behind the altimeter plot, given Bobby Kaplan—a mechanic, with access to Butterworth's plane at the critical time, and of course, what I'd found at his East Liverpool home, a veritable shrine to Adolf Hitler, and George Lincoln Rockwell.

There was still more, of course: his suspicious behavior, early arrival to work, which I'd seen his own employer question, and the proof, in the duplex, of someone contacting him about my travel plans.

Great—case solved—Nazis killed Butterworth.

Bet the Alcorn County sheriff would jump all over it, if I went back with that theory.

My job clearly wasn't done. They were going to want the details fleshed out. Like: oh say, the name or names of particular Nazis.

Back to my question:

Why would Nazis want Butterworth killed?

They might not have trusted him not be a Nazi hunter. Perfectly plausible. Even if he kept his word, didn't try to bring Valdemarr to justice, his writings still might reveal, or simply imply, Valdemarr still lived. Inducing others to go on the hunt.

Simon Wiesenthal.

The Israeli government.

Still, Valdemarr, if alive, had managed to stay off everybody's radar for twenty-three years—unlike Bormann—meaning he was very well hidden, probably quite smart, and perhaps had a lot of competent, loyal help. Why then kill a man like Butterworth? Why take the risk? Better to lay low, burrow deeper, let the matter rest. Butterworth had to give up eventually. He had a family to support, and a day job. Nobody was paying him for the book project, not after Hutcheson pulled the plug. Why go to such an expensive hazardous effort to save a sixty-seven-year-old Nazi, when it might not be necessary? When things might just blow over.

Unless of course:

That sixty-seven-year-old Nazi, Valdemarr, were of such vital importance to what John F. Graham claimed to be a well-financed conspiracy to build a Fourth Reich, that they couldn't afford, couldn't risk, just waiting.

It was dark outside.

Still flurrying.

Getting colder.

I decided to go off the clock.

Start a fire, sit by it, read for pleasure, for a change.

My brain was frazzled. I decided to spend one more day at least, tomorrow—cold, rainy, and snowy being the forecast—on Buzz Hutcheson's dime, reading more of Butterworth's files, digging into that technical stuff, between the first and second Huntsville trips. He had learned something in all of that, which put him onto Valdemarr, his wartime secret-weapons and high-technology research. Stuff that made Butterworth a target. I resigned myself to needing, unfortunately, to know what that was.

I had a couple of other things simmering too, that might tell me the next step.

My query to Alan Legate, of the FBI.

And the Pittsburgh PI, hired to sweep the Butterworth residence for bugs.

CHAPTER 31

THE FORMER SERGEANT OF THE *Das Reich division of the SS,* *a man named Kargher originally from Dusseldorf, eased his 1964* *Renault Caravelle Cabriolet to the curb in light snow—taking up* *position, this time, opposite one address to the south of that belonging to* die detektivin. *Pulling his brake gently, he then sharpened into focus a* *powerful set of Zeiss field glasses. Examined the yellow-lit windows, through* *slats of louvered blinds, at the southeast corner of the cottage where she lived,* *by his reckoning, alone. Mail addressed only to her, including a* Cosmopolitan *subscription. He'd discreetly queried, additionally, at select* *neighboring homes (claiming to be tracking down an old war buddy he* *believed lived in the neighborhood, perhaps that bungalow over there, gold* *Impala in the driveway?) assuming correctly it would mostly be women at* *home, and that a woman living alone in their midst would be an object of* *prurient interest, prying attention, gossip. No, never any sight of a man,* *except one, older than her, supposed to be her father, who infrequently stayed* *the night.*

No beau anybody knew about.

She was in fact, you know (this was how they all phrased it), a divorcée.

The girl was home, Kargher confirmed, through the glasses. He let air *out of his lungs slowly through his nose. Bothersome, her stopping like that* *at the corner, the hard eye contact. No reason to assume he was* *compromised. Probably a natural female reflex: suspicion, alertness, toward* *any male stranger, view him as potentially predatory. Like a doe in the* *forest, darting at every unexpected sound, movement.*

He'd been foolish, though, remaining stationary, one exposed position, for too long. He had figured Panama City to be the more difficult phase of this mop-up operation. As it had unfolded, however, Florida had been a milk run. If Nashville required more of his skills and cunning, so be it. Perhaps, a less-noticeable car. She intrigued him, for a woman, even an American; his nerve endings tingled, sensing the challenge. Yet, she too had been careless. Alerting him to her suspicions—if she harbored any. Suddenly she emerged onto her porch, Kargher raising the binoculars, watching her haul, grimacing, limping with the effort, split logs two at a time, inside to the fireplace.

In for the night then, he concluded, but went on observing via those windows, bending down and standing up, smacking off hands, fingering back tawny hair, puffing cheeks, determinedly getting herself a fire burning. Typically a man's job. Kargher was impassive, watching a beat, perhaps two, longer than diligence to his job strictly required.

Fetching girl.

Eventually placing the glasses on the passenger seat, he took off the brake, slipped the car into gear, and the killer of French hostages in Tulle and Limoges in 1944 drove quietly off to his hotel where he was registered as the representative of a Detroit auto-parts concern.

CHAPTER 32

I HAD JUST GOTTEN THE fire to catch half-decently, some sap oozing out the end of a log, sizzling, when the phone rang, the business line in my office. I bounded up, yanked the fireplace screen sideways into place, and scurried back along the hall. I snatched up the phone from across the front of my desk, on the fourth ring. "Russell Detective Agency," I answered, puffing, clawing back hair. "Sherry Russell speaking."

"This is Alan Legate."

I smiled, stretching the black phone cord out to remove the kinks, and told the FBI agent I hadn't expected to hear back so quickly. I made room, propping one buttock up onto the corner of the desk, listening to what he had to say. "I talked to the agent," he told me, jarringly Bostonian, "who handled Mr. Butterworth's report. And I shouldn't be relaying any of this."

"Understood," I said. "Thank you."

"Frankly, it is not clear to me why I should."

"Probably because you dream about me in those Elly May Clampett outfits you dressed me up in last year to go undercover." I brushed my bangs. "None of those Ivy League girls you're used to, could've pulled that off, I don't imagine."

"Probably it."

"So…you *have* grown a sense of humor."

"Perhaps a small one. Look, nothing I say can show up in your faatha's newspaper."

"I promise, or if it does, won't be me. In any case, I promise not to link anything back to you."

"Lot of qualifications."

"I don't have a crystal ball, Alan, to predict the future. You were a lawyer, right, before you were an agent? You understand. I don't plan to blab, okay?"

"Okay. Your Mr. Butterworth was informing upon, and requesting our investigation of, a man he'd happened to meet and recognize, and suspected of being a Nazi war criminal." He pronounced it, *NAT-zi*, accented first syllable, rhyming with *gnat*, rather than *knot*. "Suspect's name was Dasch."

He spelled it.

I lifted the cord, went round the desk, and sat, rolling my chair close, cradling the receiver on my shoulder. I pulled over a legal pad and wrote that name I already knew well, though I hadn't until now known much more than that.

"George Peter Dasch," Legate finished.

I noted the given names on my pad.

"Got it, go on."

"Butterworth said he happened to meet this man Dasch, and thought he seemed familiar, but didn't place him immediately, at the home of a Dr. Arnold Reinhard in Huntsville. He's a top rocket scientist for NASA there."

"I know who Reinhard is."

"Dasch is Reinhard's chauffeur, also gardener."

"Let me guess," I said, leaning back, tapping the arm of my chair with polished nails. "Butterworth thought Dasch was really a Nazi thought long dead, named Heinz Valdemarr. How close am I?" One of my character flaws, I admit: I relish boasting I'm one step ahead of the men, or at least, not a step behind.

"Who's Valdemarr?"

"Never mind," I said, rolling my eyes.

I straightened, propped an elbow on my desk.

"So, who *did* he think Dasch was?"

"He knew him as...let's see...a Staff Sergeant Yacobean, who served in the S-2 section of his old bomber squadron, in England during World War II."

"S-2?"

"Intelligence."

The group photo… I recalled.
Front of a Quonset hut…

"In the context of a bomber squadron, I'm told, S-2 would get first notification of the squadron's next target from the Ops section, and would prepare briefings for the pilots, bombardiers, navigators, gunners, about what they could expect, in the way of fighters, antiaircraft, so forth, on a particular mission. Turns out, this Staff Sergeant Yacobean was really Abwehr Lieutenant George Peter Dasch."

"So, Dasch *is* his real name?"

"We believe it to be."

"Abwehr?"

"German Army Intelligence. Later, part of the SS. Dasch was a deep-cover agent."

"A spy."

"Entered the United States illegally in 1922, worked as a waiter in New York City. He actually served legitimately, for a time, in the Army Air Corps. Went to college. Returned to Germany in 1936. Owing to his knowledge of America and Americans he was recruited into the Abwehr, and returned to the U.S., put ashore from a U-boat, whereupon he assumed the identity of a American citizen, this Yacobean, and volunteered, again, for the Air Corps. As an NCO in S-2 in England he had advanced knowledge of bombing targets, and for a time would have been able to transmit this information to the Luftwaffe, giving them advanced warning, aiding defensive preparations."

"He would have contributed," I said, lighting a cigarette, "to killing some of our flyers."

"No doubt. He also committed acts of sabotage—carefully, very few, so not to raise suspicions—blew up a bomb dump at the base, arranged for unexplained midair explosions, which were blamed upon malfunctioning fuses. Lastly—and this *isn't* in the official record—but your Mr. Butterworth made the accusation, in his report, that this man, Dasch-slash-Yacobean, knifed to death an Army Air Force co-pilot and a British Red Cross girl. Bayoneted them both when they interrupted him transmitting in code from a B-17's radio set on the ground, late one night. The pair were sneaking onto the plane to…"

I curled a brow.

"Advance," I said, "Anglo-American relations."

"Precisely."

"Hold on a sec, will you, Alan?"

"Sure," he said, pronouncing it, *Shoowah*.

I put the phone down on the desk and went half-running into my dining room to find the old black-and-white photo Butterworth had singled out from his files, of twenty-five men who'd served in the 303rd Bombardment Group, intelligence section, known as S-2. Their names were all penciled on the back, and I skimmed the list, returning to the phone. Sure enough, second man from the left, back row standing:

S/Sgt Claud B. Yacobean.

I flipped it back over and studied the face, before setting it aside. "How'd Butterworth," I asked, when I was back on the line, "connect Yacobean to the bayonet killings?"

"Yacobean went AWOL that night," Legate said, "eventually escaping cross-channel into occupied France. Butterworth simply put two and two together."

"So, you're investigating Dasch?"

"No."

"I don't understand."

"We took Butterworth's statement and forwarded it to Washington. The justice department filed it, and thanked us very much."

"No follow-up?"

"Correct, and your man was told as much by my colleague."

"Wait," I said, protruding my tongue, and bit it lightly, "if there was no investigation, how did you get all that information you just recited—Dasch immigrating here illegally in 1922, et cetera, et cetera?"

"DOJ had it all in a file, except the murders, which was simply Butterworth's claim, unsubstantiated. We do know Dasch returned to Germany after the escape from England, was promoted, and made aide to a top officer in the SS-foreign intelligence service."

"Butterworth," I said, "is dead now, you know."

"So you told me. That's partly why I'm divulging this."

"Why is there a file on Dasch in Washington?"

"He's a...so-called..."

He seemed to be dragging, with much difficulty, the answer up out of himself.

"So-called *what?*"

"This is the sort of thing, Ms. Russell, which cannot be in the newspaper."

I licked at some smoke I was exhaling. "Understood."

"He's a so-called, *Paperclip* dependent."

I batted eyelashes:

"Paperclip?"

My tone skeptical.

"Operation Paperclip. Full details are top secret, nothing I can get access to, not without a need to know. What I have been told is, it was started by the OSS, the American wartime spy agency—"

"What became the CIA."

"Correct. Paperclip was initiated at the close of World War II, administered by the Joint Intelligence Objectives Agency. Goal, in part, to deny German scientific knowledge and expertise to the U.S.S.R., as the Cold War was warming up."

"By bringing rocket scientists *here* to work, like Reinhard," I said. "And, Wernher von Braun."

"Yes, but not *just* rocket scientists: synthetic-fuels experts, eighty-six aeronautical engineers, sent to dissect captured Luftwaffe equipment, physicists, physical chemists, geophysicists, physicians, experts in aerospace medicine, even an optician."

"How many?"

"Classified, but, more than a thousand, I'm told. The government disbanded JOIA about six years ago. All their records, including this file on Dasch, went to the National Archives. I asked a buddy of mine to dig it out, give me what he could. I've told you, what he told me, and probably neither one of us should have been doing *any* telling."

"Why are we sitting on Dasch?" I asked, tapering the end of my cigarette, rolling it round the rim of my ashtray. "He killed people, committed acts of sabotage, espionage. Right?"

"In a war," he said, "that ended twenty-three years ago."

"Acts of war, not war crimes, that what you're telling me?"

"I'm telling you, DOJ isn't ordering an investigation."

"You said he assumed the identity of a U.S. citizen, before enlisting the second time." I cleared my throat, swallowed. "Doesn't that mean he murdered the man, a civilian, on American soil, the real Yacobean?"

"Could mean that."

"No statute of limitations, is there, on murder?"

His audible sigh came through the receiver. "Truth is," Legate said, "no one wants to rankle the Paperclip scientists right now. They're helping us in the Cold War, against the Soviets. Plus, they're vital to the moon program."

"Okay, I get that. But Dasch is a gardener and chauffeur."

"Yes."

"I'm supposed to believe—not to mention the American public—that the arrest or deportation of a NASA scientist's gardener and chauffeur, will torpedo the whole Apollo program? *I'll* drive the man to work if you want me to, for least for as long as it takes to get us to the moon."

"Humorous as ever, Ms. Russell, but Dasch also happens to be Reinhard's brother in law."

"Really…"

My eyes narrowed to slits.

"Reinhard's wife was killed by British bombs. Was Dasch her brother?"

"Maybe," he said. "I don't know."

"*Humph*… Give me his date of birth."

He gave me a date in February of 1903. Dasch would be sixty-five now.

"Thank you, Alan," I told him, "really."

"Be careful."

"Always." I hung up.

CHAPTER 33

ITT WAS DASCH.

I jumped up like a kid, pacing arm-swingingly all through my house, one end of it, to the other. George Peter Dasch had killed Ralph Butterworth. I felt sure of it. I ended up in my living room, standing before my fireplace—radiating very little heat, by the way—with my head thrown back, laced fingers cradling the nape of my neck. I then dropped my arms, and racked my hands on my hips, and sighed, staring down in great pity at my fire. I'd just gotten it to catch, before Legate's call, and it was ebbing rapidly, a patient on the critical list. I dropped to my knees, setting about resuscitating it.

Dasch was a proven killer.

Assuming Butterworth had ID'd him correctly, and I was sure he had. Too amazing a coincidence, to think Butterworth had wrongly suspected a man, who then turned out to have that background on file in Washington...

Which made me think of something else, in the coincidence department, which I didn't like, but that didn't make it not true. The coincidence that Butterworth had, apparently by chance, in the course of his research, or Nazi-hunting, or whatever he was doing—wondered if he'd known by that point—run into Dasch at Reinhard's house.

Recognized him as the AWOL murderer/saboteur Yacobean. A man from his old squadron.

I shrugged.

Striking a match to newspapers.

Dasch was a Nazi, or in any case, had worked for Nazis in the war.

He was a one-time ruthless German spy.

Living a nice life today in America.

Threatened with exposure.

He'd assume the justice department would act, even if in fact, it wouldn't. Even if not now, in the grip of moon-landing fever, they might at some future date. Butterworth would have to be silenced, Dasch would think. And, as a member of Reinhard's family, probably Reinhard's dead wife's brother, there was the added motive of Frau Reinhard having been killed in an aerial bombardment of the type Butterworth had helped to carry out. Killed in a bombing, rumor had it, deliberately missing its military target, hitting the housing area instead. In other words, George Peter Dasch, possibly acting alone, possibly aided and abetted by his brother-in-law, Arnold Reinhard, had motive to spare in killing Ralph Butterworth. And of motive, Edward Dieckmann's *Practical Homicide Investigation*, which I'd checked out of the library, not long ago, had pontificated:

> While it isn't required that you, as the detective, have to
> prove motive, it is a mighty fine thing to have
> around…It is very, very often a good springboard for
> your take-off into the investigation.

A springboard being just what I needed.

Lastly, cinching it, far as I was concerned, Ralph Butterworth had traveled to Huntsville, to meet Dasch at one o'clock, at Maple Hill Cemetery, on the very afternoon of the night of his death.

It was Dasch.

I'd bet on it.

Motive.

And opportunity.

And, he was no stranger to killing.

Once I'd gotten the fire going again, satisfied with it, I climbed to my feet. Tapping the center of my upper lip with my finger.

Making my mind up.

Before cozying up next to the fire, swathed in a knitted afghan, with a book, sipping another drink, I made a long-distance call. To Chattanooga.

Surprisingly, I got an answer at that hour.

I set an appointment for Tuesday morning.

CHAPTER 34

Like Eisenhower to Korea, I would go to Huntsville.
I would go armed with a simple plan—dangerously simple, perhaps—for trapping George Peter Dasch. First, though, I had my other case to put to bed.

I'd decided I'd knock two more fat clinics off my list. That would make eight of the ten the state officials wanted when they hired me. I could submit that report and evidence and hopefully satisfy them. Submit my bill to the state, then focus on the Butterworth matter. There were two clinics in the Chattanooga vicinity and I had an appointment at one of them for nine o'clock Tuesday morning—eight o'clock Nashville time. Admittedly I hadn't considered that pesky time-zone change when scheduling the early appointment. Didn't matter though: it was the only slot they'd had open, they'd claimed, at the last minute. Cash only, I was sternly warned, minimum of $15 to see the doctor, not including any medication prescribed. It was all sounding pretty par for the course.

It was still snow-flurrying over an hour before sunrise, my car's heater set on high, when I drove out of Nashville via Route 41, in the cold silence of that early Tuesday. Two hours and a half later I had scaled the Impala twistingly up "the mountain"— as everybody who ever drove from Nashville to Chattanooga called it—to Mont Eagle, then down the other side, in grinding low gear, white thick ice cascading down ragged granite walls, where steep ridges had been dynamited through for the highway, smelling the scorching brake pads of big tractor-trailer rigs ahead. Eventually I pulled into Chattanooga, the "Dynamo of Dixie." Despite its near impossibility to get to from anywhere, Chattanooga was one of the South's chief industrial cities, wedged down between two of the great land regions of East Tennessee—the coal-rich Cumberland Plateau to the west, and to the east, the Appalachian Ridge and Valley. Lookout Mountain stood to the south, from the top of which, on a clear day, you could allegedly see seven states. TVA dams bracketed the city as well, harnessing the Tennessee River, and controlling flooding the year round.

I found Dr. Orville J. Dewey's office—on Chamberlain, near Wilcox, north of the children's hospital—making it for my appointment with two minutes to spare. The huge WEIGHT CONTROL sign on the roof helped. I swear I had never been to Chattanooga when I hadn't gotten lost at least once. Had to do with screwy roads related to all those mountains and the forever twisting river. When I checked in, removing my double-breasted green coat, hanging it off a rack, I received a ten-page mimeographed handout to read.

WELCOME ABOARD! it began. FIRST, if you are NOT overweight by average standard I DO NOT WANT YOU TO WASTE YOUR MONEY AND MY TIME WITH EVEN AN INITIAL VISIT. At length, it went on to conclude, I do not consider you to have ANY medical overweight problem at all unless you are 15% or more over your average weight.

I did some arithmetic, figuring fifteen percent over my ideal average would be about 153 pounds. *Humph...* Since I'd never come within a dozen pounds of that in my entire life, I began to hold out hope for Dr. Dewey. Almost began to root for him. I was just doing a job I'd been hired for. I'd be paid the same whether or not I actually dug up dirt on all these doctors. I wasn't out to get them. To the contrary, I had the utmost respect for the good doctors I'd worked with as a nurse—I'd learned much from them—but I also had great disdain for the bad ones.

The pale-purple-lettered handout concluded:

BUT NEVER FEAR, overweight or obesity is a very common disorder which can be corrected WITHOUT DIETING!

One corner of my mouth knotted up.

I was called to the back.

Technicians put me through the wringer, an examination procedure that required me to undress as far as my slip, and included a urinalysis, blood drawn from the vein in my arm, weight, body measurements, BP, pulse, EKG. Dr. Dewey came in after all the above, thick-necked and heavy-browed, looking like a retiree from the Marine Corps. He had a big smile on his face and shook my hand by the tips of my fingers. I had my cream-colored, ruffled-fronted blouse back on, partly buttoned by this point, but not my skirt. He said, "you're in great shape kid, you have no weight problem."

"Oh, well, thank you, sir," I said, beamingly, resting a hand below my throat. "Such a relief."

Then without giving me any sort of exam or taking any sort of history himself, he proceeded to prescribe me progesterone—a sex steroid—and 234 other pills that included diuretics, thyroid hormone, and appetite suppressants. I was flabbergasted, and back out in the reception area paid $40—cash, gotta have that cash—wondering how many pills someone who *was* overweight got out of Dr. Dewey.

CHAPTER 35

S EVERAL EVENINGS EARLIER—THURSDAY, 14 November, with Sherry Russell still in Pittsburgh—Kargher, the chief executioner of the Sektor Amerikanisch of the ODESSA, reported to the Zyklop's Chicago office. Both men smoked and the Zyklop, fanatic and astute, in constant communication with superiors in Argentina, began the briefing with what might have been regret. "There is an unfortunate investigation into our book writer's accident," he said, sneering over the word, accident. "A woman private detective, eine detektivin." He slid a sheet containing a dozen lines of typewritten data across the desk, the killer taking it. "This is her. There isn't much. And there is, of course, the other loose end."

Kargher nodded. Since the late-fifties he had fulfilled twelve assignments for this or another ODESSA chief executive, first in West Germany—where Zyklop's opposite number was codenamed, Werwolf—then in the United States, ruthlessly dealing with those getting too close to top men, or who elected to expose their comrades, the man preferring to strangle or break the necks of his assignments, using only his butcher's hands. He was equally skilled with a gun or knife. The Huntsville job, however, had become a muddled affair in which he had not been given his usual freedom to act. He was unsurprised, therefore, over having to tidy up a mess, nodding with understanding, knowing the Zyklop shared his frustration, although neither man spoke of it. "The orders?" the killer asked, after listening to all his chief had to say.

Twin smoke streams exited Zyklop's large nostrils, a thick Cuban *rolled thoughtfully between the attorney's thumb and heavy fingers.*

"Locate and liquidate."

Kargher nodded.

Simplicity was best.

"I do regret the need to order her death," the Zyklop confided, indicating the typed profile on the Russell woman with the chewed end of his cigar, "yet she almost certainly leaves me no alternative." He could not reveal General Schrecklich's last words to him in Mexico City, in September—not about die detektivin *specifically, for she was not yet involved—but regarding certain lines of inquiry by Herr Butterworth, which had touched certain nerves, which could endanger the identity of a certain one of their Kameraden, a man of vital, absolutely vital importance.*

Schrecklich had left him virtually no freedom of decision.

The Zyklop grinned slightly over the puzzlement on his subordinate's face, making the tip of his cigar glow as he drew from it. "To kill a girl is distasteful, but at times necessary," he explained, shrugging, "as you well know. It is nevertheless problematic, in this situation we find ourselves. The killing or disappearance of a girl risks added zeal on the part of local law enforcement. Americans retain a silly bit of medieval chivalry where their women are concerned. Southern Americans particularly. You must take this into account."

"I understand," Kargher said. "I'll need money." The Zyklop responding with a wad of three thousand American dollars pushed across the desk, together with a forged Michigan driver's license.

In Nashville, Tennessee, on Tuesday, 19 November, Kargher took a taxicab, carrying a small valise, leaving the Renault in the hotel garage, to a dealership called Parkway Volkswagen, at Eighth and Craighead. He waited until they opened and spent $950 cash on a used black 1966 Volkswagen 1300 Sedan. As commonplace a car as one found on America's streets, escalating its utility as a surveillance vehicle. And of course die detektivin *knew the Renault. She had marked it on Monday, and while he had no concern his purpose had been compromised by that brief encounter, she clearly would not ignore a second appearance of the same car. He transacted his business quickly, tossed the valise in the backseat, and sped over to Grantland, which by odd coincidence was only a quarter mile from the used-VW lot.*

The valise contained a totally clean, of fingerprints that is, murderously sharp bowie knife, and fifty feet of yellow-and-blue polypropylene rope, both purchased from a hardware store the previous evening. He had decided little was to be gained by further delay. If he found Ms. Sherry Russell working from home, as on Monday, he would simply, calmly walk up to the house carrying the valise, and ring her doorbell. And that would be that. He would make certain, in light of his chief's instructions, the job was carried out in a way not obviously connecting back to any case she was currently working. Given that she was recently divorced, attractive, living alone, he felt that would not be difficult, several scenarios coming to the ODESSA killer's cold-blooded mind. The best, circumstances permitting, would be suicide by hanging, a note left in her own hand stating how distraught she was over her failed marriage, how she couldn't go on living. Slashed wrists in the tub, by one of her very own kitchen knives, would work as well, but would be more difficult to stage and coerce. Last resort, the bowie knife would gash Sherry Russell's throat from ear to ear, almost severing her head from her body, à la Jack the Ripper.

Kargher would not commit rape but once the woman was dead from the neck wound, time permitting, he would leave her unrecognizable as a human being, facial and body parts severed, liver and entrails wrenched away, intestines draped about her neck—all, again, à la Jack the Ripper. The point being to make the motive seem sexual to the Nashville police, a case of—to use, actually, a German term—lustmörd, joy-murder, rather than a murder carried out, as would be the case, for purely practical reasons, a business murder, which the Germans had no term for.

Kargher bypassed the house on Grantland, studying it.

Stunned—the gold 1967 Impala SS missing from the driveway!

He cursed and pounded the dashboard of the Volkswagen repeatedly and violently.

CHAPTER 36

I FOUND A GRANT'S IN Chattanooga, and ate at the lunch counter, a slaw dog for 35¢ and a "giant" milk shake for 45¢. When I was done and had reapplied my lipstick, I located the pay phone. I placed an operator-assisted long-distance call, charged to my home-office number in Nashville, to the next, hopefully final, clinic on my list. Ironically, I knew from the public-health department that Dr. Chester M. Thompson—in Cleveland, Tennessee, the smallest town I would visit, population just over 16,000—was the most prosperous fat doctor in three states. Over three hundred patients per week cycled through his office. I was lucky: a receptionist who sounded, I swear to God, like Gomer Pyle's sister, said they could see me at three-thirty.

Nothing earlier? I pleaded.

Nope, three-thirty or next week. I booked it and killed a couple hours riding the incline railroad up Lookout Mountain, and freezing my derrière off, strolling about the Civil War park. *I even saw Rock City!* Yep, lived my entire life in Tennessee and had never seen it despite hundreds of barns painted SEE ROCK CITY from Michigan to Texas. Eventually I drove east out of Chattanooga, taking I-75, halfway to the western tip of North Carolina, to Cleveland. I found the international headquarters of the Church of God, which I'd been told to look for, and two doors down I parked in front of the THOMPSON OBESITY

CENTER. I gave a pilfered Chattanooga address and fake phone number, after which a brown-haired woman with a face like a cartoon of the wicked witch of the west—long hooked nose, long pointed chin—told me she wanted to check my hemoglobin count. She jabbed three different fingers before getting enough blood out for her test, contritely stating at the end of my ordeal, "You just don't know how sorry I am."

Wrong lady!

I was at least as sorry as she was.

Testing resumed: urinalysis, ankle jerk, pulse, blood pressure, bust-hip-waist measurements, weight—135½ pounds. She gave me a medical history quiz, replying "real good" whenever I indicated I had no problem in the area being asked about. "My pretty…" I couldn't help tacking on to anything and everything she said. Once Queen Grimhilde was done, I was directed through a door saying DOCTOR'S OFFICE and waited twenty-five minutes for Dr. Thompson to blow in with his friendly, tad-over-familiar demeanor. His cheeks and bulbous nose were very pink; he had white hair, recessed at the temples, wore worsted-wool slacks and a bright white wraparound medical smock with short sleeves. He felt the front and back of my neck, checked my ankles for swelling. Then claimed, judging from the size of my arm, I ought to weigh 120 pounds.

"Oh dear," I exclaimed, rebuttoning the neck of my blouse.

"Eat and drink anything you want," he said, with a think-nothing-of-it hand sweep. "All you have to do is take the pills I'm going to give you, come back once a week to check your progress, and get a booster shot, and of course pick up the next week's pills."

"That's all?" I said happily. "You can really get all this weight off me?"

"Or my name ain't Dr. Tom."

"That's such a relief," I said.

It was time, he then said, for my first weekly shot.

My heart bumped sickishly.

I swallowed.

First time I'd encountered a shot.

"Oh I…don't know about that," I said, affecting my bubble-brain act. "I hate needles. I…faint at the sight of them. I really do."

"Don't waste my time," he scolded, mildly, but enough to make me jump, blinking. "I am a busy man and you, young lady"—he was wagging a finger at me, the sonovabitch—"have got to be disciplined, and committed to recover your health. You don't get this problem under control now, you could be facing a lifetime of complications: premature atherosclerosis, fatty infiltration of the liver..."

"Ewww..."

I wrinkled a nostril.

"Traumatic skeletal changes, such as hypertrophic arthritis."

"Oh dear," I said again, pretending to be cowed by his vocabulary. "But can't we just stick with pills, doctor?"

"No shot, no pills. Make up your mind, honey. I got plenty of waiting patients who *want* to be cured."

What I wanted was no part of any shot, but I needed those damn pills to take to the health department—hard incontrovertible evidence of just what kind of medicine Ol' Dr. Tom was practicing over here in Tennessee's hyper-religious fringes. "What is the shot?" I asked, meekly.

"Name of the drug doesn't matter," he said, shrugging, giving a head-shake. "You wouldn't understand anyway, but think of it as...first gear, in revving up your body's machinery. Look, try it this time." He propped one fist on his hip, leaned on the exam table, looking me straight in the eye, feigning patience, thinly. "If you don't like it, won't have to take it next time. Deal?"

I agreed.

Sighingly.

"Good." Straightening, he reached for a 2-cc syringe, two-inch 22-gauge needle attached—*ouch!*—and a glass ampule, off a waiting Mayo stand. He snapped the ampule and filled the syringe, then plucked a cotton ball from a blue jar of 70% alcohol. "Up with your skirt, honey, down with your skivvies, as we said in the army, well not—"

"What?" I squawked.

"All the way."

"Can't you inject me in the arm?"

He rapped the glass syringe back down. Marched for the door. "Obvious you don't want my help," he said, taking hold of the knob, "your choice, but you still have to pay the girl on the way out, for my consultation."

"Wait, please, doctor."

He rotated half away, then back like he was built of springs. "Yes?"

"I want the shot."

"*Thaat's* better." He grinned, and shoved away from the door, returned swaggeringly, dancingly, to the Mayo stand, taking back up the syringe. He got a fresh cotton ball from the jar and wiped the needle, and stood watching while I hauled up my camel-and-cream-tweed skirt and my slip in back. I was wearing a back-closure garter belt, got that unfastened, while still being watched, by the way, and managed to thumb down my panties, at which point Dr. Tom instructed me to bend over the exam table, on one elbow while holding my clothing up out of the way in back. Like a lewd game of Twister. He dragged the Mayo stand closer and put the syringe down on what appeared to be a clean four-by-four. My prime concern at that point being Dr. Tom's sterile technique. Suddenly though things took a stunning turn.

He told me he was looking for the best spot for the shot, and began quite zealously fondling and squeezing both my buttocks. My head flew up, blinking rapidly; I held myself rigid, unable to believe the situation. I really wasn't sure what to do. Finally he gripped my left as he jabbed the hypodermic deep into my gluteus maximus on the right—I was baring my teeth—and he pushed the plunger in, exceedingly slowly, it was seeming to me.

He withdrew the needle, eventually, placed the empty syringe on the Mayo stand, proceeding to massage the area he'd injected, with a rotary motion. With a small intake of breath, I gaped over my shoulder. "Working the drug in," he explained, "my own patented technique." With his other hand, mind you, he was still cupping, not gently either, the buttock that hadn't gotten a shot.

Eyes flicking, getting my breath, I said, "Thank you…for taking such care, doctor, after I've been so much trouble."

"My job, and my passion."

Then he spanked me on the butt.

I jerked.

"Nice," he said, "very nice."

I wondered how nice he'd think the snub-nosed .38 in my

purse was, but for the moment it was out of reach. Done at last, Dr. Tom took his crummy hands off me, carefully soaping up and washing them at the sink, as I straightened, quavering with disbelief, revulsion, a clenching in the pit of my stomach. I yanked my panties up, managed to fasten one hook at the rear of my garter belt, probably catawumpus, and threw my skirts down. He was opening the door by then and went out, twisting back to add, "Pay the girl at the desk. She'll have your pills ready. Good day."

I wasted no time getting out of there, but snatched up the empty ampule first and rotated it:

'METHEDRINE'® BRAND METHAMPHETAMINE HYDRO-CHLORIDE.

A 1cc ampul, 20mg/cc.

Shit.

He'd shot me full of the entire amp.

Twenty milligrams of speed.

Goody.

I wrapped it in Kleenex, for evidence, and put it in my purse, and paid the desk fifteen dollars, received twenty-six pills for the week: a diuretic, a barbiturate, and a red-and-yellow capsule called *Phantos*, a combination of 15 milligrams amphetamine sulfate, 1½ grains thyroid, atropine, aloin—a harsh laxative—and phenobarbital, yet another barbiturate. *Warning: may be habit-forming*, said the instruction sheet. *No kidding!* A sign at the desk read that as of January 1, 1969, prices were rising to $20 for the first visit, $10 per week thereafter.

I wanted to scream. I didn't but I did beat my steering wheel with my fists a lot once I was in my car in the parking lot. Then I brushed back my hair, huffing, and started the ignition savagely. It was dark, misting rain, close to freezing. First gas station I saw I pulled alongside the pumps, barked at the attendant to fill it, while I got the key for the ladies room, which was filthy and stinking and the toilet was clogged by a feminine napkin, but the place felt sparkling to me, stacked up against Ol' Dr. Tom's exam room. I peed and gave myself a sponge bath below the waist where he'd touched me, then got my undergarments sorted back out.

One positive about having a gluteus maximus shot full of

methamphetamine was I had no trouble staying awake at the wheel driving back to Nashville late. I studied a map, deciding going back through Chattanooga would be out of the way. Besides, I disliked interstates, and had a lot on my mind, so I'd just take the back country roads home. I drove up into Meigs County, the night moonless, and very black. Past Birchwood at the confluence of the Tennessee and Hiwassee Rivers I found, to my utter astonishment:

No bridge!

I used the Blythe Ferry, which carted me and one other car across. See the interesting things you find, off the main roads in Tennessee.

Rumbling off the ferry, gunning up the landing, I went into Dayton, picked up Route 30 to Morgan Springs, through Fraley's Gap, elevation two thousand feet, following twists and double-backs to Pikeville, up onto the Cumberland Plateau in Van Buren County. With a dry mouth and metallic taste I hit Spencer about seven-thirty, where as far as I knew, Pauline Prescott's junkie ex-husband still subsisted off all the vermin he could plink as night watchman of his brother-in-law's salvage yard, plus twenty smackeroos a month to keep his mouth shut about his past with the Queen of Country—Pauline struggling to hang onto that honorific, nowadays, versus the likes of Loretta Lynn, Tammy Wynette. Finally a decent-sized town materialized out of the pitch black. McMinnville. My heart pounded, thanks to the shot, not McMinnville. I felt my pulse in my throat, and no need to stop to eat or pee and there was more than enough gas, no stopping Sherry the Hopped-Up Road Queen. Highway 70S into Murfreesboro, then Smyrna, past Stewart air base, then LaVergne, then Una, into Nashville. A trek of 156 miles, taking three hours, fifty minutes—awfully fast, considering all the back roads, and a ferry of all things, but then I was on speed, wasn't I? Must be why they called it that. Home before ten, still buzzing, I grabbed a nurses' drug manual I kept in a drawer with my stethoscope, and ironed-stiff-and-flat origami hats, and looked up the half-life of amphetamines.

Nine to twelve hours!

My God.

Day and a half for my body to eliminate three-quarters of

that shot, as much as two and a half days to get it all out of me. No sleep to be had that night, I imagined. The time wouldn't go to waste, however, thinking it diabolically ironic—I was grinning like the Grinch who stole Christmas over it, in fact—to use the time to type up and polish up and finalize a report on my drug-seeking activities at the behest of the State of Tennessee, and capping it off with the lurid tale of my molestation by Dr. Tom of Cleveland. I was typing fast, my ordeal pouring out of me, singled-spaced, elite, onto 8½ x 11 white bond paper. But when I let my fingers finally coast to a stop, and rolled that part of document up and read it back to myself, I yanked it out, read it some more, then balled it up.

Heaved it in the wastepaper basket.

"Shit," I said.

I stormed in the other room and mixed a Dewar's and water on the rocks, returned to the office, forcing a slower pace, slurping Scotch, and thought about Dr. Chester M. Thompson. And those thoughts, that fury, honestly, got all jumbled up in my head with what Dr. Alec Longhurst had done to me five years ago at the great and glorious Hermitage Infirmary. My skin felt tight and not because of amphetamines. I sipped from my drank, then shook my head very hard, hard enough to rattle my brain inside my skull, to free it of all that…that *stuff*, get it to focus just on Thompson, how I'd love to skewer him for his wandering paws, and while I was at it, condescending damn attitude.

Except—

Was that a good idea?

Sounded like a good idea.

Felt in my gut, and my sore bottom, like a good idea.

But none of that meant it *was* a good idea.

After all, me taking on Longhurst had gone *so, so* well…

I agitated my head again.

Different situation, keep on the rails, Sherry, how'bout it.

The state had not hired me to ensnare Thompson in some sexual-misconduct beef. They wanted him nailed for being a dangerously irresponsible diet-pill monger, and if I muddied the waters with a groping charge—I had to ask, *might that endanger the primary purpose of my having gone there?*

And I had to answer:

207

Sighingly, *it probably would.*

Illegal, utterly unethical, creepy and humiliating, what he'd done to me. But the overprescribing of diet pills was a far deadlier practice to the hundreds of Tennessee women, and out-of-state women, who encountered Dr. Tom and these other fat doctors, than one molester was—hard as that was to stomach.

I finished my drink.

There were also business considerations.

My business.

This case was an opportunity.

Just as my work for Buzz Hutcheson was.

If I succeeded, reported my findings back in a professional manner, especially if we actually shuttered some of the clinics, it would boost my reputation. Bring in more investigations. Which meant money, a living. If I screwed it up—if it got screwed up, I should say, by *something*—especially if that *something* were solely related to me being a woman, my career as a detective might be in the dumper right next to my nursing one. The state prevailing against any of these doctors hinged on the solid integrity of my reporting, and subsequent testimony, if it came to that.

Lawyers for the doctors would certainly try to ding that integrity. *Ding*, hell—machine-gun it full of holes, if they could. And I already had some strikes against me:

I was a woman.

A divorced woman.

A woman in a somewhat disreputable profession, especially for a woman.

A woman nurse who'd been drummed professionally out of Nashville.

Maybe I could weather all of that.

One whiff, though, of anything sexual between me—undercover as a patient—and any of these doctors, could ruin my credibility as a witness against them all. They'd argue, probably successfully, I'd brought on Dr. Tom's behavior.

I was to blame.

I was an immoral woman. Like Eve and original sin. And if I was immoral sexually, how far behind might lying on paper be, to please clients, and lying on the witness stand?

I could not bring up the molestation.

Not now.

And if not now—

Not ever. No reputable woman, no lady, steamed up about a matter like this, would sit on it, keep silent. That's what they'd say. Pissed me the hell off, but that was the way of the world in 1968.

One day maybe I'd track down some of Dr. Tom's other molestees, and we'd get him somehow. If there was me, there were others. I sighed. Not, I think, today, however. I retyped that part of the report, finishing around three-thirty A.M.

I wasn't sleepy, still.

I took off the rest of my clothes and fogged up my bathroom getting a very hot shower. Then I packed a suitcase, and my train case, for Huntsville.

I finished *Nat Turner* and fanned the pages of two other books my father had loaned me: *The Case Against Congress*, and a novel, *True Grit*, by a newspaper buddy of his, a native Arkansan who'd covered civil rights for the *New York Herald Tribune*. Never read a western but its circa-1880's heroine, a precocious fourteen-year-old, was getting a lot of feminist hype. So, I tossed it in the suitcase, along with my Virginia Woolf book:

Orlando freed, liberated, from any constraints of time or gender.

Speaking of the way of the world:

Certainly not borrowed that one from my father.

CHAPTER 37

KARGHER IN HIS VOLKSWAGEN BURRED *along Grantland in low gear about three A.M. that Wednesday. It was twenty-four degrees. In a holster under his left armpit the executioner carried a Walther Model HP Automatic Pistol, 9mm, eight-shot magazine—civilian prewar version of the Walther P-38, which as of 1938 was the official German military sidearm. Kargher preferred the Model HP, distinguished by finer materials and workmanship, compared to wartime models. He had burglary tools, prepared to break and enter* der detektivin's *home, and learn whatever there was to, before reporting to the Zyklop.*

The lights in the little house were on!

He was stunned. The gold Impala was there. He rubbed his shaven jowls hard and deep.

Thinking.

Plotting.

The valise with the bowie knife and rope was still in car. Problem was, apparently, the girl was wide awake, despite the hour. His plan Tuesday morning had been to walk up, ring her doorbell, coax her into making the fatal mistake of letting him inside. He doubted, however, any woman living alone in her right mind would open up for a stranger, a male stranger, the size of him, that time of night.

And if he tried and failed, there'd be no running that play again.

Patience, he counseled himself, and drove quietly back to his hotel.

CHAPTER 38

O N MONDAY EVENING, THIRTY-SIX hours earlier, anticipating spending all of Tuesday, which I had, on the fat-clinics investigation, I wrapped up my reading of the Butterworth Papers. Then I dug out a tough old oxblood leather satchel of my father's, from his law-school days. I stuffed it full of the transcripts of Butterworth's interviews with NASA officials from his two Huntsville trips and threw in the Florida-trip documents for good measure. I thought they might be useful to refer to while in Huntsville, so I decided to carry them along. I decided also to gather the carbons of the investigative reports I'd typed so far, mostly from the Beaver Falls trip, into a separate manila folder, and I locked that in the heavy case with the rest. My originals I locked in my file cabinet, zipping the key inside my pocketbook, then I hauled the leather satchel to the car and locked it in the trunk.

As for the rest of Ralph Butterworth's surfeit of material that I had for the most part not digested yet in any detail, I packed it all back away in its sturdy carton with the lid the prissy bank manager in Beaver Falls had provided. This comprised most of the author's research and travels between the first two Huntsville trips. What little I'd gleaned of it was pretty bizarre stuff, which at this point I was doubting had anything to do with his death, probably murder, at the hands of George Peter Dasch, my chief suspect. Until I had it all wrapped up though, it remained premature to rule out any possibilities.

What do I mean by: *pretty bizarre?*

Well, repacking the box got me re-skimming some of it. There was the foo-fighter mystery, strange objects over Germany, late in World War II. UFOs, in effect, though that term hadn't been coined yet. It had been, though, by the time Butterworth, under a pseudonym, published his little paperback on the subject. There were plane crashes in the desert. Things called flying discs, klystron generators. Projects named *Lusty, Winterhaven, Harass.* My eye caught references to *Oxcart.* Not until years after did I learn *Oxcart* was code for a secret high-altitude reconnaissance plane—later designated the *SR-71 Blackbird,* after the Air Force took it over from the CIA. Speaking of that, there was an entire copy of an Air Force report, February 1956, titled, incredibly, *Electrogravitics Systems—An Examination of Electrostatic Motion, Dynamic Counterbary and Barycentric Control.* A corner of my mouth twisting, opposite brow curling, that was rubber-banded to a magazine, *Aviation Week & Space Technology,* August 15, 1960, an article inside marked by paperclip, discussing gravity-research programs. There was other stuff, too, nonsensical…but some of it mentioned in the Huntsville interviews, like, Nazi gold, gunrunning, murdered intelligence officers. There were two Gulf Oil Tourgide Maps—of Nevada, specifically, and New Mexico. On the New Mexico map, in red ballpoint, Butterworth had jotted two names, which I didn't recognize from anything else— let me just say, there is a lot of white space for writing things on a highway map of New Mexico—and beside one of those names, a *Maj. Jesse Marcel,* he wrote *Intell.*

Underlined it.

Also he'd circled a town:

Roswell.

I PACKED ALL THIS AWAY, jammed the lid on the box, and rat-tat-tatted it with my bright glossy fingernails twice, before caving to curiosity on just one point. In my living room, I grabbed up the Q-R volume of *The World Book,* and looked up ROSWELL, N. MEX. I'd never in my life heard of it, but there it was, all on its own in the encyclopedia—pop. 39,593—center of a great cattle-raising, farming region. Home to John Chisum, "cattle king" of the Pecos Valley. Walker Air Force Base was there. Nothing much else to speak of in the encyclopedic wisdom on Roswell, N. Mex., nothing—but possibly the base—suggesting any connection to the rest of this weirdness.

Snapping the book closed, I shoved it back on the shelf, and I went back along the hallway, and tapped my fingernails some more atop the box of papers. Filled my lungs, emptied them slowly through my nostrils, hearing the wheeze that hadn't been there before Sal LaRocca broke my nose. It was silly, but I was leaving town, first to go to Chattanooga to hunt fat doctors, then Huntsville, to hunt George Peter Dasch.

Should I leave this material just lying about?

Unless I was very wrong, something Ralph Butterworth was looking into had gotten him killed. I thought I knew what that something was—that George Dasch, brother-in-law to the director of the Saturn V program, which was supposed to be getting us to the moon, was in years past a murderous Nazi spy.

Be a mistake, however, to assume just yet that the rest of this stuff was unimportant. And if I didn't want to take it, then I had ought to hide it.

Just to be silly safe.

Probably the same niggling up from the base of my spine that had gotten me to load the satchel containing the material I did want with me in Huntsville into the car that night, meaning I was going to be hauling it with me to East Tennessee and back on Tuesday for no good reason. No harm. Didn't need the trunk space. But why?

Just to be silly safe.

Two-handedly, then, I lurched the heavy box out of my office along the hall and through the swinging door into my kitchen. With a groan, I deposited it on the floor, then shoved it with my foot across the linoleum into the tiny mud-room off the kitchen. The walls were bead-board. There were wrought-iron hangers for coats and umbrellas. An exterior door, on the right, led from there onto the adorable little awning-covered side porch, which was part of why I fell in love with the house.

To the left, entering the mud-room from the kitchen, was a hatch in the floor. It swung it up, hooking it open beneath a shelf. Down the opening, a short flight of concrete steps led into a cramped low-ceilinged cellar. The walls were cinderblock, the floor poured concrete. I pulled the chain on a naked seventy-five-watt GE bulb, illuminating a cave-like space. After checking around for salamanders, not finding any, I bounced my box half down the steps. The main floor was puddled and slimy, the sump pump working its little heart out. The propane furnace and hot-water heater were down there, which meant, once you crammed in the requisite plumbing and ductwork, there wasn't much room left for anything else. The space, what there was, was mostly useful to me as a tornado shelter. I kept a radio and Coleman lantern high-and-dry, down there, for that purpose.

On the wall of the stairwell you were looking at when facing the front of the house, brickwork filled a gap between the top of the cinderblock foundation and the underside of the floor joists supporting the kitchen. A section of that brickwork had been chiseled out by some prior occupant, creating a hidey-hole into the crawlspace, which was quite dark, beneath the kitchen. I kept a fire-resistant strong box back in there, inside which I stored some emergency cash and savings bonds, and my important papers.

I got a hammer from the mud room, and squinting, made the opening larger, not by much, just enough to shove through, clumsily, the box full of Butterworth's research, my teeth gritting with the effort. Reaching through, grunting, I pushed it deep to the right, over dirt, and shattered brick and mortar. Puffing, I piled up some of that detritus, then stuffed in an old filthy towel to boot. And while the result hardly left the box invisible, finding it would take a sharp eye, and some luck.

Not to mention somebody really tearing the place from stem to stern.

CHAPTER 39

B
Y THE TIME I ACTUALLY went to Huntsville, two phone calls made me very glad I'd gone to some trouble to hide the balance of Butterworth's papers, and think the exercise not so silly after all.

The first had been an Ansafone message from Bernard B. Petrosky left on Tuesday while I was out of town, which I retrieved at about ten that night. It said I should call immediately, day or night, and left a number. On the second ring, Petrosky himself picked up, my ear registering the Slav-accented voice of the PI I'd hired in Pittsburgh. He said he'd send his bill, and trust me to mail him a check, but he thought I ought to hear his report without delay. "Very well," I said, taking a draw off a cigarette, pulling a pad and pen closer.

"The Butterworth line is tapped," he said. "You were dead on about that, and the job wasn't worked by any amateur."

I blinked. "I'm listening."

"A Mosler TLT6 device was wired into the junction box outside. Wasn't difficult to locate, but most people wouldn't know what to look for. I mean, it would stick out like a sore thumb if you were, say, a member of a crime syndicate, alert for things like that."

"But not people like the Butterworths."

"Check."

"Pretend I'm an idiot, Mr. Petrosky. What are we talking

about?"

"A TLT6 is an automatic telephone transmitter, very versatile. Can be placed anywhere convenient in the telephone circuit, with a range of three city blocks. It's an expensive instrument—say, two hundred bucks—and purchasing is restricted: have to be a qualified federal, state, or municipal agency, or a licensed detective agency."

"Okay."

"That ain't the half of it. This one was rigged, specially, to draw DC current directly from the phone line to recharge its batteries. Whoever planted this baby wanted it active for a long while, and didn't care about committing an expensive hunk of hardware for the duration."

"What's your guess?"

I blew a lungful of smoke.

"No PI I know," he said, "myself included. Nor for that matter, in my opinion, do any local or state police have deep-pockets enough for this set-up."

"Federal?"

"That's my guess."

"FBI?"

"Possibly. There are other three-letter agencies, of course."

"Of course."

THE SECOND CALL WAS EARLY the next morning, Wednesday. How early mattered not, since, as you know, I hadn't been to bed. On the line:

Sheriff Buford Pusser.

Newell McClanahan, tow-truck driver and cockfighting aficionado, had been found dead in Panama City.

"How?"

"Broke neck, some fleabag motel."

"Broke how?"

"Somebody's bare hands," Pusser said carefully. "Pair of very strong ones."

I swallowed.

"Leads?"

"None."

"Missing briefcase?"

"Still missing."

"Thanks," I said, "for calling."

"You be careful, ma'am," Pusser said, "McClanahan did not travel in the most genteel of circles, meaning his death isn't necessarily linked to your case."

"I'm not hearing a compelling reason not to link them."

"My point exactly."

He sighed.

"If your man, Butterworth, *was* murdered—"

"And I'm more convinced of that, now, than ever."

"Then the only person we got any line at all on, who could prove it, is dead."

"You saying," I lashed, "I should've gone to Panama City?"

Just came out of me.

The speed.

Lack of sleep.

"No, that's not what I'm saying."

"I'm sorry."

"Maybe you should have," he said, "maybe not…not my case to say. You mighta tracked him down, got something, or it mighta been a humongous waste of time. What I *am* saying is, if that car crash was no accident, then McClanahan knew it, and now somebody's tied up a loose end. So, watch your step. If you're right, there are people out there who'll kill to keep the truth under wraps. And, to be honest, Miss Sherry, I'd be real sorry if your neck was the next one they got hold of."

"Join the club."

"And, ma'am, let me add, you do not want to be tangling with anybody who could snuff out, barehanded, the likes of Newel McClanahan—thirty-eight in your handbag, or not—read me?"

"Read you, Sheriff. Thanks, for your concern."

Then a thought occurred…

"Did you tell the Panama City police about me?"

"No. Left you out of it. Will, if you want me to."

"No," I said, soft and slow. "Just wondered." In my experience local cops either do nothing, or they run roughshod over everything. For now, life would be simpler, less entailed, even safer, without their involvement.

"Why didn't you, Sheriff?"

"Call me Buford."

"Buford," I said, "why didn't you?"

"Tell them about you?"

"We both just agreed his death had a fair chance of being connected to my case. Just curious. I'm quite content to stay clear of it. But wouldn't the Panama City investigation benefit from what we know?"

"That's just it," he said. "Doubt they're especially interested in investigating aggressively a skid-row motel killing—much less, pursuing it out of state. Probably ecstatic to be able to report no leads. Which is why they asked me no questions. They didn't ask and I didn't tell. I had made an inquiry about McClanahan, he turned up dead, and they fulfilled their professional obligation to me, as a fellow law-enforcement official. If they'd wanted to know more about my interest, they'd have asked, and I'd have told them everything I knew, including your pretty little name, and number."

I smiled.

"They didn't ask, I didn't tell, because they didn't want me to."

"I get it," I said.

Pusser then told me one thing they did ask him about.

He didn't know if it would help me or not, but for what it was worth...

"Yes?"

"Coroner down there counted a dozen tattoos on McClanahan."

"Charming."

"Several were racial slurs."

I nodded. "You told me he was a big-league bigot."

"Yes," Pusser said. "And three were swastikas."

I sat straighter.

Lifted my chin.

"They found a membership card in his wallet—something called, the National White Americans Party. It's a neo-Nazi group, the TBCI tells me, founded in Georgia, 1962, thought to be defunct."

My heart began to knock, hearing the word *Nazi*.

I had never told Pusser of any Nazi connection to Butterworth's death.

In fact, when I was with him, I hadn't even been to East Liverpool yet. "Thank you, Buford," I said. "Keep me posted."

When I hung up I was already on my feet.

Pacing.

Thinking about Bobby Kaplan, of the Ohio White Nationalists League.

Now Newell McClanahan, of the National White Americans Party.

MY PLAN FOR HUNTSVILLE WAS neither subtle, nor intricate. I would go to Arnold Reinhard's home, and observe George Peter Dasch's movements, Dasch who was Reinhard's chauffeur, gardener, and brother-in-law. When I thought the time right, if no better ideas had blossomed out of my blonde brain, I would approach him with what I knew, and figure out the next step, on the fly, based on his reaction. I would not, needless to say, let him get me off somewhere alone. I would go armed, totally prepared to defend myself, should any other "accidents" appear in the offing.

Wednesday morning was clear and cold.

I took my birth-control pill, made eggs and grits, lots of butter and cream whipped into the grits. Pusser called while I was stirring the grits. I read the paper while I ate, *Today Show* on in the other room talking about Red China, denied a UN Security Council seat in favor of Taiwan. I dressed in a gold knit pull-on skirt and matching top with three buttons at the neck. When it was late enough, I phoned the guy at the State Department of Public Health who'd hired me on the diet-pill case. I told him I had to go out of town on another matter. I wanted to drop off my report, evidence, and an itemized bill. He could mail me a check, and call me later if there was more they needed. He told me to leave it all with his secretary, and I drove up there in traffic, and did.

I gassed up the Impala on the way home and didn't stop off long. I called both my parents to let them know I'd be in Huntsville, and at what motel. I'd arranged with Pearl Harwell, my widowed neighbor, to get my mail again, and pick up the newspapers. I lowered the thermostat and left the outside lights and a kitchen light burning. I put the luggage I'd packed the night before into the trunk. My revolver was in my pocketbook, loaded for bear. I laid my Sears pump-action shotgun across the backseat, covering it with the afghan off my sofa. There was a full box of twelve-gauge shells in my suitcase, also a box of .38-Special. Probably wouldn't need any of it, but I'd had enough close calls and nasty scrapes, I lived by a better-safe-than-sorry philosophy. I got my shearling coat and locked up the house and backed out of the driveway. I drove south on Grantland then right on Bradford to cut over to Franklin Pike, which Eighth Avenue became just below my neighborhood, and off of which I could pick up the interstate to Huntsville, less than two hours south.

CHAPTER 40

KARGHER TAILED SHERRY RUSSELL TO *the Cordell Hull Building beside the State Capitol. She was inside ten minutes, then set off again. He watched her get petrol then return home.* Taking no chances on die detektivin *making the Volkswagen, he parked on Benton, a block and a half north. Driving downtown, she'd taken Grantland north, than left on Benton, and right on Eighth. Following the same path again, she would turn left before his eyes, he couldn't miss her. Unfortunately Grantland doglegged before Benton, meaning her house was out of his line of sight. But he was sure to be out of hers as well, and that was key. He needed thirty minutes, no more. Thirty minutes' delay, the killer decided, then he'd drive boldly down, wheel the VW up her driveway, and march to the house with his valise. Carry out the assignment. If a neighbor described the VW to the Nashville homicide men, it would be of no matter. He planned to ditch the car quickly and leave town in the Renault. All his dealings locally had used the fake name and address on the fake Michigan driver's license. He was untraceable. When reporting to the Zyklop on schedule at 1700 hours, in person or by phone, as circumstances dictated, he expected to be able to deliver his superior excellent news.*

The half-hour lapsed.

Enough time for the Russell woman to settle in, relax, have no cause to suspect a caller at the door of having been watching, waiting for her to arrive home.

He started the motor, let out the clutch, steering left onto Grantland, the bungalow on the left, 250 meters ahead. When he reached it he stomped the brakes. The little car screeched, stood on its nose, bounced on its springs. Kargher couldn't believe his own eyes, wanted to smash something to smithereens. The Impala was gone! Again! Missed her like an idiot! Left out the other way, south. Dammit to hell. Worse—her porch lights were switched on, meaning she expected to be gone until dark, if she would return at all that night. Kargher no longer anticipated his report to the Zyklop with any relish, a confession instead to his own stupidity.

Literally growling, teeth bared, he drove on, down a few houses, U-turned and pulled alongside the curb, idling for a time. Thinking, drumming fingers. The mailman strolled by on his rounds, up to each porch. Soon after, Kargher observed, an elderly woman came out of the house next door and went over and collected the Russell woman's mail.

Kargher's heart deflated.

No telling how long she would be gone. Or what she might be doing that might have been part of his mission to stop. Quickly he put the VW back in gear, swung out and gunned along, swerving in at the Russell woman's driveway. He jumped out, leaving the car running, door open as he crossed the lawn calling for the neighbor before she could disappear inside. "Ma'am, excuse me, ma'am..."

She turned.

Kargher slowed his mountainous bulk, puffing breath fog. Fortunately she was not one of the neighborhood women he'd spoken to Monday. "I couldn't help seeing you pick up Ms. Russell's mail...Ms. Sherry Russell..."

"Yes." She got a haughty look, notwithstanding Kargher's size. He had at least a foot of height on her. He handed her one of the business cards he'd collected upon arriving in Nashville for such circumstances. This one picked up in the lobby of a storefront Nationwide Insurance agency. He gave the lady the name on the card and claimed to have had an appointment with Sherry Russell to discuss upgrading her homeowner's insurance, but she didn't seem to be home. Helpfully the neighbor told him she was sorry, but the young lady had gone out of town and she wasn't sure for how long, but several days possibly. Kargher didn't have to fake disappointment. He casually asked where out of town, as if idly curious. She told him the Russell woman hadn't said.

Kargher thanked her, wished her a good day. He made a quick scan of the vicinity, once the neighbor was inside, saw no one else outside any homes nearby. He took a chance and walked up three steps mounting the side porch of the Russell home, took out his handkerchief and loosened the bulb in the light fixture by the door enough to make it go out. Checking again for nosy neighbors, he ducked around back. One window, no door, and there was a step ladder lying on its side on the ground, against the rear wall. Two sets of floodlights burned like the other exterior lights, aimed to illuminate the backyard at night. He grabbed the ladder and rapidly scaled it to extinguish all four lights, unscrewing them a turn or two like the side-porch light

Then he drove away, crammed behind the wheel of the VW.

CHAPTER 41

I CAME INTO HUNTSVILLE, THAT island of affluence afloat in agricultural Alabama, on University Drive, passing UAH. I steered down Memorial, where oddly two Holiday Inns squatted almost opposite one another. I signaled, wheeling into the one on the left, where my reservation was, and I finally smacked into that brick wall of exhaustion, bound to come, as I checked in, for $8.00 a night. I found the room, and dropped my luggage inside, slamming and chaining the door. I pulled down my skirt and stripped out of my top. I draped them about-half-neatly over the back of a chair, and fell into bed. I slept till suppertime—jolted awake by a nightmare, two vampiric women, teeth pointed, had me spread-eagle on a brass bed somewhere. Others, distinctly male, muttering and shuffling, in a peripheral blur—like an episode of *The Twilight Zone*—the only one coming, from the side, into any kind of focus, being:

Oh God!

Dr. Alec Longhurst.

Up, cold-sweating, heart-thumping...

I peed, and opened my train case and brushed my teeth. I mopped sweat from my chest, arms, and face with a white towel, and put my skirt and top back on and some lipstick, and I got something to eat. I had a beer after supper, in the thick cigarette smoke of the adjoining lounge, and added some to the smoke. The TV behind the bar played a Wednesday Night Movie with

Suzanne Pleshette in it. I was low, and tired, and lonely. No, I didn't want a pickup. That wasn't why I was at the bar, not nearly drunk enough for a repeat of Printer's Alley. Maybe that was what I was low about, the one-night stand, or that nightmare I hadn't had in a while, or maybe just the after-effects of a rump full of Methedrine. Always like the dream was trying to tell me something I couldn't get at, beyond the grasping hand of my conscious self. Only part of it ever making any sense, in the way of a real memory, was Longhurst. Back in my room, no TV or reading or drinking, I put on warm green flannel pajamas with embroidered flowers, and cotton lace, and slept—dreamless this time—until my wind-up travel alarm jangled.

CHAPTER 42

FROM HIS FIFTH-FLOOR ROOM, Hermitage Hotel—which by that time, honestly, was in poor condition, the downward spiral beginning—Kargher phoned the Zyklop on the dot of five. He reported failure, without excuses, adding his plan for remedying matters, returning to the home that night, searching for anything related to Ralph Butterworth, or of conceivable interest to the organization. The Zyklop would know the meaning of that, better, in fact, than Kargher—the liquidator's original orders from the ODESSA executive stating Butterworth was known to have had access to sensitive information—some of it, technical, some, "shall we say, operational"—words of the Zyklop— "more specific I cannot be. You understand."

The killer nodded.

"The material is of concern both to our Kamerad..."

"Yes."

"As well as to...friends."

"Friends," Kargher said, "outside the organization?"

"Yes." The Zyklop, eyes narrowing to slits, elaborated no further, but made clear the material must be recovered. That mandate had motivated the removal of Butterworth's attaché case from the wreckage of the Oldsmobile. When Kargher took possession of it from the towing-service driver—one of those American cretins fancying themselves genuine National Socialists, who were, nevertheless, of occasional use—it contained a manuscript.

Nearly five hundred double-spaced typewritten pages, Butterworth had been taking to Memphis. Kargher knew better than to read documents of *this nature without permission, or a clear need, but had skimmed it to determine its worthiness of delivery to the Zyklop. The title page made little sense, but the Zyklop had seemed pleased:*

```
            WORKING TITLE:
ROSWELL, THE REICH, THE RING OF THE BELL:
               AN EXPOSE
                  By
         Ralph E. Butterworth
```

By the time of Kargher's second briefing in Chicago, the one dispatching him to Panama City, then Nashville, the Zyklop was less pleased. The manuscript, upon analysis, was the tip of an iceberg. The original source material was still out there, still to be recovered. The Butterworth home, outside Pittsburgh, had been covertly searched—Kargher was not told by whom—but no papers were found. In Panama City, prior to having his neck snapped expertly by Kargher, that idiot drunk McClanahan had denied all knowledge of more papers.

That left die detektivin. *She might have acquired the raw research, a possibility that simply must be seen about. That Wednesday evening in Nashville, over the phone from Chicago, the Zyklop augmented the liquidator's orders, Kargher stiffening to attention, on his feet.*

If the material were recovered from the Russell woman's home, she was to be located and killed. If not, however, Kargher was authorized to employ any means...

Any technique of persuasion...

To determine what she knew.

CHAPTER 43

THURSDAY I WAS UP BEFORE five, more or less back to the ol' Sherry Louise, which I thought, more or less, to be a good thing. I showered and did my hair, putting in a yellow knit headband, and dressed quickly like a stage actress between scenes. I wore my gold Shetland-wool pullover and zip-up-the-side plaid slacks of copper, yellow and charcoal. I put in tiny hoop earrings while rushing around, eventually stepping into a pair of brown leather brogues with block heels. Lastly I tossed on my warm shearling coat, grabbed my pocketbook and pivoted out, locking the door behind me. Puffing breath fog, stretching on gloves, I was ready and raring, outside the coffee shop when it opened. A Danish pastry and coffee were all I ordered, and I took my refill in a Styrofoam cup. At a Kwik-Chek I bought a city map and a *Huntsville News*, then drove north a mile on densely commercial Memorial and took a right on Governors where stood the Siesta Motel—COMMERCIAL RATES, MODERN AIR CONDITIONED, COLOR TV, FREE COFFEE—and the El Palacio of Mexican Foods. I headed east, the hospital and downtown on my left. Governors became residential, then wooded and curvy. After three and a half miles I found my turn north onto Monte Sano Boulevard that took a steep, ear-popping, climb through and bordering a state park, leveling off in a secluded enclave of private residences, on narrow, twisty, tree-shrouded streets. The particular narrow, twisty, tree-shrouded street I wanted, I found quickly—Panorama Drive.

It looped all about the rim of the mountaintop neighborhood for a mile and a half or so. At the eastern edge was a hairpin turn, where I located 7123 PANORAMA DR., HUNTSVILLE, the location referenced by Ralph Butterworth in the transcript of his second Arnold Reinhard interview. I traveled past, tracing around, and found a cross-street, and went around the block and came back to 7123 again. I pulled the gold Impala SS into the shade of a droopy tree diagonally opposite. I unfolded my map, pretending to be studying it confusedly, for the benefit of anyone in the house I was in front of, wondering what I was doing. Which was: watching a modern sprawled-out, shades-of-orange-brick ranch, with bay windows and lots of stone and shrubbery, and a wide driveway, and a double carport. It was on a well-manicured, downhill-sloping lot, which would probably afford the occupants an incredible view out the back, of the lush and fertile mountains of northern Alabama, a view no doubt giving the street its name.

This was the home of Dr. Arnold Reinhard.

Rocket scientist, what my FBI contact called, a "Paperclip" scientist—brought to the United States in the wake of World War II to help us beat the Soviets in the Cold War. This particular Paperclip scientist had been a top official at Peenemünde—and later, at Mittelwerk, a notorious underground V-2 guided-missile factory, which had utilized slave labor, under brutal conditions.

A genocidal war crime.

Now Reinhard was at NASA.

Special Assistant to the Director in Huntsville.

Reinhard, and his boss, Wernher von Braun, both working with many of the same men they had in Germany. Except now they were working for us. The group supposedly purged, by presidential order, of all Nazism. Yet, according to Butterworth's sources, Reinhard had joined the Nazi Party in Germany as early as 1931.

A significant date:

Years before von Braun joined, and even predating Adolf Hitler's legitimate rise to power in the German government in 1933. All suggesting Reinhard, the man in charge of building

America's Saturn moon rocket, was not just some fair-weather Nazi, joining the party when he had to, for his own preservation, as perhaps von Braun could argue. Reinhard seemed, in other words, to have been an ardent supporter of the movement, at a time before anyone could convincingly claim they had no choice but to be.

I sat there an hour with nobody bothering me.

Stranger things have happened.

Not many.

At seven-thirty on the button, a pair of men appearing to be in their sixties walked creakingly out of the ranch-style home. One, dressed in black, with a tie and white shirt and black bill cap, like chauffeurs wore, opened the rear door of a long gleaming black Mercedes with a lot of chrome, and held it, waiting for the other man to climb in. The first man had, in fact, emerged briefly, ten minutes earlier, starting the big car, and backing it from the carport. He'd left it idling, warming up in the low-twenties morning, puttering condensation from its exhaust system. Now the chauffeur stood, stooped with age, though in good approximation of military attention, while the second man climbed in back. He would be Reinhard. He wore a black winter coat he seemed to be buried under. On his head, a black Homburg, white hair a bit flyaway below the brim—a bit Albert Einstein like—and he lugged a battered briefcase. The chauffeur closed the car door solidly after the man in the Homburg, then circled arthritically around the front of the big car to the driver's side. He eased himself stiff-jointedly under the wheel, and hauled shut his door, a process almost painful to watch.

That was Dasch.

George Peter Dasch.

The scientist's brother-in-law, gardener, chauffeur. By the time the stretch Mercedes was pulling smoothly and sleekly from the driveway, I had my map folded and the Impala's V-8 growling. When they'd gone past out of sight I threaded forward, following Panorama around until the Wildwood split, then intersected Monte Sano, on which I turned and came up behind the Mercedes, grinning. I should do this for a living. They followed Governors toward town and turned off left onto Whitesburg, heading south. I let a green Dodge Dart merge between us. The Mercedes was easy enough to keep in sight, a behemoth that got me wondering just how much in salary a government rocket scientist pulled down these days.

Doubted it was enough to buy what would be quite an expensive car.

We went three and a half miles past schools, shopping plazas, signs for golf courses, until we turned west on Martin Road. After Memorial we covered almost two miles of flat pastureland and marsh, in moderately heavy morning traffic going to work on the Redstone Arsenal military base. Shy of the main gate about a hundred yards, I signaled, pulling onto the road shoulder, and rested my forearm atop my steering wheel, watching. Ahead the horizon was dotted by the distant tips of enormous monolithic test stands for rocket engines. I let the Mercedes go, knowing Dasch was driving Reinhard to his office at the Marshall Space Flight Center, somewhere deep inside the installation.

I didn't know if they'd let me through or not, but this was a low-profile stage of my investigation, and didn't want anything rocking the boat. Besides, I didn't see the necessity of eyeballing a man in a big black winter coat being dropped off at a government office building.

When I could I merged back into traffic and used a turnaround to swing through to the opposite lane, accelerating back the way we'd come, going a couple of hundred yards, before parking again on the shoulder. There was almost no traffic passing now, in this lane, this time of day, leaving the bustling installation. My view ahead was of a small mountain. I adjusted my side mirror to watch the Redstone Arsenal guard post. I found a radio station playing the Tammy Wynette hit "Stand By Your Man" that was getting skewered by feminists. I grinned, finishing my coffee. The eight-o'clock news led with a mine fire in West Virginia. I was pinching a bra strap through my sweater when, after some twenty-five minutes, I spotted the square chrome grill of the Mercedes heading back through the gate, outbound, Dasch alone now, having dropped off his charge. I killed the radio during "Folsom Prison Blues" and swung in, accelerating, twisting the wheel, behind the old retired German spy, keeping a comfortable cushion between us. He went up Memorial toward town. Eventually he drove up in front of a Sambo's and parked.

I followed him inside, after two minutes, smelling bacon frying, and took a stool at the counter. I ordered and paid for a mug of coffee and stirred a lot of cream and sugar into it, tapping the spoon. I had my morning paper and read some of it. A front-page inside-section piece said Huntsville-Madison County had the highest per capita income in Alabama, a "space economy," it said, in which most worked for the federal government, or big core firms like Boeing and Chrysler. Over my right shoulder, George Dasch was sharing a large corner red-vinyl-upholstered booth with five other men of similar age and accented English—unless they broke out in full-blown German. Couple of the old geezers shot me looks coming through the door, and one was still giving me the glad eye. I didn't think it meant they knew I was following their buddy Dasch.

I thought it meant they liked the way the plaid slacks I wore fit my can.

I reacted accordingly.

By that I mean, I did not pretend not to notice.

If too forced that could invite suspicion. Rather I glimpsed ever so briefly over, meeting their leers, then away—a perfect balance of disdain, and stroked female vanity. One of these days I'd simply have to write a guide to private investigation for young women, who try as they might, were biologically incapable of blending in like a male detective would strive to. Men noticed women. Period. And it didn't matter what we looked like. Pretty hair, straight teeth, nice bottom, sure. But, Jesus, even flat-chested and pig-faced, we'd attract male attention and comment, for that!

Dasch was about five-foot-eight with a lot of paunch. On his head, a heavy mane of silvery hair grew, combed straight back, Vitalis'ed, accenting the fair amount of balding at the recessed temples. The eyes were piercing blue, the laugh robust, from down deep, when one of the others told a joke. He had a schoolmasterly face, strong pinkish hands.

Could he have murdered Ralph Butterworth?

However he appeared today—and I'm not saying there wasn't a sternness there, a potential severity—he had been a cunning undercover operative in wartime, I had to remember that, and probably a cold-blooded knife killer. On that day, at that moment, in Huntsville, Alabama, though, all he was taking a knife to was the large white oval platter he was served, mounded with eggs and sausage and brown toast, which he buttered and jammed, washing it all down with buckets of black coffee.

While Dasch and his companions gobbled enough breakfast to feed Biafra, I slipped away to the little-girl's room. Never, I repeat never, pass up any such opportunity when on surveillance, especially if you're female. Have to put that in my how-to book. The pee department, I was convinced, was a good fifty percent of why it was so much a man's world, and might always be. The male detective could sit in his car all day filling up an old milk jug or empty juice bottle or something. Hate to imagine the mess if I tried that. And don't even get me started on menstruation. Anyway, I and my bladder were ready to walk out casually, a fashionable twenty seconds behind Dasch, as the Teutonic breakfast clutch broke up, all going separate ways, all different varieties of vehicles.

I tailed Dasch back to Panorama Drive.

Picking a different low-hanging shade tree to park beneath this time, I watched him polish the Mercedes for ten minutes, then sweep the driveway, and porches, and walks to Prussian spit-shined perfection. And after having then disappeared inside for twenty minutes, he reemerged wearing a thick gray sweater and khaki trousers and took two prancing dachshunds for a walk. I stayed put, assuming the dog walk to be what it appeared to be. I made note of the time, however. If a daily routine, might come in handy when I was ready to make contact. Ten-thirty. I lit a cigarette, drummed the fingers of one hand on the steering wheel as I started to smoke it. I popped open the under-dashboard ashtray and used it, then snapped on my radio, twisting the knob. Tuning in a station, hearing "A Whiter Shade of Pale," then "To Sir with Love." Great movie, though it made me even happier I hadn't become a teacher. I was prepared to be quite bored for as long as I decided to maintain this vigil, wondering if I should try making friends with some hausfrau, who'd let me use her bathroom, maybe spy on the Reinhards from the comfort of a living-room couch.

Probably not.

Couldn't be sure I wouldn't land up in the enemy's camp. I knew from Butterworth's papers, for instance, that Erchanbolt Ritter, that other Peenemunde alumnus he'd interviewed, lived on this same—

Then something interesting did, in fact, happen.

A young woman exited the Reinhard house.

I rose in my seat, snagged up binoculars, managing a pretty good look, before she swung out of her carport, shifted gears expertly, and sped off in a sea-blue Karmann-Ghia convertible with the top down. I followed.

On instinct.

She was about a size sixteen, my height, her build what my mother would call boxy. Not fat, but thick-waisted, corn-fed, athletic. Her hair was short, straight, light brown, and boyishly cut off the ears. She was large-busted, but appeared at first less well-endowed than she was, owing to that straight torso, lack of hip definition. She could be the odd girl in the photos in bed with Ralph Butterworth.

Sporting masquerade-party eyewear and that Frederick's of Hollywood sheer nightie. The hair wasn't right, but I'd already surmised the woman in the pictures wore a wig.

That day, as I trailed her out onto Governors Drive, west toward town, she wore a jaunty bright-red beret and matching red two-piece jersey dress with a V-neck, white turtleneck dickey, and pleated knee-length skirt.

Who was she?

Reinhard's wife was dead.

Killed at Peenemünde.

No mention of remarriage in Butterworth's biographical sketch, though I didn't know for sure he hadn't remarried. This could be a wife. But, there'd been a daughter, too, at Peenemünde. Five years old then, who had barely survived the bomb strike on the family's shelter that killed her mother.

Five, in 1943…

Make her thirty today.

The woman in red driving the Karmann-Ghia could easily be thirty. I trailed her to a post office in west-central Huntsville for the 35805 zip code—which was not the zip code for the

Reinhard residence. Meaning, she should not be having mail delivered there, right? She went in wearing black gloves with a black purse in the crook of her arm. She came out carrying several thick letters. Or rather, envelopes. I knew not what they contained. We drove north to a shopping plaza on Oakwood, off University. She buzzed into a slot close to AUDREY'S BEAUTY SALON, while I took up a position in the center of the parking lot, well back from the little blue Karmann-Ghia. I stayed put long enough to be sure the woman was actually getting her hair done, meaning she'd be awhile. Eventually, I got out, crossed the asphalt, and strolled alongside the convertible's passenger side. It was sunny, having warmed since early morning, so I'd shed my shearling coat. I pretended to be admiring the sports car, the interior an easy scan, top still down. It looked new, and I found myself wondering yet again, in amazement, how much NASA paid these Paperclip people.

I didn't see the letters in the car.

A quick scan of the area didn't show me any busybodies paying attention to what I was doing, so I darted my hand in, punched open the glove box.

No letters.

I shut it back with a click.

She'd taken them inside, carried in her purse. Back in the Impala I drove to a red-roofed Burger Chef on University I'd spotted the day before. After testing their plumbing, I stood in line and ordered, to go, a Big Shef, fries, and a large strawberry milk shake. I paid the guy in the paper hat my $1.12, and ate at the wheel of my car, back watching Audrey's Beauty Salon. "Elegance in Coiffure Design," said the slogan in the window. While there I saw two different women leave, freshly elegantly designed, carrying envelopes, which could have been from the batch Fraulein Kraut picked up at the post office that was not hers. Of course, I didn't know anything for sure—still, I'd been to a lot of beauty parlors, and couldn't recall ever having left one with an envelope, much less seeing two women in a row doing so, after a third arrived with a bunch of them. Even if I had known for sure those women were carrying envelopes obtained from Fraulein Kraut, I still didn't know what, if anything, it meant. Perhaps the girl in red was president of the ladies auxiliary of the Huntsville Dachshund Fancier's Association, and she was doling out the monthly newsletter.

She came out after ninety minutes, jumping in the Karmann-Ghia. I hung back, drumming fingertips on the wheel, long enough to let a faded blue Chevy Nomad station wagon, sixty or sixty-one model, pull between me and the convertible—camouflage, so I would look less like a tail. We all turned east on Oakwood out of the shopping center then north at the next light onto Blue Springs Road. Next stop was about two and a half miles up at a State Farm Insurance office next to a YMCA.

What happened there stunned me.

I was already suspicious of the Chevy.

It seemed to be sticking to the Karmann-Ghia like glue—when suddenly, it, the Chevy, pulled off into the YMCA parking lot. Immediately after that, without having given any previous sign she would, not even a blinker, the boxy woman in red turned off, parked, and went inside the insurance office.

I drove past.

Craning back.

Jaw sagging.

The driver of the Nomad was not only tracking the Karmann-Ghia, like I was—but had known in advance of the State Farm stop! I swung around, U-turning, and coasted back partway before steering to the side, waiting, idling. Almost immediately the woman in red came out with more envelopes and drove to a small dental office, belonging to a Dr. Kashell, less than a mile away on Winchester Road, the Chevy tailing, me bringing up the rear. More envelopes.

My map showed Winchester tied up with Memorial at a point ahead roughly five miles north of downtown. Indeed, we all turned down Memorial, and eventually made a liquor-store stop at Northside Plaza. The girl in red did, that is, I and the Nomad driver just watching. The proprietor of the liquor store, a thin elderly man, with a shock of black hair, followed her out after they'd transacted business. He loaded a case of—I grabbed my binoculars, sharpening the focus—French champagne into the front-end trunk of the Karmann-Ghia, and slammed it shut. He bowed to her, smartly. At that point, I pivoted my binoculars onto the Chevy. My vantage point wasn't good, but keeping my presence, and interest in all these goings-on, a secret took priority for now. All I could tell was the station wagon was driven by another woman—girl's day out in Rocket City—and she was a tiny thing, as if she could barely see over her own dashboard.

Russet-haired.

Neck like a stem.

We were off again.

Our three-car parade snaked down congested Memorial west of downtown and went straight on through the intersection with Governors.

This took me by surprise, Governors being the turnoff back to the Monte Sano neighborhood where the Reinhards lived, and where I was assuming the Karmann-Ghia was returning to. Instead we all went another two miles south, passing my own motel, to Airport Road. Turned east. Over a railroad track, golf course on the left, shopping center on the right, we took the first left after that onto a little side street called Chateau Drive. Following that around, it dead-ended into the CHATEAU DEVILLE APARTMENTS. The Chevy and I danced our little dance of furtive parking—I was really keeping my distance by then, hard as it was for me to believe at least one of these other women hadn't yet realized what was going on. Well, only one of us had to, and I was glad it was me. The girl in the red beret carried without too much seeming strain the case of champagne, all the envelopes piled on top, up a flight of stairs to the upper-story apartment unit on the right, as I observed the building from the front. The beige brick facade had a large brass "F" bolted onto it, the roof mansard style, dark gray-brown. I'd liked to have checked what name labeled the mailbox belonging to that apartment. I didn't dare, however, show myself yet to the petit redhead in the Chevy.

Forty-five minutes lapsed.

Almost three o'clock.

I was kneading deeply, grimacing and grunting, my own neck and shoulders, and wishing I had one of those empty milk jugs to try my luck with, when Fraulein Kraut in the bright-red hat and dress emerged, locking up the apartment, and returned to the Karmann-Ghia, strutting, carrying a new stack of envelopes in one hand. I judged them to be new because they didn't appear to be as thick as the others. She drove away, west on Airport, and slid to a stop, shifting to neutral, beside one of those blue-and-red U.S. MAIL boxes, planted in the middle of the Westbury Shopping Center parking lot.

The envelopes were deposited and the three of us went back the other way along Airport, passing the Holy Spirit School, the Holy Spirit Catholic Church, the Trinity Methodist Kindergarten, the Trinity Methodist Church, Bruno's Super Market, a bank and a gas station. North on Whitesburg we passed a drive-in theater and a Church of Christ before the road went residential. Still, as we continued, there was the First Christian Church, the Huntsville Conservation Synagogue, the Redeemer Lutheran Church.

Eclectic town.

A right fork onto California got us back to Governors. This time the Karmann-Ghia indeed headed off in the direction of Monte Sano—almost certainty going home. The Chevy broke off the tail at that point, reaching the same conclusion, and drove straight north through the intersection, passing some medical buildings, and on up through a residential neighborhood bordering downtown.

I stuck with the Chevy.

My very full bladder notwithstanding.

I knew where to find the Karmann-Ghia again.

At Pratt Avenue we turned left, went half a mile, and turned north on Meridian. Where that crossed Oakwood, the southeast corner, sprawled a vast complex, I later learned was the former Lincoln Mills, a textile mill closed in 1957, and purchased by Huntsville Industrial Associates, to provide a high-technology infrastructure, that had not at the time existed, to support rocket development at Redstone Arsenal. A very space-age-looking sign with a solar system model or something atop it said:

HUNTSVILLE
H

INDUSTRIAL
I

CENTER
C

Below that, a listing of tenants:

NASA-KSC	BOEING
NASA-MSFC	BROWN ENG. CO.
	HAYES INTERNATIONAL CORP.
	SOUTHERN BELL TELEPHONE
	SOUTHERN CAFETERIA OPER. CO.
	TENN. VALLEY TECHNICAL SCHOOL

North another mile we ended up in a mid-to-lower-middle-class neighborhood of small brick homes and narrow winding streets on the northeast fringes of Huntsville. The Chevy Nomad went to a house on South Plymouth Road, and after getting the mail, the woman, who was short, slender, fine-boned, wearing a navy-blue dress trimmed with white pique around the neck, went inside. Ten minutes later, a school bus spewed out some of its load of high-school kids up the street, and two, a boy and a girl walked down together, carrying schoolbooks, and let themselves inside the house with the reddish-haired woman. The girl, a pretty brunette, wore a gold blouse, checkered A-line skirt, knee socks, and penny loafers. Her brother—I assumed them to be siblings—had a short neat haircut, gray slacks, white tennis shoes, an athletic jacket of burgundy-red wool, with white vinyl sleeves, and a varsity letter, a big "**L**," sewn to the front. I copied the address and the name on the mailbox—R. D. LINDELL—and the Alabama license of the Chevy.

I backtracked to a Shell station. They filled the gas tank while I used the relatively filthy lavatory outside the yellow, red, and white building. I returned the restroom key, thumbed some coins in a machine, and yanked out a bottle of Coke, and pried off the cap. I signed the gas ticket. The guy plucked my card from his little charge-ticket tray, and I thanked him. The charge would be recorded as an expense billed against Buzz Hutcheson's advance. Various tanks filled and emptied, well ogled by the attendant, I returned to South Plymouth Road and staked out the house until almost six-thirty. That was when a dingy white Ford Galaxie parked in the driveway, only a little newer, and modestly less shabby, than the station wagon. A tall thin man dragged out, retrieved the evening paper from the box, and slogged inside to his family carrying a battered satchel. He wore black slacks, a white shirt, a tie loosened at the neck, and a tan windbreaker. He seemed tired. I knew I was. I waited a few minutes for good measure, drove to the end of the driveway, and through binoculars read the Ford's license number, and wrote it down. Then I drove off, calling it a day.

CHAPTER 44

BACK AT THE HOLIDAY INN, I picked my feet up one at a time, hopping, prying off my shoes, then half peeled my sweater up and unhooked my bra in back, groaning. I tugged the sweater back down and brushed my teeth, and hit my hair with a brush about three times, and sprayed it. Then I paced in stocking-feet, a hand back on my hip, the other clamping my temples. It was late to be calling, but I decided to chance it, and charged to my business number in Nashville a long-distance call to the FBI Birmingham field office. After waiting on hold, I was connected with Agent Alan Legate's Bostonian brogue. "Didn't expect you there this late," I said.

"I aim, Ms. Russell, to give the taxpayers their money's worth."

"I really do, Alan, think you might be developing a sense of humor."

"Only what Mr. Hoover issues us."

I laughed aloud, in spite of myself.

"I need a favor Alan," I said, still clucking.

"Mean, *another* favor."

"Yes, that's what I mean," I said, "but it's insulting you're counting them."

"Shoot."

I gave him three Alabama license tags, asking for names, and if possible occupations, of the registered owners. They belonged to the Karmann-Ghia, the Chevy Nomad, and the Ford Galaxie, the latter belonging to the husband, presumably, of the Chevy driver. Legate asked: "This related to the matter we discussed Monday?"

"If I say, yes, does it move me to the head of the line?"

He uttered a half-amused, "Humph…"

Then said he'd see what he could do. Wasn't sure why I felt the need to be evasive, but it just felt like a good default position, since any information I might turn over to Legate, strictly speaking, belonged first and foremost to my paying client, Buzz Hutcheson, not the United States Government. I gave Legate my motel telephone and room numbers, adding, "I don't have my answering service in Nashville anymore, since I got the machine. If you don't reach me here, leave a call-back number with the front desk."

"Right."

I thanked him, hung it up, and from where I sat surveyed the room's yellow-and-beige-striped wallpaper. I was starving. Standing, I re-hooked my bra, put my shoes back on, and donned my coat, getting back to near freezing outside. I locked the door and took a brisk walk to a MR. STEAK, down Memorial. I felt like walking, looking at the stars, stretching my legs, having spent most of that eternally long day behind the wheel of my car. All this exercise would probably knock a thrombus loose, and kill me, if nobody tried to mug me first. My gun was in my pocketbook. Wouldn't help the thrombus, but would be more than a match for any muggers or rapists materializing out of the night. At the restaurant, I had two Scotches, two cups of Sanka, two trips to the salad bar, and one big top sirloin, medium-well, which I did some manly damage to, never one to eat like a bird. I skipped dessert, and strolled back on a full stomach, and didn't have to shoot anybody going or coming. Merely curious, I checked out the tenant listings of two office buildings I passed. A sampling: Martin Marietta, TRW, Thiokol, Texas Instruments, Beckman Instruments, Boeing, Vaughn Electrosources, Beech Aircraft, Pratt & Whitney, Raytheon, GE, Philco-Ford, U.S. Steel, Bell, Tektronic, Ling-Temco Vought, Bendix Aerospace, Northrop, General Dynamics, Motorola, Hughes Aircraft, Lockheed, RCA, General Dynamics, McDonnell, Goodyear,

ITT, Western Electric, Emerson, Westinghouse, North American Aviation.

I sensed a trend.

I was undressed, had a flannel gown on for bed, a Scotch half finished, and my underclothes and stockings rinsed out in the sink, drying on the shower rod—when the phone rang.

Legate.

"That was fast," I said, sitting on the edge of the bed, legs crossed, rubbing up and down prickly stubble on my shin, before reaching for the Holiday Inn memo pad, and green ballpoint, which I clicked sharply.

"Find something?"

"Indeed. Hope it's not too late to be calling."

"Not at all."

"Got a pen?"

"Yes."

"First, the 1968 Volkswagen Karmann-Ghia"—he repeated the license—"registered to a Miss Veronika, spelled with a *K*, Reinhard, same Huntsville address as Dr. Arnold Reinhard, who, as I am sure you know, is her father."

"I guessed," I said, firing up a Kent. "Thanks for confirming."

"Also, same address as our old Abwehr friend, George Peter Dasch."

"Uh huh," I said. "Her maternal uncle, I believe."

"You might have told me," he said, "when I asked."

"And rob you of the satisfaction of figuring it all out for your little G-man self?"

"Have I figured something out? If I have, pray tell, enlighten me."

"Join the club," I said, huffing.

"No occupation so far for the Reinhard girl," he went on. "The 1960 Chevrolet Nomad and the 1963 Ford Galaxie, both registered in the same name—Robert David Lindell, age forty-five." He read me the South Plymouth Road, Huntsville address I knew. "His wife is a naturalized citizen, native of Great Britain, Daphne Poole Lindell. He brought her home after the war. She's a registered nurse, works part-time, weekends, at Huntsville Hospital, when her husband can be home with the children.

They have…let's see, four, two at home."

"You know all this—*how?*"

"Seem surprised, Ms. Russell. Why cawl you if you didn't think the FBI were all-knowing?"

"You don't get this kind of information from the department of motor vehicles, especially not"—I glimpsed my travel alarm—"at almost ten at night."

"Lindell's a thermal engineer with Boeing, subcontractor on the moon-shot, at NASA, up at Redstone. We've run security clearances on all of them. There's a file on the Lindells here at the field office." I heard a shrug in his conversation. "Clean, as far as we know, if that interests you."

"Very much," I said. "Anything else?"

"Depends," he said, "on what you're looking for, doesn't it?"

I twisted a corner of my mouth. Okay, he wouldn't spoon-feed me, or maybe he really didn't know more, without more digging, prompted by yours truly. "I'll take that as a *no* for now," I said, "but I'll call back if I think of something?"

"Somebody here," Legate said, "will be able to reach me twenty-four hours a day."

My eyes narrowed to slits.

He added, "Tell you what…"

"What?"

"Use that name…you gave Monday, if you call back."

I blinked, scowled slightly to myself.

Sue Williams, he meant, though I didn't say it on the open line.

Somebody listening?

"Have a good night, Alan," I said, with an exhale.

"You as well."

Connection broken, I bolted up, rubbing my brow, then looked around, glowering at the phone. Then flinging my arms for no reason, I went to the dresser by the TV, grabbed my bottle of Dewar's, and splashed some more on top of my half-finished drink, and added ice from the bucket. I swirled the glass, and took a large slurp. Then I hauled over my portable typewriter, and started composing a set of investigative notes for the day. One leg folded under me I typed on the bed, banging keys rhythmically till the bell rang, hitting the return lever, resuming, about every other line pausing for more Scotch slurped out of the ice. All the while thinking Special Agent Alan Legate was being awfully damned helpful.

And not, I didn't think, because he was all wracked up with guilt over getting me shot in the leg last year.

Didn't know what it was.

I stopped typing.

Sighed heavily, the room's furnace cycling on.

Pressing the wet glass to my temple.

I trusted him.

Yet I didn't.

You know.

He was a good guy who mistakenly thought he could be a good guy and still be a loyal cog in the system.

I gnashed my teeth.

That was Alan Legate's problem.

That, and his crush he had on me.

CHAPTER 45

FRIDAY MORNING WAS BRIGHTLY BLUE and very cold. First thing, I drove to the house on South Plymouth in the Edgemont section of Huntsville. No sneaking around this time. I turned in, pretty as you please, and parked in the driveway of the Lindell house, nosing up to the rear bumper of the Chevy Nomad in the single carport. The Ford was gone, Robert Lindell by then having gone off to work. It was close to eight-thirty. The children should be in school. With luck I'd find Daphne Lindell home alone.

With further luck I wouldn't scare her to death, and maybe I could get some cooperation. One of those times—surprisingly many—when it was an asset in my profession not to be over six feet, big and burly. I tapped up onto a small recessed front porch and rang the bell. I held my pocketbook at my side as I waited, right hand on my hip. I wore a jacket and skirt of dark brown, and a light-gold shell, which matched the windowpane plaid on the front of the jacket. I heard a dog race to the door, nails scraping hardwood, barking, yelping, a woman's voice after it telling it to get back, be quiet. The dog turned out to be a chestnut-red-and-white Cocker Spaniel named Winston, the woman answering the door, perhaps no more than five feet tall, maybe a hundred pounds wet. She had the reddish-brown poufed hair I'd seen yesterday, and wore a red corduroy housecoat. She said hello to me with a voice of authority—far

246

from timid, despite her petite build, with an accent she later identified to me as Southern Welsh.

"Daphne Lindell?" I said.

"Yes." She bent her head back, assessing me down the length of a fine-featured nose, suddenly holding herself, I realized, as if she were tall.

"My name is Sherry Russell. I'm a private detective from Nashville."

I held out my card.

She unhooked and pushed open her screen to take it.

"May I come in?"

"Of course." She backed out of the way, and I squealed the screen door fully open on its spring, and went through. "What is this about?"

The dog came up as I pivoted, swiping my bangs, Daphne closing the door. Then she faced around, glimpsing my card, then me again. The spaniel was sniffing my skirt and pocketbook, thinking about licking them, at least I hoped that was all he was thinking. "Winston! Be good!" the lady of the house commanded, forceful, but not loud, and he scurried, toenails clicking, along the foyer to the back of the house.

"It's about," I said, "Veronika Reinhard."

She blasted a hot look up at me.

Lifting eyebrows.

Not even trying to be coy.

She said acidly: "I see."

Leading me through to a formal living room, off the foyer, she invited me to sit. The room was small and excellently though not expensively furnished, crammed with Victorian-looking bric-a-brac that would be nightmarish to dust. I smoothed my skirt behind me and took a seat upon a satin-upholstered wingback, placing my handbag on the floor, and removing my gloves. I laid them on my lap and folded my hands on top, then looked up waiting for my hostess to say more. She did, cinching her arms tightly.

"Did she hire you?"

"No," I said. "I was following her too. That's how I found you."

She grinned out one side of her twisting mouth, saying,

"Humph," with a lilt.

Then: "If you'll excuse me a few minutes," she said, "I'll dress proper."

"Certainly."

"Make yourself at home. Hot water is on the stove if you'd care for a cuppa tea."

"Thank you."

She was back in ten minutes in a red dress that was not new, buttoned to the neck, with a shirred bodice, belted at the waist. She offered me a small Danish cookie out of a blue round tin, then closed the lid carefully back, and placed the tin atop a small ornate writing desk. She settled daintily upon a love seat, the only other seating the room had space for. She crossed her legs, angled her body in the love seat to face me, and held her spine very straight. She laced her fingers and rested them on her knee. There was a large round mirror in a gilded frame above the writing desk, and a curio full of ceramic birds against the wall, to the right of the archway from the foyer. I heard the dog lapping slobberingly in the kitchen.

Daphne's eyes blinked suddenly as if she were switching on.

"Now, tell me what this is all about," she said.

"Why were you following Veronika Reinhard?"

"Why were you?" she said.

My right eyebrow lifted.

Then I glimpsed aside, flickering over an antique gold clock under a glass dome, then back. "It's complicated," I admitted. "I'm investigating a car crash in which a man, named Butterworth, was killed. My client wants to know if it was really an accident, or was it murder?"

"How very Hitchcockian."

"Yes." I smiled, washing my cookie down with a sip of tea, then leaning, I chinked the cup back into its saucer. "I have reason to believe," I resumed, relaxing back in my chair, "one of the last people to see Mr. Butterworth alive could have been Miss Reinhard's uncle, a man named George Dasch, who lives with the Reinhards, working as their chauffeur and gardener. And, possibly, Butterworth may have been with Veronika herself, the day of his death."

"I see."

I produced the snapshot of Butterworth his wife had provided (the formal Olan Mills portrait, wearing a gray suit and striped tie, not one of the ones in bed with the masked woman) and showed it to Daphne Lindell. "Have you seen him?" I asked. She took it, and studied it, taking out her reading glasses, studying it again through them, before removing the glasses, staring up at me.

"No." She gave her head a small shake as she passed it back, and I said:

"Your turn."

"I don't like Germans," she said. "More accurately, I hate them. With every fiber of my being. I hope I'm not being unclear. I don't like the way they've taken over this town. And I think they're...*up* to something."

"Anything specific?"

"I don't know what they're up to, but it is something. I have a feeling it's illegal, almost certainly underhanded. And I am not a paranoiac."

"I didn't say you were. Obviously I have suspicions, too, or I wouldn't be here. I'm hoping we can help each other, share...information...?"

I shrugged one shoulder slightly.

Behind her eyes I could see she was thinking the proposition over. After a moment she pushed out her red-lipsticked mouth, and gave me a nod. "She's a rather hideous creature," she said, taking a sip of the tea with milk she'd poured for herself, eyeing me over the rim, "don't you think?"

"Veronika, you mean? Looks like she could try out for the Russian Olympic weightlifting team, if that's what you mean. But hideous, or not, that isn't a reason to follow her all over town."

"What could you surmise from what you witnessed yesterday, Miss Russell?"

"Call me Sherry," I said.

Then inhaled deeply.

Emptied my lungs.

"I saw her," I said, "pick up a stack of mail from a zip code not hers, then go to a beauty parlor, have her hair done, and distribute that mail to other women at the shop."

Daphne Lindell gave me a look with her eyes, seeming to

indicate she might be impressed with me after all. "From there," I continued, "she picked up more envelopes from an insurance agent and a dentist, which I'm not sure *what* to make of, then she purchased champagne, and delivered it to an upstairs apartment."

She nodded.

"What you saw yesterday," she said, "was Veronika Reinhard's routine every Thursday. I've followed her, must be, a dozen times on a Thursday and seen the same. I have also, at other times, followed her to the airport, and seen her board nonstop flights to Los Angeles and Houston."

I jotted that down. "Any idea if she got connecting flights from those destinations?"

"I don't know."

I nodded, thinking.

"The women at the beauty parlor..." Daphne said, my hazel eyes flickering back. "There are ten, five every other week. They each receive an envelope, which she picks up from the post office prior to going to the salon. I have followed each of them as well at various times. All are Paperclip dependents. Do you know what that means?"

"Yes," I said.

She looked at me. More brightly than ever, nodding. "The envelopes contain money—cash—and a lot of it. I've seen enough of them opened by the women immediately, in their cars, the bills fanned greedily."

I twisted my mouth.

"That's interesting," I said. "What do you know about the apartment?"

"I know she entertains there."

"Entertains...? Meaning...men?"

"Most Friday and Saturday nights she throws big parties. Like she's the Great Gatsby or something. Men and women arrive, after dark, separately, often in groups."

"The men arriving in groups," I said, "and the women in different groups?"

"Yes."

"Arrive how?"

"Limousines. The women first, to get ready. They come after

the caterers. And they're dressed like it's for dinner and a show in Vegas, let me tell you."

"How many? Male guests, say?"

"Varies. Say a dozen, sometimes more, sometimes less."

"How late does this go on?"

"I took a thermos and stayed for the whole thing one time, earlier this year. My husband thought I was working a night shift. I'm a part-time nurse."

"I know." I gave a sisterly smile. "I'm an RN, by training, myself."

She lifted her brow.

And tea cup in acknowledgement.

"And yet," she said, coyly, "you do this?"

"Nursing has its pluses. Steady paycheck for instance. But, I guess, I'm not a good order taker."

There was a lot of understanding, as she nodded, lurking behind her look.

"How late?" I prompted.

"She was sweeping the last of them out at dawn."

I bit my lower lip lightly.

Pulling it from my teeth.

"Don't suppose you have direct knowledge of what really goes on?"

"I've not been inside, no. There's music, dancing, drinking, eating, smoking, lots of smoking. Fairly sure some of the time there's gaming."

"Gambling? Illegal gambling?"

"I can't prove that but it has seemed that way to me."

"Sex?" I asked.

"I wouldn't know, but one can speculate, can't one?"

"Indeed," I said. "Mrs. Lindell, I don't suppose you've followed any of these limousines. See where the men went back to, when the party broke up?"

"No. Believe it or not, I have a life."

"I know. I saw your children arriving home yesterday. Lovely family."

"Thank you."

"Yet, you do this."

"Yes."

"Do you know who the men are, at these parties?"

"I know they're German…" She shrugged. "Many at least: I've heard them speaking German amongst themselves coming and going. Especially going, after a night of drinking and carousing."

I nodded.

"Are they all German?" she resumed. "I assume so but I can't prove that. I know one by name."

"Oh?"

I readied my pen.

"Max Kiesel." She spelled it. "He's a Paperclip engineer who works with my husband's team at the HIC Building. That is, the Huntsville Industrial Center."

She'd pronounced it: "Hick Building."

I told her I'd seen the place.

"The Americans call him Kaiser Kiesel," she said. "It was he who set me on the path, shall we say, of my unusual hobby."

"Following Germans?"

"Following Nazis."

My chin jolted upward.

"My husband was griping one day, year or so back, about a shiny new car Kaiser Kiesel was driving. Far above his pay grade, Robert said over his eggs and ham, and look at the cars that were all we could afford. Then he said it had always been that way with them. So pretentious. In the early days, after the war, the Germans were actually hired for lower salaries, by the Army, than American scientists and engineers, because they were desperate. They wanted to be in America, out of the devastation of Europe, especially out of reach of the Soviets, who needed them as much as the Americans."

"To fight the Cold War."

"Quite. My husband got over his little snit. He's like that. But it inspired me to follow Mr. Kiesel, see what he did when he wasn't working. It was all quite a bore, actually; it wasn't until a month later I happened to spot him going into one of Madame Reinhard's parties. He drove himself by the way—you had asked me earlier if I had ever seen where the limousines pick up and drop off."

I nodded.

"Anyway, eventually I decided to follow his wife instead."

She grinned, marveling at her own cleverness. "And guess what?"

I tilted my head.

"What?"

"She turned out to have a regular every-other-Thursday beauty-parlor appointment, at that place, Audrey's, where she would meet up with..."

"Veronika Reinhard," I said, brightly.

"And receive..."

"An envelope," I said, nodding, "stuffed full of money."

"Right." She swung a small balled-up fist.

"Explaining Kiesel's new car," I said. "Probably Veronika's Karmann-Ghia."

"It was then I started to follow Veronika Reinhard," Daphne told me, "time permitting, instead of the Kiesels. And she is anything but boring. You got a taste of that yesterday."

"You follow her on Thursdays, you said..."

My eyes squinting, with a thought.

"Often," she said. "Some other days of the week as well, but they haven't tended to prove as enlightening. Grocery shopping. The library."

"It was a Thursday—October thirty-first—when she might have been with the man whose death I'm investigating. Sure you didn't see him, or a man who might've been him, at the apartment?"

"Thirty-first, you say? That explains it. I didn't follow her that day. There was a Halloween costume contest at my children's school. I went to snap pictures."

I nodded.

"Too bad," I said, with a sigh. "So, Veronika Reinhard augments the incomes of Paperclip scientists by channeling tax-free cash to them, via their wives."

"Precisely."

"Where does the money come from? She doesn't grow it in her father's backyard."

"I'm afraid," she said, "my investigative—

Pronounced in-*vest*-igative.

—wherewithal has not penetrated that deeply."

"I see." I ran the tip of my tongue along my lower lip, and placed my empty cup in its saucer carefully over onto a mahogany occasional table, inlaid with brass. There was a small lamp on it, a flowery candy dish, and a tiny brass cannon. "I'll get us more tea," Daphne Lindell said. "Come along dear."

I followed her through to the small knotty-pine kitchen adjoining the tiny living room. The curtains on the kitchen window, looking onto the front lawn, were white and laced. The smell of the dog was stronger here. I crossed my arms, bumping my brown-skirted hip against the stove while she poured from a ceramic pot, with bluebirds on it. "I like you, Sherry," she said, adding milk and sugar to the cups. "Glad you popped in. I wish it were later…" She turned with my cup and I took it. I was six inches taller than she was, not counting my heels. "If it were closer to the cocktail hour I'd treat you to one of my special Beefeater Gibsons, two onions."

She raised two fingers.

"Mmm. Alas, though, it is early, even for me."

Daphne laughed.

Laughed hugely for a small person.

"Mrs. Lindell—"

"Call me Daph, please, my dear."

"Daph, you started out, saying you hate Germans." I was pacing, slow-heel-tapping, about the perimeter of the, I'd guess, twelve-by-twelve kitchen. "Then specified Nazis." I looked at her. "Surely we can agree there's a distinction?"

I swallowed some tea.

"I'm not sure," Daphne answered.

Sourly.

"Well, we can at least agree the Nazis deserve to be hated," I said.

I was watching her from my height.

"Why might you hate Germans in general?"

CHAPTER 46

"WHY DO YOU THINK?" DAPHNE Lindell said in reply to my query about hating Germans.

"I know you're British," I said, "and were there during the war."

"I was in London, during the Blitz, taking my nurse's training."

"I can only imagine what you saw, how frightening…"

"My father was a Welsh coal miner. He became sick. Massive fibrosis of the lungs. Black lung. What they now call, *coal worker's pneumoconiosis.*"

I nodded. Unsure where this was leading.

"There was a relative lull in the bombings from 1941, all the way to '44. I was working as a nurse in a London milit'ry hospital. Life was relatively good. I brought my parents to London to live with me, so my mother and I could care for my father, who could barely breathe, practically bedridden. My sisters stayed in the country, as was common, and my brother was in the army, a paratrooper, a *Red Devil*, as we called them. Like you Yanks' *Screaming Eagles.* Anyway, the bombings started again in early 1944, but petered out, May or so. We survived that. My sisters begged my parents to return to Wales.

"I resisted. He needed so much care. Maybe I needed him, too, his strength."

My eyes narrowed.

Chin down, listening.

"Then came the Buzz Bombs, in June. In August, one hit the house we were living in. I was at work. My parents died instantly. Month later my brother was machine-gunned to death in Holland."

I blinked.

"Sorry."

"Did you lose anyone in the war, Sherry?"

"My father fought, a naval officer, the Pacific. He came home, thank heavens. I was five when the war ended."

She nodded.

"Yes, Sherry, I hate Germans. That answer your question?"

"Of course."

"I hate these rocket people most especially. How they're lorded over, honored, revered. Their butchery forgotten, in this frantic race to the moon, this over-obsession with the Russians."

"Did you know," I said, "Veronika Reinhard lost her mother to British bombs?"

Her eyes flashed.

Not, I thought, with sympathy.

"Then I suppose fate is just after all," she said, then asked:

"Do you know Shakespeare, Sherry?"

"A little, actually."

"*Lear, Act V*: 'I am no less in blood than thou art, Edmund; if more, the more th' hast wronged me. My name is Edgar, and thy father's son. The gods are just…'"

DAPHNE LINDELL HAD FORGOTTEN ABOUT her tea; it was cold when she next took a sip. She set it aside, grimacing, and walked petitely rigid back into the living room. I placed my cup and saucer next to hers, and followed.

"Just one more question, Daph, if I may…"

She folded herself back into the loveseat, and waited.

I remained standing, pacing the tiny room in my high-heels. "These *parties* of Veronika's sound like rather loud affairs," I said, "and they go on *all night*? Don't the neighbors complain, call the manager, the cops, especially if it's an every-week thing?"

"They happen every week she's in town," Daphne said, "as far as I've observed, but, yes, I do see your point."

"And?"

"First—the apartment-complex manager—he is a man named Hermann Wessel."

She pronounced the name, no doubt correctly:

Vessel.

"I see. What else?"

"You saw Veronika Reinhard go into only one of the apartments yesterday, but she actually leases all four apartments in that building. The one she entered, upper floor, right side..."

"Yes."

"That's the one she uses when it's just her, daylight hours, her base of operations, I s'pose. Single women do live in the other three, to make everything appear legitimate, but I've followed them, as well. Each is employed as a housekeeper, or in one case a nanny, in a Paperclip scientist's home. And I've seen all of then dolled up, wearing trollopy French maids' uniforms, for the parties. I assume they serve drinks and hors d'oeuvres to the guests. And, to cycle back to your point, yes, I suppose they do have to keep it all down to a dull roar, don't they, so's not to disturb the rest of the complex intolerably, but nobody's having to hear it through a wall, or across a breezeway."

"You've been very thorough, Mrs.— I mean, Daph."

"Thank you."

She flickered a brow.

"I'm well motivated."

"What were you planning to do," I asked, "with all this, had I not come along? You've invested quite a lot of time and effort, after all."

"Well, one must be practical, mustn't one? My husband needs his job, and there aren't a lot of other moonshot programs around, are there?"

I nodded.

Knotted my arms.

"So," she went on, "I can't make too many waves on my own. I suppose I figured I'd learn as much as I could, and wait for the right opportunity, if that ever came. Perhaps if a scandal of some sort broke out, through no fault of my own..."

"You'd be ready and willing to fan the flames."

"Precisely. Oh, and Sherry, you asked about sex, at the

parties?"

I curled a brow.

"Speaking of scandal...yes?"

"I have seen a number of couples go in and out—one couple at a time, mind you—in and out of the upper left apartment. Across the breezeway from the one Veronika entered yesterday. Pardon me, for having a dirty, filthy mind."

I nodded.

"Thank you," I said, and put my notepad and pen in my pocketbook and hooked it in the crook of my arm, starting for the foyer. "I'll leave you to the rest of your morning."

She darted up.

Rather desperately, I thought.

"Was I helpful?"

She threw the words out.

"Very."

I stopped, pivoted.

"In fact, you can take the weekend off."

"*Pardon?*"

"I'll attend the party tonight," I said. "And tomorrow night."

"May I help?" Daphne asked, bursting her eyes.

They were jade.

I filled my lungs slowly, blew them empty. "I want to know where the limousine or limousines pick up and drop off the men and the women." Then I blinked, bending my head to the side. "No, the women first, and most importantly," I said, facing her back. "It's probably an escort service, or something."

She nodded, eagerly understanding. Like twenty years melting off her. "The men would be a nice bonus," I said. "You'll have to follow the limos back and forth, starting from the apartment, when they drop off the women."

"Yes," she said like a pistol shot.

"You may have to follow when they take the women away tomorrow morning, to see where they end up. Or perhaps I can do that?"

"No, I'll do it."

"Ookay, you do it; I'll watch the party, get the lay of the land before Saturday. You stay away from there Saturday, though, completely away, unless you hear different from me."

"All right," she gasped.

"Whatever you do, stay away from me. *Don't* look for me; definitely *don't* try to contact me anywhere on the apartment-complex property."

"I understand."

"I need the name of the escort service or whatever there is to know about where the women come from as early as possible tomorrow, Saturday."

She snapped one nod.

"How do I contact you?"

"Saturday dawn, when the party breaks up, I'll return to my motel, Holiday Inn-East, on Memorial, and wait for your call." I gave her the phone and room numbers jotted on the back of one of my business cards.

CHAPTER 47

I NEEDED TO SEE INSIDE THOSE apartments. Shoot some photos, if lucky. The fledgling, slightly nutsy, definitely risky plan geminating in the womb of my little brain was to learn as much as I could staking out the party tonight, then attempt to crash it on Saturday, in the guise of one of those party girls. The case of champagne suggested the festivities were indeed on for the weekend. I was hoping of course the bevy of girls each night was some random selection of escort-service workers, even hookers. If there was a regular group, well known to each other, to Veronika Reinhard, to her male guests, I was sunk. I'd only need a few minutes in each apartment though.

It would be easier, naturally, and safer, if I could gain access some other way, when no big party was in progress. The four apartments, all except the upper-story-right one Veronika used as an office, were occupied, according to Daphne Lindell. But those women would likely be out currently, working their domestic-service jobs. It was about ten o'clock in the morning as I hummed away from the Lindells' average little neighborhood in northeast Huntsville. Too much to ask that one or more or all had left their front doors unlocked, anticipating some sneaky private eye wanting a looksee. I wasn't counting on that, but it would be crazy not to check, just in case, instead of spending two days and nights preparing for and executing my extremely dicey party-crasher scheme. What I wouldn't do was break and enter. Not that I was above bending the law, but nor did I have any desire to be arrested, off my home turf, out of state even. I couldn't pick locks, and even if I thought I could get into one apartment, somehow, with a reasonable safety margin, four apartments were out of the question. All the more in broad daylight.

First off, I drove out to Monte Sano, up to Panorama Drive.

The Karmann-Ghia was in the carport.

Bingo.

Veronika Reinhard was home, meaning the one apartment she used, at least, would be empty. I could probably bluff my way past anybody else I ran into. I accelerated back into town along Governors, down California, merged onto Whitesburg heading south, and took a right at Airport. I turned off, navigating through the Chateau DeVille Apartments. I first scouted out a place to park later, out of the way, yet affording a view of the comings and goings from the F section apartment houses. The complex comprised six sections of two shrub-hugged beige-brick buildings each, four units to a building. Generous parking marked off with sidewalks and grassy islands branched off one direction or other from a two-lane tree-lined drive winding back through the complex. Sections A and B faced one another across one of the car parks, C and D the next, lastly E and F. At the rear, each building sported patios and balconies, and a large tree-shaded lawn. It was a nicely manicured, likely more-expensive-than-average-to-lease-from complex. There was a pool, tennis courts, and a clubhouse/office between the B and C apartment houses. The F section was the rearmost with a tall wooden privacy fence behind it. Beyond that, best I could tell, was nothing but pine forest.

I parked between sections C and D and strolled to F, to the second building in. I was carrying my clipboard prominently with the RCA Victor Record Club life-membership application on it. If anybody asked, I was going door to door, starting from the back of the complex. *What, no soliciting? I'm so terribly sorry, I'm an idiot, I must've missed that sign. Have a lovely day anyway!*

I pranced into the breezeway all perky, like I belonged there. The four apartments leased in the name of, or at least for the use of Veronika Reinhard, were F-5 through F-8. Set into the brick wall of the breezeway across from F-5 was a bank of locked steel mailboxes of the tall skinny ilk. Three had slips of paper or rectangles of index card fitted into slots with occupants' names on them. There was no overt appearance of them having been produced at the same time, by the same hand, by the same writing instrument. One box was missing its name, which meant nothing, I shrugged, par for the course in these situations. I wrote each name that was there in my notebook, and the corresponding apartment number. The only one the least bit interesting belonged to F-7. That happened to be the apartment Veronika Reinhard had taken the champagne inside, and worked on the those envelopes of hers in, so I assumed it the nerve center of whatever went on. Lettered elegantly with a black felt-tip, in what could almost be called calligraphy, the name attached to F-7 was:

DR L THEOFILA

How odd.

I grimaced, then boldly, exactly, copied that name onto its own fresh page, which I'd flipped over to.

The doors to all the apartments, two down, two up, were locked. Figured. I shrugged a shoulder of my brown-and-yellow jacket, turning my head, scanning, thinking. I'd rapped on each along the way, using the brass eagle door knockers, as I would have were I really a door-to-door seller of record-club memberships. No one answered. I clipped back down the steps, gliding a hand down metalwork railing, and looped around at the bottom, strolling out back. One gray-painted wooden patio door was locked from the inside with a hook. The other was not, and I went through it. The sliding plate-glass door into the apartment *was* locked. Back out onto the going-brown-for-winter lawn, I studied the rear face of the building. Screens covered all the windows and no sashes were raised. I saw nothing useful when I tried peering through them. I sighed, glimpsing around, feeling sun on my back.

Truthfully, if it had been in me to commit burglary, had I been dressed for it, for example, the set up couldn't have been better. I was invisible from the parking area as well as the side windows of the neighboring apartment house. Behind me stood that tall privacy fence, with woods beyond that.

But—I'd have to cut screens and break glass, even if just chiseling out a small bit to get to the latch with a screwdriver. I'd be leaving evidence, which might scare them off from having the party that weekend. So, even if I didn't get arrested, a break-in or two might be very counterproductive. Plus it would only get me inside the ground-floor units, when it was the upstairs ones that really interested me. The one belonging to "Dr. L. Theofila," and the one across from it Daphne Lindell had suggested to me might be Madame Veronika's own private bawdyhouse.

I gave up the idea therefore, and having accomplished all I could there, I got in my car and drove around the corner to the Westbury Shopping Center, on Airport, where it crossed Memorial. That was where Veronika had used the mailbox the previous afternoon, before returning home. I looked for a public telephone and found one and got out, leaving the Impala idling.

I checked the directory.

Under PHYSICIANS & SURGEONS.

No *Dr. L. Theofila* listed in the Yellow Pages

No last name *Theofila* anywhere in the book.

I had time to kill before my dusk-to-dawn stakeout of Party Kraut, so, naturally, I went and had my hair done. I went up to Audrey's on Oakwood, to where I'd tracked Veronika Reinhard the previous day. I assumed they must be good, if she and the Paperclip wives saw fit to use it. Secret payoffs notwithstanding, no woman would frequent a bad hairdresser, or convince others to, if there were alternatives. When I arrived I told the girl up front I'd wait, since I didn't have an appointment.

What did I want done?

My hair colored honey-gold, I told her, straight on top, parted over my right eye—demonstrating with much flowing hand gesturing up around my twisting head and face—oh yes, and lots of ringlet curls cascading down the sides of my face, fixed so I'd look like Marlene Dietrich, the *Blonde Venus*.

Singing "Lili Marleen."

Not too surprisingly, they'd had that request before.

CHAPTER 48

I BOUGHT AN EYEBROW PENCIL, some mascara, and deep-red lipstick at a department store on the way back to the motel. I napped for a couple hours, banking some shuteye, anticipating pulling an all-nighter on stakeout at the Chateau DeVille Apartments, watching Veronika Reinhard's party, which in fact, I did. I broke up the excitement with occasional stealthful strolls about the grounds, staving off drowsiness, and deep-vein thromboses, all the while trying to keep warm, and get used to my new hairdo.

It all unfolded as Daphne Lindell had described. I saw her dutifully behind the wheel of the blue Chevy Nomad bird-dogging the limos. There was a catering truck. There was music, but not too loud. This wasn't a rock 'n' roll crowd after all. I saw wine and cases of German beer wheeled in. I saw couples furtively, gigglingly, disappear into F-8, the unit Daphne thought might be used for prostitution. Actually, before the women's arrival, already after sunset, I worked my way in close—wearing black stalking clothes, including a black crocheted wool turban pulled down over my new bright-blonde coif—and was down on one knee, concealed by the shrubbery, poised to study the girls passing under the floodlights outside the apartment house, as they entered.

There were seven, all wearing stiletto heels. Pretty much what I expected, bubbly and curvy, classy in a rough-cut way. Top tier, or at least middle tier, compared to the hookers I'd met in Biloxi working The Strip. If they were hookers. Might not be, I shrugged, but I wouldn't bet my last dollar on it. There was a mix, blondes, brunettes, mix of ages, too. Full spectrum of the twenties. One might've been thirty-five. She might've been forty, if you gave her makeup extra credit. I could smell their heavy perfumes from where I was, carried by the breeze. I wasn't wearing any for exactly that reason, though I doubt they'd have noticed a single added scent, within that cacophonous assault on the olfactories. There were jumpsuits, with plunging necks. One of stretch corduroy, one very Jean Harlow, flowing, white with flared legs. There was a metallic-gold crop top, double-ruffled three-quarter sleeves. There was a red chiffon go-go-dancing dress, flashing rhinestones. There was a black crepe V-neck, and a black one-sleeved sheath, rhinestone trim, one shoulder completely bared. There was a black spaghetti-strapped job, covered with fringe.

Most important to me, and this was no more than a vague impression: they didn't seem particularly friendly to one other. Not a tight-knit group, not a team. They were each others' competition for that night's crop of sugar daddies. None of that confirmed they didn't know each other, but I thought it might just be possible to slip a stranger amongst them—that being me, of course—without causing too much of an uproar.

The limo carrying the girls departed with the diminutive German-hating Daphne in tow like a Chihuahua, at 5:45 A.M., an hour before sunrise. Veronika Reinhard came out not long after, in a figure-fitting—her odd figure, that is—royal blue, all-over sequined dress, sparkling with her every move, a semi-scoop neck at the top, trumpet swirl at the bottom. She buzzed away in the Karmann-Ghia, and I drove, struggling to keep awake, to my motel up Memorial, so exhausted, I took off my shoes and went straight to bed. I was still wearing my clothes, turning off the lights and pulling the covers over my head to shut out the glow of dawn in the window. I quickly fell asleep.

Thirty minutes later the phone shrilled, and I sat drowsily up in bed, coughing a little.

"Hello," I managed.

Daphne Lindell.

I wrote down the information she had to tell me, though barely legibly. The women were dropped off as a single group, at a downtown hotel, the Morganton Arms, all then going their separate ways. That sounded good to me. The men were handled by the same limousine service, picked up from a restaurant and lounge called King Arthur's Round Table, which had torches burning out front. I told her she'd done good, sternly reinforcing my instructions for her to stay away that evening, Saturday. She gave me her number, if I needed her. I thanked her, hung up, and slept again until my wind-up alarm woke me at noon. After showering and putting on fresh clothes I went to the restaurant, which by then was serving lunch. I ate a BLT with potato chips, and drank a lot of coffee.

I smoked two cigarettes while finishing the coffee.

I had a dress in my closet back home I thought would pass muster for Veronika Reinhard's party.

It was 110 miles to Nashville. If I floored it, played fast and loose with the speed limit, I could get there and back, stopping only long enough to pee and grab the dress, by not much after four-thirty. That ought to leave me sufficient time to get dolled up and make what I was estimating to be a 6:45 pickup for the girls, here in Huntsville, at the Morganton Arms Hotel. I was basing that on their arrival time Friday, and Daphne's assurance the Friday and Saturday parties ran on identical timetables. A race to and from Nashville beat lounging around the Holiday Inn, dreaming up reasons not to go undercover as a high-class prostitute for a pack of ex-patriot Nazis. Rank ordering said reasons by relative risk to life and limb. Speaking of risks to life and limb, I managed 85 or 90 much of the way, without getting a speeding ticket—blondes really do have more fun—and that had me wheeling into my driveway not much past two-thirty, believe it or not.

CHAPTER 49

MY BEAUTIFUL HOUSE HAD BEEN wrecked.
    I almost died there on the spot, when I entered and saw it, emitting a strangled guttural sound, balling my hot fists up around my ears. A pressure in the core of my chest like an inflating balloon threatening my suffocation. Then my knees began to piston me up and down like I was trying to jump out of my skin.

Letting myself in the side door, through the small mudroom, my first sign of something wrong had been a smell. Sweet, vinegary, cloying. Then I saw the mess spread all over the kitchen. A smashed ketchup bottle, its spattered contents dried a gummy dark red onto the blue-and-gray-tile floor pattern. Same had been done to jars of French's mustard and Duke's mayonnaise. A jar of strawberry jam had been thrown against the stove, chipping off some enamel, the stove appearing to have bled. A half-carton of extra-large white eggs I'd had left had been thrown, one by one, broken against walls, doors, and the floor. A box of Corn Flakes emptied, shaken out. Dishware pulled down from the Hoosier cabinet, glasses and plates, cups, cooking pots, shattered and broken, the floor covered with shards, chunks of Desert Rose. I was crying. There was wild spray paint on some of the cabinetry.

The refrigerator stood open.
Kids!

My first explosive thought.

You heard from time to time about this kind of vandalism. I got my wits about me finally, though, and dropped my keys and drew my gun out of my bag. I sidled, front of the sink, along the Hoosier cabinet, avoiding stepping in the disgusting morass, made all the more disgusting by ants and shiny-backed cockroaches teeming over the mound of spoilage, my mouth curling up as I hopscotched to the swinging saloon door, entering the hall. I closed the refrigerator door on the way by, incidentally, wondering if anything in it could still be good. Gripping my gun tight, steeling myself to check the rest of the house, it occurred to me I was probably in no danger. That mess had been a day old at least. Be that as it may, I aimed the Smith & Wesson as I swung left, letting it lead me into the living room. I grew increasingly sick. Pillows sliced open, stuffing everywhere. Spray paint on furniture. Half the books tumbled out of the built-ins onto the floor, glass in the doors broken out. Ashes from the fireplace ground into the rug, scattered over pages of books. I lowered the gun stiffly beside me, clutched my elbow with my other hand, and swallowed back something trying to come up in back of my throat. I rotated, stared through the archway into the dining room, my ribcage pumping. I'd deliberately avoided looking there coming out of the kitchen. Everything was swept off the sideboard.

Breakage strewn over the entire hardwood floor.

A heavy knife had gouged a deep line across the top of my dining table.

I exhaled quaveringly.

Blinking.

Along the hall to my office, I stood in the door, dazed. Worst yet. I collapsed onto my knees with a whimper, sat back on my heels, balling by then. Great heaving sobs, which angered me almost as much as the wonton destruction. All my file cabinet doors were open, files dumped on the floor. The drawers had been locked. The lock broken with a crowbar. *My* crowbar, incidentally. When I spotted it, I got up, picked it up, looking around, then tossed it back down on some papers. My desk drawers had been torn through, all the items on top of the desk pushed off. My favorite ashtray broken. My typewriter and its stand toppled on the floor, on their sides. I went out, spray paint on the hallway wall, and some pretty pictures I had up, and I saw water on the floor, end of the hall, coming out of the bathroom. Some of it had evaporated but from the damage to the floor finish, there had been more. My estimate of how long ago all this had happened bore revision. Two days, perhaps. I stepped through, sloshing, and stood in a puddle on the black-and-white-diamond tile floor, in my tan Merri-Mocs with the buckle and black stitching.

Some cretin had emptied a box of twelve Kotex napkins into the toilet.

Tried flushing them. "Shit!" I screamed.

They had a lot of sick fun in my bedroom.

Every bureau drawer pulled out, dumped. I breathed scattered potpourri. Slips were ripped in half, most of my bras. A pair of scissors out of my office lay open on the rug, amongst panties and girdles whose crotches were cut out. The bed was stripped, a big "X" slashed in the mattress with a knife, same one I supposed, used to mar my nice table in the dining room. I checked the closet and chifforobe, then the closet in the guest bedroom, where I kept some dresses.

The guest room hadn't been touched.

Closets and chifforobe, too, left alone. Small favors, I thought, lightheadedly, and sank onto the edge of the bed in the guest room, elbows on my knees, burying my face in my hands. "Oh my God," I muttered, feeling myself squirm, the narrow bones in my ribcage tremble. Then I thought of something, and slowly stiffened my spine, sat upright. After a deep quaking breath, I pushed up and grabbed the gun and was out the door, along the hall, back through the kitchen. Circumnavigating the swarming putridity, I dropped the gun on the kitchen table with a clunk as I went by, going in the mudroom. Grunting with the effort I hauled up the cellar door, and hooked it open on the second try.

And climbed down.

"Goddamn sons of bitches!" I screamed.

Hammering the brick down there with my fists.

"Shit!"

The box containing Butterworth's research—

What I hadn't taken with me in that satchel to Huntsville.

—was gone.

The strongbox with my own important papers and mad money remained. Pivoting backward I half-sagged, half-sat down on the concrete steps. Deflating, I glowered at the furnace in front of me. They had gotten Butterworth's papers. Whoever *they* were. They had searched my house for them—my beautiful house—leaving a modest mess, no doubt, then when they had found what they wanted down here, where I thought I had been so clever to conceal them, they went back through the house committing all that sickening destruction. Just to cover up their real purpose. Kids. Not Nazi conspirators. Baring my teeth I smacked the heel of my hand three more times with all my might against the rugged concrete wall until it bled. Then I cried some more, into both my hands.

Eventually dragging myself to my feet, I slogged up and out, letting the cellar door slam. Going outside, onto the side porch, I leaned atop the little wall to think. Clear and warm for a late-November in Nashville, sunlight meandering through the bare limbs belonging to a big oak grown up beside my neighbor's house. To make Veronika Reinhard's party, in the other -ville, Huntsville, I'd have to go back inside, get that dress I'd come for and a pair of shoes to match, and hightail it back to Alabama post haste. If I did the sensible thing most people would do coming home, finding their dwelling ransacked, like calling the police, and an insurance adjuster, I'd miss the party.

I'd miss a chance—even if only slight—of striking some kind of blow against these people, these heartless brutes, who did this to me. Destroyed my home, my lovely little bungalow—*mine*—I'd worked so hard crafting. Holding my stomach, I turned, and reentered weak-kneed. I emptied a can of roach spray over the mess in the kitchen. Should've seen them scatter. I got some bath towels out, laid them down in the hall and bathroom to sop up the remaining toilet overflow. Then I got the party dress from the guest bedroom closet, draped it over an arm, and some black strappy sandals with heels, and took them to the car, high-stepping through and around the mess. The bodice was white rayon chiffon over taffeta, with a ruffled collar and cuffs, and sheer sleeves. The belt and knee-length skirt were black rayon and acetate.

I went back, in sudden afterthought, for a pair of sheer black stockings. Then I had another slightly devious glimmer, and grabbed down from the top of my closet my black quilted vinyl handbag with the gold-chain shoulder strap. It wasn't formal but it looked good enough to carry with the party dress, and there was room in it for my gun, my small Instamatic camera, and two flashcubes, no more. For camouflage, I stuffed in on top a pair of black bikini briefs—which still had a crotch, actually—and—

Had to scan around—

There. My black strapless bra.

It had been ripped apart. I stuffed one C-cup of it into the purse and closed it. Only for show anyway, and it was just as well—wouldn't have been room enough for the whole bra.

I left a spare key under a flower pot outside and made it back to the Huntsville-East Holiday Inn in time to dress for the party and apply some of my new lipstick and eye makeup. I also, crossing my legs and grabbing a smoke, managed to get hold of Ely Deegan of the Metro Nashville Murder Squad. "Thought Tom told me you got married to some country boy?" he said, in a voice that was world weary. I'd only ever seen the detective wear black, and thought, give him a long-handled scythe, he'd make a pretty fair Grim Reaper. Tom, by the way, was my cheating ex-fiancé, current city editor of the *Banner*.

"I did," I told him. "I'm divorced now."

"Sorry."

"Why? I'm not."

"Ooo-key."

"Look, sorry to rush, Ely, I don't have much time, and I'd like a favor."

"If I can."

"It's really nothing underhanded, though I am back doing what I was before."

"Gumshoeing."

"Uh-huh. I'm on a case. Out of town. Not going to tell you where, but I had occasion to return briefly home this afternoon. I found somebody had broken in while I was away. They tossed the place, pretty badly. Vandalized it. I'm pretty sick about it"— my voice cracking up, my cigarette quavering—"tell the truth."

"Sorry," he said.

"I figure it's kids."

"Maybe. What about this case you're on?"

"Doubt that has anything to do with that."

"And you're not going to let us to determine that?"

"I'm not asking you to."

"What are you asking?"

"I need a police report for insurance, right? Can you just send a cop over there to make a report. I'll come in, sign the complaint when I get back in town."

"Humph," he gruffed.

"See, nothing underhanded," I said, fingering the sweep in my hair. "Just asking you to help grease the wheels, dealing with a case of hooliganism, while I do what I have to do here."

His sigh was heavy into the phone line.

"Anything missing?"

I pictured the box of Butterworth's bizarre research, including an Air Force monograph on...*what was it? Electrogravitics? Dynamic Counterbary?*

"Nothing. Not that I saw."

"All right," he said. "We'll take a look."

"Thank you. Key is under an empty flowerpot on the side porch. You don't have to kick the door in or anything."

"How do you think cops get their exercise?"

"Not my problem. Goodbye Ely."

And I hung up.

Without telling him how to reach me.

Nor even what state I was in.

CHAPTER 50

A BROOD OF OVERDRESSED WOMEN, seven, like the night before, lounged on some deep-pile furniture in the Morganton Arms Hotel lobby. Most were smoking, one or two watching their ankles rotate, swiveling high-heeled T-straps. They looked like party girls waiting for a pickup, probably by a limo, possibly by any man on the make, who looked rich enough. For a bunch of females there wasn't much conversation: two weren't even facing the others, nor each other. I recognized two from Friday. At least two I was sure hadn't attended Friday's party.

The setup was perfect.

I stretched my lungs, slowly exhaling as I began to move toward them, my steps across the lobby small, sharp, and pecky. "Can we help you?" challenged a woman, who unfolded, standing as I approached the group. It was the older one, from last night, probably at least forty, possibly mid-forties, now that I saw her close. "This the mustering spot," I asked, hip-swaying to Tony Bennett's 'Boulevard of Broken Dreams,' in my head, "for the Reinhard party?"

"Who wants to know?"

She twined her arms.

Stopping my dance, I said with a haughty, barely bothered look:

"Same query back at'cha, lady."

"Liz," she said, hooking back a sheaf of blonde as platinum as my mother's engagement ring.

"I'm Sue," I said. "I met Veronika Reinhard at Audrey's Beauty Salon. My friend, Rachel, does hair there. She suggested I come tonight, told me to meet you all here—see how it worked out."

"Peggy know?"

I shrugged.

My heart tripping over itself.

"Search me," I said, and made myself swallow. "That would be between Peggy—whoever she is—and Fraulein Reinhard, wouldn't it?"

Liz shrugged.

Seemed bored. Drew off a cigarette held between two straight fingers.

Puffing a plume of smoke sideways, she looked me up and down, and said, "Peggy makes sure we get what we're owed, so you should find out who she is."

"I'll look into that, thank you."

"My name's Sue as well," a seated brunette said, glowering up from under. "Some coincidence."

"Isn't it? Guess I'll be *Blonde* Sue. You can be *Brunette* Sue."

"Call yourself whatever the hell you want, sister woman—jus' stay outta *my* action."

"Naturally," I said.

Then smirking, I grazed the new curls, lightly hair-sprayed, springing to my shoulders.

"Speaking of blonde…" I quipped, like Mae West or something.

"If you're natural blonde, sweetie," the other Sue said, "I'll eat this pack a' cigarettes."

"Maybe you two can score a ménage à trois," a short redhead added to the exchange. "See for yourself, and let us all in on the secret."

Several laughed bawdily.

Liz, the mother hen, twisted: "Can the talk like that, Cinnamon."

"Oh pooh," she pouted.

"Loose lips sink ships."

The limo's arrival was ten minutes after mine. It took us all in one trip though it wasn't unlike being in a sardine can. There was a reeking mixture of perfumes, not all from the dime store, but there was some of that. There was a lot of Arnel polyester and velour date-bait, ruffles and lace and leopard-print corduroy and rabbit fur and mesh and Watusi fringe and rhinestones, and oh yes—revealing décolletage out the wazoo. Not me. I wore a shallow V-neck with a tiny diamond pendant on a chain. "What's in the suitcase, sweetie?"

It was Brunette Sue, from the facing leather limo seat. She meant my handbag, which was larger than any of theirs. Unhesitatingly I opened it, flashing them coquettishly a glimpse of the panties and ripped black strapless job I'd stuffed in on top of my Instamatic camera and revolver. I concealed, quite obviously, the fact the bra was torn, and really only half there. I closed and fastened the flap. "Case a change of costume is called for."

Brunette Sue rolled her eyes.

"Anybody mind if I smoke?"

When we were disgorged at the Chateau DeVille, Liz, the mother hen, held me back, a gentle hand wearing a couple of glitzy rings pressing the blousy chiffon of my sleeve. I looked her in the eye, peering through the dark, praying the fear sending my heart into flutters was adequately concealed.

Had I erred?

How?

"You know, you're just what most of them are looking for," Liz said.

I exhaled gently through my nostrils.

My you're a coy little she-devil aren't you Sherry?

I saw Liz's eyes, heavy with mascara, flicker over me again. "Much more so than the others."

"I'd hoped." I smiled. "Thank you."

"Well," she said, "let's not keep our hostess waiting."

"Liz, wait."

She turned, listening.

The other girls were twenty feet ahead on the sidewalk, stopping, staring back.

"I lied to you," I told her.

"Big surprise."

"Rachel *is*…a friend. And I have seen Miss Reinhard at her shop. But we never talked and she didn't invite me here tonight. I was hoping to worm my way into a nice gig. Can you blame me?"

"Hey," a shout came from the group, "little cool to be spending the damn night out here, in *these* getups."

"Relax," Liz called, huskily over a shoulder, never fully taking her look off me.

She asked:

"Why tell me?"

"Don't rat me out to Veronika. Don't tell her I don't know…*this* Peggy."

"Okay," her abundantly lipsticked mouth said. "You know what you're letting yourself in for?"

"I think so."

She nodded. "Well, something told me, not much mind you, you weren't a virgin."

I blinked.

"I'm *not*."

"Then, let's go a-entertainin'."

And she twirled and began to slink ahead of me in the night, like she had to prove something, or teach it, to the younger brood, going toward the floodlights over the apartment breezeway. I followed suit, tawdry and seductive, and we all entered the ground-floor apartment on the right.

F-5.

Nothing remained inside of 1960s leased residentialism. The place was a…a nightclub…a cabaret…that was it…a pre-war Berlin cabaret. Small dance floor, little round tables. Zebra-striped settees lined the walls. There were tiny white winking Christmas lights providing most of the illumination, what there was. Dark blue satin fabric suspended on wood strapping inches below the ceiling intensified the intimacy, an illusion of the heavens on a starry night. The entire two-bedroom apartment was renovated like that, an establishment for drinking, cards, and companionship. A nice hi-fi piped music around that was old and full of oboes and trombones and saxophones and viols and low and high drums. The converted kitchen was a bar stocked with gins and liquors, cordials long forgotten, a variety of bitters, imported beers in bottles on ice. There was a hired barman in a tuxedo, ready with his limes, lemons and oranges. Olives and maraschino cherries abounded too. A glistening smorgasbord on silver platters, delivered by caterers before our arrival: celery with Roquefort cheese, mushroom salad, lobster mayonnaise, ox tongue salad, egg salad, tuna and sardines in oil, smoked herring and salmon, sliced salami and ham, roasted oysters on the half-shell, goose liver paté, stuffed tomatoes, aspic-glazed shrimp, a variety of canapés, olives and small pickles, served with dark bread and butter. The under-lit, exotic atmosphere evoked Fred and Ginger, in Rio or Morocco, all points warm and balmy, anyplace but modern Huntsville, Alabama. Veronika Reinhard was there: fussing over everything, exploding like a dragon lady anytime something wasn't perfect.

Liz introduced me as the new girl Peggy sent.

Adding, "Isn't she just puurr-fect," talking like Catwoman.

Veronika wore lush brocade. As I had from a distance I judged her about a size sixteen, to my twelve. The dress was shimmering aqua with a plunging neckline halfway to the waist. There were built-in bra cups, and wrist-length tight mesh sleeves. The same aqua mesh formed a bust inset that filled the neckline. Her hair was in a French twist, and blonde, the color of champagne. It had to be a wig over the shorter darker coiffure I'd seen Thursday. Her eyes darted me over, creepily, the odd woman agreeing that I was, in fact, perfect, then telling Liz—in the tone of a stern order—she'd better show me the whole operation, before the gentlemen arrived.

So we went, Liz and I crossing in our heels to Apartment F-6, a mirror image, naturally, of the floor plan of the first apartment, but with an entirely different decor. Walls dark burgundy, gold-painted trim. Numerous potted plants stood around, in brass planters. A bar smaller than that across the way was set up. The front room housed a billiards table, cue sticks racked on the wall. There was a round card table in one bedroom, with a green-felt top, ready for bridge, or poker, or gin rummy. A craps table was in the second bedroom. Liz explained I didn't have to serve drinks; they had two bartenders and a cocktail waitress for that. I was just supposed to circulate, keep the men happy and content, drink with them, light their cigarettes, or let them light mine, as they preferred, play cards with them, sit on their laps for luck. Were I propositioned, there was a room upstairs she'd show me. It stayed locked for privacy, the key on a hook outside, which if missing signaled, in its subtle manner, the room was occupied. "You keep any tips, guy slips a poker chip in your brassiere or something," she said, and I nodded. "You turn a trick, most of the guys will slip you a little something. Say, a twenty, if he liked it. More if he liked it a lot or you did something…special. You can keep that too. But let's be very clear…"

"Yes."

"They *don't* have to pay."

"I don't understand?"

"It's part of the service. They're the hostess's guests."

"The hostess being, our Miss Reinhard."

"Yes. They get anything they want. Anything. We get paid very generously by Peggy at the end of the weekend, and no doubt Veronika pays her a hefty markup over and above what we pocket. You know that drill, I'm sure. But in return, there ain't no saying no to these men. No matter what they want—or how rough, or how strange, they want it."

"I see."

"That's what I meant back in the parking lot."

I lowered my chin.

"Understood."

"Still want in? I'll cover for you if you don't."

"I'm good," I said quietly.

"Okay. I'll introduce you to Peggy tomorrow. You'll have to square things with her, but I'll put in a good word, if I think you deserve it."

"I'll do my very best."

"That's exactly what these people want. The best. Of everything. And they are very Old World."

Festooning the walls of the gaming parlor were Nazi and World War II paraphernalia, including a German Navy recruiting poster, and a huge flag covering one whole wall—you know, the red one with the center white circle with the swastika in it. Most incredible, was a display in the poker room, on an occasional table in a corner. Upon a lace doily, stood an ornate gold picture frame propped on an easel-type stand. The frame held an old creased black-and-white photograph. There were two men in the picture with a little girl of perhaps three. One of the men was half-bald, flyaway dark hair on the sides and back of his head. He was twenty-five or thirty years younger than the NASA publicity photo I had seen in Butterworth's interview files, but I was certain it was Arnold Reinhard, smiling and laughing with the other man. The little girl was on the second man's knee.

The second man was Adolf Hitler.

There was another photo, more startling even than the first.

It hung on the wall catty-corner to the Hitler picture, blown up the size of a large poster and framed. "My God, is that her?" I caught myself asking.

Liz said it was.

"Her too?"

I indicated the little girl.

"Yep."

The blown-up picture displayed the full-length of a standing posing woman, whose legs and arms were rather thickish, mannish, wearing a black one-piece swimsuit, hands propped upon her not-too-curvy hips, atop a plain plywood pedestal. She wore tan sandals with wedge heels; her breasts were pointed and heavy, her short hair boyishly cut. She was smiling, a large outsized smile, standing in near-profile, head canting toward an audience. She wore the famous Nazi armband around the biceps of the bare left arm. The stage backdrop she stood before was the red Nazi flag with the swastika, the swastika as big as she was from the waist up, and she was poised so she mostly stood to the side of it, her bustline just crossing the rim of the white circle, in the photo, and the tip of one arm of the swastika, that ugly black symbol of Nazism.

The poster was labeled, lower left hand corner:

**MISS
NAZI
1968**

I kid you not.

"Where was this?" I asked, glimpsing Liz.

"Santiago, Chile, they tell me."

I nodded, facing the picture again, studying it, knotting my tweezed, dark-penciled brows.

Presenting this year's Miss Nazi:

Veronika Reinhard.

CHAPTER 51

WONDER IF NASA HAD ISSUED a press release on that?
Directly above us was Apartment F-8, the one Daphne Lindell had, correctly, surmised to be a bordello. Following Liz up the outdoor stairs, I asked her about the other second-floor apartment. The one belonging to Dr. L. Theofila, according to the mailbox.

None of us were to ever go in there, I was scolded.

Men either, for that matter, other than one or two at times.

Veronika's private sanctuary.

She let us in F-8 taking the key from the hook on the wall to the left of the door. The front room was yet again decorated differently from the others. This one as a parlor for intimate entertaining—a deep leather couch, actual bearskin rug, another bar, this one featuring champagne on ice, in a large steel basin, romantic music, mood lighting, wall-mounted electric fireplace. One nice cat house, I thought. "Bedrooms are identical," Liz said, twisting back, leading the way through a short hallway, our skirts rustling. She disappeared to the left, entering a room at the end. The first door to the right as one passed along the hall was a full bath, the second bedroom coming next on that side, directly across from the first, which Liz had gone into, and was showing me. Inside was a bureau and a bed with a decorative swirl-design metal headboard, made up with silk sheets. "Two can be used before a maid has to run up here and change sheets, which they do all through the night."

"Classy."

"We don't have to do that either. All we have to do is—"

"I know," I said. "Keep the Paperclip men happy."

Liz stiffened.

Her head tilted, squinting.

"How'd you know that word?"

"Paperclip?" I said.

"I've heard it around," she said. "Even I dunno what it means."

"You didn't just fall off the turnip truck, Liz—think I just stumbled into the reigning Miss Nazi's beauty salon by accident?"

Her look soured.

"I...I suppose not. You a cop?"

"No. I'm not a cop. I swear. But if the night goes well, and you introduce me to Peggy, with a good reference, I'll tell you all about Paperclip. Deal?" I curled a brow at her, then shouldered past her, out of the room. Liz spun, slack-jawed, staring me between the shoulder blades, as I strode determinedly, crossing the hall, to give a looksee to the other bedroom. As I surveyed it, high and low, Liz stopped behind me in the doorway, confused, eyes narrowed. Folding her arms, she bumped a shoulder against a doorjamb. I ignored her—almost one hundred percent certain this was the room, that was the bed, which had been the setting for the boudoir photographs of Ralph Butterworth with a woman not his wife.

Photographs received in the mail by the woman who was his wife, the day of his funeral, and snapped most likely the day he died.

I was also almost one hundred percent convinced that Miss Nazi 1968—aka, Veronika Reinhard—was the woman in those photographs in bed with Butterworth, wearing the black, sheer, baby-doll nightie, the almost G-string, and a carnival mask.

And I thought I could prove it.

CHAPTER 52

I NEEDED SNAPSHOTS.

I asked Liz if it would be okay if I used the can—that was how I said it—before going back down, joining the others. She said she guessed so, and I said, "Oh, please don't wait; I can find my way back."

She said: "No…" thoughtfully. "I'd better stay. I'm taking an awful chance vouching for you. If I'm wrong, the least to happen to me will be losing the best job I ever had, and there ain't a lot of call for forty-three-year-old harlots around here—not, anyway, in places where you'd want there to be."

I nodded slowly.

"Suit yourself," I said, and pranced out and shut myself in the bathroom, sighing, racked by guilt. Didn't seem too likely there was any scenario, good or bad for me, that wouldn't land Liz into trouble. I couldn't let that be my problem though. I had enough of them. Running the faucet at a trickle, I pretended to be "freshening up." There was a medicine cabinet on the wall. Quickly, quietly I decided to check it out, long as I was in the neighborhood. Truthfully an idea had occurred to me, long shot though it was. Inside the cabinet was about what you'd expect: condoms, some Listerine, powder, perfume, toothpaste and brush, couple shades of lipstick…

And—*bingo!*—a brown pint medicine bottle with a measuring spoon.

I rotated it by the neck.

DORMAL, 500 MILLIGRAMS PER TEASPOON.

It would be a clear syrup.

Perfect for mixing.

It was chloral hydrate.

Knockout drops.

They'd been used, that very bottle probably, on Ralph Butterworth. And that was something I *would* be willing to bet my last dollar on. It wasn't something the Alcorn County coroner in Mississippi would have tested for, I expect, not having reason to suspect it. I carefully clicked closed the cabinet, flushed a perfectly clean toilet, and shut off the faucet. I rejoined Liz in the front room, no words passing between us, as I followed her downstairs, the party getting rolling.

How the hell was I going to get back into that room?

Without, that is, having to sleep with Adolf Eichmann?

Well, I bided my time being a conversationalist, a good-luck charm for a card player, arm candy, dance partner—I'd have to give my mother a dozen roses and a kiss for making me take those old-fogy dance lessons: the Foxtrot, the Tango. Not the ballet ones. I was yet to find a practical application for them. What I was gleaning, without being too pushy—it helped that men liked telling well-made-up young women about themselves, all the more so, when they were boozing and cooing—these men, Veronika's party guests, were all from Germany, came to the United States after the war, all in some engineering and/or scientific capacity, although one confided, while trying to plant a hickey atop my shoulder where it joined my neck, that he had pulled the wool over the foolish Americans' eyes. He had been passed off as having some highly specialized technical expertise, when in fact his university degree was in archeology.

"Oh isn't that interesting," I said, detaching him, with a gritting of front teeth, smilingly taking his glass to refresh his champagne. "When I come back, you simply must tell me all about digging up"—I was all atingle, flashing my eyes—"mummies and things."

Ann-Margaret—

Eat your Bye Bye Birdie heart out.

Something else interesting, though I didn't know what it had to do with my case, probably nothing. Most of the fifteen men we girls were fraternizing with lived in Huntsville, and were regulars at Veronika's bashes. Two, however, turned out to not be local. One flew in special from Dayton, Ohio, another, from Maryland. The Maryland guy got pretty wasted, and bragged to me that, while he really shouldn't be saying anything, of course, he was doing top-secret work for the Americans at Fort Detrick. A lab there.

"Oh, my," I said, bubble-headedly, "mean like a science lab, a chemistry lab?"

"No, no, a vi-*rology* lab," he exclaimed.

Slurringly.

I grinned with one corner of my mouth.

Lowering my brow on the same side.

About one o'clock A.M., the cigarette smoke hanging very heavy, Veronika Reinhard found me in the casino apartment, summoning me away from a four-seat poker game, and told me to come with her out into the front room. Every player protested my departure, claiming I was bringing them luck. Wasn't quiet sure how you brought all the players luck in a poker game. My Wonder Woman-like superpowers, I supposed, my golden lasso looped round them all, transforming even losing into a happy affair. *You'll try in vain; you can't explain; the charming, alarming blonde women*—mouthed a leggy, sultry Marlene Dietrich, *The Blue Angel*, 1930. Leaving the chip-clacking game my heart was of course in my throat. Turned out, though, Veronika told me, facing me, pivoting, out by the billiards table, I was doing very well.

Quite the attraction, in fact.

"You are a fine-looking girl," Miss Nazi added, staring, probing me with incandescently blue eyes, reaching and feeling my arm, with a strange delicacy, my look going to the place she touched. "Thank you, ma'am," I replied, taut with wariness, giving what I hoped passed for a nervous, deferential curtsy, simultaneously taking my arm back. Casual but decisive, rubbing my chiffon sleeve, intensely cold there.

"You're German?"

"Oh, no ma'am," I admitted sheepishly. "I only wish."

"Explain."

A voice of authority, of a senior officer.

"I'm mostly Irish," I said, "on both sides."

Truth.

"But I'm…ashamed, of that heritage."

Lie.

"Shiftless, drunken, losers, the lot. I've *vished* I was German instead, ever since I was a little girl."

"All right."

She smiled at me.

Wearing Chanel No. 5.

Perhaps I had another calling—acting—if this detective thing didn't work out.

"There is a very important man," Veronika said smoothly, "who believes you to be German. Let him keep thinking so. Tell him you came to the States after the war as a little girl, as did I. That explains why you don't remember much, don't know the language. *Nein, spechen sie deustch?*"

"No, I don't."

I sipped from a fine goblet of champagne.

"Pity."

"I agree." I flickered a brow. "You mentioned, an important man…?"

"He has offered our…our project, two thousand dollars in cash, if you will sleep with him. Now. He's waiting upstairs."

"Two thousand."

Guess I had even broader career options.

"I'll give you half," Veronika said, "provided, you keep it between us."

I curled a dark thin eyebrow. Then pretended to catch myself—nodded smartly, almost clicked my Nazi heels. "Ferry generous of you, Fraulein Reinhard, but my understanding, from Liz, was I could not refuse your guests." I swept my champagne glass, pinched by the stem. "Refuse them *anything*. Free of charge."

"My dear, you've been refusing my guests, ever so subtly, and cleverly, and slipperily, all night. You are like a human eel."

"No."

"*Ja!* And…I understand."

"Well, the man enjoys it all the more," I said, "if there is challenge, as if it's a hunt. Don't you agree?"

"I do. But in this case…"

I said, evoking not-too-thinly disguised skepticism, "Which *one* is he?"

"Gray three-piece. Gold tie. Watch fob. Not too much hair."

"That's because his head's covered with little brown wrinkly bumps," I said, "spouting hairs all their own, warts or moles or something. That's *Methuselah* you're talking about: not my name for him, I assure you, one of the other girls. I would not be so presumptive, ma'am, in referring to one of *your* guests."

"Quite. Nevertheless, you might buff your opinion of this particular, geezer. He's Colonel Feuerstein."

I tipped my chin.

"So?"

"Ranking officer in the trenches in World War I," Veronika said, "if you can believe that."

"Seeing, in this case, is believing."

She found that amusing, Veronika having an oddly large mouth that opened very wide when she spoke. "He was Rommel's right-hand man in the Afrika Korps," she went on, sipping at last from a tiny cordial glass of green liqueur, then switching the glass to the other hand. "Later he was a loyal member of the Führer's personal staff. It is said he helped expose the plot against the Führer, in which Field Marshal Rommel himself was implicated."

"Terrible."

"Yes. Point being, he was in the Führerbunker, in Berlin, until a very few days before the end."

"I see."

"He's rather like royalty in our circle."

"I've seen your poster, Fraulein," I said. "I think I know what your circle is."

Militaristically she placed a hand behind her, small of her back, still cradling the little cordial glass in the other, as she rose up slightly, lifting her high heels from the floor. "And?" she said, her voice like the bark of a Bavarian Mountain Hound.

After a half-second of thinking I pulled straight, faced front, and snapped my right hand up and out, in a rigid storm-trooper salute. "My loyalties, ma'am," I told her, "are to the Führer."

"I see."

Adding quickly, latching my hazel eyes onto her blue—we were of equal physical stature—"The Führer, that is, ma'am, of the past, of the present, perhaps? And of the future."

My bizarre adaptation of Dickens' ghosts of Christmas. Had I really that reference in mind when I, in the blink of an eye, conjured up that Nazi patriotic hogwash, hoping to bond with Miss Nazi. Or had it just seemed so, thinking back. Nevertheless, Veronika seemed to swallow it hook, line, and sinker, returning my salute.

"Excellent."

"I will go up now," I said, "and do my part for the...project."

"*Sehr gut.*"

"And the thousand dollars. A girl must eat, no matter her politics."

SPEAKING OF SLEEPING WITH ADOLF Eichmann...

Colonel Feuerstein wore a silk lounging jacket, black with a silver pattern of X's-and-O's. It had a shawl collar, wide cuffs, and a tie sash in solid lustrous black. The lighting was subdued, orange flickerings of the electric fireplace splashing walls of pastel blues and browns. At the man's neck was a silver-gray ascot, believe it or not. He was stretched like a sultan upon the black leather couch on my left as I entered. Seeing me he grinned, flashing gleaming dentures, and rose up, spanking twice the cushion beside him. Swallowing, breathing heavy in and out, I snicked the door locked behind me, indelibly seductive, bearing all the exotic, erotic secrets of old Europe. I slinked over, swaying arms, kissing his lumpy mottled forehead, when I reached him, fingering his scalp, the rim of an earlobe—then slithered away, before he could pull me down on top of him with that ropey-veined, liver-spotted grasping hand.

I went to put on a record: Gene Austin, "My Blue Heaven."

"Come, my dear," he said, beaming the teeth again like a Halloween skull.

I put a manicured finger up: *patience, Colonel, patience, good things come to those who wait...*

And I popped the cork on some champagne.

I placed the bottle back on ice, then said: "I'm so sorry, Colonel…"

"Please, call me Jürgen, my dear."

"All right, Jürgen…" Blazing my most coquettish smile. "I am so sorry, but you really must excuse me, to the little girl's room. To freshen up." I was really emoting. Even blew him a kiss, with exaggeratedly pursed lips. "Back in two minutes, promise."

I was back in two minutes.

Grinning, sexy walking back round to the kitchen/bar, the little brown bottle of chloral hydrate and the medicine spoon concealed in the folds of my black skirt. I half-twirled—Jürgen leering from the couch, like some grizzled, mummified satyr—and I disappeared into the kitchen. "Just one more second, darling," I chortled, on tippy-toes, getting down two deep crystal champagne goblets. Quickly I put one and a half teaspoons of the clear syrup in one of the glasses. The old bastard was close to eighty, if not older, and might for all I knew, suffer heart or kidney disease. Plus, he'd been drinking, and I would be generously nurturing him with more alcohol.

I didn't *think* 750 milligrams of chloral hydrate would kill him.

Half the dose they warned you about in the nursing manuals.

But I damn sure wanted it to be enough. If I got lucky he'd be out like a light, and I'd have all the time in the world, Veronika Reinhard and the others assuming I was entertaining the old coot to death. When really, I would be gathering evidence in the murder of Ralph Butterworth.

For I was now convinced beyond any doubt it was murder.

It worked.

The drug, that is.

Eventually.

We kissed and necked and I had to let Jürgen Feuerstein feel me up more than I would have preferred in this lifetime, possibly the next, but eventually he did tire, and I cooed, "That's all right, Colonel, you're in my hands now, *darlink*, just relax." I massaged cavernously sunken temples, then Gunter's sock feet, then he was asleep, wheezily snoring, skeletal legs across my lap. I sighed, waited, a full sixty seconds more by my watch, taking a couple of sips of very good—non-drugged—champagne as I did. *Be careful when you meet; the sweet blonde stranger; you may not know it; but you are reaching danger...* I looked at him, looked at his deep, even breathing. Pressed the pads of two of my fingers over his radial pulse, which felt regular. I wormed out from under, then stood, bent, lowering, carefully his heels onto the couch. I spread over him a velvet throw I'd grabbed off a chair, then snatched up my heavy purse and stalked scamperingly back along the hall, entering the bedroom at the end on the right. On the way I returned the Dormal bottle and spoon to the medicine cabinet in the bathroom.

In the wake of it all, hopefully, the assumption would be the old man simply fell asleep on me. First I switched on all the lights, then I took out my Instamatic, popped on a flashcube, and snapped two shots of the bed, one from across the room, one a close-up of the headboard, its white wrought-iron scrollwork. Moving quickly then, I searched the closet, and a chest of drawers. In a drawer I found the sequined, beaded, feathered carnival mask worn by the woman photographed in bed with Ralph Butterworth. The baby-doll nightie, black lace woven with silver Lurex, hung in the closet with a selection of negligees and gowns. The black Cleopatra wig was on a Styrofoam head up on the top shelf. I took all of this out, arranging a display on the bed—EXHIBIT A—adding, a last-second afterthought, the brown bottle of chloral hydrate, retrieved back from the bathroom—and I took photos of all this, snapping on my second flashcube after the first two, total of four pictures, always sure to get the unique scrollwork of the headboard somewhere in each shot, an edge or corner. So no smart lawyer could convincingly argue I hadn't found the right place, the setting of the Butterworth photographs. All these elements in one place—the bed, the mask, the wig, the nightie, the drug used to render Butterworth unconscious—simply could not be a coincidence, nor fabricated, part of some sleazy PI trick, not easily anyway. I spent all my flashes. I would love to have gotten a shot of the Miss Nazi poster downstairs, but saw no way to pull that off with the party going.

I got everything back how I'd found it, including the Dormal bottle, back once again in the medicine cabinet, and my camera, and the charred flashes, four to a rotating cube, stuffed back down in my bag with the black bra and panties on top, and went out to check on Colonel Feuerstein. He was, I'm happy to report, sleeping like a baby—good respiratory pattern, strong pulse.

What next?

Standing, shouldering my bag, I half wanted to return to the party. Maybe get a picture of the Miss Nazi poster—one of the men did have a Polaroid, I thought with a flicker of an idea, some of them getting pictures taken with a girl around his neck, or sitting on his lap, or teasingly flashing a nipple—maybe I could finagle somebody posing with me beside the poster on the wall, then plead cooingly for a second snapshot, for me to keep, a memento. Also I thought, if I stayed longer I might manage a peek inside the other upstairs apartment, Veronika's sanctum sanctorum, attached to the odd name, Dr. L. Theofila. Yet another reason to stay: I feared what might happen to Liz if I bugged out. Not to mention, my premature disappearance could put them onto what I'd done, before I could get the film developed, and figure out the next step. They could cover up. Or simply disappear.

Still…

Remaining was too risky.

I'd lucked out so far. But anybody discovering I had a camera and gun with me might cause things to take a very ugly turn. And staying would seriously press my luck in two or three other important ways: (1) somebody might figure out I'd slipped Colonel Jürgen Feuerstein a Mickey Finn; (2) worse yet, the horrid old zombie might wake up, still wanting to have sex with me (I'd sooner have intercourse with Cecil the Seasick Sea Serpent); and (3) no guarantee, as the hour grew late, I could continue to evade the carnal advances of any number of the others, all men expecting to have nothing refused them.

No, I'd gotten most of what I'd come for, and wouldn't pay to be greedy. Time to bail, and, too bad, but warning Liz would be foolhardy. Next issue: my car was miles away, downtown. I really hadn't formulated a mid-party escape plan. I'd have to hoof it. If I were missed quickly, the danger realized, I might easily be chased down in a car. But if I did manage a clean getaway, it was a half a mile, an easy hike, to the Westbury Shopping Center, where I knew there to be a payphone. A taxicab could be called, perhaps Daphne Lindell, for a pickup. Giving the old man a last looksee, satisfied he'd be fine, I started for the door, crossing carpet in sandal-feet, Marlene Dietrich curls springing at the sides of my face. *They fascinate, they captivate; beware the amazing blonde women…*

I was reaching to unlock the door and let myself out—

When I heard footsteps—

Two people.

One heavy.

One less so.

Man and a woman.

Ascending the stairway outside. Breath became trapped in my throat and my heart jumped like a rabbit. I retreated mid-room, feeling heat from the flame-effect fiberglass logs, from the black-and-brass wall fireplace. I managed some deep breaths, calming myself. Just a matter of sitting tight, waiting for the amorous pair to go off, disappointed, but patience is a virtue right? More, perhaps, so than chastity? Colonel Feuerstein and I had the key. When the key was missing from the hook outside, it was a signal the apartment, the bordello, was *occupato.*

Equivalent of a DO NOT DISTURB sign.

All was peace for a couple of seconds, the walking people halting beyond the threshold, inches on the other side of the door. I waited, listening and squinting. No more than another second or two, I knew, before I would hear them return from whence they'd come, resolving to try back later.

My ears pricked then.

A hand flying to my sternum.

With sounds I had decidedly had not expected.

Muffled by passage through the door, but sounds of unmistakable identity. The slow actuation of a type of mechanism, as if the effort were being made to be quiet about it all, to be furtive, to take us by surprise—

Followed quickly by a harsh metallic slapping or slamming noise.

The sequence happened twice.

The first lighter, snappier than the second.

Feminine and masculine, like the footsteps, the feminine leading, by the way, in charge.

The noise was the racking of the slide, the jacking of a cartridge into the chamber, from each of two semi-automatic pistols.

One small, like a purse gun.

Another larger, heavier.

CHAPTER 53

I SPUN AROUND, SKIRT SWIRLING, bolting at a dead run down the soft-lit hallway toward the two bedrooms. I slammed my shoulder into a wall with a shock of pain as I heard the tickling of a key nobody was supposed to have, unlocking the apartment. Shoving off one wall, teeth gritted, I flatted my back against the other, listening, as my chest rose and fell, spastically, feeling like there wasn't enough oxygen in the air. I sidled over till I was abutting the bathroom doorframe. Managing to think suddenly, my eyes flickered down at my pocketbook, which I was clutching white-knuckled, and I drew my revolver from it. The black panties and black strapless bra cup went flying. By then, though, I didn't care about that. What I did care about was my precious photographic evidence—proof Veronika Reinhard was with Ralph Butterworth, in this apartment, probably the day of his death, probably having drugged him into unconsciousness.

Time permitting I'd have lobbed my entire handbag, camera, film, and all, like a grenade, out a back window, over the top of that privacy fence into the woods. Just then the exterior door swung open, banging off a wall, and obviously time had run out for that. I simply flung the bag by its gold-chain strap through the door into one of the bedrooms, then stalked back along the hallway toward the living room, staying to the left, which gave me the best concealment from the intruders' perspective. Edging past the bathroom door this time, I for a fleeting instant considered ducking through, but that would just get me trapped, nowhere to run. My clothes made a lot of rustling and swishing sounds as my body moved around inside them, this outfit hardly meant for stealth. I could tell they were listening for that, because I didn't sense they were moving. I might've heard breathing, and held my own breath, confirming it wasn't me. I stopped inches from the corner, hugging the wall where the hallway opened up into the living-room/kitchen area. My revolver was aimed forward, tucked up close to my body. I could smell my own perfumed sweat, felt the nylon tricot of my slip sticking to damp skin. There were no shadows yet being cast onto the part of the far wall I had a view of, meaning they hadn't advanced far into the apartment, hadn't crossed in front the electronic fireplace that was the main light source.

I knew they had guns. The fireplace didn't illuminate things all that much, and what it did throw off was quite orange and flickery. It would be disorienting, at first. They would be cautious. I could surprise them. If I got up the gumption. Staying low, I figured, I'd be a more difficult target. Raising my skirt one-handed, I lowered to my knees, and crawled—and I swung my .38 and half my face and blonde curls, up from almost floor level into the front room.

Vacuuming into my visual cortex whatever there was to see out of that bizarre flame-effect-splashed scene. Might as well have been high on LSD. Veronika Reinhard was there, turning, eyes bright and scanning, in that shimmering aqua brocade of hers, gripping a brand-new fashion accessory, though one quirkily appropriate for Miss Nazi—a shiny black Walther PPK.

The pistol waggled as she infiltrated forward, halting center-room, attention snagging onto, scudding over the sleeping, wheezing Colonel Feuerstein. I heard her curse. George Peter Dasch was behind her. He had a Luger, arm bent at the elbow, aimed at the ceiling. Low, and watchful, the experienced hunter. He half threw, half kicked the door shut behind them. Veronika barked she couldn't see a damn thing, for him to hit the overhead lights.

I shouted.

"Don't!"

A sudden-lit-up room would blind me, if only for a second, giving them an edge that might be all they'd need to take me. Gun in one hand, grabbing my skirt up with the other, chest tight, I scrambled to my feet, and sidestepped boldly out, into the open, in the room, weak-kneed, tingling. With my elbow locked, I twisted so that my arm was in line with my body, and pointed the hammerless Smith & Wesson, with the blade sight, drawing a bead onto the center point of Veronika's sternum.

More precisely the V of her plunging neckline.

From less than five feet away I could hardly miss. Even if my aim was off there was still an excellent chance off shooting off one of her boobs. She knew that, plus I'd positioned myself such that she was linearly directly between Dasch and me, meaning he couldn't shoot me without risking shooting his niece. "I'll kill you first Veronika," I said, overexcitedly, through my teeth, "either you twitches a muscle. And you, Mr. Dasch, if you make any move, either side, even shift your weight to a different hip—got it?"

He growled, accentedly:

"I am not moving, Ms. Russell."

One of my cheeks ticced at the sound of my own name.

How'd he know?

I was expecting it when my peripheral vision detected a tensioning of Veronika's grip on her little PPK. The gun was hip level. She'd have to arc it thirty degrees, Miss Nazi twisting at the waist, or externally rotating her arm, to target me. "Don't, Veronika. You *might* get lucky, but there's a good chance of me putting a bullet through your cold, cold heart before you get a shot off. Or at least at the same time."

I saw her flicker her eyes, onto my stainless-steel revolver, then on my face again. "One other thing," I said. "Kind of natural for a man to hesitate killing a woman, even if for a second. Don't count on that second from me. I'm not that partial to women." Almost imperceptibly, her chin lifted and fell, her body letting out some of its coiledness, though there was hate there, lurking back of her eyes, heating up. "Drop the guns," I said. "Both of you. Nice and easy."

Dasch obeyed first.

I knew he would.

The Luger, he lifted it. Clicking down the safety catch, he tossed it as if it radiated heat, the pistol thudding onto the carpet. He wouldn't put Veronika's life at risk, some Prussian chivalric code, plus he was a professional, or once was, an ex-cold-blooded-German spy. He would summon up his training and experience; he would innovate and adapt; he would yield, unemotionally, to the practical. He wore a light-blue windbreaker, tweed newsboy's cap, black loafers. Veronika kept hold of the Walther. Convincing her to not try to shoot me was an easier sell than out-and-out surrender:

Miss Nazi was a fanatic, a sincere true believer.

Stalwart persistence would be a virtue for her.

Compromise, a failing.

Besides that, a woman, any woman, especially one like her, used to ruling the roost, being fawned over, would fear loss of control far more acutely than any man. George Dasch knew that, too, and said:

"Do it, Ronnie."

Back of her, gutturally, like Curt Jurgens in *The Enemy Below*. She glimpsed her uncle over a shoulder. "No choice," he told her, dentures gleaming downward, brightly white. "She got us. This time."

Smirking now, she replied my way, "Indeed."

He added:

"Our day, shall come."

And with a nodding jerk of her head, she raised, clickingly de-cocking, the PPK.

Tossed it onto the carpet and I backed away, slinkingly, toward the kitchen-turned-bar, out of reach of any Miss Nazi roundhouse kick, or some lunging attack. "Okay, one at a time," I said, puffing, still aiming my gun, waist level now, "first Veronika, kick those guns, carefully, my way." They did, and as they did, I kept a wary eye on the pair. Then I stalked in a half-circle, keeping to the outer edges of the room, snagging up the pistols, then retreating, and pitching both deep back along the hallway. There was a heavy clatter and some knockings against drywall. "Now, Mr. Dasch"—I straightened, facing them—"you may turn on the lights, but slowly, keeping your hands up, where I can easily see them."

"*Ja*," he said, walking ataxically backward, doing as he was told, how he was told.

Squinting then, adjusting to the ceiling lights, I ordered both the Germans onto the floor.

Face down.

Spread eagle.

They did so, and I lowered my gun, exhaling, feeling like I was deflating myself, weight of the revolver sagging down alongside my thigh. With my other arm I mopped my brow, then folded it across my body, beneath my bustline, clutching its mate above the elbow. I melted a little against the wall that divided the kitchen from the living room, bumping a shoulder. "What now, Ms. Russell?" Veronika asked, sternly, twisting up, looking at me, with that face, like an evil large-mouth bass.

Her tone startled me away from the wall, and I began to pace, my gun raised, aimed from the hip again, to about midway between her and where Colonel Feuerstein was quite rhythmically snoring. Ironically, I was trying to slow, regulate my own breathing. I'd had little experience holding people at gunpoint in my life—my father was right, I should get out more—but seemed to me I should be the one giving orders, setting the pace. To hear Veronika, it was…like she was scolding me.

Like: *Here we all are Sherry, get on with it, I'm getting bored.*

"For starters," I said, "no moving around, and if I even think you're contemplating getting up from that floor, I'll shoot—him or her, no difference—no warning. That's a promise. Let me make it perfectly clear, to quote our new president-elect, I have no intention of ending up dead, after a visit to this apartment, like Ralph Butterworth did."

"Who?" she asked.

"Don't bother, Veronika."

"I don't know what you are blithering about."

"It was you in the pictures, with Butterworth, mailed to his wife, as a smokescreen. I know they were snapped in a bedroom down this very hallway." I thrust my chin that direction. "Perhaps your uncle here, Mr. Dasch, was the photographer, perhaps not. But I found the carnival mask, the wig, the rest of the outfit. I'm also ninety-nine percent sure Butterworth was drugged in those pictures, with the choral hydrate in the medicine cabinet, in that bathroom along the hall. I don't believe he ever had sex with another woman, other than his wife, or if he did, not with anyone connected to this caper. Like I said, it was your idea of a smokescreen. It worked to a point. I do believe, however, he was still drugged, comatose or close to it, when you staged, or had staged, his *drunk-driving* accident. I'm going to do everything I can to get Butterworth exhumed, Veronika, and toxicology-tested, to prove that part of it."

Veronika asked, had I used the same chloral hydrate on the colonel, thus avoiding having intercourse with him. "Yes," I admitted, "I slipped him a Mickey. Don't worry too much. I'm a nurse." I shrugged. "I think he'll be all right. As far as knocking him out, avoiding sex wasn't my only motive, but it was a good one."

Veronika laughed.

"So it was. Does it not bother you, Ms. Russell, that we know who you are? Know your name? That my uncle and I knew to come up here, catch you at whatever it was, you thought you were doing?"

I paced in my heels, gun swaying at my side. "A little," I said, looking at her, fingering my hair. "But, why be surprised? I know for example, Mr. Dasch here, George Peter Dasch, is your uncle, your father's chauffeur and gardener, yet in a previous life: a member of the Abwehr, later close to the top of the SS foreign intelligence service. And you people obviously know about me, my involvement in the Butterworth investigation. My house was burglarized, ransacked. Bobby Kaplan, an American Nazi in Ohio, was alert to my visiting Butterworth's wife. You all are probably using *him* as some sort of pawn. Then there's that ultra-sophisticated phone tap."

"What phone tap?"

"Butterworth's home, in Pennsylvania."

"I know of no tap."

"Why deny it?"

"I've denied nothing to this point, Ms. Russell, nor have I assented to anything. Can we two women agreed upon that?"

"All right," I said. "What's your point?"

"I am prepared to swear that neither I, nor anyone I am

directly involved with, has had the late Ralph Butterworth's home phone tapped. Ever. And that should bother you, Ms. Russell."

"I'm listening."

"I am done talking. Except to say you should immediately give up this insanity of holding us—*me!*—at gunpoint. I am, whatever else you think I am, the beloved daughter of the special assistant to the head of your country's moon-rocket program. Now get out of here, now, and I give you my word as a loyal German, a loyal *National Socialist*, we will not stop you. Not tonight. My word."

Through teeth, I said:

"I'm not going *any*where."

"Then you are a fool."

"Perhaps. Butterworth was to meet Mr. Dasch, here, at Maple Hill Cemetery, in Huntsville. During or after that meeting, I believe he, Dasch, or both of you, lured Butterworth to this apartment. He was a pretty-good lush. Wouldn't have been difficult. You gave him a drink, laced with that chloral hydrate, and once he was unconscious, you and Dasch stripped him, put him to bed, with you in it. Compromising photos were taken, which made it look like he was making love with you."

"You cannot prove that."

"What makes you say I can't?"

"You, yourself, talked of a carnival mask," Veronika said, viperously, up from the floor, "sounding to me like there would be no way to prove the identity of the woman photographed."

"Baloney. I can prove it happened here. I've told you how. I can prove it was you."

"How?" She spoke from down deep.

Like a harsh cough.

"Your Miss Nazi poster."

"What?" she grunted. "I...don't understand..."

"Your poster," I said.

"*What* about my poster?"

"You wore the Nazi armband, swastika, even during your swimsuit competition. In the warm sun of a late Chilean summer. It left a tan line. A most unusual tan line, which shows on the arm of the woman in the photos."

After looking away, giving a couple of nods, she turned toward me again.

"Most clever, Ms. Russell."

"Thank you."

"Okay, we took photos. But, if, as you say, we wanted this man dead, why would we risk exposing ourselves with such a tactic?"

Horn music, like Lawrence Welk, emanated from one of the lower apartments. My LP, on the hi-fi, had finished, the set shutting itself off. "You wanted the death to look like an accident. That was important. Otherwise it would lend credence to his investigation, his research. You wanted him out of the way. *And* discredited. The wife would be the most likely party to challenge an accidental-death ruling, so you took out insurance. If Myrle Butterworth thought her husband was having an affair, you figured—correctly, by the way—she wouldn't ask questions. She'd be angry, feel he deserved what he got. And if he could cheat on her, his wife of twenty-two years, commit that moral turpitude, how difficult to accept he'd get so drunk he'd drive his car into a billboard stanchion. That part of your plan worked: Mrs. Butterworth cares noth—"

Suddenly we all were jolted.

Two great shattering crashes downstairs, in quick succession. Like small bombs. It was the doors of both downstairs apartments being kicked in.

Muffled screams of surprise, hue and cry, cops yelling:

"All right! Everybody freeze!"

Pandemonium up through the floor.

Goddamnit Daphne! What'd you do?

CHAPTER 54

THREE THINGS HAPPENED NEARLY SIMULTANEOUSLY in the bordello apartment while all hell broke loose downstairs, police kicking in doors, subduing suspects, who preferred not being subdued.

Firstly, Veronika Reinhard cried uncle.

That is, she screamed an order to Dasch, her uncle:

"Onkel George, kill the *licht!*"

Licht is German for light—she was telling him, "Kill the light." Moreover, it is my belief, in hindsight, she was using him to distract me, give me a moving target to worry about, possibly shoot (*could she be so cold-blooded as to sacrifice her own uncle that way?*), whilst she took action of her own.

Secondly, Dasch—who was sixty-five years old and probably hard of hearing to begin with, then in the midst of the bedlam downstairs, the uproar coming through the floor upon which he lay face down—I think, misunderstood his niece's command. I think he thought she said, "Kill the bitch!"

Licht and *bitch* coming close to rhyming, if you confuse things with some accent and noise.

The bitch of course being me, and the overweight, retirement-age, former spy wasted no time mustering all his loyalty and training, surging surprisingly quickly upright, not however without having to brace against a wall, cupping one arthritic knee with a florid hand, and pushing down upon it with all his effort, getting to his feet. I was aghast he would try anything. His age, unarmed, police closing in. I raised my gun.

"Halt, Dasch! Stop!"

He didn't and I admit I didn't shoot, all my bravado notwithstanding.

Should I have? Old and decrepit or not, he was a big man, and I retreated, eyes agape, my back coming up against a wall as he staggered my way, hands balled threateningly into enormous fists. He was circling to my right, taking the long way, passing in front of Feuerstein. I might have shot him then, hesitating that time because I might hit Feuerstein, asleep, prostrate on the couch, in my line of fire.

Thirdly, Veronika Reinhard.

The reason of course Dasch had to take this clumsy roundabout path of attack trying to get at me was because his niece was lying flat on the floor between us, directly in the way.

Except, once she knew Dasch's feint—her diversionary ploy—was afoot, she rolled suddenly up onto her arched back, bending both knees in the air. I had no clue what she was doing when she reached both her arms behind her knees, and anyway I had Dasch to deal with, repeatedly demanding he stop, training my gun around on him. From the floor then came a jagged sound of dress fabric ripping.

Veronika had grasped, I realized, both sides of the slit up the back of her tight skirt. It was a pencil skirt so slim and body-hugging as to fetter, I well knew, most physical activity—especially kicking and fighting, and for that matter, getting up off of a floor agilely once one was down there. However, Veronika Reinhard was dauntlessly splitting her own skirt up to the waist in back—disencumbering the thick-muscled lower half of her odd but clearly powerful body.

Rolling up onto her haunches next, smelling of Chanel, she was poised to lunge at me in a feral attack; however in doing so she had unintendedly thrown herself in the path of her own uncle's foray, also directed, of course, against yours truly.

"You fool!" she blistered, as he toppled over her, completely over, like a kid turning a somersault. His hat flew off, and his head hit the floor, the rest of him coming down in a heap. He lay on his back, rolling his head side to side, half-stuporously. His legs were bent every which way, the big shoes with his feet in them jammed up against a baseboard.

Veronika jumped up and staggered back, her lips bared from her teeth, her pointed breasts rising and falling. She was in front of the hi-fi, near the dinette table where they had the basin of chilling champagne. I half expected her to start grabbing bottles by the neck and hurling them at me mercilessly. I was happy she hadn't, realizing she couldn't make me out well, back along the shadowed hallway I'd retreated down, as I presaged her and Dasch's collision.

For what it was worth, I was safe from harm, for the moment. Veronika was facing me, seething, crouched with her arms held out like a wrestler's. But there were over a dozen feet between us, and both the Germans' guns were back here, behind me, where I'd tossed them earlier. She would know, or at least have to assume, I was still armed, which I was, and would shoot her if she tried charging me across that distance—enough distance that she could be pretty fast and I still wouldn't have to be Wyatt Earp, and I wasn't, to drop her in her tracks.

Same if she started flinging bottles of bubbly, with any accuracy at all.

However, I probably wouldn't shoot her as things stood. Too much like cold-blooded homicide, not to mention the police, who'd be on me in ten seconds, under the circumstances.

So, that's my marginally respectable excuse I maintain to this day for not having shot her when I could've. I'll add to it, I was utterly flummoxed by there having been a police raid—*that* night, of *all* nights! And, anticipating cops bursting upon the scene any second—wasn't sure I wanted to be the first spied with a deadly weapon, much less trying to shoot somebody with it, even if that somebody *was* Miss Nazi, 1968. That seemed a formula for getting shot by the police, and while I had been shot before, never by the police, and I sort of wanted to keep it that way.

Miss Nazi, though, got her wits about her before I did, and vanished from view—to my left, which meant she could be going for an escape, out the front of the apartment. Or she could have something else up her sleeve, lying in wait.

She didn't go out the door.

I'd have heard that.

What I was hearing was a storm of men ascending the iron-and-concrete stairway outside. Suppose the smart thing to do would've been to stay put, or hole up in one of the bedrooms, until they swarmed in. I was safe from Veronika, and didn't think Dasch was in any shape to hurt me, but I wanted her—her at least—in hand before the cops took over. I didn't want her escaping out right, or telling some really good story getting me arrested and thrown, as my mother said, "under the jail."

Or killed.

So, I went full tilt out into the front room—like an idiot.

Veronika was ready for that and made a forward leap like a lioness on the Serengeti. Quick, big-boned, Amazonian, she attacked low, head-butting me just beneath the bosom, knocking the breath out of me, slamming me against the wall with a thud that shook the apartment. My skull bounced off plasterboard, and I felt a shooting pain, back of my head. Shaking that off I tried to move away from the wall, but Veronika's clawed hands flashed out together, one clasping my right wrist, the other around my throat. I felt her thumb and forefinger squeeze the soft spots beneath my ears while the palm forced me back, compressing my trachea, my tongue popping out of my mouth. Gagging and coughing I had my gun but she had a tight grip on my wrist and my arm pulled up, hammerlocked to the wall. I was no match for Veronika in terms of physical strength. My revolver was rendered utterly useless, as a firearm, or even just something to club her with. And, yes, if you're keeping track, I did have one hand free. That was grappling with the stranglehold she had on my neck—an effort proving every bit as impotent as those focused on the Smith & Wesson.

My temples began to pound.

The world around me starting to blur.

Never a cop around when you needed one: *What the hell were they doing out there? Taking a smoke break?* I grabbed her hair but her French-twist wig came off in my hand. I cursed, managing only a strained guttural wheeze, then viciously yanked her real hair, balled it in my fist trying to rip it out of her scalp. Veronika gave a yowl of pain. There was an animal snarl of hot breath, spraying of saliva in my face, as she let go my neck. Air came into my lungs in gulps, with a peculiar rasping. Up and over the other woman's fist lashed, exploding beneath my left eye. My body jerked, my head whipping around. Momentarily blinded, I saw purple and yellow globes of light, feeling something sticky and thick. It was wet. It was blood. My cheek—it bled—cut by what proved to be a large blue star sapphire, set in Veronika's ring.

She followed that up with a swinging blow to the side of my head, which jerked around again. It felt like being struck by a sledgehammer. Still I had the gun, had her by the hair. She twisted under my arm, slugging me brutally in the ribs. I turned guardingly, protecting my abdomen and breasts, caught her thickset wrist above the fist that was punching me. Straining with all my might to twist that arm up behind her back. Without success.

Lips drawing away from horrible white teeth, Veronika then smashed again and again the fist with my gun in it against the wall, battering my knuckles bloody. And when that failed to knock free the gun she stretched my arm to the corner, where the wall ended, and she began a very earnest effort to shatter my metacarpal bones against the ninety-degree angle.

I squirmed, gasped, desperate to throw Veronika off, sobbing now, my eyes blurry, stinging with tears, sweat and mascara. She was too heavy, shoving me back violently. My knee flew up and caught her in the symphysis pubis hard. Her body jolted, she gave a wounded cry, crashed on her back, pulling me down on top of her. The chiffon sleeve of my dress ripped like tissue paper. My face bleeding red onto the glimmering aqua front of her dress, as we simultaneously battled for oxygen in each other's faces, bellowing, spewing hot breaths, cloying with our mingling perfumes.

We were bottling up the hallway meaning George Dasch—upright by then, wavering, clamping the dome of his head, desperate to aid his niece—couldn't get to the PPK or Luger back there where I'd hurled them. Veronika's silver-manicured fingers, lashed out at, trying to dig nails into my breast, but I grabbed her wrist down, using my weight, gravity to advantage now, gritting teeth, pinning the stronger woman's arm to the carpet. Her thighs were as muscular-hard as a man's, and she pounded me in the side, with the inside of her left knee, thudding heavy blows at my flank and ribs. Dasch was hovering, arms groping, shuffling—like an aged boxer, dancing in the ring—working out just how to pull me off Veronika without me shooting her.

By then the door frame was shattering.

A terrific thunderclap.

Squad of Huntsville police pouring through.

"Freeze, mister!"

"Hands back of your head, fingers laced."

First voice then louder:

"*Turn A-round!* Now!"

Clothes rustled, men around us. I saw spit-shined black low-quarters, tailored blue wool trousers, sharp creased. Veronika spat a curse, balls of muscle at her jowls, and shoved at me, ceasing her struggling with a growl, and a face that would curdle milk. The muzzle of a police Smith & Wesson, gleaming blue-black with gun oil, six-inch barrel, pressing the artery throbbing wildly in Veronika's temple.

"Give it up, ma'am," a voice, kind, but hard told the German. I surrendered my weapon to a second officer, a tall slim Negro, who wore his uniform well, whose hand carefully closed round the gun, dislodged it from my grasp, using a slight twisting motion.

I was helped up, quite wobbly, catching my breath, blood spatting down the double-ruffle white collar of my dress. I tried to staunch it, pressing my left cheek, my throbbing eye. Two officers took me under the arms, a wide hand cupping the small of my back, helping me sideways to the leather couch. They half-sat, half-propped me upon the big overstuffed arm, air filling and emptying my lungs hungrily. Wincing, I clutched my right side, doubling over, savagely battered by the inside of Veronika's knee, feeling the area, worried one of my ribs might be broken, gnashing teeth. The length of the couch, I glimpsed over, coughing, was occupied still by a snoring Colonel Feuerstein. George Dasch and Veronika Reinhard, shackled behind their backs, were being herded out. Surprisingly no one was cuffing me—the one with the gun, and far as anyone other than George and Veronika knew, just a fancy prostitute. *My injuries?* Bleeding from my face! The colored officer gave me ice from the basin the champagne was in, wrapped in a dish towel, to hold against my eye. "Thank you," I managed, flinching.

Suddenly I looked over, called, constrictedly, to an officer with sandy hair and freckles, trailing the Germans out. He was telling Veronika, adjusting his hat, "Don't worry, ma'am, we'll get you some safety pins for your dress." She was wearing fishnet black tights with bikini panels, the cop getting a good look, through the self-inflicted tear up the back of her skirt. "They're murder suspects, Officer," I said, short-winded. "I'm a PI, licensed by the Metro Nashville DA. Hold them, please…till I can make a statement."

"We know, ma'am."

It was Killian, the Negro's partner, looking down on me with an easy grin.

I looked up, blinking, hurting my eye to do so. He might be six-four. He had a round, florid face, a hard mouth and cold eyes, with sideburns, and longish gray-fletched hair. He wore the blue uniform, a tie, a tie clip, and open windbreaker, with a police badge above a breast pocket, a sleeve patch with crossed swords, and glinting H.P.D. pins fastened to the collar points of the shirt.

"You *know?*" I said.

"He told us."

Killian indicating the doorway George and Veronika had just exited.

CHAPTER 55

FBI SPECIAL AGENT ALAN LEGATE.
Birmingham Field Office.

Shoulder bumping the doorjamb, hands in trouser pockets, he wore his trademark evil-clown grin. He had a gaunt symmetrical face, stacked with angles: a jutting chin, the grin, long satanic nose, horn-rims, thickset eyebrows up out of deep creases above the bridge of the nose. The brown hair was Vitalis'ed, widow's-peaked between high flat temples. He was a tall, clean man, five-foot-nine-inches of immaculate brown suit, white shirt, French cuffs, conservative gold-striped necktie. He looked steam pressed, despite the hour, which had gotten on towards two A.M.

First time I ever met Alan Legate, answering his knock at the Tuscaloosa Holiday Inn last year, it'd been even later—after *four* in the morning—and he'd looked every bit as spiffy then, as now, strolling inside the brothel apartment, lankily, loose-jointedly, hands still pocketed. Killian and the Negro officer, whose name was Hammer, made way, Killian thumb-hooking his Sam Browne belt. "He all right?" the agent asked, tipping forward on one leg, gazing the full length of Colonel Feuerstein.

"Appears to be sleeping, sir."

Legate found that amusing.

Gave me a nod, coming round close, and squinting as he brought my chin up with the light pads of his fingers, checking

309

beneath the ice-towel compress I held against my eye.

"Ms. Russell."

"Alan," I replied.

He gingerly thumbed the laceration.

Sucking through front teeth, I blenched.

"Sorry," he said. "Going to have a black eye."

"Yep."

"That cut needs stitches."

"Figured."

He took up my hand like he was going to gallantly kiss it, hesitating, seeing the bloody pummeling my knuckles had suffered. "This lady, officer," he said, lowering my hand, patting it, then swinging round, facing Killian, "is a registered nurse by training." The Kennedy-esque brogue came through loud and strong. He tapped his glasses back up the hooked nose, cufflinks simple gold-plate disks. "A very good one, matter of fact. I've see her jury-rig a chest tube out of a Bic pen."

The senior cop tipped back his beefy head, pulling his mouth as if impressed. "If the old gentleman snoozed through a police raid," Legate went on, "likely he had help. Better get him checked out."

"Yes, sir."

Killian then shot me a look. "Well?"

There were laws, I suppose, against what I'd done, my first instinct being to admit nothing in mixed company. But the little caregiver angel on my shoulder began whispering in my ear, and I fessed up:

"Chloral hydrate, 750 m.g.'s. In the champagne."

"Holy mackerel," Killian recoiled.

"Should be fine," I added, fatiguedly, "in eight to twelve hours."

Hammer was keying his walkie-talkie, ordering an ambulance, Legate's shoulders bouncing with suppressed laughter. He pocketed a hand then, and took me aside, toward the kitchen, the champagne basin, letting me lean on him. When he faced me, bent low, he asked was I okay, besides the obvious. "I think so," I said, glimpsing up. "Might've known this was you. How'd you find me?"

Brows flickering, sweeping the room, he half-whispered:

"Tell you when we get outta here."

I nodded.

Shrugged then, haplessly, looking down at my party dress. Very bloodstained.

Sleeve torn. "Every time I get involved with you, Alan, I end up bleeding."

"*Post hoc ergo propter hoc?*"

"Excuse me?" I sputtered a laugh in spite of myself.

"Latin," he said. "*After this, therefore because of this.* It's a fallacy in logic: just because a thing happens before another thing, does not necessarily establish a cause-and-effect relationship." He shrugged lightly. "One thing might have nothing to do with the other, your bleeding, for instance, and my involvement."

I shook my head, still with a half-grin.

"Anything's possible. Get me the hell out of here."

He plunged back down into the ice some champagne he'd lifted out, rotated, dripping, to examine the label, then he strode around me back to Killian. "I'm taking Ms. Russell to Huntsville Hospital for stitches, Officer, and a lookover. We'll go in my car. Immediately after which, we'll both present ourselves to police headquarters."

Hammer, the Negro, curled a brow at his partner.

Killian met his look, then turned back to the FBI agent.

"Of course, sir," he said. "Care for a code-three escort?"

"Code two will be sufficient."

"Very well, sir."

"Doesn't want us out of his sight, Alan." I vamped up from behind. "Doesn't trust us."

Legate's spine drew stiffer, straighter, if that were possible.

He fussed at his French cuffs.

"Indeed," he said. "Officers…"

They postured to listen, most unobsequiously, however. It came as no surprise to me, there being no general love lost between Southern law enforcement and the FBI. "The bureau," Legate began, "and I can speak for Washington in this matter, would consider it a large favor if you would keep our Ms. Russell, here, clear of any of these"—he fluttered hands—"unseemly prostitution and gambling charges. Not to mention"—he scudded bespectacled eyes over Colonel

Feuerstein—"assault, attempted-poisoning, et cetera, et cetera. For the record, you may consider Ms. Russell to be a…a paid civilian consultant, to the Federal Bureau of Investigation."

It hurt to flicker my brow.

But I did, upon hearing this revelation. Pinching the brim, Killian adjusted his hat back, and blew up and emptied his big chest, then pulled the hat more firmly down, the two heavy-lidded eyes half covered. "Understand, Mr. Legate, we must clear such a—favor—with our sergeant, and likely's not, the district attorney will have to be consulted."

Legate blinked.

Gave the evil-clown smile.

Nodding.

"We, of course, understand that. Meanwhile, I will carry Ms. Russell to the hospital, under escort, and we'll meet back up at your headquarters after." He didn't seem to be waiting for an answer, as he pressed the small of my back, starting to walk me out. "One moment, Alan," I said, a placing a hand on the front of his shoulder.

He turned, and I explained, "These gentleman have my revolver, and I'm happy to let them hold onto it, as a show of good faith. But I would appreciate being allowed to go back down the hall, to get my pocketbook…?"

I made it a question for Killian and Hammer.

They looked at one another, shrugging, Killian nodding, gentlemanly, smiling, saying, "Sure."

"Thank you kindly," I said, delighted when no one followed me. I retrieved my half a strapless bra, and black panties, off the floor along the corridor as I went, then hunted for what I was really after: my purse with my camera and photographic evidence inside, which I'd tossed into one of the bedrooms for safekeeping. I panicked a little when I went into it, and didn't spot the bag immediately. Then I glimpsed the gold-chain handle tangled under the foot of the wrought-iron bed. "Oh," I gasped, going over, snagging it up. I knew from the weight the camera was still inside, and I stuffed the black underwear pieces on top, arranging them, camouflaging the camera as I'd begun the evening doing, then fastened the clasp. When I rejoined Legate and the cops in the front room, babying my cheek, I carried the vinyl-quilted bag over my shoulder, knocking against my left hip as I walked, heavier than it should have seemed, but the men paid no attention to that. Five minutes later I was the front-seat passenger in an all-black 1968 government Chevy, the heater blowing, pressing fresh ice against my cheek. Legate at the wheel trailed at moderate speed a Huntsville PD radio car, up a nearly silent and traffic-less Memorial Parkway. "Daphne Lindell spill the beans?" I asked, glimpsing over.

"Not…exactly," Legate replied, twisting the steering.

"Said you'd tell me."

"Actually, Ms. Russell, it's a fairly long story."

"Then get started."

He glimpsed sidewise.

"Feel up to it?"

"Look," I said, grating with frustration, "you may not believe this, but I had things pretty well in hand before your little police-raid stunt threw a monkey wrench into everything, as a result of which Veronika attacked me, and gave me this eye, and the need for stitches in my face—*my face, Alan*—so, yes, I damn well do want to know what happened."

"Ookey," he said, funny sounding. "Let me see, how far back to go…?"

"The beginning?" I said.

He darted a look, then back to watching the mercury-vapor-lit street.

He asked:

"Know who Martin Bormann is?"

CHAPTER 56

I HUFFED, SHAKING MY HEAD.

"Perhaps you're right."

I was winding some of my over-blonde hair around an index finger, watching Legate do the driving. "I just might, indeed, be too tired for a story opening with, *Do I know who Martin Bormann is?*"

"Do you?"

"Yes. Hitler's number two. Possibly alive and well in South America. Ralph Butterworth—"

"The motor-vehicle accident," he looked over, confirming, "Corinth, Mississippi."

"Correct. Only I'm dead sure, at this point, it was no accident. He was murdered. Anyway, Butterworth was interested in Martin Bormann. Might be some of what got him killed, but it's not all."

"J. Edgar Hoover," Legate said, "is likewise, interested in Bormann."

I bent my head.

"The FBI is hunting Bormann?"

His head shook. "Quite the contrary."

"So I was led to believe."

"But," he said, "Bormann is a fascination of the director's, a hobby, you might say. As a criminologist, he's curious to know the solution to the mystery. Did he survive the war? Escape?

Where to? There has been a standing order, at the bureau, going back twenty years, to route to Mr. Hoover's personal attention, every scrap about Bormann. Must be quite a file by now, most of it rubbish."

A lit-up bank sign we passed displayed a temperature of 39°F.

"Not following," I said. "What has this, to do with tonight?"

He looked over, and back. "Told you it was a saga. Heard of *Odessa*?"

I blinked.

"Yeah," I said, "city in Tex— No, wait—" Twisting suddenly in my seat, I peered hard at Legate through the darkness, dashboard lights reflecting in his eyeglass lenses. "Simon Wiesenthal's memoir..." I began to dredge it up. "ODESSA...was a secret organization, consisting of former SS members."

"Yes."

"They got Nazis out of Europe, war criminals, after World War II."

"Giving them new identities," Legate said, "and protection."

"Legal protection?"

"Yes. They have defense lawyers. They provide fake passports, the like, but when necessary, they play rough. Use muscle, even murder, if the threat is serious enough."

"Wait," I said. "ODESSA still exists?"

"It does."

I faced forward suddenly.

Exhaled.

"My God."

"And," he said, "they were *quite* interested in your Ralph Butterworth."

"He was asking the wrong people about Bormann, I know that," I said, "and another man, a war criminal, many think also to be dead, but never a body, just like with Bormann. A Heinz Valdemarr. Heard of him?"

"No. Except from you. You mentioned him on the phone."

He looked.

Shrugged.

"Really, Sherry, I never heard of him. Nazi hunting isn't my specialty."

"Is it anyone's?"

Shrugged again.

"Search me."

"Humph," I said.

"If I may be so bold," Legate said after we were quiet for a time, "you might be wrong about something."

"What's that?"

"Butterworth asking the wrong people."

"Yeah?"

"Maybe he asked the right people."

"And it got him killed," I said. "Right for his investigation. Wrong for staying alive."

"Could be."

"ODESSA killed Butterworth? That what you're telling me? Staged his car crash? Makes sense. There's good evidence they tried once before, to cause his plane to crash, a sophisticated type of sabotage." I nodded thoughtfully. "ODESSA sounds like it might have those kinds of resources."

It made sense.

"I don't know about that." Legate gestured with his hand on the wheel. "Might be right, but all I really know, for sure, is their interest in Butterworth, ODESSA's interest in him, that is, and Butterworth's interest in Bormann, all has come to the attention of..."

"Of who?"

"Central Intelligence."

CHAPTER 57

I DARTED MY FACE.
"The CIA?"
"Yes."
"*The* CIA?"
He gave me a nod. "*The* CIA."
"Not the Community Improvement Association?"
"Ahh, no."

We stopped for a red light, at Governors. Rolling up behind the police car's glowing red brake lights. "Now," Legate was going on, "haven't the foggiest idea how…"

I wasn't listening. I was staring ahead, heart pounding out of my throat. Crazy as it seemed, it was like I'd been dropped in the midst of a Matt Helm movie.

Sherry the Slaygirl.

This revelation actually jibing quite nicely, though, and disturbingly, with what Bernard B. Petrosky, the Pittsburgh PI, had reported about the bugging of the Butterworth home. "Wasn't through regular channels," Legate was saying, and I was hearing him again, "nor do I know what it contained, but FBI Headquarters somehow got hold of an internal CIA memo about Butterworth and ODESSA, a connection. And *because* that document mentioned Bormann, it was forwarded to Hoover, per that standing order, and…"

"Yeah?"

"Blew his stack."

"Hoover?"

He nodded.

"Why?"

The light blinked green.

We growled off again, steering a right. "Butterworth was an American," Legate explained, "a U.S. citizen, never left U.S. soil during the period of ODESSA's interest, far as we know."

"Far as I know, as well."

"Well, CIA's charter forbids it to operate on U.S. soil, right?"

I nodded.

"Only overseas. Very least, CIA was legally and procedurally obligated to have passed the ODESSA matter off to us immediately. They didn't. And Mr. Hoover is this close"—he displayed his thumb and forefinger, as if pinching something— "to ending all cooperation with CIA. On anything."

"Can he do that?"

He bent his head.

"Very little Mr. Hoover can't do, ma'am, if it's important to him."

"So, whatever else is happening," I said, "there's an FBI/CIA turf war in the middle of it."

"That, Miss Sherry, is about the size of it."

I sighed.

Head shaking. "Jesus Christ."

We were swinging up the hospital driveway, marked EMERGENCY.

"And that gets us almost up to you, tonight."

"Don't stop now."

"In response to the leaked memo," he said, "Mr. Hoover, less than two months ago, modified his standing order about Bormann. He was to be forwarded, to his personal attention, *all* German Nazi-related material."

"No longer," I said, "just mentions of Bormann."

"Correct."

"Go on."

"You contacted me twice this week."

My head twisted away, nodding.

"Once on Monday," he said. "Second time, Thursday."

"Monday, I asked you why Butterworth contacted your office. You replied, giving me George Dasch's history."

"Yes," he said. "And I flagged a memo, about your interest in Dasch, to Hoover."

"Because of Dasch's Nazi background."

"Yes."

He slipped us into a hospital parking spot, braking, and threw the gear shift into park. He faced me.

"Let me guess," I said, eyes flashing, hard edged, a sense of betrayal blossoming, "you did the same with my request for a license and registration check on Veronika Reinhard's Karmann-Ghia."

"Yes."

"Because her address is Dasch's address."

"Yes. Sorry, Sherry. My job."

I inhaled slow.

Let it out fast.

Nodded.

"I get it."

CHAPTER 58

A T THE HOSPITAL LEGATE GOT us shed of our Huntsville PD chaperones, claiming the case involved national security, arguing if he had to, he'd wake his SAC to have their chief contacted directly. Killian rang up his sergeant in response. There was talking back and forth, before he gave the phone to Legate, who reiterated his pledge to deliver me to police HQ, adding "before sunrise" to the arrangement. That dealt with, Legate threw more Federal weight around, getting me back to see a doctor PDQ. I made the man assure me he wasn't taking me ahead of some crushing chest pain or railroad spike through the brain, and he assured me, cheerfully, it was fine, it was a quiet night. Grimacing, I got my cheek laceration irrigated, painted with tincture of iodine, infiltrated—gritting my teeth some more—with Xylocaine, and finally closed with seven interrupted 5-0 Dermalin sutures.

Fresh with a dressing of Telfa and a rolled-up gauze two-by-two and tape, and feeling ever so beautiful—all the more for my increasingly blacking-up eye, bloodstained dress, not to mention the same dress's missing sleeve—I let Legate wheelchair me backward through a swinging set of doors exiting the emergency room. We wound, at a leisurely pace, through bright corridors, eventually finding the hospital's chapel. We had the place to ourselves at that wee hour. Refusing to be coddled, I pressed down on the armrests of the wheelchair, hoisting to my feet.

Then, cradling my side, sore despite the doctor's and my agreement that I had not in fact broken any ribs—I knew what broken ribs felt like, thanks to Biloxi, to Sal LaRocca—I eased onto a front pew, groaning. Then I crossed legs, smoothed the black rayon of my skirt, and rested my elbows up along the spine of the pew, hands drooping relaxedly from my wrists in front of me, and I waited, bright and attentive.

For the FBI man to resume his story.

Of how he and a police raid happened to converge upon the Chateau DeVille Apartments that night of all nights.

How it might "not exactly" be Daphne Lindell's fault.

Legate came around facing me and planted a cordovan-brown Corfam wingtip on the front edge of the bench seat, cupping his kneecap with one hand, hip-pocketing the other. His suit jacket, swept back, exposed a snub-nosed .38 with a walnut grip, butt-forward, holstered on a shiny brown belt, with a bright gold buckle. "I knew," he said, and cleared his throat, "you were in Huntsville."

I nodded. "I told you, Thursday on the phone."

"Right. It was Friday when I forwarded your interest in Veronika Reinhard to Mr. Hoover's attention. Tuesday, when I forwarded the Dasch report."

"Okay."

It hurt to blink.

"My office got a call Saturday, early," he said, "less than twenty-four hours ago, from a man identifying himself as Special Agent Tom Rhodes. Claimed to be from Headquarters, Washington, wanting to know the nature of our query into the Dasch file."

"*Claimed?*"

I twisted my head, shifted my body a bit. He went on as if I hadn't spoken. "The Birmingham agent getting the call reached me, as I'd instructed. Told him I'd handle it, and accepted responsibility. I was suspicious from the get-go: my report forwarded to Hoover's office had covered all that. And"—he shook his head—"be no other reason for the Bureau in Washington to know *any*thing of the matter."

"Okay," I said.

"I called Headquarters myself, talked to the switchboard. The call-back number left by the man identifying himself as Rhodes *was* a downtown Washington line, but not at the FBI building. And, when I asked for Special Agent Rhodes, turns out, there is a Tom Rhodes assigned to Headquarters, but not only was he not in on Saturday, he was off on vacation. Visiting family in Oklahoma, for Thanksgiving." Legate flung an open hand. "So, I had the operator use the reverse directory, give me the address belonging to the number given by the caller, the man calling himself Rhodes. It was on Pennsylvania Avenue, the Benevolent Literary Society."

"That's strange."

"Indeed. Then I had the operator transfer me to the Domestic Intelligence Division."

"Ahh, your old pals"—I smirked—"in the dirty-tricks department."

He let that go.

"I reached Sullivan, William C. Sullivan, division head, associate director, one of Mr. Hoover's key lieutenants. I told him the story, and he confirmed what I suspected."

"Which was…?"

"The Benevolent Literary Society is a front for the CIA."

"My God." I lowered my head, giving a slow, disbelieving side-to-side waver. "The CIA wanted to know about me," I muttered, "and Dasch."

"The CIA," he agreed.

Standing then, pacing stiffly, buttoning his coat.

"Or somebody the CIA is in bed with."

I glimpsed up, following him with my gaze.

Then it hit me.

"ODESSA," I said, softly.

"Might be."

He turned.

"Why?" I asked.

"We don't know. However, Director Sullivan and I did theorize along those lines. He told me to stay by the phone, and he'd get back to me within the hour. It was more like two, but when he phoned back, he told me he'd spoken to both Hoover directly, and to a special C.I."

"C.I.?"

"Confidential informant."

My good eye narrowed.

"I don't know for a fact," he said, without waiting for me to ask, "but I suspect it's someone inside CIA, probably high up."

"I see."

"You did not hear that," he said, "from me."

I looked at my lap, sighing.

Smoothed my skirt some more. Then I fingered my pocketbook, before remembering I was without cigarettes. I'd been bumming them all night from feel-copping Germans. Suffice it to say, come morning, not all my bruises and marks could be blamed on Veronika. Anyway, I dropped my bag, and Legate, reading my mind, shook me out a tan-filtered smoke from his pack. Thanking him, I put it between my lips. He got out his lighter, fired mine up, then one for himself. I refreshingly puffed a plume of smoke past pursed lips, before quipping: "I suffer from selective deafness."

"Good."

My disgust, though, at the whole crazy system, was brought to new heights.

The FBI having its own spies inside the CIA...

Clapping closed and pocketing the lighter, he put his cigarette in his mouth and stared at me, dragged his own lean chest deeply full. Then he deflected away like suddenly something had bounced off me and he was seeing where it went. When he came back into my face, twin streams jetting out satanic nostrils, again the eyes, somehow, ricocheted. He couldn't make himself look at me. The hand in which he was fingering the Kool Filter King flailed, and he went off pacing some more.

"What is it, Alan?" I said.

He stopped, three-quarter faced away, and spoke.

"Sullivan was told," he said, "you were a target."

My heart bumped.

"Me?"

"You." He pivoted on heels, focusing squarely again.

I ran nails through my mussed, too-blonde, curls.

Wincing from my eye, asking:

"Target of whom?"

"That's all he knew, or—"

He shrugged.

"—at least, all he told me."

I nodded, smoke floating dimly from my cigarette. I waited through several cycles of respirations in and out, breathing I was more conscious of than I should have been. "Sullivan asked," Legate eventually said, "if I could locate you."

I looked at him.

"I said I'd try. My orders were to notify him, directly, when I had a location."

"On me."

"Yes."

"*Moi*, who you had just been told was a target."

He trod softly over the carpet of the chapel, puffing silently off his cigarette.

"Yes."

"Please tell me, Alan, you trust this man implicitly."

"Director Sullivan," he said, "specifically, sternly, ordered me not to bring you in."

I swallowed.

Looked.

"Or *warn* me?"

"Or warn you."

"Why would that be?" I said softly, evenly.

No answer.

We both just kept smoking our cigarettes.

CHAPTER 59

I CALLED YOUR HOUSE," LEGATE said, once we both had fresh smokes.

"My house?"

"Long shot," he said, "in case you'd finished up in Huntsville, gone home. Seemed a logical first step. To my surprise, though, who picks up the phone? Not you. Not your answering system. But a Nashville Murder Squad detective, name of Deegan."

"He's a friend," I said.

"Uh huh."

"To be more accurate, he's a professional acquaintance."

He huffed, grinned mildly.

Bittersweetly?

"I...think I understand."

"You should," I said. Then:

"I suppose Ely, Ely Deegan, explained I had a break in."

"Yes."

"Bastards trashed my house. I asked him to cut through some red tape"—I shrugged—"that's all, get me a police report for insurance, while I was tied up down here. That's the truth. Whole truth. So help me God."

I blew smoke.

Tapped my ashes.

"Nothing missing, you told him."

"Yes."

"That true?"

I slowly shook my head.

"It's true that's what I told him."

"Something *was* missing?"

"A box of Ralph Butterworth's research."

The tapered chin lifted, and fell. "I guess," I sighed, "they tore my house apart looking for those files. When they found them, took them, they tried to cover up, make it look like kids, vandalism."

"Probably."

My eyes blurred.

Stung wet, salty, with tears.

I quavered at the shoulders.

Legate approached gingerly, cupped me by a deltoid.

Squeezed. "Sorry," he whispered. I nodded spastically, inhaled, blinking.

When I could manage, I looked up and told Legate that, on a positive note, they hadn't gotten everything. Nothing, in fact, of what I considered key in the lead-up to Butterworth's murder. "I have all that with me, here in town."

"Where?"

"Bus station locker."

A lie, one seeming prudent.

"Everything," I said, "about his interactions here with these Paperclip people."

Then, hardening my gaze:

"And that's something I want *you* keeping under *your* hat."

"I…"

"Tell no one, Alan. Especially not, this…this, Sullivan."

The hand caressing me, rather pleasantly, went away.

He tossed it in the air, reeling on his heels.

"Not this Sullivan," I blasted, raw-voiced, "who didn't even want me warned, who went out of his way to make sure you didn't get the bright idea *to* warn me, if you could. And let me just say, you ought to appreciate the great-big benefit of the doubt I'm tossing your way, in all this."

"Sherry."

"You owe me, Alan. So does Hoover."

"Provided," he said, twisting back, "I'm not asked pointblank. I won't lie to Headquarters."

I raked back my curls.

Nodded.

"Fair enough."

"I'm sorry, Sherry. For a lot."

"You haven't said how you found me. You talked to Deegan, but I made a special point of keeping him in the dark. Could've been in Moose Jaw, Saskatchewan, for all he knew."

"At that point," he said, "I could assume you were still in Huntsville, poking around Dasch and the Reinhards. So, I drove up. Paid an official call on Daphne Lindell, and her husband, who was home, it being a Saturday."

I nodded.

"My DMV query."

"Don't want a professional to find you, Ms. Russell, don't leave a trail of clues."

I sneered. "Don't think I could've found you given the same info?"

"Perhaps."

I huffed.

Finished my cigarette.

"Mrs. Lindell was only too happy to tell me what you two were up to. Where you were. Also about the prostitution and gambling. Don't blame her. I made sure they both got a good look at my badge, and I wasn't pretending to play nice."

I nodded.

"I...might've made a veiled threat against her husband's job."

"Of course you did."

I rearranged on the pew, listening.

"You were already in by that point," he said. "I phoned Director Sullivan from the Lindells', told him where you were and what the set up was. He ordered me to sit on the location, with Huntsville PD standing by, to raid the place. For prostitution and gambling. Then, he told me his scheme..."

"Yeess?" I said, skeptical.

"I'm sorry. I know..."

He sighed.

"Seems like the Klan matter, all over again..."

"Doesn't seem like that yet, Alan. You haven't told me anything."

"Sullivan's plan was to leak your location. Exact location. What you were doing, your cover, to the agency. To CIA. Didn't say how he was going to manage that, but it's part of my basis for concluding he has a mole, a spy if you will, on the inside."

"Pretty hard," I said, "to imagine a more screwed-up government."

He let that go.

"My tasking was to sit tight, watch, see what happened."

"See if somebody killed me."

"Sherry…"

"Go on."

"Well, what happened was, after just about two hours, George Peter Dasch tore into that apartment complex, entered one of the downstairs party rooms—and moments later re-emerged, Veronika Reinhard leading, both brandishing firearms. They raced upstairs, to where I now know you were supposed to be entertaining the old…general, or whatever he was."

"Alas," I said, "only a mere colonel."

"By then, I'd pulled the trigger on the raid. The rest, you know as well as I."

I waggled my head.

"How do we," I asked, "connect these dots?"

"Explain."

"One: FBI leaks to CIA I'm at the Chateau DeVille Apartments. Two: George Dasch scurries down from the Reinhard house, warns Veronika, and the two of them charge upstairs to nail me. What's the missing link, between step one, and step two?"

"We don't know."

"We can speculate."

"Can't take speculation into court."

"FBI rulebook," I said, "doesn't permit brainstorming?"

"Okay," Legate said, splaying hands. "Brainstorm away."

"Missing link: ODESSA."

"Go with that."

"You told me, Alan, you and this Sullivan theorized that the CIA might be in bed—*bed*, the term *you* used—with ODESSA."

"Indeed," he said. "What's *your* thinking on that?"

"Well, it's not rocket science, no pun intended. I suppose anything is possible in a world where the FBI spies on America's own spies, but I'm not at this point willing to assume George Peter Dasch is hardwired into the CIA." I shrugged, with one shoulder and a brow. "Maybe I'm wrong—he *was* in intelligence—but seems more probable to me, the CIA contacted ODESSA, and they in turn, dispatched Dasch. Whether as a stopgap, or perhaps he's a full-fledged—like the Mafia calls them—*made man*, in ODESSA. Maybe they got him bodyguarding Reinhard and the girl."

"Hah," Legate reacted.

Then became quiet.

"What do you know about *made men*?"

"I know things, Alan. I know people. I had a very full life before we ever met, chockful of disreputable characters."

"Like who?"

"It's another story, Alan. Maybe, I'll tell you some day."

There it was, the evil-clown grin, above it an eye narrowing down.

It was a line of curiosity that I had reasons of my own for squelching.

"You're full of surprises, Sherry."

"All real women are. Can we stick with one web of deceit at a time?"

"Sure."

He nodded, blinking, still with the maniacal smile.

"Actually, you make a key distinction," he said, "for our purposes: is Dasch CIA, or is he ODESSA?"

"Uh huh…?"

I looked up.

"If Dasch is CIA, we'll hit a brick wall."

"Get nowhere."

"If he's ODESSA, with enough evidence, we might have a chance."

"If," I said, "Dasch and his connections are a gangrenous appendage, rather than part of the body, they might be amputated."

"Excellent metaphor."

"Thank you," I said. "So we assume Dasch is ODESSA."

He nodded.

"Otherwise, we're sunk."

"Logical."

"For a girl?" I said.

CHAPTER 60

FOR EXPEDIENCY, THEREFORE, IT WOULD be assumed that the conduit leading from (1) the FBI's leak to the CIA to (2) my confrontation with the Germans, Veronika Reinhard and George Dasch, in the bordello apartment, was ODESSA.

The missing link.

An organization of former SS members dedicated to concealing and protecting, by subterfuge if possible, force if necessary, their former brethren—all crown princes of evil, having branded their mark, perhaps still doing so, upon a century that had run little more than half its course, yet had already proved unprecedentedly violent. Ironic, considering our veils of civilization, modernization, compared to say those medieval sword, pike, and battleax centuries of yore.

ODESSA was an organization shrouded in secrecy, yet known to be operating to this day in Europe, and which apparently had metastasized across the pond, to America, carried perhaps by the Paperclip scientists.

Operating perhaps in their service.

Perhaps at their behest.

"If ODESSA sicced Dasch on me," I said, "I need to know who else they contacted."

"What are you thinking?" Legate said.

Legate was sitting now, bent forward, elbows on knees,

331

flatfooted on the floor, socks argyle, looking at me sideways. "Somebody else is out there," I told him, a little desperately. "A big man, driving a Renault, blue, Illinois plates. I think I'd recognize him if I saw him again. I think he wrecked my house, took Butterworth's research. I think he was watching me."

My head shuddered. I despised how vulnerable I felt suddenly, not a competent nurse, not an intrepid detective, here in a hospital chapel, beside a man, not a colleague, a man who I, a woman, with a black eye and torn dress, and an invaded, ransacked house, suddenly longed to be held by, protected by.

"I want to know who he is," I said, sputtering, "and I want him, goddamn, gone, out of my life."

The crying angered me, the last straw. I rocked forward, up off the pew, standing, a little wobbly, but up on my own two feet again.

And when I moved, so did Legate.

I refused his help, his reaching for my arm. Instead I plodded around, facing him, grasping the polished side and back of the pew for support. "Thing is," I said, voice clogged, though I'd gotten the waterworks stifled, "if you're right, your CIA contact was right, and I am a target of ODESSA's, it's probably this man, the Renault man, and he's still out there. He killed Butterworth, either setting up or helping Veronika set up, the Corinth, Mississippi accident scene."

"Could be."

"I really believe Dasch's stone killer days are over. The mind willing perhaps, but the body's, from what I've seen, a little too arthritic. And there's more to Veronika than meets the eye, more than just parties, mail drops, money laundering. For starters, she doesn't confine herself to Huntsville, Alabama. She travels. I don't know where all, but I do know she's plugged into, and in no trivial way, that nest of Nazis in South America."

I shrugged. "Maybe Bormann himself."

"Interesting."

He lit a cigarette and smoke it, pacing, a hand pocketed, listening as I ran through quickly, for his benefit, Veronika Reinhard's Miss Nazi crowning, in Santiago, Chile, and my investigation of Bobby Kaplan, of the Ohio White Nationalist League, and of the altimeter sabotage, what I knew, and suspected. I tacked on the end, Butterworth's encounter with a "Dr. Schmidt," in Florida. Three locations, at least, in the United States, and one in South America, where there was direct evidence of Nazi activity.

And that was just what I had uncovered.

How much more iceberg must be still hidden?

When I got through, there was silence.

Only the PBX operator murmured overhead until Legate finally unfolded, giving me a level, nodding look. "We'll sweat the Reinhard woman," he said, "and Dasch. It's a start."

"*We?* Mean, I'm included?"

"If I can swing it. You, Ms. Russell, know the case better than anyone." He shrugged. "Provided, of course, you feel up to it?"

"Wouldn't miss it."

My gaze, though, narrowed. "How long before NASA puts the kibosh on us? Gets them released? Lest some Paperclip scientist gets so upset, he suffers a hangnail, and the whole moon program has to be scrubbed."

Evil-clown grin.

"Let's find out."

THE PUBLIC SAFETY BUILDING WAS downtown on Gallatin Street, a hop, skip, and a jump north of Huntsville Hospital. We arrived before five A.M., beating our Sunday-dawn deadline. Walking through glass doors into the lobby, I wore a trench coat of Legate's over my shoulders like a cape, covering my ruined dress. No cops pounced me, took me in a choke hold, or anything. At the desk, Legate folded open his badge case, flashing the gold Federal star, and introduced us. We were directed to the third floor, to a Detective Sergeant McClashon's desk. He took a #2 pencil out of his mouth, and rolled it, looking at the teeth marks. Then looked up at Legate. Then me. His eyes went over me, exploring, noting me, cataloguing me. He invited us then with arm gestures, to take seats in two guest chairs upholstered in blue vinyl, proceeding to inform us, as I'd feared:

NASA was raising holy hell.

McClashon had been on the phone twice already, with his

chief, a man named Dyar—who in turn had been talking with the mayor, who had, together with the district attorney, received deeply concerned calls out of the night from none other than Wernher von Braun.

Mr. Space himself.

The upshot being no prostitution nor pandering charges would be filed. No one, after all, had actually been caught in a sexual act. The DA would mull over some misdemeanor gambling beefs, but everyone, the men and women, meanwhile, would be released on their own recognizance. "Including," I blistered, "Veronika Reinhard, George Dasch?"

His large eyes peered at me.

"Including Miss Reinhard," he said, with slow movements, voice toneless, flat, uninterested. "She is, as we speak, being out-processed."

I exhaled heavily.

"Sergeant, I have good evidence linking her with a probable murder."

A pair of bristly eyebrows moved.

Albeit slightly.

"Murder you say…"

"The victim," I said, "a man named Butterworth. Ralph Butterworth."

"Butterworth, huh…"

"That's right."

He tipped back, creakingly, in his chair, twisting the pencil in his fingers. "Not to mention," I plowed on, "I was assaulted by her highness, the Countess Veronika." I gestured flailingly up around the battering of my face, the bandaged cheek, bruised eye. "Evidence of which, you can plainly see, if you're not blind."

McClashon cleared his throat with a snort. He reached his pipe off the desk. Knocked it out and refilled it, looking sidewise at Legate, while tamping down the tobacco with the brass end of the pencil. He lit it then, with a struck wooden match, looking back at me, and blew smoke, before beginning to talk again. "No one, ma'am," he told me, "is slamming the door on any legitimate investigation, or charges. The city, and county, are simply doing NASA a favor, letting them have the benefit of any doubt."

"A self-serving favor," I said, "considering the space economy here, the local job market."

He gave a slow nod, a dark stare, smoke drifting from his pipe.

Then, a barely perceptible shrug.

As if saying, *Touché, mademoiselle.* "You wish to view it that way," he said, pipe clamped in his teeth, "suppose there could be truth in that position."

I nodded.

"I'm sure there is," I said. "And it's understandable."

He took the pipe out of his mouth.

Leaned back, staring more, different angles. Wasn't sure he wouldn't relish beating my teeth out. Or maybe it'd be enough just to blacken my other eye, even me out, symmetry being, after all, the essence of beauty. Something was stopping him. Perhaps nothing other than an FBI Agent sitting there cross-legged beside me, in his pressed suit and tie. My bodyguard. He certainly wasn't speaking up any more than a mere bodyguard, permitting me the initiative. To sink or swim. McClashon puffed on the pipe stem again, blew a little smoke from the corner of his mouth.

He asked me: "What you want?"

"To talk to them," I said. "Or at least sit in, while you or one of your men do. Or Agent Legate."

I smiled, testing my mother's adage about catching more flies with honey than vinegar. "No can do," McClashon said, shrugging with eyebrows and pipe. "I'm sorry. Orders. Nobody talks to them. Not this weekend. Beside, as I said, the girl's on her way home."

"Sergeant—"

He halted me with a mildly lifted palm.

"Nevertheless, Ms. Russell," he said, "Chief Dyar has instructed me to make assurances to you, the district attorney will, in due course, view all your exhibits, and entertain your story."

I blinked.

Swallowed.

"When might this be?"

"Soon." Another shrug, the pipe all by itself. "Not before Monday."

I glimpsed Legate, silent as a statue.

"You're giving them time," I told McClashon, "to cover up."

"I don't know that you aren't right, ma'am, but those are my orders." His eyes heavy and motionless, smoke wisping out of the bowl of the pipe. "You spoke of favors, Ms. Russell. Favors to NASA. Well, we're just chockful of favors this morning. The DA's willingness to talk to you, personally, is another. Except that was a favor to the FBI." He glimpsed Legate. "A call from Washington I might add, not Birmingham, confirming you, ma'am, to be a consultant."

Legate suddenly did pipe up in that brogue of his:

"We appreciate, Sergeant, your cooperation." I looked at him, then McClashon, thanking him as well. I wanted to talk to Veronika and Dasch, that was true. On the other hand, I really didn't care about the assault charge, as annoyed as I was about my face. I'd reiterated Veronika attacking me only out of desperation. If I'd pressed it, she'd counter that I'd been holding them at gunpoint—which would be true—and claim she and her uncle felt their lives threatened, and were just defending themselves. She could probably make that story stick, all things considered, so I did have to count myself lucky to not be in police custody. I wasn't sure why, but seemed like the FBI—not simply Legate, one agent, who might be carrying a torch for me—was throwing up enough of a smokescreen to keep me on the good side of the Huntsville constabulary. Otherwise they'd have squashed me like a bug, or at least shooed me off, in yet another favor to NASA, to von Braun, to Mr. Space. "You specified," I groaned, rearranging in my chair, trying to ease the aching in my side, "Miss Reinhard, was being released, when I asked about her and Dasch."

"Yes." McClashon shrugged forward all of a sudden.

"What," I asked, "about Dasch?"

"He's staying."

"Why?"

"Confessed."

"To what?"

"Murder."

My jaw fell open.

"What?"

He consulted some jottings in a green folder.

He was a burly man, sagging heavily back in his swivel chair.

"The murder, some weeks back," he said, "of a party you know, Ms. Russell…"

"Yeah."

"Ralph Butterworth."

CHAPTER 61

"MY GOD," I SAID.

Not original, but my reply was spontaneous. They were still keeping him under wraps. Even Legate, for now, denied access. Dasch had confessed and would neither seek nor accept bail. He was stoically refusing to answer questions, wishing to see no one. The city would honor that request at least through the weekend, and sort things out after the first of the week. "It's dicey for us," McClashon acknowledged, "to your point, Ms. Russell, about the local economy, local politics…"

I nodded.

"This man Dasch being the brother-in-law, forcrissakes, a member of the household, of Dr. von Braun's top deputy. We're all on eggshells here, if I may be candid, and off the record."

"I get it," I said.

Legate said nothing, having barely uttered a word since we'd all exchanged introductions. Breathing quietly, listening, immaculate hands laced before him. I pressed gingerly over the dressing below my eye, found the tape secure, and proceeded to inform McClashon there was reason to believe George Peter Dasch, formerly of the Abwehr, and SS intelligence, had cold-bloodedly murdered a noncombatant, knifed a British Red Cross girl, no less, in England, during World War II, perhaps also, prior to that, an American civilian named Yacobean. Both killings surely war crimes, in and of themselves. I might be right, the detective acknowledged, adding, it surely wasn't his call to make. Anyway, plenty of time for all that. Dasch was going to be held, pending a quick extradition—which he had also pledged to not oppose—to Alcorn County, Mississippi, which had full jurisdiction for now over the Butterworth death.

"Ahh…" I nodded. "I see."

"See *what*, ma'am?"

"You and your bosses," I said, "liking nothing better than a quick, quiet foisting of this entire mess off onto Mississippi."

"What of it?" He blew smoke with a backward jerk of his head, looked at the mouthpiece of his pipe, and continued: "Justice is served, and it's lawfully appropriate."

"And doesn't have you too much ruffling NASA's feathers."

He bit down on the pipe stem, staring again.

"Can you at least tell us," I said, "what happened when Mr. Dasch was brought into the station, what exactly was said."

"No harm in that, if it would be helpful."

"It would," I said, and crossed my legs, smoothed my skirt, and waited.

Listened.

The old German undercover agent broke down, it seemed, upon arrival, sobbing, claiming to have, three weeks earlier, walked in on Miss Veronika Reinhard and Ralph Butterworth, in bed, in that very apartment he and Veronika had just been hauled out of. Veronika, mortified, had covered her nudity, before her uncle, protesting the intoxicated book author had blackmailed her into sex, into performing repellant acts of depravity, in fact—otherwise he would have, in print, accused her father, a high-ranking NASA official, of Nazi war crimes. Dasch then, in a fit of rage, attacked Butterworth, killing him, after which the road accident was arranged as a cover up. Arranged by Dasch and Dasch alone. That was his story. Not to save himself, but to shield the Reinhard family from scandal— Veronika, and her father, his brother-in-law, a brilliant scientist who had been kind enough to take in Dasch and his beloved wife, Martha, give them a home in the States, when they were refugees from war-torn Europe. He would not have any of them suffer, he emphasized, for his own rash, violent act.

CHAPTER 62

"Y<small>OU</small>," I <small>FUMED</small>, "<small>WERE A</small> *big* help."

Outside, well past dawn by then, it was cold and cloudy, the Sunday before Thanksgiving. Legate lit me a cigarette, in apology, and another for himself, spewing the smoke out, the wind taking it rapidly off. "You managed okay," he said, snapping his Zippo closed.

"Thanks."

"Besides, I didn't believe you wanted men leaping to your rescue all the time."

I looked up.

Looked him in the eye, narrowing my good one.

"Half surprised," I breathed, "you comprehend that."

"You are quite competent, Ms. Russell."

My lower lip quavered.

I was silent, still studying him, feeling my heartbeat.

Then I dropped my gaze—stunned, really.

"That…" I stuttered, "might be…the most…important thing anybody ever said to me."

"It's true."

I smiled.

"Well, for the record, Alan, while you *are* right, generally speaking, about my opinion of unsolicited rescuing, I was quite okay last year"—I took a puff, blew the smoke—"with you and the cavalry showing up, when the Ku Klux Klan had me trussed up to a tree."

His shoulders jumped, a chuckle huffing through his hooked nose.

"You thought it was *you* we came for?"

He gazed off, toward Big Spring Park.

"Naw. Lee Autrey. He needed rescuing."

I began to laugh like a loon.

"Long as it wasn't me," I snorted.

"Scout's honor." He put up the three-finger salute.

Then plucked the cigarette from his mouth, flicked the ash.

"This," he said, "wraps up your case doesn't it?"

I had drawn his London Fog coat, shruggingly, more tightly around me.

"Does it?"

I looked up.

McClashon had had one of his officers type up my statement. I'd signed it. It was brief and limited to my presence at the party, my drugging of Feuerstein, and confrontation with Veronika Reinhard and George Dasch. I listed the items from the bedroom—wig, baby-doll nightie, so forth—establishing the setting of the blackmail photos sent to Butterworth's wife. I was assured the items would be seized and tagged. I said nothing about my camera or the photos I'd taken of the aforementioned items. I wanted insurance in the, as I saw it, likely event of a cover-up.

Perhaps I was just a paranoiac.

"Butterworth was murdered," Legate said. "It's official. Is not that what you were hired to learn?"

I blew smoke from the side of my mouth.

Licked chapped lips, sighed.

"Doesn't clear him of marital infidelity."

"Is that what you were hired to do?"

"No. But it *has* become important. For me, at least. I don't believe for a second Ralph Butterworth blackmailed that woman into sex with a threat to expose her father. He may *well* have been intending to expose her father as a war criminal but I believe him to have had more integrity than to offer the family that kind of out—or perhaps any kind of out."

He downward nodded, thoughtfully.

"Not his style," I said, "as I see it, anyway."

I pulled a drag from my cigarette, that hand outside the coat, the other hugging it around me. Legate shrugged. "You're discussing motive. I acknowledge, Dasch is probably trying to protect his accomplices, his family members, but do you doubt his guilt, motive aside?"

"Don't look confessions, like gift horses, in the mouth?"

"Something like that," he said, grinning.

"My theory of Butterworth's death has long been that either Dasch killed him to keep knowledge of his World War II activities suppressed—knifing the Red Cross girl for instance— or that Dasch, or someone else, killed Butterworth to protect Heinz Valdemarr. A top Nazi war criminal, right up there with Martin Bormann. Butterworth believed *him* to be in the United States. Not in some deep hidey-hole in South America, like Bormann. Probably this Valdemarr has some new identity, probably created by ODESSA, judging from all you told me."

"Possible," he said.

"This confession—false confession, partly anyway, if you ask me—makes perfect sense in light of all of that."

"Elaborate."

Squinting, he puffed his cigarette.

Pinched it aggressively from his lips.

"He's loyal to the family," I said, thinking it out, "probably to Veronika, in particular. Nor do we have any reason to believe he's not a loyal Nazi."

Legate was nodding.

"His confession, the way he framed it, protects Veronika from a murder charge, even an accessory charge. In his version, she's a sexually exploited dupe in Ralph Butterworth's blackmail scheme. In mine, she, Dasch, maybe somebody else, maybe from ODESSA, conspired to kill Butterworth, then muddy the waters, making it look like there was an affair, when there hadn't been."

"I see your point."

"His confession," I said, eyes sparking, "makes the whole thing personal. Makes it, hot-blooded, murder in the heat of passion. Takes ODESSA, whatever larger Nazi conspiracy there might be"—I spread my arms—"if there is one, out of the picture, off the hook."

"Okay." He scraped the thumbnail of the hand holding his cigarette along his lower lip. "What do you do next?"

"Tell my client what he wanted to know. Butterworth was murdered. Then, submit my report, my bill, get a fat check, minus advances. Then, I'm going to tell Mrs. Butterworth I don't think her husband was having an affair, or even that he was blackmailing another woman into sex, and I'm going to continue working to prove that."

"If you're lucky," Legate said, twisting his head, "she'll hire you."

My mouth twitched.

"If I'm lucky. Regardless I'm going to try. Call me a romantic. I don't think this was a man who would cheat on his wife. Do you think we can manage an interview with Dasch, in the jail? Get permission?"

"Doubt it," Legate said. "They'll use the fact it's Sunday to drag the red tape out."

"Yeah."

It was starting to occur to me, no longer the Pollyanna I once was, that my old buddy Alan Legate might just be running interference, following orders, say, out of Washington. Help her just so much, but no more. He himself, after all, had suggested a connection between ODESSA and some Washington faction, some faction, mind you, within our own government. "No matter," I said, darting the cigarette onto the sidewalk, grinding it beneath my shoe, glimpsing up. "I can wait till he gets to Alcorn County. The sheriff there and I are like *that*..." I raised an index and a middle finger, side by side, two peas in a pod.

Smirking.

No, I was not Sheriff Grady Bingham's favorite individual.

And having a confessed killer extradited into his lap, after his department ruled the relevant death accidental, might or might not improve his disposition towards me. Still, I had an ace in the hole, I thought, in that neck of the woods.

A Tennessee sheriff by the name of Pusser.

Legate drove me to my car. Around the corner from the Morganton Arms Hotel, where I'd joined up with the Nazi party girls, not much more than twelve hours earlier, though it felt far longer. He asked if I could drive, holding open the door of the

Impala for me, as I grimaced, sliding behind the wheel. I promised him I was fine. He shut my door, and followed me to my motel down Memorial. He made a call from my room, then watched Lawrence Spivak moderating *Meet the Press*, while I changed, got cleaned up, my body livid with bruises. I emerged from the bathroom, however, turning a pirouette, nigh on presentable, if you got past the black eye and stitches, wearing a burgundy pullover, tweed slacks, even tasteful spritzes, inside the wrists, at the neck, of Eau Sauvage.

We ordered room service.

The FBI stenographer he'd sent for arrived equipped with a reel-to-reel recorder. I gave them everything I knew and suspected about what might be a well-financed conspiracy to build a Fourth Reich, to which Heinz Valdemarr, current identity unknown, might be of vital importance. I gave them what I knew and suspected of Veronika Reinhard, crowned Miss Nazi 1968 (the steno glimpsing up at that, flabbergasted, the efficient woman's only overt reaction to any of it), who appeared to be running a network of illegal mail drops all over Huntsville, funneling funds—funds for sure, possibly information, possibly directives—to Paperclip scientists, via their wives, via Audrey's Beauty Salon. Funds from where? South America? For what purpose? Legate speculated, wildly, he admitted, they could be transferring information, classified data, from say, our space program, between German rocket scientists at NASA, and counterparts working for the Russians.

Whatever Veronika was up to, seemed to be operated out of that private apartment, whose mailbox sported the name *Dr. L. Theofila.* Legate said he'd run a check on the name, apply for federal warrants to search the apartment (no probable cause to do so vis-à-vis the gambling/prostitution raid involving the other units), and the suspected mail drops. He'd subpoena the Paperclip families' bank records as well. "Think you're going to get all *that*?" I asked, showing my paranoiac stripes. "We'll see," he said benignly, evil-clown grin. I told them about the loose-lipped virologist bragging about top-secret work at Fort Detrick, Maryland. I gave them what I knew about Bobby Kaplan: Kid Nazi from East Liverpool, Ohio. I told them about the altimeter sabotage, the opinion of the Barfield Instruments technician. I left Vince Petrolino's name out of it, just in case. I told them about tow-truck driver Newel McClanahan, another American Nazi, who probably helped stage Butterworth's car accident, later found murdered in Panama City, Florida.

We finished around three.

The steno left. Legate turned, asking if I wanted protection. I said no, I'd be returning to Nashville early Monday. I'd drive back down whenever, if ever, the Huntsville DA really wanted to talk. Meanwhile—exhausted from two all-nighters, babying my eye and bruised side and knuckles from my fight with the reigning Miss Nazi (thinking I'd acquitted myself rather well against an opponent capable of winning such a title)—I planned to drink a couple of Scotches, in my room, then get a decent night's sleep. I promised not to get blitzed out, to keep my door locked and chained, my gun on the nightstand. The police, by the way, had returned it to me. I asked what Legate planned. He said he'd keep the information I'd provided confidential, until he knew what was best, had things more figured out.

Clearly there were risks, care must be taken. I told him I agreed. He said he'd consult privately with his SAC, whom he assured me, could be trusted—a man named McNeill, Gerry McNeill.

I asked, pushing my chin toward the door, what about the steno? She would give him all her notes and tapes, and of course the typewritten statement, which, eventually, I would have to sign. He would keep a copy and leave the only other with McNeill. The steno would say nothing, ever. If asked, by anyone, outside of a courtroom, she would report the inquiry to him immediately.

"What," I said, "is she a robot?"

"A little bit."

"Just like you, Alan," I lilted.

"That what you think of me?"

"Alan, y—"

He tried to kiss me.

I darted my head back, mouth agape.

My splayed hand pressing Alan Legate's necktie, suddenly but gently separating us. And he let me, hands releasing, falling away, ratchet-like, hands that had eagerly, almost brutally, grasped me above both elbows, bunching my shoulders up to my ears.

"Sherry—I'm sorry."

"A-Alan…"

"Oh my God," he said. "I'm sorry."

He spun away, then back, seized the doorknob, as if to flee, in utter mortification.

"Alan wait," I demanded, coming forward. "It's okay."

Hands out, gesturing.

"I'm sorry," I said.

"No. I got carried away. Forgive me."

"Nothing to forgive. I'm flattered. Really. Taken off guard. But flattered."

"But, not interested…"

"No. I mean, that's not it."

"Forget it, please, Sherry." He was vacillating, a rat in an electric-shock experiment, between where I was standing, and the door to the outside. "I've ruined everything."

"No, Alan. I'm just not ready. It's me, all me. I like you, Alan. I appreciate you. I just haven't been divorced that long. I'm not ready to jump into anything—another relationship—yet."

My shoulders shrugged, hands flung.

"You can see that…"

"Yes," he said, sagging. "Of course."

"Thank you."

"Just," he said, smoothing his hair, "I…I have fond memories…that little spaghetti joint in Columbus. Mississippi."

I nodded.

"More the company," he added, "than the food."

"Me too. Both were okay, as a matter of fact, in my book."

I sighed, knotting my arms, pacing.

"Well, well, isn't this a surprise."

"Pleasant one, I hope?"

I held a look on him, exhaling.

Nodded.

"Course it is. Look, Alan, I'll think about it. I promise. I will."

"May I wait awhile, and call you?"

I swallowed.

"Okay."

"Good."

"Just...give me some time."

He nodded, tormentedly.

"I won't forget," I said, "I promise."

"Okay." I barely heard him.

"I swear. I won't go off"—I flung an arm nonchalantly—"marry somebody else, without telling you."

"Not exactly the assurance I'd hoped for."

"I know."

I smiled.

Demurely.

He took my hand. Gently kissed the back of it, cupped his other atop the kiss.

"Be careful, Sherry."

He left, driving away.

Neither of us saw the blue Renault Caravelle Cabriolet parked out front of the Pizitz Tire Center across Memorial. Nor had we seen it track us from police headquarters to the Morganton Arms, then to here. The driver released the brake, worked the shift, and tailed after the black government Chevy as Special Agent Alan Legate of the FBI pushed south on Route 231, back toward Birmingham. He got gas at an American Oil station outside Cullman, uncharacteristically petulant with the attendant, and preoccupied, then set off again, now without the ODESSA executioner in pursuit. Kargher having, quite furtively for a large man, absconded with the station's copy of the credit-card slip, from the office, with Legate's name and license written on it.

CHAPTER 63

TOOK ABOUT A WEEK FOR my homeowner's insurance— my agent was my father's drinking buddy, naturally, which hurt nothing—to fork over the check covering my ransacking damages. I made the man take an oath not to say anything to daddy, even in passing, about my claim. My parents had a dim enough view of my neighborhood. Detective Ely Deegan, bless him, had personally paid a plumber to unclog my toilet, and arranged for a cleanup—for which I, appreciatively, reciprocated with a fifth of Jack. He'd called upon one of those crews homicide cops know, who tidy up violent-crime scenes, the messes people leave when, for example, they kill themselves by blowing their brains out with .357 Magnums, sawed-off shotguns, and the like.

Home from Huntsville Monday just past nine A.M., I managed to flip my slashed mattress, clumsily, but managed it, to where I could sleep on the intact side. I made the bed with undamaged linens. I checked all back through the house, assuring all doors and windows were secure. The screen was off the back window over my claw-footed bathtub, a pane partly chiseled out. A screwdriver, inserted through that opening, used to work the latch, was how he got in. That's how I would've done it, I thought, shrugging with eyes and mouth and bitter irony. Cardboard was taped over the opening. I called a glazier to fix that, arranging for first thing Tuesday afternoon. I was uneasy, I admit. Scared, to be completely honest. Despite the seeming resolution of the Butterworth case, whoever had burglarized my house *was* still out there. *Could* still come back.

Somebody from ODESSA almost certainly. Dasch was in custody, but far as I knew, he'd never left Huntsville, nor did I think him fit enough to climb through my bathroom window. Veronika Reinhard was, but she'd been managing her parties. And while she could have raced to Nashville just as I had, there was utterly no rational basis for believing she had.

Almost certainly then, a third perpetrator remained at large. A third perpetrator who was an aider and abettor with George Dasch and Veronika Reinhard in the Butterworth killing, and then tied up a loose end, killing Newell McClanahan in Florida.

Barehanded.

Broke his neck, Sheriff Pusser told me.

Bobby Kaplan?

Gave my head a shake.

I doubted Kaplan had the physical strength to break the neck of a rough-and-tumble denizen of the State-Line area like McClanahan. Actually, a theory I was germinating gave Kaplan and McClanahan essentially equal status in a greater Nazi-run conspiracy: I figured them both pawns of ODESSA, low-rent local talent, recruited p.r.n.—nurse-speak for, *on an as needed basis*—from domestic neo-Nazi and other white-supremacist-type groups, for specific tasks. In Kaplan's case, the Ohio White Nationalist League. In McClanahan's, the National White Americans Party.

Which begged a question:

What was I, if not low-rent local talent? Cut from better cloth than Kaplan or McClanahan, I was willing to maintain, but ODESSA was a clearly international conspiracy. Then there was Legate's assertion of a CIA connection *forcrissakes!*

The point being, I sighed, was I out of my league?

Wouldn't be the first time.

But that didn't give me carte blanche to be stupid.

Should I cut and run?

Let sleeping dogs lie?

THE DRESSING BELOW MY EYE needed to stay in place another

day, the sutures a total of three to five. They could come out the day before or after Thanksgiving, and I wasn't above snipping them out on my own. But they were minuscule, and quite close to my eye. I figured I'd be a good little patient and find a steady-handed doc to pluck them out. I probed, in the mirror, up close, with fingertips all about the eye itself, the socket, without flinching too much. It and the cheek, though, were thoroughly bruised.

Yet again I would have to think up some excuse about not seeing my parents until the discoloration faded, at least somewhat.

Then, I remembered *Thanksgiving!*

Screamed, "Jesus Christ," through my teeth.

Cross that bridge later, I decided, rubbing circles in my temples. For now neither mama nor daddy knew I was back. I'd leave it that way. I perked some coffee. I read the paper while I drank it with sugar, no cream. I'd sniffed, the cream curdled and reeking, spoiled, victim of my vandal attack. The paper said three U.S. planes were downed over the weekend, three weeks into LBJ's bombing halt. Since 1965, 918 American aircraft, lost in Vietnam.

After taking some aspirin I lay down awhile. Getting beat up by an Amazon Nazi takes the starch out of you, even if you do sort of win the fight. Up at one o'clock, I gargled and swiped a brush over my hair in the mirror. I hated my hair this way, the Marlene Dietrich coiffure. For years I'd had a standing hair appointment on Wednesdays, day after tomorrow being no exception. I supposed I could wait that long to get it colored, shampooed and set, put back as correctly as could be managed, without witchcraft. Then, donning a windbreaker, slipping on a pair of Foster Grants, to obscure my bruised eye—the big dark ones Raquel Welch modeled with the sailing ship tattooed on her deltoid—I went over and got my papers and mail. Having an afterthought, I twisted back from my neighbor's porch steps, and called through her closing screen. "Mrs. Harwell, pardon me, but by chance did you see anybody strange hanging around my house while I was away?"

"Well…the police…on Saturday. You knew that."

"Yes, ma'am."

"Now…" She was thinking, tapping rapidly the center of her upper lip.

"Yes?" I encouraged.

"Just, that insurance man."

"Insurance man?"

"He said he had an appointment. Asked if I knew where you were. I said you were out of town. Is that all right?"

"Of course. When was this?"

"Day you left. Wednesday?"

"Must've slipped my mind."

"Oh, that happens, dear."

"I don't even remember his name."

"I have his card," she said. "Would you like it?"

"Oh, yes, thank you."

I climbed back onto the porch. She disappeared into her foyer. A desk drawer scraped open. She came back with a business card for NATIONWIDE INSURANCE, 1808 WEST END. Salesman's name, DONALD ISBELL. I asked her for a rough description. "Very tall," she said, "broad shouldered, too." She made her voice deep and stuck out her elbows. I grinned. "Do you watch football?"

"Some," I said.

"He was like that…that Dick Butkus, plays for the Bears."

"Same age?"

"No. Older."

"Gray haired?"

"Yes."

"Long?"

"No. What do they call it? Crew cut."

"What kind of car?"

"Lemme see…"

She tapped her lip again.

"Foreign?" I asked, thinking of the man I'd seen packed into that Renault, before my trip. I'd not seen him terribly well, but what I had seen fostered in me no belief he might not be capable of breaking a man's neck barehanded, even one such as McClanahan. "Well, yes, now that you mention it," she said, finally, getting my attention back, "I suppose they are foreign. It was a Volkswagen. Black, I think."

"A VW. A Beetle?"

"Yes."

"You're sure?"

She recoiled.

Insulted.

"Certainly think I know one of those Love Bug cars when I see one."

"Of course. Thank you." I went back in my house, piled the mail and papers onto the dining-room table and dialed in the number on the Nationwide card. I asked the receptionist if Donald Isbell was a big man, over six feet, close to 250 pounds, like Dick Butkus. "Oh my no," she told me. "Mr. Isbell is a rather smallish man, perhaps five-five, rail thin, mustache, and large bald spot."

"Thank you, I thought so. Goodbye."

I hung up.

Rat-a-tat-tatted fingernails upon the telephone receiver. Then went in the kitchen. There was tomato soup in the pantry. I fixed that, and spent the rest of the day and evening piecing my house back together, making lists of what needed replacement. I went Tuesday to H.G. Hill in thirty-six-degree weather, in my dark glasses, and grocery-shopped. The bathroom window pane got replaced that afternoon. Nobody, Dick Butkus-looking or not, broke in that night to snap my neck barehanded. That didn't keep me from a fitful night's sleep, however, worrying about the prospect. Wednesday dawned at long last, proving thoroughly unpleasant, raining three inches. I got my hair done at nine, which improved my disposition. I bought some pretty new clothes and undergarments from Sears and Castner-Knott. I ate at Morrison's in 100 Oaks Mall, going through the line, ordering dark-meat fried chicken, greens, mashed potatoes—yes, to gravy—cornbread, a large wedge of devil's food cake. When I got home there was an Ansafone message from Alan Legate. He said it was important. That was his way of telling me, I guess, it wasn't him calling back already about a date. I sighed. He was right, goddamnit, he *had* ruined everything.

I returned the call. Stretching out my knotted phone cord, waiting to be connected, my heart thudding, by the FBI Birmingham division switchboard.

When he picked up there were no pleasantries.
George Peter Dasch had hung himself in his cell overnight.
He was dead.
"Well," I said, "ain't that convenient as all hell."

CHAPTER 64

M Y EYE DIDN'T HURT MUCH but in the mirror remained fairly ghastly looking. I'd arranged to see a surgeon I knew first-thing Friday for suture removal. Thanksgiving was a problem, of course, but I would just have to bite the bullet, have turkey with my father and Evelyn and her brother and sister-in-law and their twenty-five-year-old studio musician nephew, who my father was getting in the reserves to keep him out of Vietnam, of all the ironies, and later more turkey in Murfreesboro with my mother and her family, and at both meals explain how I got a black eye, in spite of being the prettiest girl any of them were related to, if I do say so.

The holiday went as well as could be expected, considering on top of everything else, I'd taken the last pill in my Ortho-Novum Dialpak the previous Saturday, waking up that Thursday with my period starting. That was the most regular thing about me. News of the police raid on Veronika's party had been suppressed—no surprise—by NASA. Thus, nobody spooning out cornbread dressing and green-bean casserole and whipped potatoes knew anything about the previous weekend's festivities in Huntsville. This gave me free rein to brilliantly concoct an entertaining story full of half truths about how I'd been punched in the eye by a foreign beauty queen, wearing a big fat gemstone, when I'd exposed her scheme to blackmail, with faked photos of a love affair, the man I was investigating.

Rousing stuff.

THE WEEK AFTER THANKSGIVING MY father called middle of
the day from his office at *The Tennessean*. "That FBI agent you
worked with last year, on the Klan matter," he began, speaking
in a tone an octave more serious than the one he usually
reserved for me, his little DD, *debutante daughter*.

"Name was *Legate*, right?"

"Yes."

"Alan Legate?"

"Yes," I said, narrowing my eyes to slits.

"Sorry to tell you this, punkin', but he's dead."

"What?" I burst.

"Just got it off the AP wire."

A look of utter horror came into my face, and I sat down
slowly on the floor. I didn't fall. I slow bent my knees and sank
down in a sitting position, leaning to the left, my left hand on the
floor for support, my right still pressing the telephone to my ear.

"How?"

"Blew his car up."

My eyes wrung shut.

"Who?"

"Klan they think. You know, they never captured John Riley
Hobbs."

"I know," I said.

KKK Imperial Wizard.

I sighed heavily. "Last I heard," I said, "FBI thought he'd
skipped to Rhodesia, got work as a mercenary."

My father said: "Sounds like the sort of fellow who'd blow
up an FBI agent, one who'd ruined his plans to assassinate
Martin Luther King. His anyway. Only takes one successful try."

"Yeah. Could be."

Told him I'd be right over. I lived two-and-a-half miles from
the paper. I walked straight into my father's office and took the
three-foot-long yellow AP teletype he passed across his desk to
me without my asking. I sat, reading down it, horrified, frankly
choked up. My father saw the tears, repeated he was sorry. Just
then a lean tall man I knew to be a reporter appeared in the
doorway next to me, with longish hair, sideburns, a wide wild

necktie. I couldn't recall his name.

"Yo, Charlie," he said.

"Yeah." My father's gleaming bald dome glimpsed up from the editorial he was editing with a dark-red wax pencil. "Said you'd be interested, more came over the wire on that FBI bombing in Birmingham—*Bombingham*, that is." I twisted up, suddenly, wide-eyed through the sunglasses I still wore so I didn't look like I lived with a wife beater. "Whatcha got?" my father said.

"They got the guy."

"Already."

"Blew him all to hell actually."

I took the teletype.

"S'okay, Ken, that's my daughter. Thanks."

"Sure thing." He snapped a nod. "Ma'am."

And he was gone.

The updated wire-service report said an anonymous tip led a heavily-armed, bloodthirsty contingent of FBI special agents, Birmingham police officers, and Alabama troopers to a small home near the city limits, where they engaged "Dynamite Jim" Chambers in a brief intense gun battle, killing the notorious Klan bomber—out on bail, awaiting trial on reduced charges in the Jasper Holiday Inn bombing, after testifying in a host of other Klan prosecutions—hitting him, thrashingly, with five shotgun blasts, and nine handgun rounds.

Couldn't've happened to a nicer guy, I thought.

But if he'd blown up Alan Legate…

I'd play Lady Godiva, on horseback, around James Robertson Parkway.

To be continued…

In the next Sherry Russell Thriller:

Die Detektivin

SUGGESTED READING

Stages to Saturn: A Technological History of the Apollo/Saturn Launch Vehicles by Roger E. Bilstein (NASA SP-4206), 1980.

The Hunt for Zero Point: Inside the Classified World of Antigravity Technology by Nick Cook, 2001.

Power to Explore: A History of Marshall Space Flight Center 1960–1990 by Andrew J. Dunar and Stephen P. Waring (NASA SP-4313), 1999.

Aftermath: Martin Bormann and the Fourth Reich by Ladislas Farago, 1974.

Secret Agenda: The United States Government, Nazi Scientists, and Project Paperclip, 1945 to 1990 by Linda Hunt, 1991.

Secrets of the SS by Glenn B. Infield, 1982.

Operation Paperclip: The Secret Intelligence Program that Brought Nazi Scientists to America by Annie Jacobsen, 2014.

The Rise of the Fourth Reich: The Secret Societies that Threaten to Take Over America by Jim Marrs, 2008.

The Murderers Among Us: The Wiesenthal Memoirs, edited by Joseph Wechsberg, 1967.

ABOUT THE AUTHOR

James K. Rone is a physician and writer living with his wife, Susan, on their farm outside Nashville. He is a native of South Carolina, son of a newspaper editor, and has also lived in Mississippi and Texas. He is honorably discharged from the U.S. Air Force, having served eleven years on active duty, rising to the rank of lieutenant colonel (select). Dr. Rone is an amateur military historian, widely read on the history of World War II and the American space program.